FOLLOW THE WIND

ALSO BY JANELLE TAYLOR

SAVAGE ECSTASY

DEFIANT ECSTASY

FORBIDDEN ECSTASY

BRAZEN ECSTASY

TENDER ECSTASY

LOVE ME WITH FURY

GOLDEN TORMENT

FIRST LOVE, WILD LOVE

SAVAGE CONQUEST

STOLEN ECSTASY

DESTINY'S TEMPTRESS

SWEET SAVAGE HEART

BITTERSWEET ECSTASY

FORTUNE'S FLAMES

PASSIONS WILD AND FREE

KISS OF THE NIGHT WIND

WHISPERED KISSES

FOLLOW THE WIND

JANELLE TAYLOR

ZEBRA BOOKS
KENSINGTON PUBLISHING CORP.

ZEBRA BOOKS

are published by

Kensington Publishing Corp.
475 Park Avenue South
New York, NY 10016

First printing: November, 1990
ISBN 0-8217-3204-8
Printed in the United States of America

Dedicated with love to:

my husband, Michael,
my two daughters, Melanie Taylor and Angela Taylor Reffett
and my son-in-law, Mark
And with
much love and pride for my first grandchild,
Mark Alexander Reffett

Acknowledgments and Thanks to:

the staffs of historical Forts Concho, Davis, and Stockton in Texas; the wonderful people in San Angelo and San Antonio; the staffs of the Texas tourists bureaus and chambers of commerces across the Lone Star State; and to the many friends we made as we researched and camped along my characters' trail. The staff at Fort Davis was particularly helpful with books and information. We arrived during a historical celebration that featured reenactments and demonstrations of fort life, 1800s clothing and weapons, riding formation-saber-pistol-cannon demonstrations, and much more. "Fort Davis is today one of the most complete surviving examples of the typical western military fort to be found" (*Fort Davis: Historical Handbook Number 38,* by Robert Utley). It was fun and educational to be present on such a special occasion. Thanks to all you Texans who made my research there so pleasant and unforgettable.

A special note of thanks to my in-laws, Joe and Betty Taylor, and to my friend, Terri Gibbs Daughtry, for teaching me so much about the courage and humor it takes to overcome disabilities. They were inspirations for Tom and Navarro.

FOLLOW THE WIND

CHAPTER ONE

"A cold-blooded gunslinger is exactly what we need, Papa. A man who can strike as quickly and accurately as a rattlesnake, one without a conscience."

"Men like that can't be trusted, Jess. We'd never be able to control him. The way my luck is running these days, he'd rope up with Fletcher and betray us."

"Papa, you always said even a bad man has a crazy streak of loyalty toward the man who hires him or when he gives his word on something. If we pay him enough, he can be bought. If we don't get help soon, Wilbur Fletcher will own this land and we'll be buried on it. Or left to feed the coyotes and buzzards; that would be more like the evil bastard."

"Jess!" her father shouted in dismay. "Watch your tongue. Your ma and me never allowed you children to speak such words. This trouble is weighing heavy on all of us. It's got us to thinking, talking, and acting loco." Jedidiah Lane wiped the sweat and dust from his wrinkled face and took a deep breath.

"That's my meaning, Papa; we have to stop it soon or be destroyed. I know you don't want a dangerous gunslinger around and I know how you hate to seek help, but we must. The soldiers and Sheriff Cooper can't do the job, and we can't handle it alone. What else can we do?"

They had had this disturbing talk several times before, but Jed was still reluctant to admit he could not defend his land and family against the easterner who had itchy hands for his ranch and seemed ready and willing to do anything to get it. Jed ran his dirty fingers through graying auburn hair, then drew a bucket of water. As they did every day, he and Jess had halted at the well behind the house to wash up before going inside for their evening meal.

"Listen to me, Papa; the time for talking and praying is over. You know I would never suggest such a desperate plan if there was any other way to defeat Fletcher. What's so wrong with it? He has gunslingers on his payroll. We need a man who thinks like they do, a man who can outwit and outgun them. We can't fight and take care of the ranch at the same time. This is one of our busiest seasons. If we hire a gunslinger, he can handle Fletcher and his men for us while we tend to the branding and planting. At least he can teach us how to thwart him."

As Jed rolled his sleeves, he reasoned in a weary tone, "What can one man do, Jess? We have fifteen hands and it's made no difference. Fletcher still does as he pleases. If Sheriff Cooper or the Army gave us a little help, we could trap and stop that sorry bas—" He halted before saying the same crude word he had scolded Jessie for using. "Over the years we've endured many hardships, but this trouble is different. We know Wilbur Fletcher is behind it. No month passes without another offer from him to buy our spread."

Jed splashed cold water on his face. His joints ached and he moved slower these days, reminding him that he wouldn't always be around to protect and provide for his loved ones. If only Alice were at his side. If he lost his mother, his children, and the ranch . . .

"Papa, you aren't listening," Jessie said, tugging at his arm and worrying over another of these recent withdrawals into dreamy distance. "The Army and the sheriff told us they can't do anything without proof. They won't even look for any until they have 'just reason.' I understand they can't camp here to observe; Fletcher would only lie low until they left. But they're the law; they should do something, anything. While they're waiting for him to make a mistake, he's getting stronger and bolder, and we're getting closer to that cliff he wants to push us over. Please let me ride into San Angelo and search for a gunslinger. I'll be gone less than two weeks. Then we can have this trouble settled before summer."

Jedidiah Lane looked at his daughter with indecision in his dark-blue eyes. Her reddish-brown hair hung to her waist in a thick braid that had loosened itself during her labors. Her face was flushed with excitement and anger. Jed shook his head when he saw that her sky-blue eyes that should be filled with peace and joy instead sparkled with determination and hatred. His gaze swept the petite body clad in men's clothing. She looked so fragile, but he knew she was strong. He was so used to having Jessie at his side and doing a man's share of work that he often forgot she was a girl. No, he corrected himself, at twenty-four, she was a young woman, a beautiful creature. He often worried that some man would steal her from him, and he didn't know how he would exist without her. "You can't go into a rowdy town like that, Jess. I'll send Matt or one of the hands."

That wasn't what Jessica Marie Lane wanted to hear. She needed distance to cool her anger and clear her head. She had to find a way to help her father. She also wanted time away from the trouble and her responsibilities. Though she loved the ranch and her family dearly, she needed time to relax and think. Jessie wasn't sure if her father realized just how dangerous Wilbur Fletcher was. It had been she and their foreman, Matt Cordell, who had convinced her father that Fletcher was behind their recent troubles. Her father had created the Box L and had made it succeed through many lean years. In a way, Jedidiah Lane didn't think anyone or anything could wrestle it from his grasp. It sounded as if she finally had persuaded him they needed outside assistance, and she wanted to select the best man for the job.

"I stand a better chance of finding and hiring the right man than any of them do, Papa. You know I can take care of myself. I'll take Big Ed with me and be on the alert every minute. You need Matt and the others to remain here to run the ranch and watch out for Fletcher."

"Maybe you can locate a retired Texas Ranger," Jed replied as a concession. "You know how skilled they are."

Her tone was respectful but firm as she said, "No, Papa. A Ranger has law running through his veins. He would try to handle this matter like an assignment, like a lawman. We need a man with a killer instinct, one who follows our orders, no matter what they are. We might have to do things a Ranger wouldn't allow. Fletcher doesn't respect or obey the law or any code of honor, and we can't either. Good men don't always win, Papa. Nor can we take a Christian attitude and turn the other cheek. This trouble isn't going to stop until one of us loses. To win, we have to fight like he does: mean, dirty, and clever."

Jed stiffened. "We aren't like that, Jess. We're good, honest, hard-working folk. If we start breaking the law, we're no better than Fletcher is. This thing has to be handled right."

"Good won't win over Evil this time, Papa, unless we fight Fletcher on his terms. You always say, 'When a man wallows in the mud, he gets up dirty.' The truth is, mud will wash off, Papa, but six feet of dirt can't be pushed away from the inside. We have to face bitter reality: it's kill or be killed."

Jed sighed wearily. "In the past, I've used my wits and courage to defeat strong forces, like those Apaches and Comanches and rustlers and even nature. Blood has rarely been shed on my land. I kept praying that Fletcher would give up his hunger for the Box L Ranch, might even return East or move to another area. Perhaps you're right in saying the man will never give up. If so, you must be right this time, too. I depend on you, Jess, and trust you completely. You're smart. You're proud and tough like me, but gentle and wise like your ma was. For twenty-six years, this has been my land, my heart, Jess. After I made claim on it with the government's approval, my Alice used her inheritance to buy our first stock and supplies. We worked side by side creating this spread. We faced droughts, rustlers, sickness, hunger, cattle disease, poverty in bad times, and my pa's death. Until we built this house with our bare hands, we lived in a tent, then a shack. We watched two sons die and we buried them out there. I watched my sweet wife suffer and leave me, and my hands were tied by God. Fate dealt me many crushing blows, Jess, but I overcame every one. Sometimes I'm too stubborn, and even reckless, but I won't give up to nothing and nobody. My sweet Alice and two sons are buried on this land; so is my pa. I'll be buried next to them one day."

Jed's voice grew hoarse with emotion. "Sometimes I got depressed and tired. But I haven't felt this helpless and angry since Alice and the boys died. Ma is getting old and weak, and Pa's been gone a long time. You've been like a son to me, Jess. I taught you to do anything a man can do, sometimes even better than most men, so you can take care of this spread when it's yours. If I have to die for my home and family, so be it. But I won't die without doing all I can to stay alive and to hold on." He drew another deep breath and wiggled his sore shoulders to loosen his muscles. "You best

leave at first light before I change my mind. I'll go tell Matt and Big Ed our plan. Be real careful-like, Jess. If anything happened to you, I couldn't bear it. You're the rose of my heart and life, girl. When your ma was taken from me . . ."

"I know, Papa," she responded, hugging him in gratitude and to bring him solace. "I still miss her, too. I'll be fine. Before you can round up the calves for spring branding, I'll be home again, with help. You'll see, Papa, that rattlesnake won't bite us again without suffering several strikes in return."

Jessie watched her father head for the bunkhouse, his shoulders slumped and his expression somber. He hadn't reminisced this way before, and now she knew what had been on his troubled mind. Although they were closer than most fathers and daughters, Jed usually kept his worries and fears penned inside. Jedidiah Lane was a strong, tough, independent man and he had taught his heir to be the same way; but this frustrating situation was overwhelming him, and that saddened her.

It also made Jessie feel guilty about the many times she had resented being depended upon so much. She resented the fact that her older brother's death had caused this duty and burden to fall on her back, forcing her to make herself tough enough to bear them. She resented being a "son" instead of a daughter. She hated those feelings, but couldn't help them.

She wanted romance, love, marriage, her own home and children. But there was little chance of meeting and marrying anyone if her life didn't change. Even if she did meet a man, how could she *leave* with him? What would happen to her father, her grandmother, to her disabled brother, to this beloved ranch, to her immature sister until Mary Louise wed? If her father had an accident, who would take care of him and the Box L Ranch? Gran and Tom couldn't, and her self-centered sister wouldn't. She was trapped here by her responsibilities.

Besides, her blood, tears, and sweat were on this land, too. She loved it as much as Jed did. It would belong to her one day. She knew her father hadn't meant to cause her pain. He loved her even more than his other two children because she was so close and helpful to him. Jessie knew that her father had difficulty expressing love since her mother's death. She believed that he was afraid that whomever he loved deeply would be taken from him.

No doubt, she mused, her father yearned for a love to replace the wonderful one he had lost. Surely there had to be more to life than hard work for both of them. But how, when, and where could she find a true love?

By all accounts, Jessie fretted, she was a spinster! Was it, she asked herself, so terrible to experience nibbles of resentment once in a while? Was it so awful, so wicked, so selfish of her to sometimes think, *What about me?* To sometimes want to live her life for herself instead of always for others? Maybe someone special would ride into her life one day. *Stop dreaming, Jessie. You have work to do.*

"Father said you can do *what?*" Mary Louise shrieked.

Jessie glanced at her younger sister, whose dark blue eyes were wide with astonishment. "Ride to San Angelo to hire help against Wilbur Fletcher," she repeated.

"That is ridiculous! You and Father will get us all killed."

"It's the only path left open to us. I'm tired. We'll talk later," she said, hoping to end the conversation before an argument could begin. "We've been repairing cut fences and gathering strays since sunrise. I have to get packed. I'm leaving at dawn."

"I'm going with you," Mary Louise stated.

"You can't. We have to ride fast and hard. You know what that terrain is like. Besides, there isn't time for shopping or playing."

"I never get to go anywhere or do anything fun!" Mary Louise pouted. "I'm stuck in this godforsaken wilderness without friends or diversions!"

As she gathered clothes for her journey, Jessie reasoned, "One day, all this trouble will be over, and you'll have plenty of both. Be patient, Mary Louise."

"Never! It's too spread out and wild here. We're practically cut off from life by mountains and deserts. The only close neighbor we have is Mr. Fletcher, and you two think he's our enemy. None of you care if I grow old and die here. I hate it. Father should sell out and move us back to civilization."

Jessie knew it was futile to debate Mary Louise's last statement. Continuing to pack, she replied, "You're exaggerating. There are several towns and posts within a day or two of us. We go there for supplies and holidays. And there are other ranches within a few days' ride. We aren't that secluded, little sister."

"What good are they to me? I'm never allowed to visit them for more than a few hours or overnight. And there's no one proper to meet there. We have no entertainment, as you can't call barn dances much fun. I'm lonely and bored."

"There's plenty to do. For one thing, Gran needs help in the kitchen. You know she can't get around like she used to. She's seventy now and needs help. If you'd stop complaining all the time, you'd find plenty to keep yourself busy."

"With slave labor? I shouldn't have to feed chickens, milk cows, grub in the vegetable garden, clean house, and do washing. Father can hire servants to tend us. All my friends at school had them. We aren't poor, you know."

"We don't need to fritter away hard-earned money on servants when we can do our own chores. Besides, we don't have an extra room for a female helper, and she can't live in the bunkhouse with fifteen men."

"If Tom went off to school as I had to do, she could use his room like Rosa did before she ran off to marry that drifter."

"He wasn't a drifter. He was a seasonal wrangler, and she loved him. It was time for Tom to move out of Gran's room; they both need privacy. And you know why he can't go off to school. The boys would give him a hard time, and he'd be miserable. You're smart, little sister. If you help me with Tom's lessons each day, he'll learn far more than I can teach him alone. That would give you something important to do."

Mary Louise glared at Jessie, then flipped her sunny curls over her shoulder. "I'm no schoolmarm, and I won't be treated as one."

"Teaching your own brother isn't going to make you a schoolmarm. He needs help, Mary Louise. Between the two of us—"

"No. I do enough work around here as it is."

Jessie looked at her sister's perfect features, currently hardened by a pout. Mary Louise was two inches taller than her own five feet four inches. On occasion Jessie wished she had her sister's tame golden tresses instead of her own auburn hair that sometimes frizzed into small, loose curls or tufted on the ends to do as it pleased unless controlled by a snug braid. Her sister's eyes sparkled like precious jewels, expensive sapphires. The lucky blonde had an attention-stealing figure, whereas—even though she was four years older—Jessie was less filled out in the bust and hips. Men always noticed Mary Louise in a crowd. The bad thing was that Mary Louise was too aware of her exquisite beauty and the power it gave her. When it suited her, she used those charms and wiles without mercy. Jessie was glad she didn't have her sister's sorry attitude and personality, or Mary Louise's insensitive and selfish nature.

Annoyed by now, Jessie responded a little harshly, "You do very little, and you know it. Gran isn't a tattler, but I know she covers for your laziness many times. What have you done today? From the way you're dressed as if for a party, I doubt very little. It isn't fair to put your work on Gran's tired shoulders."

"It isn't fair to force me to live here and work like a servant."

Provoked, Jessie asked, "If you want to leave so badly, why don't you accept a position as schoolmarm in a large town or in a private school like *you* attended? It's a very respectable job. You're smart enough to do anything you wish."

"Smart enough to find a way out of here one day, but not by teaching brats!"

"I'm sure you will, little sister. Just make certain the trail you take from home is a good and safe one. Life isn't as easy as you think." Jessie realized that her sister was more bitter, spoiled, and resentful than she had imagined. That troubled her deeply, but she didn't want to deal with this constant irritation tonight. "You've been home from school for nearly two years, Mary Louise. It's past time to forget the East and stop making yourself so miserable."

"I am miserable. I hate it out here. There's nothing but heat, work, and solitude. I'm beautiful and educated, but how can I meet a proper husband or friends in this wilderness? I will not wither and die as a spinster, Jessica!"

Ever since she'd come back from school, Mary Louise had been different. She called Papa "Father" and Jess "Jessica." The girl made everyone miserable!

The blonde continued. "This harsh land killed Mother. Look at pictures of her when she was young. She was beautiful and shapely. When she died, she looked old and worn. That isn't going to happen to me. She never recovered fully from Tom's horrible birth. It's too hard on a delicate woman out here, and I refuse to live and work and look like a man as you do, Jessica Lane."

"Tom's birth was difficult, but Mama died of a fever she caught from that drifter. You can't blame Tom," she scolded.

"If he'd never been born, she wouldn't have been so weak and gotten sick."

"Mary Louise Lane! That's a horrible thing to say."

"We're lucky we weren't born deformed, too. Mother had trouble bearing children; she lost two others, you know that. Father treated her as one of his brood mares. She was too frail after Tom to risk another child, but he didn't care."

"That isn't true," Jessie countered. "Davy died when he was two, and the other baby shortly after birth. Tom was seven years old, so Mama wasn't still ailing from his hard birth. That's a mean thing to say, little sister, and a terrible thing to think."

Undaunted, Mary Louise retorted, "If Davy hadn't died, you wouldn't be Father's son. You would be married and have children. If Mother were still alive, she'd have forced him to leave this ranch land by now."

"Mama loved it here. We all do, except you."

"If she were still alive, she'd hate it, too. She would realize what it was costing her to remain. It will steal our beauty and drain us dry, Jessica, if we don't get away soon. Talk to Father; he listens to you. We could have such a grand life near a big town."

"I love this ranch as much as Papa does. I'm sorry home and family don't mean the same to you any more. And I'm sorry you've been so unhappy since your return. We missed you those five years you were gone. You might be happier if you tried."

Chilliness filled the girl's eyes and tone. "If I were missed and loved so much, I wouldn't have been sent away and kept away for so many years. I can't be blamed for falling in love with civilization. I feel like a stranger, an intruder, here."

"That's your doing, little sister. But you were loved and missed. Mama wanted you to be educated as a lady in the way she was. Before she died, Papa promised her he'd make sure you were. If I hadn't been eighteen already, he would have sent me, too. The only reason I didn't go was because when I was the right age the war had just ended and there was still trouble back there. And we couldn't afford it after the war took its toll on everyone. Mama did her best to teach me here, just as I'm doing with Tom. Besides, Papa and I couldn't take care of you, Tom, and Gran properly while working the ranch. Gran was sick back then and had her hands full with Tom. Papa didn't send you away to be mean, Mary Louise. How can you resent the years back East? You so clearly love them as the best in your life."

"You wouldn't understand, Jessica. You've never seen the places I have or done the things I have. You've never had friends around all the time. I miss them. Letters aren't the same, and Father refuses to let me go visit them. If you knew what the outside world was like, you'd do anything to get away."

Jessie was aware she didn't have any close female friends, but she did have some nice acquaintances who she saw occasionally in town or on special occasions. There were plenty of men on the ranch and in town, but it was true that none of them courted her. Here, the hands sometimes treated her as a sister, but more often as "one of the boys" because she worked with them daily doing the same tasks. Only infrequently had a seasonal cowpuncher paid attention to her as a woman, but she had never been tempted to encourage one beyond a stolen kiss.

Sometimes, Jessie admitted, she did want to see other places, make real friends, do exciting things, and find love like she read about in books and old magazines. Maybe that was another reason why this trip to San Angelo was so important to her. But her place was here, and she had accepted that, not threatened to find a way to change it as Mary Louise did. Yet her sister was accustomed to another kind of life. Jessie was trying to understand her feelings, but Mary Louise was so greedy and rebellious. If that was what "civilization" did to a woman, Jessie concluded, she didn't want it.

"We're so different now, Mary Louise, but we *are* sisters. If only you would—"

"Sisters help each other, Jessica. If you truly love me and want what's best for me, you'll convince Father to send me back East, at least for a long visit. His stubborn selfishness is going to get us all killed."

Jessie knew if the girl left, she would never return, and perhaps that would be best for everyone. But she didn't want Mary Louise hurt or endangered in her desperation to escape the life she hated. The girl couldn't be reasoned with, so Jessie decided to drop the distressing matter for now. "I wish you didn't feel that way. I have to finish packing. Please go help Gran with supper."

"It's *dinner,* Jessica. How like a rough, unmannered man you've become over the years without Mother here to guide you."

Vexed, Jessie snapped, "What can you expect after being Papa's 'son' since birth and working every day like a man?" She instantly regretted her words and continued in a softer tone, "But you're wrong; I know I'm a woman. I want to find love and marriage one day, but first this trouble has to be settled. And it will be after I return with help."

Mary Louise grinned with satisfaction at Jessie's irritation. "How can you find a decent husband? All you see are crude cowboys, penniless drifters, and rough soldiers. If you married one, like moon-eyed Matt, you'd be stuck here forever, slaving on the land and pushing out babies. Not me, Jessica. I'm going to leave. I'm going to marry a rich and handsome man. I'm going to travel and be pampered as I deserve. Look at yourself in the mirror. You're as tanned as a cowboy. You wear your hair braided, and you hardly ever don a dress. The sun and work are sapping what little beauty you have. In a few years, even that will be gone. Perhaps even old Mathew Cordell won't desire you then."

Jessie gazed at Mary Louise, who was standing with hands on shapely hips and a devilish gleam in her deep-blue eyes. A challenging expression was on the blonde's face, but Jessie responded calmly. "Matt is our foreman and my friend, nothing more. He's never tried to catch my eye, not that he isn't ruggedly good-looking. I respect him. He's dependable, hardworking, and kind."

Mary Louise laughed mischievously. "And nearing forty. Of course, you are only ten to fifteen years younger! When Father dies, you'll need a man to help you. Matt's already well trained, and your choices are few. By all accounts, big sister, you're already a spinster at twenty-four."

The redhead frowned at those mean words. Jessie wondered what her sister had noticed about their foreman that she hadn't. Or was it a joke, an attempt to point out that the best choice of husbands was a man Mary Louise considered beneath them? Matt was a good man, but there was no magic between them, only friendship. "Why do you keep teasing me about him lately? Does he appeal to you too much for your liking, considering he's too poor and honest to be useful to you? I can't wait to see whom you choose to fulfill your dreams."

"It won't be a cowpuncher with dirty fingernails and dusty clothes. My choice won't stink of horses, sweat, and manure. He won't be uncouth and uneducated. He'll be wealthy, powerful, and educated. He'll adore me and spoil me."

Spoil you? You're already spoiled more rotten than old eggs in an abandoned nest! "I wish you luck, little sister. Until you find him, you have work to do. Papa will be angry if you don't get busy helping Gran with supper."

"Luck, Jessica, isn't what I need. I have wits, beauty, and determination. What I need is opportunity, and it will knock on my door one day very soon."

What you have are dreamy eyes, little sister, and enough greed to fill a thousand bottomless barrels. You're lazy, vain, and defiant. Who will want to tame a selfish critter like you? I wish Mama were here to straighten you out!

Jessica Marie Lane sat at the table with her father, sister, brother, and grandmother. Her emotions were in a turmoil after her talk with Mary Louise. To distract herself, she remarked, "The chicken and dumplings are wonderful, Gran. I wish I could cook like you. Every time I try, it never turns out like yours."

The older woman smiled. "I'm glad I cooked your favorite tonight. You be careful on this trip, Jessie. We'll miss you and pray for you."

Jed had told his mother about their plans before Jessie joined them at the dinner table. He glanced up from his plate and said, "She'll be fine, Ma."

Mary Louise scoffed, "I think it's an absurd idea, Father, and a dangerous one. When Mr. Fl—"

Her tone and words stung Jedidiah Lane. "It's not for you to correct me, girl. This is the only thing I can do to keep my land and family safe."

Jed's rebuke provoked Mary Louise to defiance. "You can sell out, Father. We could move to a more civili—"

"Hush such silly talk, girl. I claimed this land and made this ranch from blood and sweat and hard work. No man is going to drive me off it. You should be more like your sister," he added unwisely.

"I'm not Jessica, Father. You know how I feel about living in this wilderness. Let me visit Sa—"

"You've bellyached enough for everybody in Texas to know how unhappy you are. You've been stickier than a cactus since you came home from that fancy school. If I'd known it was going to ruin you, I would never have kept my promise to your ma to send you there. I'm tired of your grumbling and laziness and having to tell you ten times to do something or make you do it over to get it right. I told you a hundred times you aren't going back East to get worse, so don't ask again. I'm warning you, girl: correct yourself and stop this whining or I'll straighten you out with a strap." Jed wasn't one to strike his children, but his younger daughter's disobedience and haughty manner had worn thin.

"But, Fa—"

"No buts or arguing, girl. I didn't raise you to be a weakling or a griper."

Mary Louise fell silent, but her eyes exposed the fury within her to everyone.

It was obvious to all present that Martha Lane tried to hurry past the awkward and fiery moment by questioning her son and oldest granddaughter about their plans to thwart Wilbur Fletcher. The talk went smoothly for a while.

Tom, the girls' thirteen-year-old brother, was excited and pleased about the decision to hire a gunslinger. "I can't wait to meet him, Jessie. How will you pick him?"

Jessie's sky-blue gaze met her brother's greenish one, and she smiled at him with deep affection. She saw him squint to see her clearly; the round glasses he had gotten from the doctor at Fort Davis were not strong enough to correct his bad vision. Jessie loved him dearly, and she wished his twisted foot and bad eyes had not made such a terrible mark on his young life. She knew that Mary Louise was embarrassed by their brother's disabilities, but she had not known how deeply the girl resented Tom. Jessie gazed at his freckled face and tousled dark-red hair. No one was more aware of Tom's problems than Tom himself, and that saddened her. Jessie's smile broadened and she said in a whispery, playful tone, "I'll play the fox, Tom, and sneak around watching them. Then I'll make my choice."

"I wish I could help," Tom murmured. "That Fletcher wouldn't give us trouble if I was big and strong and good with a gun. If I could ride and shoot, I'd take care of him for you and Pa."

"The best you can do for now, boy, is keep to your studies."

"I will, Pa," the boy replied in disappointment and with a hunger for approval.

Jessie looked at Tom's lowered head. "I'm sure you would be a big help, Tom, but you're a mite young to be taking on gunslingers and their evil boss."

Tom knew age wasn't his problem; his disabilities were. He smiled at his older sister who loved him and helped him more than anyone else. His forefinger pushed his straying glasses, for what little good they did him, back into place and he returned to his meal.

"You've been quiet, Gran. Are you tired, or just overly worried about me?"

Martha Lane looked at her eldest granddaughter. "Only a little, child. If there's one thing about you, Jessie, it's that you get done what you set your mind to doing. If it's a gunslinger you need, you'll come home with one. And I've no doubts he'll be the best man for the job."

"Thanks, Gran," Jessie responded gratefully.

After the meal and dishes were finished, Tom returned to his attic room to complete his studies. Jed went to his desk to work on the ranch books. Mary Louise, as usual, retired to the room she shared with her sister to write letters to old school friends and to daydream or plot an escape from the ranch. Jessie and Gran worked in the kitchen, preparing and packing supplies for her journey.

"You know this has to be done, Gran, don't you?"

"It's sad to admit, child, but it's true." A wrinkled and gnarled hand caressed Jessie's cheek with softness and love. "You have your pa's strength and your ma's gentleness, Jessie. You're a special girl. You've been a blessing to my son and this family. The Good Lord knew what He was doing when he gave you to Jed as a helpmate. Without you at his side, he might have given up during hard times. I know this secluded life is hard on a young woman, but times are changing. When Thomas and I came here with Jed and Alice, there was nothing but the land. Jed and Alice worked dawn to dark building this spread. Me and Pa helped as best we could. It's one of the finest in Texas, in the whole west. This home was built with love and care. Every board and stone was handled by a Lane. Every mile of this ranch has Lane tracks on it. To think of that evil man taking them away makes my heart burn with hatred and anger, and the Good Lord knows how I resist such feelings. Find us help, Jessie, but don't lose yourself in this bitter war."

"What do you mean, Gran?" Jessie asked.

"Fighting evil has a way of making a person grow hard and cold and ruthless. To battle a man like Wilbur Fletcher means you have to crawl into his dark pit to grasp him and wrestle with him. That takes a toll, Jessie. You get dirty. It changes you. Whatever happens, you can't allow it to change you in the wrong direction. Always remember who and what you are: a Lane."

Jessie eyed the proud woman who could be so tough when the occasion demanded it. She was lucky to have Martha as her grand-mother, to be able to speak most of her mind to someone who cared and understood, who could be trusted. "I promise, Gran; the only thing that will change around here is Fletcher."

When they were done packing the supplies, Martha retired to her bedroom and Jessie went to sit on the floor beside Jed's chair in the large living area. The March night was cool, and a fire had been lit to chase away its slight chill. Jessie rested her head against her father's knee as she had done for years, though not lately. She felt as if he needed her closeness and affection tonight before her departure, and after his harsh words with his younger daughter.

As when she was a child, Jed stroked her loosened hair and murmured, "Come home safe, Jess."

"I will, Papa. Soon this trouble will be past. Be careful while I'm gone. Fletcher's daring and greed make me nervous. We have to work fast to win."

"I wish Mary Louise was more like you, Jess. What's wrong with that girl? She balks at every turn worse than a stubborn mule. She's been a splinter in my side ever since she came home. I wish I'd never sent her to that school. They ruined that girl. They filled her head with crazy ideas and dangerous dreams. She's so bitter and rebellious now. I don't know what to do with her. Every word I speak has to be mean and cold or she won't obey me. I think the girl hates me."

Jessie replied with care. "She's having trouble adjusting, Papa. Life here is so different from what she was used to in the East. It's remote and lonely without her friends and diversions. She had those things at school. She wore beautiful clothes, received lots of attention, and it changed her. She's not a Texan anymore. We can't blame her for being the way she is now. She was away from our love and influence too long. Be patient and gentle with her. Maybe that will help."

His voice cracked with emotion and fatigue as he said, "She won't let me, Jess. Every time I try, she takes advantage. It's next to impossible to get her to do her chores. I never have to ask you and Tom more than once to do something, and it gets done right the first time. Maybe she thinks I'll give up if she keeps battling me and making mistakes. She struts around like a spoiled lady. She's rude to the men and disrespectful to me and Ma. Sometimes I'm tempted to switch her good, but I'm afraid if I do, I'll be so angry that I'll really hurt her. If she keeps pushing me and testing me, I don't know how I'll behave, and that's bad."

"I understand, Papa. I pray that time is all she needs."

"That's what we need, too, Jess. Time to defeat Wilbur Fletcher."

"We will, Papa; I swear it." She yawned and stretched. "I need to go check Tom's schoolwork for today and give him assignments for when I'm gone."

Jessie halted before leaving the room and said, "Papa, if you can find something for Tom to do while I'm gone, it would help him. He feels so badly about being too young and unable to assist us."

"What can he do, Jess? It's too dangerous for him to ride herd with us or to help with the branding. He can't move out of danger fast enough. I can't even let him carry the pail after milking 'cause he trips too many times. I wish he had been born whole, Jess, but he wasn't, so we have to protect him."

"I know, but it's so hard on him . . . Good night, Papa."

"Good night, Jess."

Jessie walked through the kitchen and eating area and up the corner steps to Tom's attic room. She recalled with dejection how many times the railing had been loosened and repaired from Tom's pulling at it as he struggled upstairs with his clubfoot. She wished he could run and play and ride like other children. Most tried every trick to get out of chores when Tom would give anything to be normal enough to do them. She tapped on the door, opened it, and entered the cozy room. Two lanterns gave brighter light than the average person required for reading, but Tom's bad vision made it necessary.

Jessie walked to the small table he used for a desk and fluffed his wiry hair. Tom removed his almost useless glasses to rub his tired eyes, then smiled at her through a narrow squint that created creases between his brows and around his eyes. She teased her fingers over her brother's freckled nose and cheeks. "Ready to get busy?"

After they went over the lessons Tom had done that day, Jessie told him to work on reading and on memorizing his times tables while she was gone. She instructed him to write down every word he had trouble saying or did not understand so she could explain them and give him the correct pronunciations later. She wished Mary Louise would work with him during her absence, but she knew the selfish girl would not. She dared not suggest that Tom ask for help and get his feelings hurt.

As she was about to leave, Tom asked in a pained voice, "Will I always be this useless, Jessie?"

Jessie's clear blue gaze met his anguished one. "You aren't useless or helpless, Tom. Please don't feel or think that way."

"I can't help it. I can't do much here. When we go someplace, I have to sit in the wagon and watch the others have fun. Look at what I have to wear," he said, pointing to the thick stocking over his clubfoot that Gran had made for him because he couldn't get a boot or shoe over the badly twisted foot. "People laugh at me, Jessie. They don't want to be near me, like they can catch it or something. I wish they could, so they'd know what it's like!"

"Sometimes people are cruel without meaning to be so, Tom. There are things they don't understand, so it frightens them. If life had turned out different, they could have been you. To hide their fears and relief, they joke about it."

The boy turned in his chair and stared down at his desk. "Please don't let anything happen to you, Jessie. If you and Gran left, I'd be here alone with Pa and Mary Louise. They don't like me. They're ashamed of me."

From behind, Jessie lapped her arms around Tom's chest and rested her cheek atop his head. "Papa loves you very much, Tom. He feels responsible for what happened to you, and it hurts him because there's nothing he can do to correct it. I know it's hard, but a person's behavior and attitude sometimes control other peoples'. If you act ashamed and defensive, they'll react the same way—or even worse than they normally would. Show how brave you are. Don't let this get you down or stop you from trying anything you want to do. It will be harder for you than for others, but your perseverance will reveal your strength and courage to everyone. Treat your problems with humor; that relaxes people. Sometimes you can hush mean people by saying, 'God gave me this busted foot. I haven't figured out why yet, but I know He must have a good reason.' Or say, 'I'm slow, but I'll get there eventually.' Always laugh, even if you're hurting inside. If you show you can overcome your problems or accept them, others will. Everybody has flaws and weaknesses, things they can't control, and it frightens them."

Tom loosened her affectionate grip and looked up at her with shiny eyes. With enthusiasm and confidence, he said, "Not you, Jessie; you can do anything."

Merry laughter came from the redhead. "I wish that were true, little brother. If so, I wouldn't be leaving in the morning. My weakness is in being a woman. If I were a man, I could battle Fletcher."

He looked puzzled and surprised. "You don't like being a girl?"

"I didn't mean that. I just don't feel like a whole woman. I've been a tomboy and cowhand too long. Now I don't fit into either sex. I had to be boyish to work the ranch with men, and I had to learn to do everything better to be accepted. One day I'll be their boss, so I need their respect and trust. I can do almost any man's chores, but I'm not man enough to challenge Fletcher and his hirelings alone. It feels kind of like that half-breed who worked here a few years back; you're in the middle with no real claim to either side." Jessie laughed and teased, "Why am I rattling on with silly female talk? I have to get some sleep. Work hard while I'm gone. This isn't playtime, young man. Always remember, Tom, a smart brain is better than a perfect body. What you can't do physically, learn to counteract mentally. A smart head can open some doors that strong bodies can't. Learn all you can, as fast as you can. One day, you'll be glad."

"I love you, Jessie. I'm so glad I have you for a sister."

"I love you, too, and I'm glad you're my brother."

"Even though I'm nearly blind and crippled?"

"But you aren't blind, and you can walk; those are blessings, Tom. Think of your troubles as challenges, never as ropes tying you to a post. Look what strength and courage they've already taught you; it can be more, if you let it. If I know my brother, one day he won't let this foot and these eyes bother him. Until then, young man, study hard and don't lose heart. Promise?"

"I promise. You always make me feel better. I just forget it when I'm around other people, especially when we leave the ranch." Tom hugged Jessie and kissed her cheek. "Be careful, Jessie. Come home safe, and soon."

"I will, Tom. I have more lessons to teach. Good night."

Jessie went to the room she shared with her sister, who was either asleep or pretending to be so. She donned a nightgown, put out the lamp, and got into bed. She was both excited and tense about her journey. She hoped nothing would happen tonight to prevent it. Fletcher had kept them busy for the past two days with his evil mischief, so hopefully he would be quiet for a time, at least long enough for her to get away unnoticed.

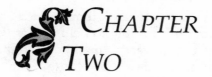# CHAPTER TWO

Jessie saddled her horse, a well-trained paint that balked at anyone riding him except his beloved mistress, and secured saddlebags and a supply sack. A bedroll was attached behind the cantle, and two canteens hung over the horn. An 1873 fifteen-shot Winchester rifle was in its leather sheath. Belted around Jessie's waist was a Smith & Wesson .44 caliber pistol that loaded rapidly and easily and fired six times. She carried ammunition in one saddlebag and in her vest pocket. She knew, if a horse had to be dismounted quickly to take cover from peril, survival could depend on having a supply of bullets within reach.

Jessica Marie Lane was anxious to get on the trail before the hands returned from their nightshifts and reported any threat that would halt her departure. With the sun attempting to peek over the horizon, she had to hurry. Just as she was ready to leave, she heard men approaching her.

Jed employed fifteen regular hands, then hired seasonal help during the spring and fall roundups. Half of the men rode fence and did chores while the other half rested from theirs. The night/day schedule altered each week. As soon as the hands in the bunkhouse finished dressing and eating, they would replace the others to do the same before yielding to much-needed sleep.

The hands who gathered around to see her off and to wish her good luck were among Jessie's favorites and best friends. These seven men were unflinchingly loyal to the Lanes and had been with them for years. All were skilled at their tasks, and all were amiable men who loved practical jokes.

Rusty Jones was laughing as he joined her. The bearded redhead told them, "That biscuit shooter is airin' his lungs deep. I told him I was starving, but he ordered me out of the cookhouse till he sang out that vittles are ready. Come back fast, Jessie. I'll have a hot iron waitin' for you," teased the expert brander.

"We'll start bringing in the cavvy today," Jimmy Joe Slims said.

Jessie smiled, sorry she wouldn't be able to help gather the wild and half-broken horses to get them ready for the roundup.

Carlos Reeves, a skilled broncbuster, lit a cigarito, then rubbed his seat. *"Sí, amigo,* I haven't tasted dirt in a season. There's one stallion I'm eager to get my gut hooks into. I never could break him last time. I'm not over that defeat yet. That *diablo* is *demente.* Ride with eyes and ears to your rear, *chica."*

John Williams, a huge and strong black man who labored mostly as their blacksmith, said, "Miss Jessie, you be careful allee time. We'uns'll work hard tilst you git back. I gots yore hawse shoed good and ready to sling dirt if needs be."

"Thank you, Big John."

"Lasso us a real tough *hombre,* Jessie. Just tame him before you get him here," jested Miguel Ortega as he settled a sombrero on his broad back.

"Jamas!" shouted Carlos. "We don't want him tamed, Miguel. We want him eager to spit lead at anybody riding the Bar F brand."

"I'll be jumpy as a prairie dog with a rattler in his role until you get back," Jimmy Joe declared.

"Hold your reins, sonny," Rusty replied. "Ever'body knows those two abide each other 'cause the dog don't know that rattler is feeding on his pups."

"Biscuit!" Hank Epps shouted from the cookhouse, "Git yore grub whilst it's givin' the steam!" Yet the crusty and jolly old cook hurried to join them.

Jefferson Clark, another black man, said, "We was jus' tellin' Miss Jessie good-bye. She'll be gone nigh unto two weeks."

"Eh?" Biscuit Hank responded, cupping his ear as if his hearing was bad, but all the boys knew it was fine when Hank wanted to hear something.

"I'll be mounting up, Papa, so the boys can fill their bellies and get busy."

Jed embraced his daughter and urged, "Be real careful-like, Jess."
Mathew Cordell ordered Big Ed, "Take extra good care of her."
The burly man mounted his large sorrel. "I will, Boss."

Jessie smiled at Matt who was fingering his mustache. He had
never been one for many words, but this morning he seemed more
talkative than usual.

"You sure you don't want me or one of the boys to go with you
two? That's a long and dangerous trail, Jessie. I'll be worried till I
see your pretty face again."

What her sister had hinted at last night kept flickering in her
mind. As she had told Mary Louise, Matt was good-looking. He was
steadfast and loyal, but a mite serious and quiet when compared
to the other hands. A breeze played in his hair and something curious glowed in his eyes of a matching dark-brown color. His gaze
was deeper, longer, and stranger than she had noticed before. Or
maybe she was looking too hard because of her sister's implication.
"Don't be worried, Matt. I have to go," she told him.

"I figgered you would from the first time you mentioned seeking
help," the soft-spoken foreman replied. "I've seen how your clever
head works."

"A man don't stand a chance against Jess when she makes up her
mind about something," Jed added. "Not even her pa."

"I knew she would win," Matt responded, grinning.

Jessie wondered if that was a soulful expression in his eyes when
the foreman ordered, "Let's eat, boys. Jessie has to leave, and we
got work awaiting."

Jimmy Joe nudged the half-Mexican and teased, "Yeah, Carlos
is eager to git his britches warmed, his bones rattled, and his butt
sore before dark."

"I'll take the spit and fire out of any horse you bring in, *amigo.*"

"Why don't we start with that stallion who tamed you last time?"

"Hopping onto his saddle will be easier than getting into a bunk
with tied-down covers. I was so tired last night, I didn't even loosen
her reins before I jumped on her. Which of you *amigos* hobbled her
so good and tight?"

The men laughed and glanced around, but no one laid claim to
the joke.

Gran and Tom joined the merry group, but Jessie's lazy sister was
still dressing. Mary Louise had been told to take over Jessie's morning chores during her absence but claimed she was "kind of behind"

today. Jessie had awakened Mary Louise in ample time, yet her sister had not heeded her urgings to arise and get busy. Obviously Hank or a hand had done the milking and egg gathering. Jessie was glad she would be gone when their father learned of the girl's new disobedience which would surely provoke more anger and harsh words. The redhead didn't know what it was going to take to quash her sister's stubborn defiance.

Embraces and words were exchanged. Then Jessie mounted the piebald animal and bid them all farewell. Off she and Big Ed rode on their adventure.

For the first few hours, the riding was easy as they traveled over grasslands and hills that were scattered with short trees, scrubbrush, and yuccas. Here and there they encountered cactus: mostly prickly pear, ocotilla, and cholla. The area was lush and green, and Jessie always marveled at its beauty. Several buzzards circled high above in the clear March sky as they searched for food. Graceful antelopes darted about during their early browsing. They were plentiful—thankfully, more so than the many skunks and porcupines!

About twenty miles eastward was the old Comanche War Trail. The Indians had used that trail from North Texas for their raids into Mexico, particularly during the feared "Comanche Moon" in September. But Colonel Mackenzie had defeated the last big band in the Palo Duro Canyon in '74, two years ago. The survivors had been placed on a reservation in the Oklahoma Territory.

Jessie knew how lucky they were that her father had made a truce with them in the beginning, just as he miraculously had done with the hostile Apaches who sometimes rode to the west of their ranch. Both truces had proven to her that peace was possible when each side was honest and willing.

After a rest and water stop, they rode another two hours. The Davis Mountains were to their left and the Glass Mountains to their right. The Del Nortes near the Lane Ranch were left behind, as was the Bar F Ranch which they had skirted cautiously. In the distance, the mountains—that were mainly brown up close—looked purple. In every niche and cranny, wildflowers bloomed across the landscape, as spring was this area's most colorful season.

Jessie and Big Ed rested longer on their second stop and prepared a light meal. She was glad it was not summer, as this southwest section of Texas could blaze with life-sapping heat during that time. The terrain had begun to change; it was now semidesert. Many hillsides were dense with yuccas. Soon it would be desert with only occasional hills, mesas, and desolate scrubland. And soon they would be able to see for miles without obstructions on the flat and dry wasteland that would demand a slower pace as they weaved through wild vegetation.

From past trips to the town near Fort Stockton, Jessie knew that only one more stop in two hours or so was needed, then it would be another two hours' ride into town. If they encountered no problems, they should be there by five.

Jessie was right. Shortly after five, they made camp beyond town on the Comanche River. This area was known for Comanche Springs, a main stop in the parched Trans-Pecos region for the San Antonio–Chihuahua Trail, both upper and lower San Antonio–Èl Paso roads, the old Butterfield Overland stage, and the Great Comanche war trail. Fort Stockton had been constructed in '58 to protect the vital route and its travelers against Indian hostilities, one of a chain of posts and camps built and manned for that task. During the war between the North and South, it had been occupied briefly by Confederate troops before the embittered Apaches almost destroyed it. In '67, it was rebuilt and heavily garrisoned, mostly by black "Buffalo Soldiers." Afterward, the small town of St. Gall nearby had flourished. With Pecos County officially organized last year and with St. Gall made the county seat, Jessie had no doubts the town name would soon be changed to Fort Stockton, as most already used that name.

Weary, but stimulated to be on the trail, Jessie ate little and slept little. By dawn, they were traveling again. They had avoided town, in case Wilbur Fletcher or any of his men were present. Jessie did not want her plan unmasked to the villain, who might follow them to discover the reason for such a journey.

The mesas and hills in all directions on the desert terrain would have slowed them if not for the rugged road. With luck, they would encounter little traffic this time of year: Butterfield had ceased its route in '61, any wagon trains from back East had not made it this far west yet, freighters usually passed earlier in the week and most used the lower road, and soldiers from Forts Stockton and Concho had little trouble with Indians to keep them on the move.

Because of the scarcity of water in this arid region, they could not head directly toward San Angelo. It was necessary to ride northeastward to Horsehead Crossing on the Pecos River, then along the upper road toward their destination. To avoid contact with possible trouble, as soon as they reached the middle Concho River, they would follow its bank into town rather than remain on the road.

They followed the same schedule of yesterday: ride two hours, rest, ride two hours, eat and rest longer in the heat of the day, ride another two hours, rest, then a last two hours before camping. That way, they would not overtire the horses or themselves.

Horsehead Crossing on the Pecos River was made easily in three hours. After watering their horses and refilling their canteens, they forded the shallow river and continued past mesas, hillocks, and an area where more yuccas and green amaranths—future tumble-weeds—grew in abundance.

The landscape rapidly drifted into a drier terrain that was sliced by intermittent arroyos that warned of flash floods to the unwary traveler who ventured into them at the wrong time. Except for the dirt road, this area was covered densely with mesquites, rocks of all sizes, and prickly pear cactus. In olden days, such obstacles would have made travel slow and difficult. The land was flat and the vegetation short, giving them a view of the harsh region surrounding them. At times, they could see in any direction for twenty miles or more. Winds gusted on occasion and stirred up dust that coated them and tickled their throats. What grass there was grew in bunches in the sand-colored earth. No clouds could be found in the azure sky, and the day was the hottest they had experienced so far.

Five hours later, they camped on the Concho River. In two days, by Sunday night, March twelfth, they would reach San Angelo. They were tired, and Big Ed wasn't much of a talker with women, so they ate and turned in for the night.

Up at dawn and after a hot meal, Jessie and Big Ed broke camp and mounted. They followed the winding bank for hours. Jessie was glad they were near the river where plenty of water was available for them and the horses. It was hot and dry beneath the sun, and perspiration formed quickly. It dried rapidly on their exposed flesh, but their garments were damp. She had not had a bath since leaving home, and was more than ready for one. She wished she could strip off her clothes and boots and take a swim, but knew that was unwise.

They made their last camp on Saturday night, thirty-six miles from their destination. Big Ed whistled and grinned while he tended the horses and Jessie cooked their meal. The redhead guessed how eager her partner was to reach town. She had given him five dollars for being such a good companion and guard; she knew where and how he would spend the money. She would pretend not to notice when he left her at the hotel to visit the local saloon and brothel to indulge in masculine pleasures. While he was doing so, she would finally take a long bath, enjoy a delicious meal, and get rested for her task on Monday.

The following morning, they rode through the area near the river. It was so dense with bushes, oaks, cottonwoods, and willows that they were forced to slip back into the rugged terrain nearby. The mesquite was thick, prickly pear cactus was more than abundant, and rocks of varying sizes and shapes were everywhere. At times, they lost sight, but not sound, of each other as they rode single file.

Big Ed was leading the way, and it was time for their first rest stop. Suddenly Jessie heard his sorrel whinny in terror. She heard hooves clashing against rocks. A loud thud reached her alerted ears, followed by a yell from her companion.

Jessie had been around broncbusting long enough to know when a man had been thrown. She called Big Ed's name, but received no answer. Evidently the wind had been knocked from his lungs and he couldn't respond yet—or he had been rendered unconscious. She urged her splotched mount forward as rapidly as possible. When her line of vision was clear, she saw the nervous sorrel backing away between mesquites from a cluster of rocks. The sound that caught her attention didn't need explaining: rattlesnake. Jessie drew her rifle and fired twice, striking the viper both times and nearly decapitating him. His body thrashed wildly as his life ended, but his muscles continued to work involuntarily.

Jessie sheathed her Winchester, then dismounted. She rushed to Big Ed's body. When she turned him, she saw the bloody wound on his temple. She couldn't awaken him. She bent forward to check for signs of life, finding none. The redhead settled on her haunches, resting them on her boot bottoms. She stared at the dead man. Although Ed had not been a close friend of hers, he was a good hand. She had chosen him because he was big and strong and dependable, and because she had known he wouldn't give her any problems on this job by trying to help her with the selection of a gunman. She had also wanted as much peace and quiet as possible for thinking, something none of her good friends would have allowed.

If only they had stuck to the road or she had come alone or they had taken a rest stop sooner, he would still be alive. What to do? she wondered. There was no point turning back, as she was too close to San Angelo and her crucial mission and Big Ed was beyond help. Should she carry him into town for burial? Would that bring too much attention to her, something she needed to avoid, especially now that she was a woman alone? She could not carry the body back to the ranch, a four-day ride that would attract buzzards and coyotes. Neither did she want to camp with a dead body each night. Big Ed had no family to notify. Wasn't burial here as good as in a strange town?

The sorrel's anxious prancing and erratic breathing seized Jessie's attention. The smell of blood and death made the beast nervous. Quickly she went to him to soothe his fears. When he was calmed, Jessie checked his legs for bites. She was relieved to find none. After tying his reins to a mesquite, she began the grim burial task.

Jessie took Big Ed's bedroll from his saddle. After removing his gunbelt, she rolled him inside the roll and bound it securely with Ed's rope. Locating an indentation in the earth, she struggled with the heavy burden until she had dragged the body there. For over an hour, the redhead gathered rocks and piled them atop the body until the mound was thick enough to keep animals away. Binding sticks together to form a cross, Jessie maneuvered it between rocks at one end of the stony grave, then placed Big Ed's hat upon the highest point. She said a brief prayer for him while trying not to feel blame for this fatal accident.

Jessie was exhausted and sweaty after her labors. She grasped the reins of the sorrel and her paint, then headed for the river. Locating a spot where they could make it to the water, she let the animals drink. Afterward, as the creatures grazed on grass nearby, Jessie knelt and splashed water on her face and arms, cleansing away the dirt and sweat and dried blood. She drank from the cool river, then filled her canteens.

She had seen men die before. One broncbuster had broken his neck during a fall. Another hand had been gored by an enraged longhorn. Her grandfather had died when she was young. She had been at her mother's side when Alice had left this world. Since then, she had worked hard to prove herself, to be the "son" her father needed. She knew Jed was leaving the ranch to her, as Tom couldn't handle it and Mary Louise hated it. She had to learn all she could, as her responsibilities were great. Now, a good man had been killed while helping her carry out her plan. She leaned against a tree and closed her eyes, feeling the need to have a good and cleansing cry for the first time since her mother's death.

By dusk, Jessie entered the town of San Angelo and saw a small hotel. First, she went to the livery stable to have the two horses tended. If the man was overly curious about her, he didn't show it. Taking her saddlebags, she walked a short distance to the hotel. This time, the clerk was very nosy about her reason for being there and for being alone. To silence him, she claimed she was visiting her brother, an Army officer at Fort Concho across the river.

The post had been built in '67, and Santa Angela had sprouted nearby, to be renamed San Angelo years ago. The area was lush and green because the three branches of the Concho River fused there. According to what the men on the ranch had told her, Concho Street was noted for rendering services and pleasure to off-duty soldiers. The men had also told her the town was famed for its near-lawlessness, making it the perfect place to locate a gunslinger, which surprised Jessie since it was so near a symbol of law and order. There were other reasons for the town's development, since it was on the route of the upper road and several forts were, or had been, nearby.

Jessie glanced around the room she had rented for a few days. It was furnished sparsely, but was clean. She had wanted to relax in a long bath in her room, but the clerk informed her she had to use the bathing closet at the end of the hall, one shared by the other guests on that floor. As the eating area had closed, he permitted the cook to warm leftovers and bring them to her room for an extra fifty cents.

As soon as she finished the meal, Jessie gathered her things and took a short, rushed bath. Fortunately, no one disturbed her. She brushed and rebraided her long hair, in her room, then, exhausted, the redhead went to bed, shutting out thoughts of Big Ed's death and the noise from down the street.

Jessie waited until late afternoon before venturing out to complete her goal. She had studied the town from her window. Some areas were rowdy, while others were less so. She didn't notice a church or a school nearby, and hoped that didn't mean these people were as bad as the boys had warned her.

She took several precautions. After banding her small bosom to her chest with a strip of snug cloth, Jessie attired herself in loose jeans, a roomy cotton shirt, and a brown vest that concealed her feminine figure. She used scissors to clip wisps of hair atop her head and alongside her face, hair that curled almost mischievously against her flesh. After positioning her hat, she fluffed the shorter strands around her face so it wouldn't be obvious that she was a girl with long locks stuffed out of sight. She unfolded the dirty bandanna and made smudges here and there on her face to detract attention from her clear, rosy complexion. Lastly, she strapped on her gunbelt, pushing it lower on her right hip.

Jessie eyed herself in the small mirror, and was pleased with her disguise. She inhaled and exhaled several times to slow her breathing and pounding heart. She didn't know if intimidation or panic or excitement ruled her senses.

Everything was ready. She closed her door and left the hotel.

Jessie slowly walked down the planked sidewalk, making certain she moved and carried herself like a male. She noted every wooden and adobe structure surrounding her. A few people passed her, mainly merchants and cowboys and soldiers. At the far end of the dusty street was a raucous saloon and brothel. Music and laughter wafted out the open door. Men entered and departed. A scantily clad female leaned over the second-floor railing to speak with a customer in the street. Gunshots rang out, then loud laughter.

Halfway down the street was another saloon, a quieter and cleaner-looking one. Jessie saw only three men enter it and none depart. Horses' reins were secured to hitching posts, most being at the end of the street. The nervous redhead didn't have to ask herself twice which saloon she would try first.

Jessie parted double doors—too high for someone five feet four to see over, and looked inside. Freshly washed lanterns—suspended from the ceiling—were aglow. A long wooden bar stretched nearly the length of one side, with an aproned bartender leaning negligently upon the shiny surface. Behind it were shelves containing numerous bottles of assorted liquors. Before it were tables and chairs, some occupied and many not. Two soldiers were drinking at the bar and chatting in low voices. Two girls swept down the steps, giggling and motioning to the uniformed officers, and joined them. Soon, the clinging couples vanished upstairs. At several round tables, men sat gambling, drinking, and talking. The smell of tobacco smoke filled the air, as did the odors of sweat, leather, the furniture oil that was used to replenish ever-thirsty wood in this arid region, and that particular smell that only western dust has.

The bartender glanced her way, then returned his gaze to the room. Jessie moved inside and sat at a table away from those occupied ones. She did not remove her hat, as cowboys rarely did so except in church or at home. Most just shoved them back on their heads, keeping them on as if the hats were part of their bodies. Even while sleeping in a bedroll, most covered their eyes with them.

Jessie tried not to appear nervous, but she felt herself quivering. She hoped no one would approach her, as she only wanted to observe every man with a gun strapped to his waist. One man had to be a professional gambler, she decided, from his fancy white shirt, black silk vest, and black trousers. He fingered the cigar in his mouth as he studied his cards before placing his next bet.

An old man wearing a blue cotton shirt, baggy trousers, and red suspenders entered from a back room. He took a seat at the piano and began to send out playful tunes. The conversations became more difficult to hear over the music. Glass clinked against glass as more drinks were poured.

The bartender finally came to her table and asked what she wanted. "I'm waiting for someone," Jessie told him, "if that's all right."

He looked her over before asking if she wanted a drink. When she shook her head, he shrugged and returned to his former position.

A man arrived who must have just left the other saloon, as he walked none too steadily. He made his way around the room, speaking to almost everyone. From the customers' reluctant responses, Jessie assumed he wasn't well liked.

Time passed. The sated soldiers reappeared, had a final drink, and departed. The inebriated man was talking and laughing loudly in one corner with another cowboy. Snatches of boastful claims reached Jessie's ears. Or perhaps they weren't all boast, considering the cautious way he had been greeted earlier. The men present hadn't been rude to the obnoxious drunk, and an aura of tension had been in the air since his arrival. Yet, even if he were as good with his guns as he claimed, he wasn't the kind of man she was searching for. A man who loved drinking that much couldn't be trusted to remain sober at vital times.

Two men wore their gunbelts strapped snugly to their thighs, the usual sign of a gunslinger. One had a knife scar down his left cheek, telling her someone had bested him at one time and could probably do so again. The other appeared too nervous over the card hand he was holding, a good indication he couldn't bluff easily. The gambler with his sly grin and flashing dark eyes looked too deceitful to be trusted. There wasn't a good choice here. Perhaps she should visit the other saloon, Jessie reasoned uncomfortably.

The "soiled doves" returned and moved around the tables to obtain more business. They had approached the crude man first, but he had sent them scurrying away with insults and shoves. Jessie watched the females for a time, wondering what had driven them into such a degrading life, though a woman alone in the rugged west had little hopes of supporting herself respectably without a family.

A third woman came down the stairs. She halted at the bottom and studied the room of men, frowning in distaste as she noticed the intoxicated ruffian. Like the other girls, she was dressed in a satin-and-black-lace dress that reached halfway between her knees and ankles, but hers was a sapphire blue while the others wore fiery red. The woman in blue circulated through the area, stopping here and there to speak to customers she knew. She teased her fingers over the gambler's cheek, then bent forward to whisper something in his ear. The man looked up, patted her buttocks, and grinned broadly.

Jessie tensed when she headed her way. The woman smiled seductively as she took a seat facing the disguised redhead. Feathers in her blond hair fluttered as she leaned forward and propped her elbow on the table, then rested her chin on a balled fist. She licked ruby-red lips and spoke in a husky voice.

"My name's Nettie. What's yours, son?"

Jessie tried to lower her voice as she replied, "Jess, ma'am."

Nettie chuckled at the show of good manners and anxiety in the person she assumed to be a young man seeking his first experience with a woman of her skills. "This your first time in a saloon, Jess?"

"Yes, ma'am." Jessie shifted nervously in her chair and wanted to flee. This situation was crazy, but there were things she needed to learn and do here. She had to be brave and cunning and steadfast in her mission.

Nettie stroked the protruding flesh revealed by her indecently low bodice, a trick to lure men's eyes and heat their desires. "Calm down, son. Nettie can relax you real good upstairs. You ever had a real woman before?"

Jessie flushed a bright red at the unexpected mistake and lewd implication, a reaction she couldn't remember having to any situation. What to do? she wondered. If she didn't stick to her plan, this trip and Ed's death were for naught.

Nettie laughed again, a throaty and sultry sound. "You've come to the right woman, Jess. I've broken in more young pups than a dog has fleas. You want a drink to settle you down? There's no need to be shy or scared. I'm the best in town."

"I . . . I . . ." Jessie stuttered as she tried to decide how to extricate herself without being unkind or exposing her sex. If she revealed she was a female, this woman would be embarrassed and angered. Worse, her ruse would be exposed. That could lead to failure, and to trouble.

"You don't have to say or do anything, son. I know everything. You'll leave here smiling as bright as the sun and feel as loose as a busted feather pillow. Why don't we head upstairs and get acquainted in private?"

"I got money, ma'am, but what I need to buy is information, not . . ."

Curiosity filled the prostitute's eyes.

Jessie hurried on. "I'll pay you five dollars if you can tell me who's the best gunslinger in town. I don't mean a bragger, but a man proven to be an expert."

Nettie leaned over to peer under the table. "You're packing iron, son! You ain't looking to earn a reputation here, are you? You'll get yourself killed."

"No, ma'am. I want to hire him for a job. Rustlers are raiding my pa's ranch. We need a man good with a gun to defeat them."

"That's a job for the law, son. Why did your pa send you here?"

"The law can't stop 'em, ma'am. We know who it is, but we ain't got proof. A gunslinger could kill 'em or scare 'em. I rode a long way to hire help."

"You ain't from around these parts?"

"No, ma'am."

"Do I know these bad men?"

"No, ma'am. They live where we do, far away."

"Five dollars for a name?" Nettie glanced at the bartender to see if he was watching them.

Obviously the woman was tempted by the idea of cash for no work, especially money she could hide and keep. "I need a man we can trust, one who'll obey orders."

Nettie's voice was low as she leaned closer to whisper, "I know the man you need, but he ain't in town yet. He comes in with his three brothers every few days, but the other three ain't worth their salt. Josh is as good as a gunslinger comes and he's loyal to who hires him. His brothers are trash, but Josh would kill any man to protect them. Josh don't let 'em work with him, but all other times they're as tight as a noose at a necktie social. Their ma gave 'em all names starting with J: Josh, Jim, Jake, John. He's the man you want, son, fast as lightning and no heart against killing."

"I can wait around to meet him. What's his last name?"

"The money first. But don't let anybody see you give it to me. My boss won't take kindly to giving out such help."

Jessie pulled five dollars from her pocket and crushed it in her palm. She extended her balled fist across the table. Nettie's eager hands covered it, and the money was passed along without anyone's notice. The sly woman secreted the cash into her cleavage, then grinned.

Before Nettie could reveal the gunman's name, the half-drunk man came to their table and jostled it as he staggered. He seized Nettie's wrist and yanked on it. "Come on, Nettie. I dun paid fur you. I need release bad."

"What you need is a long piss, Jake. I'm busy. Get one of the other girls."

"I want you, woman. They ain't good like you is."

"I'm busy here, Jake. You'll have to wait a while."

Jake looked Jessie over with red-streaked eyes and a surly expression, then howled with laughter. He grabbed at Nettie again, but she scrambled out of reach and glared at him. "You turnin' down a real man for a snot-nose kid?"

"Behave yourself, Jake Adams."

Jake tottered to Jessie's chair and shoved on her shoulder. "Git outta here, boy. Git home to your ma and pa where you belong."

"Leave him be, Jake. We've already struck a deal, so you'll have to wait your turn."

"I ain't beddin' no whore after no boy just diddled her. Git, afore I'm riled."

Jessie saw trouble in the making. Several men had ceased their games to observe the action. The bartender was staring at them, but made no attempt to deal with the smoldering situation. The old man at the piano halted his fingers. Silence and tension filled the room. Everyone's expressions warned the redhead this was not a man to fool with. "You go with Jake, Nettie," Jessie said, "We'll talk when you finish. I'll wait here for you."

"Ain't no need to wait, boy. I dun rented this whore all night."

Jessie tried to appease the belligerent man. "What if I come back tomorrow, Nettie?" she asked the woman.

Nettie ruined Jessie's attempt by saying, "Don't be rude and stupid, Jake. This customer asked first, so he's next with me. Let's go upstairs, son."

"Ain't no way, woman, even if he only takes five minutes—if he's got that much strength. You git out of this saloon pronto, boy. Come back when you're dry behind the ears. Fact, you git out of town and don't come back. If you do, I'll whip yore arse all over this saloon."

Jessie had to cool the man's temper. She could see Nettie tomorrow. "No need to get upset, mister. I didn't mean no harm."

Jake punched her shoulder roughly. "Nettie belongs to me and my brothers when we're in town," he said. "Ask anybody, boy. Now git! Move faster, boy!"

Jessie stood, her right hand unthinkingly and unwisely settling on her gunbutt.

Jake backed off a few steps. With a threatening scowl, he shouted, "You challenging me for this whore, boy? I'll kill you where you stand!"

Jessie jerked her hand away from the pistol and half raised both hands, her palms facing the man. "No, mister. I don't want no trouble. I just wanted—"

"I don't care what you wanted!" Jake grabbed a handful of vest and shirt and yanked her toward the nearby doors. "Git movin' afore I use you to wipe dust and spit from the floor. Hell's fire, that's what you need, a good lickin'."

Jake balled his fist to strike Jessie, but Nettie seized his arm. "No,

Jake! He's just a kid. Don't beat him! Somebody stop this crazy fool!" she shrieked, but no one came to Jessie's aid because the customers knew Jake Adams and his mean brothers too well to interfere.

With force and roughness, Jake threw Jessie against the slatted doors. Something kept them from opening and her from falling outside on her rear.

Jake mistook his thwarted effort as resistance from Jessie. "I warned you, boy. Now, yo're gonna git it. I'm takin' you outside to settle this. If yo're too yellar to draw against me, I'll whop you good. I'm gonna break yore fingers and yore laigs and make you crawl home. You won't never wanta come here and cross Jake Adams agin." He lifted his balled fist to begin his threatened task.

Before Jessie could react in self-defense, a man parted the doors and captured Jake's fleshy fist in midair. In the excitement, no one had noticed the stranger who'd been watching from outside.

"Leave the boy alone, mister. He'll leave peaceably."

Jake was enraged by the daring interruption. He jerked his hand free and glared at the man who stepped inside. "Yore nose don't belong in my business, stranger. Git movin' or you'll answer to me and my guns, too."

The challenger didn't back down. "Let the boy go," he ordered.

Jake backed off a short distance and planted his boots two feet apart. He placed his hands on his hips, near his guns. "Says who?"

"Me. No real man picks on a harmless kid. Don't shame yourself in public. Get back to your whiskey, cards, and woman. I don't like seeing boys pushed around or mistreated. He'll go home and there'll be no trouble."

Jessie couldn't take her blue gaze from her rescuer. His hazel eyes revealed no fear, only slow-burning anger and determination, a warning Jake ignored. Black hair peeked from beneath his light hat and lay against a darkly tanned face, one more handsome than Jessie had ever seen. This, she decided, was a real man. He was tall, brave, powerful, intimidating, and confident. With him assisting her, she was no longer afraid, but her wits were reeling.

"I'll give you one chance to git, mister," Jake said, bringing Jessie back to reality as she stood between them. "If'n you don't, we'll have to tangle."

"There's no need for us to fight. Let the boy go home, then I'll buy you a drink to make peace. We'll play cards and get acquainted."

Jake fumed. He shoved Jessie at the stranger to throw him off balance and get the upper hand, then grabbed for his gun. "No man—"

The stranger pushed her aside and she stumbled, then straightened herself. The black-haired man was holstering his gun before it seemed possible for anyone to draw and fire. Two shots had rung out: the stranger's accurate one and Jake's wild one as he fell backward, dead on impact with the floor.

Nettie smiled and said in a voice only Jessie and the stranger could hear, "Good riddance. You two best git fast. It was a fair fight, but his brothers won't see it that way. They're meaner than cornered rattlers. Nobody here will go against the Adams boys to help you. Hurry. They could be down at Luke's saloon. Sorry, Jess, but Josh wouldn't take your job after you got Jake killed."

"Thanks, Nettie, but I don't think I'll need him now," the redhead remarked, then sent a side glance at her champion to make her point to the woman.

Nettie smiled. "You're right, Jess. Get moving before his brothers come."

Obviously the stranger didn't want more trouble or attention, either, as he said, "I'm leaving, boy, and you should, too. No need to wait for trouble to strike if you know it's ahead and you can ride another trail just as easy."

Jessie watched him head down the street toward the stable at an easy stride. Nobody tried to stop him or to avenge Jake. She wasn't about to hang around and court danger, either! She ran to the hotel, stuffed her belongings into her saddlebags, and left by the back door. She rushed to overtake him before he left town. The stranger had paid for his horse's care and had mounted to leave.

"Wait!" Jessie yelled to him. Catching her breath, she added, "Let me ride out with you. I just have to fetch my horses."

The stranger glanced down the street and didn't see anyone coming after them but knew the boy might need help and protection for a while. "Hurry."

Jessie claimed her horses, paid the man, saddled her paint, and mounted. She joined her rescuer and off they rode with Big Ed's sorrel in tow. The redhead knew this was the man she wanted for her job. Somehow she must convince him to come to work for the

Lanes. She never stopped to think of the peril in heading for the wilderness with a dangerous and mysterious man or imagine what he would and could do after discovering she was a woman. She was too excited and enchanted to think beyond, *I've found him.*

# CHAPTER THREE

They had galloped for twenty minutes before Jessie yelled to the man beside her, "Wait up! We're going in the wrong direction. I live the other way."

The stranger reined in his mount and looked at her. "This is the way I'm heading. You best skirt town and get home fast."

The redhead knew she had to talk fast. She saw surprise fill his hazel eyes when she blurted out, "You need a job, mister? My papa is looking for a man good with his gun. That's why I rode into town to search for the right one. Nettie was about to give me a name when that drunk interfered. We have big trouble with a man named Wilbur Fletcher who wants our land. With your skills, you can scare him off or teach us how to beat him. The law can't help us. He's tried to buy our ranch, but we won't sell. Now he's trying to scare us off or break us with losses. We need help before he kills us."

"I don't get involved in other people's troubles, boy. I saved you once, so git home while you're in one piece. I won't fight over you again."

"But you got involved back there even without my asking or paying."

"If Jake had tossed you out or only roughed you up a bit, I wouldn't have intruded. He was going to hurt you badly or kill you. I don't like to see young boys mistreated for no reason; it riles me into not thinking straight. Stopping Jake's hand was like giving him a challenge. I got you outta there in one piece. No reason for me to take more risks for a stranger. Jake caught me tired, thirsty, and mean. All I got back there was a bath and food. I didn't even get a glass of whiskey or rest. You got the wrong man. I take care of myself, nobody else."

Jessie had witnessed a slight reaction to her story, as if the gun-slinger was moved by it and didn't want to be or show he was. "We can pay you good," she pressed. "You can pick any horse you want from our stock. We'll buy you the best saddle made. If you can't stay long, just teach us how to fight. A man like you has dealt with bad men before, so you know what to do. We don't. Please come home with me."

"Your ma and pa will whip you good for bringing home a man like me. You don't even know me, boy. I could be dangerous. I could rob you and leave you here dead. Everyone would think that drunk's brothers did it. Or I could ride home with you, do in you and your family, and blame it on that landgrabber."

Jessie shook her head and refuted, "You're a threat only to men like that bully and men like Wilbur Fletcher. If you wanted to harm me, we wouldn't have gotten this far from town, and you wouldn't have saved me back there if you're as bad as you think. If the law's after you, mister, we don't care. You'll be safe at our ranch. We need help real bad. You're the best gunslinger I've seen. You're fast and you're clever. A wicked man wouldn't stop to reason with an enemy before drawing his guns. He wouldn't waste time and trouble talk-ing before he settled the matter with his pistols or fists. You left town easily and quickly so you must want to avoid trouble and at-tention. I'm sorry if saving me spoiled your plans for rest and a good time."

"You're wasting your breath, boy. The answer's no. My only con-cerns are my neck and freedom. I don't endanger them for anybody or anything. I keep to myself and stay on the move. All I got in the world is right here with me. It's time you learn nobody does any-thing for anybody without a selfish reason."

Jessie recalled her description of a gunslinger to her father, but her gut instinct said little of those harsh words were true about this man. Except, she thought, he did have keen wits, iron guts, and ex-pert skills. She remembered what her grandmother had said about fighting evil—that it make a person hard, cold, and ruthless. A man like this must have done it plenty of times. He must be so alone, and couldn't be happy. That moved her deeply. She wondered what pain and hunger drove him onward in such a miserable existence. What was he searching and starving for? Himself? Importance? Some lost truth? Peace? Yet he didn't seem as hard, cold, and uncaring as he acted and believed. Maybe his fatigue had lowered his guard around her. Maybe he was trying to hide or control all good emotions so he couldn't be hurt. Whatever he had to prove, he could do it against Wilbur Fletcher!

"You do have a selfish reason to help us," Jessie persisted. "I can offer you a comfortable bed, hot food, rest, and money. All you have to do is protect our ranch and hands from that greedy bastard. Your horse looks ready to drop dead and that cheap saddle can't sit good. Stay long enough to earn new ones. When Fletcher sees we have help and won't be scared off, he'll have to give up."

As the man shook his head, she extended her hand and said, "I'm Jessie Lane. My father owns the Box L Ranch thirty miles east of Fort Davis, four days southwest of here. What's your name? If you have a famous reputa—"

"I don't, and I want to keep it that way," he interrupted, his eyes chilling. "Men with names don't get any peace or privacy. I'm not from around these parts, and I don't ride anywhere picking trouble. Name's Navarro, boy."

"That your first or last name?"

"Just Navarro." It didn't matter if he told the boy that much, as the law was seeking Carl Breed, Junior, and that wasn't his name. Even as he refused his offer, he realized a secluded ranch might be the ideal hideout for a while. He needed to replace the stolen horse and saddle, and to rest. He had escaped four months ago and put distance between him and that cruel northern Arizona prison he'd been in for two and a half years. He told himself to take what he needed and to ride on, but there was something about the boy's innocent face and pleading blue eyes that reached deep inside him and yanked at his feelings, emotions he thought he had destroyed or repressed long ago. This boy loved his family and was desperate to save them and his home, something Navarro didn't have. *Why not use them to help myself?* he asked. *It's his fault I didn't go unnoticed back there, so the little firehead owes me.*

"I won't mislead you; Fletcher has hired guns working for him. He's mean, evil, and dangerous. This job won't be quick or easy. But we'll stand a chance of winning with you on our side. Without you, we'll lose everything."

Navarro removed his tan hat with his left hand, mopped his brow with his other sleeve, and replaced it. Indecision filled him. This Fletcher sounded like a Carl Breed who needed and deserved punishment. What good had it been to rescue this boy if he allowed that bastard to terrorize and murder him? He knew what it was like to be used and mistreated by a cruel man, and bitter hostility surged through him. "What if Fletcher doesn't give up or I get killed by his men?"

"I'll kill him. I won't let him steal our ranch or harm my family. I would have taken care of him by now if it wouldn't get me into jail. My family depends on me. I can't help them from prison. We can't get any proof against him, but we know he's guilty. You can help us prove it or destroy the snake. You won't have to do all the work or take all the risks. I'll ride with you. Whatever happens, we won't let you take the blame and get into trouble; you have my word on it. Please, Navarro, take the job. I need you."

Navarro shook his head as those blue eyes pulled on him like a strong current and the sweet voice washed over him strangely. *You must be exhausted!* he reasoned to himself. "How would you kill him, boy? You can't even take care of yourself."

Jessie pointed to a broken branch at a distance. "See that busted limb?"

Navarro's narrow gaze located it and he nodded.

"Keep your eyes on it." Jessie pulled her pistol and fired. She pointed out five other targets and skillfully struck each one.

As she reloaded and holstered her weapon, Navarro remarked, *"Shu!* You didn't need my help back there. That gun's no stranger to your hand. There's something odd about you . . ." he murmured, staring intently at her.

From the Apache guests they'd had at the ranch, Jessie recognized the Indian expletive, but said nothing to the man. "I was trying to avoid trouble because I had to go unnoticed back there so no one would discover my mission or my sex." She removed her hat and allowed the long henna braid to escape confinement. "I'm Jessica Lane, but I'm called Jessie. Men like Wilbur Fletcher aren't afraid of a woman, no matter how good she shoots. And his men wouldn't hesitate to kill one if she got in their way. I'm good with a gun and horse, Navarro, but the odds are against me. With your help we can halt that bastard. Are you for hire? Name your price. My papa will agree and pay you."

Jessie knew it was daring and maybe crazy, but she casually loosened the plait and freed her hair into an auburn cascade that flowed down her back. Perhaps a woman would be more persuasive than a "boy," and she had to use all she possessed to ensnare him. After all, if he took the job, he would learn her sex soon. As she fluffed her locks, she heard Navarro murmur, "An *isdzan*. . . ."

Navarro's mouth hadn't closed yet. "Jess" was a *woman*, a beautiful woman. Her eyes were as light a blue as a spring sky. Her hair was the color of a chestnut mare under a brilliant sun that freed its fiery soul. The loosened flow of reddish-brown against her flesh softened her features. The startled man watched her use a bandanna to wipe dirty smudges from her silky skin. Her nose wasn't small and dainty, and looked as if it had been broken long ago, but it sat nicely on her smooth face. Her full mouth was appealing and inviting. He felt his breathing and heartbeat quicken as he gazed at her parted lips. Her eyes were large, too, but expressive and captivating, the kind that could draw a man into them like an enticing pool during summer heat. Her jawline almost traveled to a point at her chin but had been softly rounded at the last minute of creation. Her height must be about five three or four. Compared to his six two, she was a little bundle. Whyever, he worried, would a good father let her—

"What have you decided, Navarro? We need to get moving before we lose all light." Jessie felt strange under the scrutiny of those hazel eyes that were more brown than green. "Are you going to refuse your help and let Fletcher murder us or do you want to earn a nice payment for the use of your guns and wits for a while?"

Navarro let out a deep breath. He knew what hired guns would do with this beauty, and it angered him. He also knew what it was like to be totally helpless. She needed him, believed in him, and must even trust him to have discarded her disguise like this.

He couldn't do anything about his problems except try to outrun them, so going with her was as good as anything else he could do for a while. Luckily he came along while that drunk was attacking her. For all the help she was getting from the cowardly men present, Jake could have dragged her upstairs and . . . "Are you crazy, woman? Why would your father let you go into a rough saloon to hire a gunslinger? I should heat up your britches for pulling a stunt like this. Ride home before you get into more trouble. I can't fight beside a female. We'd both get killed." Yet he knew that female warriors could fight as well as men, sometimes better, as the Apaches were one of the few tribes who allowed skilled women to go on raids or into wars.

"Then I'll battle Fletcher alone. Hiring a gunslinger was my idea, but Papa finally agreed with it. I'm not reckless, Navarro; I wasn't traveling alone. I brought Big Ed—one of our ranch hands—with me, but he was killed in an accident yesterday. His horse was spooked by a rattler and he was thrown. I buried him under rocks about twenty-five miles west of town. This sorrel was his. I was too close to town to turn back, and what I have to do is important. You may not love or need anybody, but I do. I'll risk anything for my family and home. I'm sorry about whatever or whoever hurt you so badly that you lost all feelings of compassion. If you need another reason to help us, it's a high-paying job."

Jessie noted his defensive reaction to her perception of him. Quickly she went on. "Everybody knows San Angelo is a rough and ready town. That's where you find gunslingers, and it's closer to the ranch than El Paso or Waco. I was keeping to myself, watching and waiting for the best man to arrive. He did, when you appeared. If your answer is still no, then I'll head on to another town to continue my search. I can't go back to San Angelo and risk being recognized. But I'm not going home without help," she stated with determination.

His gaze darkened. "That's rash and dangerous, Jessie. The men you'll meet on the trail and in rough towns won't hesitate to use you any way they like. You're a beautiful woman, and all alone. It's crazy! You can't do it."

Jessie warmed at his compliment, unbidden concern, and smoldering gaze. "Then, help me. That way I won't get into any more trouble."

Navarro appeared surprised. "How do you know I'm any different, any safer to be around?" he reasoned, looking frustrated and uneasy.

"If you weren't, we wouldn't be sitting here talking like this. You strike me as a good man who's had a lot of bad luck. For some reason or reasons, you don't want anyone to get close to you. That's your business, Navarro, and I won't pry. But you can use this job, can't you? Is it so bad to help someone who needs you desperately while you earn a living?"

The desperado wasn't sure if he liked the way she made him feel.

It was scary, and he hated being afraid of anything. If this woman knew the truth, or even *half* the truth about him, she would take off like a scared rabbit. "Don't you have any brothers? What about your father? Ranch hands?"

Jessie decided she had to be totally honest to win over this wary man. "Papa is getting old and stiff, and he's no gunman. My only brother has a crippled foot and doesn't see well. Tom can't run or ride or fight. The children at school teased him and picked on him, so I teach him at home now. We have fifteen men working on the ranch, but Fletcher has about twenty-five. Our hands are good men, but only two of them are highly skilled with guns: Miguel and Jimmy Joe. Papa's afraid if we do too much shooting back or if we attack them, it'll cause more trouble and danger."

Jessie's gaze remained locked with Navarro's attentive one. "We don't want to endanger our hands. They're more than our working men; they're friends. At first, Papa ignored their bouts of rustling and fence-cuttings, but it got worse. Sometimes they simply shot steers or horses and left them to rot as warnings. The men try to avoid Fletcher's hirelings in town, but it's hard to take humiliation for a long time, and those bastards keep provoking our hands. We've had men shot at while guarding the herd at night. We've had fires in the sheds, foxes locked in the chicken coop, herds stampeded—and more. Last week we found calves driven into mud and fighting for their lives. There were tracks all around the area. I don't know what he'll pull next. In fact, I don't think Papa realizes just how evil and dangerous Fletcher is. Papa's a strong and proud man, but he can't battle such odds, and that hurts him. I'm scared, Navarro, scared my family will be killed. I hate being afraid and feeling helpless. I'm not a coward or a weakling or a fragile female. I work as hard and long as any man on our ranch, but this is one trouble I can't handle for Papa. I know this is a desperate act, but it's the only way I know to solve it. When I thought Jake was going to kill me, I lost my wits and courage. The minute you walked in and took control, they returned. I need you as my partner in this."

Her confession and pleading expression caused him to admit, "Nobody has ever needed me, Jessie, just used me. I . . ." Navarro twisted in his saddle and looked to their rear. "Riders coming fast. Could be trouble. Let's get out of sight."

Jessie led the sorrel into the trees and scrubs. Navarro moved in behind her, but it was too late. Gunshots headed in their direction.

Jessie yanked her rifle free and dismounted quickly, dropping the horse's reins to the ground. Navarro did the same. They prepared to defend themselves.

"Probably Jake's three brothers," she surmised accurately.

Their pursuers dismounted and claimed the other side of the road not far away where better concealment and protection than their location was offered. Gunfire was exchanged.

"Your brother drew first!" Navarro shouted. "I tried to talk him out of it! Ask anybody in the saloon! He roughed up this girl, was about to beat her!"

To avoid a fight, Jessie added, "Jake attacked me! He was drinking and mean! He tried to kill us! We only defended ourselves! Ask Nettie and the others!"

"You killed my brother, and you'll die for it!" came the expected reply.

"We shouldn't have stopped so long to talk," Navarro murmured. "I had you on my mind and dropped my guard. That could have been anybody overtaking us."

"I'm sorry if I distracted you," Jessie replied, "but I had to get your help before you rode off. Now I've endangered you again. Look, they're splitting up."

Navarro noted movement in several directions. He had to clear his head of this tempting female. "They'll try to encircle us. Take the one moving to the left; I'll take the right. We can't let them cross the road and flank us."

The man in the middle opened rapid gunfire to give his brothers coverage, and Navarro had to respond. Bullets zinged and thudded on rocks and wood too close to ignore. Navarro returned what she concluded must be Josh Adams's fire. Jessie could imagine how good he was since Nettie had claimed Josh was the best. Was her partner, she worried, as skilled as their attacker?

The man to their right darted across the road. Jessie aimed her rifle and fired, catching him in the chest. He spun sideways and struck the dirt. Navarro did the same with the racing target to their left, causing each to fire in front of the other. As Jessie attempted to move out of Navarro's way, she placed herself in Josh's sights. The gunslinger lifted himself to get a clear shot. Navarro's instincts warned him and he shoved her to the ground as he jerked his pistol in that direction. It wasn't fast enough, and Josh fired first.

Navarro fell backward, his pistol falling aside. Jessie saw the bloody wound on his temple and was reminded immediately of how lethal Big Ed's had been. She prayed she hadn't gotten another man killed, especially this one.

Cursing filled her ears. She whirled back to see Josh heading her way, about to open fire on her again. She hit the ground, rolled several times to a clearing in the scrubs, and fired.

Josh gaped at the wound to his stomach. Every gunslinger dreaded a gut shot. He placed his hand over it, but blood gushed between his fingers. With hatred hardening his gaze, he headed toward Jessie once more.

"You're wounded!" she shouted. "Let it go! I won't shoot again if you leave!"

Josh knew the man with her was down, probably dead. Yet he had only one bullet left in his pistol and no time to reload in the open. He assumed she was too scared to fire again. "Hell no, bitch. You're dead!" He could see Jessie clearly by now, but her beauty and sex meant nothing to him. He had to kill her in revenge before he suffered a painful death.

Jessie's breathing was labored. Her eyes were wide. Her heart pounded. Her mouth was dry. The wounded gunslinger was dangerous and deadly. She didn't know how many bullets she had left, and there was no time to look or to fetch more. She couldn't risk wounding him again. Enraged, he would keep coming, even on a crawl. This time, she must take aim and—while looking into the man's face—pull the trigger and slay him. It was harder than returning fire or hitting a target she couldn't quite see. But if she didn't, Josh would kill her. The redhead did what she must. She squeezed the trigger and took Josh's life.

Jessie returned to Navarro's side and knelt. He wasn't slower than Josh Adams, but he couldn't kill two men at the same time. He had been struck while saving her life. If he hadn't pushed her aside. . . . She leaned forward with trepidation and listened for a heartbeat. Finding one, she nearly shouted in joy. Hurriedly she yanked her shirt free from her jeans and struggled to remove the binding around her breasts. She had tended enough injured men and animals not to be sickened by blood and wounds. Using a knife, she cut a length to bandage his head. The bullet had creased his temple deeply, but had not lodged there.

Navarro stirred and moaned, but didn't fully awaken. He roused just enough to help Jessie get him onto the saddle of the sorrel. To keep him from falling off, Jessie secured his hands and legs with cut strips of rope. She knew they had to get out of this area before someone came along and more trouble started.

The redhead unsaddled Navarro's horse and freed him. There was plenty of grass and water nearby, if someone didn't find him and keep him, but the mount was too old and tired to be of use to them during this emergency. Jessie quickly tied Navarro's belongings onto the sorrel and dragged his worn saddle into the concealing scrubs. She gathered and replaced their weapons, after reloading them. She swung onto her paint's back, grasped the sorrel's reins, and headed off to skirt town. With luck, no one would see them and she could find a safe place to camp on the Middle Concho River before nightfall.

An hour later, Jessie halted to check on Navarro. He was breathing fine, but still unconscious. There wasn't much light left, but she decided it was best to keep moving as long as possible, to get farther away from town and their deed.

Finally she was compelled to stop because it was too dangerous to push on in the dark. If it weren't for the short vegetation and seemingly endless horizon, she couldn't have traveled this far before night. Even if there had been a full moon overhead, she couldn't journey farther. With the mesquites, rocks, and cactus so abundant, another accident could occur. Too, dangerous creatures roamed at night in their search for food: deadly snakes, spiders, scorpions, and such. She wasn't afraid of coyotes; they were usually cowardly creatures.

She worked their way to the riverbank, feeling it was safer than the desert terrain nearby. Jessie knew that her piebald, Ben, was sure-footed, intelligent, and unskittish, but she didn't want to risk an injury to him or to the sorrel. She dropped the reins to both horses and dismounted. She cut Navarro's bonds, and the injured man's weight assisted her with dismounting him. He slid out of the saddle and landed atop her as she intentionally broke his fall with her body.

Jessie moved from beneath him and straightened his arms and legs. After unsaddling Ben and the sorrel, she let them drink and graze nearby. It wasn't necessary to hobble them or tie their reins to a bush, as Ben would never leave her side and the sorrel would remain close to the other horse. She placed Navarro's bedroll near him and worked him onto it, then positioned her own beside it so she could keep a vigil over him during the night. Head injuries were curious wounds that must be watched closely.

She dared not light a campfire, but longed for a cup of strong coffee. She looked in her supply sack and withdrew two cold biscuits. She searched Navarro's. Jessie grinned as she realized both had been prepared for a quick flight.

Hot and dusty from her exertions and ordeal, Jessie stripped and bathed quickly, knowing Navarro would probably sleep until morning. Besides being injured, he looked tired. No doubt he had ridden a long way before reaching San Angelo. She donned a clean shirt and jeans that fit better than the loose ones she had used during her disguise, but left off her boots. She knelt again beside Navarro, and carefully she removed the stained bandage, tended his wound, and rebound it.

Jessica Lane studied him in the dim light. His midnight hair was silky and nape-length, and looked freshly trimmed. It was cut to comb backward on the sides. A right part caused the top to sway to the left across his forehead in almost a playful manner. His thick brows were far apart, and they, she recalled, hooded deep-set hazel eyes. His straight nose flared slightly at the base. His tempting lips were full and wide, his cleftless chin below it strong. His cheek and jawbones were prominent, creating defined hollows between them that her fingers couldn't resist traveling.

Jessie's enchanted gaze slid over him. Navarro was tall and muscular. Her hands felt his arms to find them hard and well defined. He looked to be in his midtwenties. His skin was smooth and bronzed, and enticed her to caress his cheek where no stubble grew tonight. The white bandage made a striking contrast against that black hair and darkly tanned face. She wondered if he had Indian or Spanish blood, as his features hinted at one or the other. No matter, she didn't care.

He was dressed in a blue shirt, tan vest, and black pants. Without disturbing him, she removed his gunbelt. After laying it aside, she unbuttoned the top portion of his shirt. She could not resist slipping her fingers inside the cotton material to feel his flesh. His chest was hairless. It was smooth, yet hard. His skin was cool to her warm fingers. He was a magnificent specimen, like a wild stallion who roamed the wilderness alone, one who couldn't be captured and tamed unless he was willing. Asleep, his features were relaxed and softened. He was so handsome that her heart pounded and her body flamed with desire. He wanted to be so tough, yet something wouldn't allow life to harden him completely, and she was glad.

Jessie's gaze returned to Navarro's arresting face. He was her captive of sorts. She had him at her mercy. She was taking him home with her. She had saved his life, as he had done for her—twice.

She wondered if he would still refuse her job when he awakened. She wondered how he would feel about getting shot and then being saved by a woman. Some men would be embarrassed and riled and accuse the woman of being to blame. When a man was angry and ashamed, he often became defensive, even cruel, to hide his exposed weakness. She couldn't imagine how this gunslinger would react.

Jessie let her fingers trail over his bold features, and she enjoyed the contact with his flesh. If he knew, no doubt Navarro would think her wicked and brazen for touching a stranger in this intimate way. She had been around men all her life, but she had never experienced this overwhelming urge to examine one. The emotions surging through her mind and body were unfamiliar, but not unpleasant, though a little scary. As her fingers journeyed over his full lips, she imagined how it would feel to kiss him, to *really* kiss him. She lifted his hand and studied it. It was large and strong and bore marks of hard labor. She found that curious for a gunslinger, but her mind was thinking more of how it would feel to have those hands caressing her than for what purpose they had been used.

"Are you dangerous, Navarro?" she murmured dreamily. She removed a gun from its holster. It was a Colt .45, kept in top condition. "How many men have you shot and why? Who are you? Where do you come from?" She fluffed his dark hair and smiled. "What will you say in the morning? Will you help us? I hope so; I truly do." She replaced the pistol.

Jessie eyed him one last time before moving away. She wanted to learn about him. She wanted to be with him. That thought surprised her, considering he was close to a stranger. But there was something about this man, something that appealed strongly to her, something more than his exceptional looks. "Maybe you are dangerous, Mister Gunslinger. I've only known you a few hours, but no man has ever made me feel more of a woman than you have, and most of that time you thought I was a boy! The way you look at me makes my heart race like a wild mustang. I must be loco to carry you home."

Settle down, Jessie, she instructed herself. *It's probably because he saved your hide two times and you need his help . . . No, it's more than that, and you know it. But what? How should I know? How many men like him have you known? None. Get to sleep, girl, before he awakens and finds you fondling him. If he's going to work for you, he has to see you as a boss, like a man. What good in blazes would it do if he did see you as a woman? You can't lasso up with a gunslinger. Mercy, girl, why are you even riding down that silly trail?*

Jessie curled to her side on her bedroll. She snuggled under her cover and went to sleep. She knew Ben would warn her if danger approached.

Navarro awoke early the following morning. His head hurt, but not unbearably. He knew what it was to endure pain, so he suppressed it now with an iron will. His hand went to the injured area and made contact with the bandage. At first he was confused. He wasn't in a dark and musty cell. He smelled fresh air and saw pale blue sky above him. He remembered he was free. He turned his head to look at the beauty lying next to him. She was on her side toward him, cuddled under a blanket. Long, thick tresses of wavy auburn nestled around her neck and half obscured her face. He remembered getting shot, but not coming here. He knew the river was to the west of town and they had been riding eastward. She must have tended his wound and brought him here.

He lifted his head and glanced around. The paint and sorrel were standing nearby, unsaddled and grazing. His stolen mount was not in sight. He knew she must have released him. Dizziness forced Navarro to lie back again.

They were on bedrolls, side by side. He wondered how she had managed this feat. She must be stronger than her size and sex implied.

A morning breeze wafted over them. He couldn't resist cautiously moving aside her straying locks to gaze at her. Jessica. It was a lovely name for a beautiful woman. She was the kind of creature raiding Apache warriors would have captured and enslaved. The morning light adored her red hair and rosy-gold flesh. Her lips were parted, and he wanted to steal a kiss from them, but he controlled that wild urge. Jessie was most unusual. It was strange and stimulating being this close to a woman like her. Feeling aroused by their close proximity, he looked skyward and took a deep breath.

He had wanted to avoid trouble following his escape, but had landed right in the middle of hers. He told himself he should be hightailing it farther east, but he couldn't seem to force himself to leave his bedroll or her side. He was a long way from his trouble and peril, but he couldn't decide how determined the law would be to locate and recapture him. Yet he couldn't run every day and night. He needed time to rest and relax, to enjoy his costly freedom.

What, he admitted, he would like to enjoy most was the woman beside him. How sweet it would be to taste her lips, to stroke her skin, and to enter her body. He could rob her, rape her, kill or capture her as the Apaches had taught him, but somehow he couldn't do any of those things to Jessie. It wasn't because she had saved his life or he needed her job; it was something else, something odd. Besides, this lovely creature had enough pains without him giving her more, and he knew plenty about suffering. It had never bothered him to do what he must or wanted, but this situation was different.

Navarro was glad his wound was on his head instead of his torso. If she had removed his shirt to doctor him, she would have seen the lash marks on his back and shoulders, gifts from a brutal guard who loved inflicting torment and humiliation. He would have deserted Jessie rather than explain those scars.

Navarro's mind drifted to dark days in his past. He had been given a twenty-year sentence for a gold robbery committed by the Breed gang, his father's men. He had escaped prison once but had been too weak from hunger and the beatings he had endured there to get away. Things had been worse for him afterward: filthy clothes and cell, whippings for the slightest offense, starvation or inedible food, rats and bugs, forced labor under a desert sun without water to drink, the summer heat and winter cold of his cell, trips to the "black hole" for defiance, sickness without care, and no family or money for bribery of the guards. It had seemed hopeless, a death sentence.

The worst part was being closed in, locked in a tiny and dirty area. Sometimes he had looked forward to the hard labor just to get outside in the fresh air and sunshine. He would never go back to that hellhole. He would kill or die to stay free. If recaptured, this time he would hang for murder, as he had slain a guard to escape. His path was set now—stay ahead of the law and hangman's noose.

Bitterness gnawed at him. No one had ever loved him or wanted him his entire life, not even his mother and father. They had endured or mistreated him. Nobody had helped him during his troubles, not even when he broke free of his old life. If only he hadn't ridden with his father to punish him, to prove he was more of a man than Carl Breed was! It was bad enough to be either a half-breed or a bastard, but to be both was torment and shame. He had meant nothing to his own parents, so why should it be any different with strangers?

Yet Jessie had risked everything—her life, escape, her mission—to help him. She could have left him there to recover and flee on his own, but she hadn't. Why? Because he had saved her twice? Because she needed his aid at home? No, she had saved him from Josh Adams as repayment. She could have tended his wound, concealed him, then left him behind. She could have left the sorrel and saddle as payment of any debt she felt she owed him. Too, she could find a gunslinger who'd be happy to take her job for the price she was offering, one far better and more experienced than he.

Navarro was bewildered by her behavior. He didn't know much about caring, self-sacrifice, and friendship. He had been taught by his parents, the Apaches, and the whites he'd met that he was a worthless half-breed bastard. He had given up trying to prove them wrong. Yet Jessie wasn't a quitter, and she believed he was worth having around. Should he risk all to help her? What would await him at her ranch? He couldn't make friends there because he had trouble trusting people. He had to stay on guard every minute against recapture, and she would distract him. Even before prison he had to make excuses or tell lies about his past. He had been made to feel inferior, hostile, wary, and defensive. *Why chance being hurt and used again?* he asked himself. *If she knew the truth, she wouldn't want me.*

Sometimes he still had nightmares about horrible periods in his life. Sometimes his entire past was like a long bad dream. But he had learned that good dreams—you tried to seize them and make them come true—were like water that slipped through your fingers no matter how tightly you cupped them. No, a dream wasn't real and couldn't be captured, so it was foolish to try.

Since his second escape, he had survived by robbing a store for food, weapons, and clothes and by setting a false trail northward. He had lain low while they pursued him, then stolen a horse to make distance. Those actions made him a thief, as well as a murderer and a fugitive. He didn't know where to go or what to do—other than to keep moving, to stay on alert, and to keep to himself.

So why get involved or halted by this desperate woman? He glanced at her again and saw she was awakening. Even so, he kept his troubled gaze on her.

Jessie rolled to her back. Accustomed to rising early even if exhausted, the redhead stretched and yawned. The moment her eyes opened and sky was viewed, she jerked upward and scanned her surroundings. Her wide-blue gaze settled on the man who was watching her. She took a deep breath, then smiled at him.

"I was startled for a moment. How do you feel?" she asked as she sat up and straightened her twisted shirt and finger-combed her tousled hair.

"Like I've been shot," he replied, the smile he returned feeling strange and tight on his face. "Thanks for saving my hide back there . . . Why *did* you?"

Relieved he wasn't angry and resentful, she smiled again. "I always pay my debts, Navarro. You saved me twice, so I still owe you. I released your horse; he was in bad shape. You can have Big Ed's sorrel and saddle. Papa won't mind, even if you refuse our offer of a job. I put your belongings over there," she said, pointing to his saddlebags.

He noticed his gunbelt to his left. "That's generous of you, Jessie, but I owe you more than what little help I've given so far. You got a taste of what it's like to almost get killed. Still want to challenge this Fletcher and his boys?"

"We have to, or lose our lives and ranch. We won't be pushed out, Navarro. I doubt you know what it's like to be afraid. You can take care of yourself or move on. We can't. Sometimes I'm tempted to sneak into Fletcher's home and kill him. Yet, as bad as he is, that seems like murder to me. I want to get him in a fair fight or catch him red-handed for the law. After that trouble yesterday, I know I can kill him if I must."

"Then I guess I'll have to help. But you should know there have been times when I've been scared. Nobody wants to die. Only a fool is fearless all the time. The trick is to use fear to make you careful, but never to let it control you. You're real smart and cunning. Your trick in town would have worked if not for that Jake fellow."

"It worked out for the best. I got you instead of his brother Josh. That's who Nettie told me to hire. I had to kill Josh to save us. I left them lying there. I'm sure somebody will find the bodies and bury them. We're several hours west of town, so I think we're safe.

You should rest today. Then we'll move out at first light tomorrow. That's a nasty wound you got. It scared me."

"I'll be fine," Navarro said as he tried to rise. "We can . . . Oh," he muttered as he touched his head and flattened out again at the wave of dizziness. "Whew, it's spinning like a dust devil. Pain don't matter, but I'm not steady yet."

"That's expected. Hard as it is for a man to lie around, that's what you need today. If anybody's searching for us, it's in the other direction. I'll make coffee and breakfast. You stay down a while."

Navarro was reluctant to obey her gentle order, but he did so nonetheless. He saw her disappear into the scrubs to gather firewood and to be "excused." Battling his condition, he did the same nearby during her absence. It felt good when he reclined once more. He hated feeling weak. His mother's people had taught him to ignore heat, cold, wounds, thirst, and hunger. No matter the suffering and hardship, an Apache warrior never complained. Morning Tears had told him that from birth, but his white outlaw father had never learned to do so. Navarro knew there was only one period in his life when he lost his strength. During his imprisonment, he had allowed the constant torment and cruelties to break him. Never again, he swore coldly, then suppressed memories of the brutalities he had endured there.

If anyone besides this woman was present, he realized he would force himself to his feet. Yet he was enjoying her tender care and genuine concern. It felt good to have someone make him feel so important.

Jessie returned with an armload of scrubwood. She built a fire near the river's edge. While it was burning down to cook level, she prepared the pot to perk coffee. Taking a knife, she sliced strips of salted meat and placed them in a frying pan. Pouring water from her canteen, she mixed a bowl of johnnycakes. While Navarro observed her, Jessie cooked their morning meal.

She moved his saddle to his bedroll so he could prop against it, which he did. She poured coffee into a metal cup and passed it to him. As he sipped the hot liquid, the redhead dished up their servings of meat and bread. Jessie settled down on her bedroll and devoured hers, as she was hungry.

"It's good," the black-haired man murmured between bites.

"Thanks. Now that we're friends and partners, how about a last name?"

"Navarro suits me fine. People get too close when they know you too well. I like to keep to myself. Hope you don't mind."

"No problem, Just Navarro," she teased. "I know how men like their privacy. That's about all I've been raised around, so I know how they are."

"You married?" he asked unexpectedly.

"No. You?"

"Nope."

"How old are you, Jessie?"

"Twenty-four. You?"

"Twenty-seven."

"Any family, Navarro?"

"None."

"Besides Papa and Tom, I have a sister and grandmother."

"How old?"

"Who?"

"Your brother and sister."

"He's thirteen. She's twenty. Unmarried, too."

Suddenly they both grinned at their sparse sentences. Jessie put aside her dishes and located a stick. She sketched a map in the dirt and said, "This is where I live. It's good grassland, and we have plenty of water. That's why Fletcher craves it so much. He's backed up to the mountains here," she revealed, pointing to the location. "He can't expand unless he gets our holdings. He also has to depend on windmills for water. They can go dry at anytime."

"That's in the middle of Apache and Comanche territory."

"You've been there?" she asked.

"Nope."

"The Comanches were defeated long ago, so we don't have trouble with them. Actually, we never did. Papa made a truce with them when he first arrived. He got the idea from John Meuseback in Fredericksburg. In '47, Mr. Meuseback made a truce with them and they never raided in his area. Papa earned their respect and friendship early on. Whenever they were in the area, he gave them tobacco, beads, cloth, blankets, and cattle, but never whiskey or guns. He always kept goods on hand as gifts for them. They trusted him and liked him. He wasn't a threat to them, so they were never a threat to us."

Navarro was intrigued. "What about the Apaches? I hear they still roam that area sometimes. They live by their own code: rob, but don't get robbed; kill, but don't get killed; capture, but don't get captured; trick, but don't get tricked. Most tribes prize cunning and deceit in a man more than raw courage or great prowess. A brave warrior is needed and followed only in times of danger; being a cunning and successful thief is more important to them."

"What about right and wrong? Honor? Don't they fear God's punishment?"

"None of that matters to them. They don't worship the one Great Spirit like most Indians. They believe in a Good Spirit and an Evil Spirit. They think the Evil Spirit rules the earth. They pray to him before heading into battle. That's why peace with them is so hard. They're too different from whites. I'm amazed you haven't been attacked."

Jessie wondered how he knew so much about the Apaches, but didn't ask him. He had volunteered more information than she'd expected, and to question him might silence him. She wanted to keep their talk light and easy, with the hope he would continue to open up to her. "The Apaches were harder to deal with . . ." she began, then halted to pour them more coffee.

"Papa came to that area on a military expedition with two engineer officers. They left San Antonio in February of '49 and headed for the Davis Mountains. Their mission was to plan out a road between San Antonio and El Paso. There were thirteen of them: the two officers, a guide, nine frontiersmen, and Papa. He was to record everything that happened for General Worth. Before they could pass through the area, they were surrounded by two hundred Apaches. The Indians escorted them to their village for a talk. There were five acting chiefs among them. When the officers convinced the Indians they were no threat, Papa's party was allowed to leave unharmed. While he was among them, he made friends with the five chiefs, and even with Gomez, a troublemaker who spoke against a truce. When he returned there in '50 to settle, the Indians remembered him. Of course, Papa tricked them a few times."

At Jessie's laughter and grin, Navarro asked, "How? They're masters of trickery. Gifts are fine, but once they're used up, they're forgotten. Just like a man is once he's served his usefulness to them. They live for robbing and killing; it's in their blood and upbringing. If they even suspect an enemy has a weakness, he's attacked. I've roamed enough to know you never let your guard down for a moment—like I stupidly did several times since I hooked up with you."

To stop him thinking about that brief weakness and to learn more, she asked, "What do you mean? They never tricked us or attacked us. Maybe because they believed Papa possessed magical powers."

"An Apache never attacks unless he's sure he'll win and without suffering losses. Each man is free to do as he pleases. They only choose a chief for a short time to lead a certain raid or battle, then he's a regular warrior again. If travelers or soldiers don't stay on alert and appear well armed—like your papa's group must have been— they're attacked without mercy. Once you enter Apache territory, you're spied on all the time. You never see them until it's too late. They watch everything and everyone. They're very patient and cunning. When they bite into a prize, they won't let go until death, like the badger. They learn how many men you have, what arms, what belongings, and your schedule. If you reveal strength and care, you're safe, even if they outnumber you. An Apache never takes a risk of defeat. If the plunder and odds are to his liking, you'll never survive his assault, even ten to one. Cheis, the one whites call Cochise, was a master of such strategy."

"Perhaps that's why they respected Papa so much," Jessie confessed. "He used deceit numerous times. Maybe they feared to harm him, for they are superstitious. He's told me stories many times about those days."

Jessie raised her knees and locked her arms around them. "He used a magnifying glass to show them how it could enlarge objects. He made fires by calling down the sun's power through a burning-glass. He also used safety matches, 'spirit sticks' they called them, to light fires. He pulled tricks with gunpowder inside gourds, and with magnets and a compass. He let them look through his fieldglasses, and that was big magic. It even frightened some of them."

Jessie grinned in amusement as she imagined such a scene. "One time he placed a white flower in his inkwell and let it turn black without dying. They couldn't believe a man could change nature's colors. He made them think his coat was powerful enough to defeat rain, but it was just an ordinary slicker. Papa always asked questions and listened, treated them with respect, and enticed them to show him their skills. He was good at sleight-of-hand; he made them think he could pull a coin or bullet from behind their ears. That amazed and frightened them. They believed he was a medicine man of great power and cunning. He gave the five leaders special gifts before he left, mostly the so-called magic items. He gave his metal hatchet and such to other important warriors. He knew he could replace them in El Paso, and he wanted these men on his side for the time he returned to settle there. He presented Gomez with a horse—they view horses like we do money. The leaders gave Papa a necklace with each one's mark on it. They said it would protect him from all Apaches. It did; not even renegades raided us. When the Indians rode in our area, they never harmed anyone or any animal with the Box L mark on it."

"That's amazing, Jessie. He must be a very clever man to outsmart them. He was wise to use his wits instead of strength to win their favor. They're taught to hate all races, especially the whites and Mexicans. They're raised from birth to see everyone not Apache as the enemy. It's easy to understand, since the Mexicans paid bounties for Apache scalps of any age and sex and the whites stole their favorite lands and made truce with the Mexicans. Farther west, grass and water are prized areas; those are the ones the whites stole from the Indian. Do you know that bad behavior in children is controlled by threatening them with the names of white men, like your bogeyman serves to frighten white children?"

"I've never heard that before. You've learned a lot during your travels, Navarro. I've never been many places or met many people. It must be exciting to see and do such things, to be totally free."

"A man can't always go where he pleases or do anything he wants."

Jessie noticed the bitterness in his tone. "Where are you from?" she asked.

"Here and there, everywhere and nowhere. I stay on the move."

"You don't have any place to call home?" she asked carefully.

"Nope. No home and no family. Just me and my itchy feet."

Without thought or hesitation, Jessie made an offer to the desolate man. "You can stay at the ranch as long as you like, Navarro. Our hands think of it as their home and us as their family. Most of them have been with us for years. It must be tiring and lonely not to have anyone or any place special."

"I've never noticed," he alleged, trying to sound harder than he felt at that moment with her gazing at him with those soft blue eyes and radiant face.

"Everybody searches for love, peace, and happiness in their own way, Navarro. Maybe that's what you've been doing all these years. Maybe you'll like the ranch and boys so much that you'll stay."

"Nope. I get nervous when I hang around the same place and people too long."

"Maybe you've been hanging around the wrong kinds too long," Jessie teased.

"I won't argue that truth, woman. But a man don't change easily."

"I'm sure of that. I live around fifteen to thirty men all the time. I know how stubborn you men are about changes of any kind or size. It's like a war."

"We have too few things in our lives that remain the same, Jessie, or too few things in our control. We like things that are familiar and easy. That way, we don't have to stay on edge or get into trouble so much."

"Little corners of peace in a room full of trouble and darkness?"

He mused a moment, then remarked, "That's a wise saying."

"Gran says it to us when we have problems. She says there are always bright places where we can find peace and safety in this large world of peril and sadness."

"Who is Gran?"

"My grandmother, Papa's mother. She's getting old, but she's a wonder. She's gentle and wise. After Papa, she rules our house."

Navarro studied the woman before him. *Tough but gentle,* he thought. Could she and the ranch be his little corners of peace during his time of trouble and darkness? He had known and enjoyed few bright places in his life. Maybe it was reckless to enter this one. He could be lulled into dropping his guard. Jessie had a power about her that was magical and intimidating. Maybe he would start wanting this woman and her peaceful surroundings too much, and he knew he couldn't have them.

"Navarro? Are you feeling all right? You look so strange. Maybe I should check your wound again." Jessie moved to her knees, closer to him.

Navarro held himself still and silent as she unwrapped the bandage and studied the bruised and torn area. He wanted this contact with her. Her touch was gentle. He closed his eyes and envisioned her as she worked on his pliant body. He heard her reach for her saddlebag. She smelled fresh and clean, and he knew she had changed her clothes during the night. He noticed her garments now fit snugger than before. He felt her fingers pressing the jagged edges into place for healing. Carefully she smeared medicine on the throbbing location, then rebound his head.

The redhead rested her buttocks on her bare heels and gazed at him. He almost appeared to be dozing. Her bold study of him last night surfaced in her mind to enflame her. For some ridiculous reason, she trembled. She felt as if she were near a roaring fire. Her knees were touching his hip, and the area was warm. She couldn't understand how *her* clothed flesh against *his* clothed flesh caused such tingles and excitement to race through her. She knew she should move away, but she didn't want to. Jessie told herself how crazy and dangerous such behavior was. "Is that better?" she finally asked.

Navarro opened those engulfing hazel eyes. "Yep."

As Jessie started to move away, the gunslinger captured her hands and lifted them in front of his face. Jessie watched him as he looked at her hands.

"Working hands. Gentle and kind ones," he murmured. "Thanks, Jessie," he added, then released them as swiftly as if they suddenly had burst into flames.

Jessie felt tense in this unfamiliar situation of being alone with an irresistible man. Their contact caused strange and powerful emotions to surge through her. Gran had always told her that it was dangerous to tempt a man with something he couldn't have. She knew little about this mysterious stranger's character and nothing about his background. Navarro could be dangerous. Yet the kind of peril she sensed had nothing to do with her physical well-being. It felt as if she were quivering from head to foot, as if her body were suspended over smoldering embers. She didn't know what to say or how to behave. From his expression, neither did Navarro. Yet they seemed to have matching needs, troubles, and hungers that drew them to each other.

Jessie could not blame the man for being aroused by the situation. They were adults. They were alone in what seemed more like a romantic setting than a desert wilderness. Though she knew she wasn't beautiful—even though he had said she was—she *was* pretty. No matter if she was dressed as a man, she was shaped like a woman. Gran had told her that sometimes it took very little to stimulate some men's passions to a hazardous peak. She wondered if Navarro found her desirable, then scolded herself for even thinking such a wicked thought.

Navarro broke into her mental dilemma. "Do I make you nervous, Jessie?" he asked. "Are you afraid of me? There's no need."

In a hoarse tone, she answered, "I'm not scared of you, Navarro. I'm just tired. These last few days have been very difficult for me." Rising, she added, "I'd better get these chores done so . . . so we'll be ready to move out if trouble strikes." Jessie pulled on her boots. She began to gather and wash the dishes in the river.

Navarro watched her intently. Unless he was mistaken, she had lied to him for the first time. He *did* make her nervous, just as she made him nervous. Even if for the same reason, he shouldn't do anything about it. Jessica Lane was a special woman. He liked how she made him feel like a special person, too. Crazy and impulsive though it might be, he wanted to be around her longer, and knew he couldn't if he took advantage of her.

That thought surprised him because he had been raised by his outlaw father and his mother's Apache people to take what he wanted and when he wanted it. And he did want Jessica Lane. He wanted her more than any woman he had ever met, almost more than anything in his life. He didn't know about the white man's ways of courting, but he did know that any decent man wouldn't toss her on the bedroll and take her by force or try to persuade her to yield to him using deceit in order to win his help, which she so desperately needed.

Maybe he could trick her into surrendering to him, but it would be wrong. That word thundered through his keen mind. *Wrong?* He had been taught by both sides of his family that doing wrong was the best way for a man to behave. To be successful at it was the highest honor a man could achieve. Still, Navarro could not seem to accept or believe that. Maybe that was why he had never fit in on either side, though he had broken laws in both the red man's and white man's worlds, laws that made him an outcast and a wanted man. What did it matter to anyone, he fumed, that he had been forced to do so to survive?

Jessie completed her task and wondered what else to do to fill her time, thoughts, and energies. She wished they were on the trail homeward. Without a doubt, this was going to be a long and difficult afternoon in camp. She didn't even want to imagine the night ahead, alone under the crescent moon with him.

# CHAPTER FOUR

Navarro pretended to nap with his head on his new saddle. He felt as if he had talked too freely with Jessie. He worried over the way she drew him out so easily, as deftly as a sharp knife working on a hide. But that was the center of it: she was easygoing and straightforward, and he hadn't been around many people like her. She had a way of making him tense at times, and totally relaxing him at others. The redhead was beautiful and desirable, but those weren't her main attractions; her inner beauty was that. He couldn't imagine what it would be like to be around her for a long time or how it would affect him. He knew he couldn't ever lower his guard completely, and she was smart enough to realize he was holding back emotionally and keeping secrets. When a person didn't know something, they always suspected the worst.

Navarro was annoyed with himself for revealing his knowledge of the Apaches, and wondered if she suspected the truth of his shameful birth. If other people could look at him and tell he was a half-breed, she could, too. So why didn't it matter to her? Most didn't want breeds around. *Shu.* Even his name branded him as the "entrails of the earth." Maybe he should change it, as his parents were never married; Carl Breed didn't think it was necessary to wed his Apache squaw, even after she bore him an unwanted son. The desperado knew he had to set some rules with Jessie; privacy was a must. Yet it was going to be hard to back off even a few steps. And for once, he didn't want to retreat.

Jessie sensed that Navarro was awake and deep in thought. As she filled the canteens, she reflected on what little she had learned about him. She tried to grasp hints from his past words and expressions. She couldn't forget what he had said just before their attack by the Adams brothers. What had created such bitterness, such an empty feeling of nobody loving or needing him? Something terrible had caused him to harden his heart, or to try to deaden it. Yet he seemed so forlorn and vulnerable, so hungry for affection, attention, and respect. He seemed so confused, so alone. Whether he knew it or not, Navarro needed to be needed. And she needed him.

Jessie wondered why he appeared poor, why he couldn't afford a new horse and saddle. His hands were calloused from hard labor, so why didn't he have money? His clothes were decent, his hair recently cut, and his weapons were new. Yet his pouches were so small to carry all his worldly possessions. She wished she had looked inside his saddlebags while he was unconscious, but snooping went against her upbringing.

Before it was time to begin their evening meal, she took a walk, being careful on the rocky terrain.

When she returned to their campsite, Navarro was gone. She listened, but heard nothing. She glanced around, but saw nothing. She knew he hadn't left, because the sorrel and his possessions were still there.

Jessie walked to the paint, who was grazing leisurely near the riverbank. She stroked the black-and-white stallion's neck, then hugged him. As he nuzzled his head against her shoulder, she whispered, "Can we trust him, Ben? A man like him can be unpredictable. Why in blazes does he make me feel so—"

Navarro came into sight not far away, and she fell silent. She watched him walk toward her, his gaze locked to her face. Those crazy tingles and hot flushes troubled her again. She focused her attention on her mottled horse.

Navarro joined her on the other side of the animal. "Does he bite?"

Jessie continued to stroke the loyal steed. "Not usually, but he isn't around strangers very much. He's very protective of me and won't let anyone ride him except me. Ben has a keen nose, so he'll warn us if danger approaches."

Navarro noticed the quavering in her voice. "He's good horseflesh. So is that sorrel. You sure your father won't beat you for giving him away?"

If Navarro's last sentence was meant as a joke, it didn't sound like it. "Certainly not. Papa lets me do what I think is best most of the time. He'll probably say the horse isn't reward enough for saving me twice. Papa never whips us, though I think he's tempted to do so these days with my younger sister. She can be unbearable at times. She's very beautiful and educated, but she's so spoiled and defiant." Jessie sighed in dismay as her rebellious sister came to mind. She wondered what Mary Louise would think of the handsome and mysterious Navarro, and what he would think of her beautiful sister. Jessie glanced down at her male attire, then envisioned her sister's lovely dresses and ladylike ways. How could she compete with such beauty for Navarro's eye? Her gaze locked with his watchful one again. She blushed at the line of her thoughts. "I'm sorry. I shouldn't have said that about her. It's just that she's been giving Papa such a hard time since she returned from school back East."

Vexed by the ridiculous jealousy and rivalry for this hired help, she pushed aside worries about Mary Louise. "Papa bred both horses. Carlos helped me break him. Of course Ben allowed me to tame him. He's one of those wild creatures who must be willing to change before he'll yield."

Jessie's blue gaze fused with Navarro's hazel one over Ben's splotched back. The closer they were to each other, the more the curious tension between them mounted. The gunman's hand slowly drifted over hers where it rested on Ben's withers, as if he hadn't noticed it there while stroking the animal. They stared at each other for a few minutes before both simultaneously looked away.

He wondered if her last sentence held a dual meaning, one about him. "A loyal horse is important. He can save your hide. A bad one can make you lose it."

As his gentle touch won over Ben, Jessie asked, "Are you angry I released your horse? I had no right to free him without permission. I was rushed and distracted."

"He was old and tired, Jessie. I only had him a short while, so we weren't old friends. My regular horse was stolen a while back, and he was the only one available at the time." He gazed off into the distance and inhaled deeply. It was crazy how lying to her made him feel bad. "I really couldn't afford a new one. I haven't worked in a while. Been moving around. That's why I decided to take your offer. The money, that sorrel and saddle, and creature comfort sound mighty appealing."

Jessie tried to hide her disappointment that his words hadn't mentioned compassion. "We didn't discuss your salary. Do gunslingers get paid a lot?"

Navarro watched the setting sun enhance the gold spirit in her red hair. Her blue gaze was guarded now. Her body appeared taut, as did her voice. "Don't know. I'm not one. Too dangerous. I like to stay alive."

His succinct and unexpected responses intrigued her. She stared at him for a moment, then reasoned, "But you're so fast and accurate. You're holstering your gun before most men clear leather."

Navarro shrugged. "Adams was drunk and slow."

"That doesn't change your abilities. I witnessed your reflexes back there. Don't men challenge you all the time?"

"I try to keep my skill a secret so they won't."

Befuddled, Jessie asked, "How do you survive, if not by your guns?"

"I bluff or keep to myself. I don't show off in towns. I keep my nose out of other people's lives. It usually works. If it doesn't, I move on."

"I meant, what work do you do for money?"

"Whatever strikes me when I need it."

"Anything illegal?" she hinted, boldly.

Navarro sent her a sly grin that softened his mouth and eyes. "I thought you said that didn't matter to you, that you wouldn't pry. You've already learned more about me than most people know. I've talked more to you in two days than I've talked to others in three years. I'm a loner."

Jessie flushed again; she'd blushed more since meeting Navarro than she had in years. "I'm sorry. I didn't mean to be nosy. I was just trying to get acquainted. For someone who doesn't like to talk much, you're very easy to talk to, Navarro."

He realized he had hurt her feelings. In a gentle tone, he replied, "Talk to me all you want, Jessie, but don't always expect answers. Too many questions make me nervous. Makes my feet itch to move on. Can't help it. That's the way I am. I feel relaxed enough around you to share a few words, but not more than that."

Jessie was relieved at his last words, but still she coaxed, "Please don't let my reckless mouth and forward manner drive you away, Navarro. I'm used to speaking my mind around men. About the only strangers I meet are some of the ones Papa hires as seasonal rovers to help with the spring and fall roundups. Some of them are the same men who return every season. We only keep fifteen regular hands year round. I'll try not to probe again. I'll make sure Papa and the hands don't bother you, either. But it will be hard. They'll make you nervous until they get used to you and you to them. They're a friendly group of men. They're always playing jokes on each other. If they do it to you, it means they like you and trust you and accept you as one of them, so don't get mad and quit." Jessie laughed and remarked, "I remember one joke they played on Big John. He's a black man who works mostly as our blacksmith. He used to be a slave, but Papa bought him and freed him. Big John is very superstitious. One of the hands dressed up in a white covering like a ghost, a 'haint' Big John calls them. The rest of the men pretended they couldn't see or hear the ghost as he moved around the bunkhouse. Jefferson—he's another black man who works for us—told Big John that only a man marked for death could see and hear Old Haint. They let him worry for hours before they revealed it was a joke."

Jessie laughed again before adding, "But Big John got them back. One night he yelled that Indians were attacking. While the men were running around outside checking out the danger, Big John filled their bunks with burrs. You should have heard the yells and curses when they crawled back into their prickly beds. Big John chuckled and told them Old Haint had done it."

"Don't the men ever get mad at each other for being tricked?"

"Of course not. They love practical jokes. It's a crazy way of showing affection and releasing tension from all the hard work. They never do anything mean or harmful or vindictive." Jessie inhaled deeply. It was getting late. "I'd best cook supper so we can turn in. If your head's all right, we'll leave early in the morning."

"It's a little sore, but I'm fine. The dizziness is gone."

"I should check it out and change your bandage."

"No need. It's best to leave it be tonight. I don't want the wound reopened." What Navarro didn't want was to get aroused by her touch again.

After a meal of beans, fried bread, and hot coffee, Jessie washed the dishes in the river and put them away. They had eaten in silence.

In the last light of the day, she gathered scrubwood for the morning fire. While Navarro was out of camp, Jessie moved her bedroll away from his. Now that he was well, it was dangerous and improper to sleep so close to him.

Upon his return, the desperado noticed her attempt to put distance between them. He said nothing and took his place.

Jessie slept soundly all night, perhaps because she had slept little last night while holding a vigil over him.

Navarro observed her for a time. He knew he had to keep to himself at the ranch. He decided it was best to make up a story to tell her father and the men about his past to prevent suspicion. Maybe he should just kill this Fletcher, take the salary, and move on quickly. That way, neither he nor Jessie would be endangered by each other or that landgrabber or the law. No, he argued; he should help her outwit and defeat the villain to avoid attention from anyone. Maybe he should just ride in a different direction from her tomorrow. No, he argued again; if he did that, she had to ride home alone and face that bastard alone.

Besides, he liked Jessica Lane and enjoyed being around her. What was the harm in prolonging that rare pleasure for a while as long as he was careful?

Their third day together began with a quiet meal and some stolen glances. After they were packed and the horses were saddled, they headed westward along the Concho River. Jessie told him the direction she and Big Ed had taken and where they had stopped to camp. Navarro requested no changes in the route.

Jessie let Navarro take the lead, as men usually felt that was their job. The riding wasn't difficult, but they couldn't move along swiftly on the rugged terrain. The sun at their backs wasn't blazing down heat yet, and the spring morning was pleasant beneath a clear sky. She watched him whenever he was in sight, though mesquites often obscured her pleasing view. His shoulders were broad and his back was straight. He rode as a man born to the saddle.

While she was washing the dishes and packing her supplies, he had disappeared downriver to bathe and change clothes. He now wore a pale-blue shirt with his brown vest and jeans. His tan hat stood out against the midnight hair around his collar. Navarro's two holsters were strapped securely to well-muscled thighs. But not once had he glanced back at her so she could admire his face.

During the first break, he had barely talked. It was the same at midday and their afternoon stop. He was different on the trail than in camp, was on constant alert. Maybe he thought the law from San Angelo was searching for them, or some of the Adamses friends out for revenge. He frequently glanced around in all directions, but tried to keep his eyes off her. She knew that from the way his gaze darted away when she looked at him. Jessie feared he was withdrawing into himself again. Perhaps he had known few women, and didn't know how to react around them. She prayed that his feelings about people wouldn't change his mind about the job before they reached the ranch.

As dusk approached, Navarro chose a campsite. "This spot all right?"

"Looks fine to me. I'll get supper going while you tend the horses." Jessie looked at him and smiled apologetically. "Sorry. I'm used to giving orders to the hands, so don't mind my bossy manner if I forget myself with you."

"You *are* the boss, Miss Lane, and I'm the hired help. Don't fret over it."

Jessie smiled at his agreeable attitude. "The hands call me Jessie, not Miss Lane, so you needn't be formal when we get there." Hesitantly she added, "If you change your mind about the job before we get home, I'll understand. It's hard to take life-threatening risks for strangers. I'll still pay you for the safe escort home. The horse and saddle are yours, no matter what you decide."

"You changing your mind about me already?"

"Of course not. But I sort of pressed you into taking the job in a moment of weakness and gratitude. I was afraid after you thought it over carefully, you'd see how dangerous your task will be."

Navarro pushed his hat back from his face. "If I backed out now, you'd race off to another town the minute I was out of sight."

Jessie didn't break their locked gaze. "No, I wouldn't. Jake and his brothers taught me a good lesson. If you have to leave, I'll deal with Fletcher, me and the boys. We've endured his threats too long trying to prevent more trouble and bloodshed. It's payback time."

"How would you do that?"

"Do to him as he's doing to us. Take a lesson from him this time."

"That's what I was going to suggest when we made our plans

against him. He'll get the message. Whatever he does, we do back, only twice as bad. We'll call his bluff, Jessie, then carry out our warning if he doesn't back down. We only have to make sure he can't prove it was us. You don't want the law winning his battle for him."

"We'll make certain we don't land in jail while that villain goes free!"

He saw anger and determination enlarge and brighten her blue eyes. "What if we do slip up and get caught? Jail ain't a place for a woman."

Jessie frowned at the possibility. "Don't even think such a horrible thing. We'll be clever and careful."

"It happens, Jessie. Prisons hold lots of innocent men, or men who were doing what they thought was right, or things they were forced into doing—or even tricked into doing. Why didn't you hire a lawman? Or someone with authority to battle him legally?"

Jessie explained to him what she had told her father about lawmen.

"You're even smarter than I realized. Sometimes the law can't be trusted."

"Does it bother you to think we might have to break the law?"

"Not if we don't get caught."

"Good. I don't like it, but it may be necessary," she admitted.

"You willing to do anything to defeat that landgrabber?"

"What do you mean by anything?"

"Anything, Jessie, anything to win."

He hadn't clarified, so the redhead wasn't sure of his real meaning. "It's like with Josh and his brothers: kill or be killed. Yes, Navarro, I'll do anything to keep my family alive and our home safe."

"What if Fletcher wanted you in exchange for a truce?"

That question took her by surprise. Jessie was amazed that he was talking so freely once more after such a quiet and distant day. "Never," she replied. "I'd die first. I'd never let that bastard touch me."

Her last words stung the desperado, who viewed himself a half-breed bastard. "But you said *anything*. Your family could die, too, if that's the price he demands."

"My family wouldn't expect such a sacrifice from me. They wouldn't allow it. Papa and the boys would gun down that bastard before letting him take me. I meant anything but that. Besides, Fletcher hasn't shown any interest in me."

"That doesn't mean he doesn't have any. Is he married?"

"No, he isn't. He's in his midthirties, rich, and from a good background. Too bad it didn't have a better effect on him. He's been there two and a half years. But he's greedy. He wants to build a cattle empire in our area. He craves power. He has about a hundred thousand acres, and runs about thirty thousand cattle and horses. But he chose a bad spot to create his big dream. He can't expand without taking our ranch. He keeps about twenty-five regulars hired year round; that's a lot for a spread his size. It's clear he has so many men for a particular reason. To fight us."

"Seems crazy to box himself in like that. You sure there isn't another reason he wanted his land, or why he wants yours?"

"Not that I know of or can imagine. I hadn't thought about it that way. There is silver in the mountains southwest of us, but none near us that I know of. We do compete for beef and horse contracts at the army posts in our area. Sometimes that's a lot of money, but he's already rich."

"Is a man ever satisfied with how much cash or holdings he possesses?"

"No. But, most of them don't go around killing and stealing to get more, do they? I suppose I really don't know. I haven't left the ranch much."

"Would you marry a lawman for his help?"

Again, Jessie was stunned and intrigued by his line of queries. What was he seeking? Was he an undercover lawman? Was his style of life a ruse? Was that why he had helped her and hadn't harmed her? After hearing her story, was he going to the ranch to investigate her claims? If all that were true, which she doubted, what should she respond? Navarro made her feel safe, desirable, womanly. He often looked at her as if his gaze were a physical caress, as if he couldn't control his eyes and interest.

"Well, would you?" he pressed when she remained silent.

Jessie began unsaddling Ben as she replied, "Does anyone know what they would do to survive until the moment confronts them? I killed Josh for survival. I suppose it would depend on who he is and how desperately we needed his help." She placed the supply sack nearby. When Navarro didn't continue the conversation, she went to gather scrubwood for the fire to cook supper.

Navarro unsaddled the sorrel and let both horses drink and graze. He vanished into the treeline along the bank to excuse himself and to think while walking. When he joined Jessie at the campfire, their meal was almost ready.

As she handed him his cup and plate, their hands touched twice. "That means, you wouldn't marry a villain, but you *would* wed a lawman?" he asked.

Jessie glanced at him as he took up the conversation where it had left off earlier. She couldn't surmise his motive. She sat on the ground, crossed her legs Indian-style, and sipped her coffee. "I hope I wouldn't tie myself to a villain through desperation or ignorance," she answered. "Everyone has flaws and weaknesses, but that doesn't make a person bad, or all bad. As for a lawman, I can't imagine myself getting bound to one of them, either. Why do you ask?"

"Just testing your feelings about good and bad. I wanted to know how desperate, rather how determined, you are to win. I like to know a person's motives and restraints beforehand. I wouldn't want to risk my neck, then have you surrender to the enemy to make a truce to keep from being pushed off your lands. That kind of survival isn't worth the price you pay."

Jessie had the strange feeling his words applied to more than her predicament. "You mean like the Indians did when they went to reservations just to survive?" she said, taking a bite of the salted meat.

He shrugged. "I guess it's the same thing. Sometimes survival costs a person a lot. Makes you wonder if it's worth it at any price."

"It's a shame the way the Indians have been treated. I suppose peace is never easy."

"Nothing is ever easy, Jessie, nothing worth having."

"You're a very intelligent man, Navarro. We'll have no trouble defeating Fletcher with you on our side."

"You'll have plenty of trouble, woman. He won't be stopped easily. Don't have too much confidence in me. I'm only one man. How do you know a drifter like me won't take off if it gets too bad?"

"Sometimes all it takes is one good man to win a battle."

"How do you know I'm a good man?"

"Good or bad, all I need is a smart and brave man. You're both. I've seen it."

"You could be wrong."

"Am I?" she challenged.

"In all honesty, I don't know. Never had to take sides before. Always fell in the middle or outside of both. What if this Fletcher offers me more to work for him than you're paying me?"

"Papa said that was the danger in hiring a gunslinger who could betray us. But you said you aren't one. If you did move to Fletcher's side, I'd have to kill you if the time came and we battled face-to-face. Or rather, you'd kill me. I wouldn't stand a chance of defeating you. I could be wrong about you, but I don't think I am. I hope and pray I'm not. If you think there's any chance you'll cross over to the enemy, please don't ride any closer with me."

The desperado was moved by the unshed moisture that glistened in her eyes. Her voice was hoarsened by emotion. "Would it bother you to shoot me?"

"Yes, and it would bother me to see one of the hands do it. I know we're almost strangers, but it doesn't seem that way, except when you pull into yourself for hours. We've been together for three days, but it seems so much longer. We can be friends, Navarro, good friends. I'm sure of it. You might even like the ranch and boys and decide to stay a long time, even for keeps."

"I can promise you now, Jessie, I won't be around longer than it takes to do this job. Then I'm on my way. No matter if I did like it, I couldn't stay. I've never been able to hang around a place long. Don't say, give it a chance. It only causes me problems if I don't stay on the move. I don't make friends easily, so don't expect too much from me. I can promise you something else: Fletcher will never lure me away from you. I'll do your job any way I have to. Once it's done and you're safe, I'm gone. Don't beg me to stay. I can't."

Jessie was touched that the job now meant her safety to him. Still, he was warning her to keep her distance. Few men had made romantic gestures toward her, so why should Navarro? Yet, she wished he would. "How can you be so sure about what tomorrow will bring?"

"I'm twenty-seven, so I know myself and life by now. I can't ever shake the trail dust from my boots."

"Because you want it that way, or because something makes it that way?"

"Getting nosy again, woman," he scolded softly.

"Sorry again, Navarro. Let's finish eating and turn in. I'm tired and tomorrow's a long day."

"As you said, how do you know what tomorrow will bring?" he quipped.

"Some things in life are for certain."

He shrugged. "You're right, unless you die first."

"Dead or alive, tomorrow will still come."

Jessie did her chores when she finished eating. Afterward, she washed her face and arms and tired feet in the river. She brushed her hair, which had remained loose, and braided it. Navarro was lying on his bedroll with his hat over his eyes, so she claimed hers.

"Good night, Jessie," he said without moving or lifting his hat.

"Good night, Navarro," she responded, then shifted to her side so she wouldn't be facing him, wouldn't be tempted to stare at him. She mused in slight annoyance; for someone who didn't like talking and prying, he certainly did his share when it came to her. *Some things in life are for certain, unless you die first,* echoed through her mind. For certain, Navarro teased her heart with crazy feelings. For certain, she didn't want to halt those budding emotions. For certain, despite his warning, she would entice him to stay. For certain, she didn't want to die before experiencing the passions he flamed within her.

They followed their same pattern on the trail: Navarro rode in the lead and was silent again today. He said his head was fine, and removed his bandage during their midday break. Since his dark hair concealed the wound, she took his word and didn't insist on checking it. He liked the sorrel, and from the way it nuzzled his hands during stops, the animal took to him. Navarro stayed on alert, and Jessie was glad he was so skilled and cautious.

But each time they halted, he seemed more and more restless. He walked around and tried to avoid her gaze. They reached the end of the river before sunset. Navarro suggested they follow one of the side creeks before camping, since anyone coming from the other direction would be eager to halt at the river nearest the road. It was still early, so Navarro took his rifle and went hunting for fresh meat.

"I'll be gone a while, Jessie, if you want to take advantage of the water."

Jessie hadn't had a thorough bath since Monday night while Navarro was unconscious, and today was Thursday. After she hurriedly collected firewood, she gathered her clothes and looked for a private spot. Navarro had been a gentleman so far, so she trusted him not to spy on her during such a private moment. She stripped off her garments and entered the shallow water. It was chilly, and she shivered. She bathed with speed, dried off, and dressed. She freed the braid and brushed her hair, allowing it to remain unbound. The shorter pieces—cut for her disguise—she fluffed around her face, and they curled fetchingly.

Awaiting Navarro's return, she mixed bread to fry and put coffee on to perk. When he did appear, he was carrying a skinned rabbit in his right hand and his rifle in his left. He came to a stop when she looked up at him from her chore. He stared, then shook his head. As if suddenly reluctant to approach her, he did so slowly. He held out the rabbit, and she took it.

"Thanks. It'll be nice not to have salted meat again tonight."

As the creature was exchanged, their fingers grazed each other's.

"I'll wash up while he's cooking," Navarro said. He moved as if anxious to get out of camp and away from her. He didn't return until the meal was ready.

Jessie handed him his plate of meat, bread, and beans. She noticed how he made certain their flesh didn't make contact. He sat down with his side toward her and began to eat. Was he trying to prevent himself from making advances? Or was he trying to show he wasn't interested in her as a woman? Or did he fear she wouldn't be receptive? Maybe she had duped herself into thinking he was just as attracted to her as she was to him. How embarrassing it would be to entice him if he wanted to be left alone!

The meal ended in strained silence. Jessie did her chores, then after checking Ben, she sat on her bedroll. "What's wrong, Navarro? You've been quiet all day." Usually he passed the ride in silence, but not all evening in camp.

His tone was gruff as he replied, "You relax me too much. I say too many things. I get too comfortable around you."

Jessie smiled, mostly to herself. "Is that bad?"

"A man like me can't stay alive that way."

"How will us becoming friends endanger you?"

"It lowers my guard. You're a beautiful and tempting woman, Jessica Lane, a damned distracting one. I've never known a lady before. I'm not sure how to behave around one. It isn't good for us to be out here alone."

Jessie's pulse raced. "I haven't been told that many times. Thank you, Navarro."

His surprised gaze shifted to her lovely face. He felt his heartbeat increase and his body tense. "You don't have a man at the ranch?"

"No. The hands are like my brothers, and there aren't many others around."

"Are those cowpokes blind or crazy?"

Jessie laughed to ease the tension within her and between them. "I've been raised around them and work every day with them, so they think of me as Papa's son or their little sister. I'll be their boss one day: Papa's leaving me the ranch. Tom can't run it, and Mary Louise would sell it to escape."

"I doubt many of them see you as a sister, Jessie," he refuted.

"If they don't, they keep it to themselves. Maybe they don't want to offend me since they'll be working for me one day. We ride herd and fence together, tend sick animals, help with foaling and calving, do roundups and branding side by side. Maybe I work them too hard for them to have time or strength to treat me as a woman. I don't mind; it gets the job done."

"How do they keep their eyes and thoughts off you long enough to work?"

Jessie glued her gaze to her half-empty plate. "When I'm filthy and dressed like them, they probably don't remember I'm not a boy. I fooled you and the others in town. I'm not very feminine."

"Where did you get that crazy idea?"

Jessie glanced up. He sounded angry. "The mirror and past experiences."

"Both lied to you. You only fooled everyone back there because you're clever and you wanted to trick them. If you wanted to play the woman, you could do it better than most. You stay Papa's son because you think it's expected of you. You have confidence in everything, except what you are and what you want. What *you* want, Jessie, not your family, not your duty."

"My sister is very beautiful and ladylike. Nobody ever forgets she and Gran are women. It's different with me."

"Only because you forget it, too."

"It's hard being a ranch hand and woman at the same time, Navarro."

"What's hard is being a son and a daughter at the same time."

"How would you know?" she snapped, irrational anger filling her.

"By listening to you. Everything has been for your family. You would sacrifice anything for them. What would you sacrifice for yourself?"

His last question haunted her, as she didn't know. "I have everything I need, a good home and a wonderful family. They would do the same for me."

"Even your sister? Would she die for you, Jessie? Would she do anything to protect your family and home? Would your brother? Your grandmother? Your father? Or would they surrender if the odds became overwhelming?"

Jessie knew he was serious. She asked herself what the others would do if defeat was imminent, if certain death would result if they didn't yield. "Mary Louise would surrender, but Papa, Gran, and Tom wouldn't. Neither would I."

"If your father loves you so much, why does he risk your life?"

"He doesn't; *I* do. You sound awfully cynical about home and family."

"I don't have either, so how would I know about them? I'm trying to learn what drives you and them before I get there."

"Love, honor, pride, and the hunger for peace, Navarro. Do you know about them?"

"Very little."

"Perhaps that's why you can't understand them."

"Perhaps."

She put aside her plate. "I'll teach you, if you're willing."

"Like that wild stallion, I have to be willing to be corraled and tamed?"

"That isn't necessary. You can still have those things and be free. Some of the men at the ranch have known hard lives before they came to us. Big John was a slave. Jimmy Joe's father beat him and worked him like one until he ran away. Miguel is probably still wanted by the law in Mexico; he was framed by a man who wanted his family's lands. His family was killed. Then Miguel was accused of murdering one of the landgrabber's men. If he hadn't escaped, he'd have been hanged. Others have bad pasts, too. We've never judged them. The ranch is their home. They're safe and happy there, and free to leave whenever they wish. Whatever made you so bitter, it will destroy you if you don't get rid of those feelings. Gran says that having to fight for yourself all the time makes a man cold, hard, and ruthless. Don't become like that. Find a place where peace lives, Navarro, before it's too late. If not at the ranch, then somewhere else, and soon." Her entreating gaze was locked with his tormented one.

"There is no place like that for me, Jessie."

"There could be, if you allowed it."

"I *can't* allow it."

"Why not?"

"Don't wait for me to answer, Jessie; I can't do that, either. Let's just turn in."

"All right, Navarro, we'll drop the talk. I don't want you losing your tongue again. More coffee?"

He extended his cup to her and she refilled it. "Thanks."

"You're welcome." Jessie carried out her chores and claimed her bedroll. "Good night, Navarro."

" 'Night, Jessie." He finished his coffee, rinsed the cup, and lay down.

The following day they journeyed for monotonous hours over a terrain that grew desolate. The road was dry and dusty, and the countryside was deserted. Winds frequently whipped around them and tugged at their hats and clothes. The mesquites and cactus were abundant. The landscape stretched out for miles around them, offering lengthy visibility. There were no clouds to shade them, but fortunately the day wasn't terribly hot. They passed buffalo gourds running along the rocky ground and prickly pear growing in clusters. Bunches of grass waved in the breeze. It was quiet, almost deathly quiet.

Yuccas appeared. Soon, mesas were seen in the distance with their flat tops. Hillocks broke the flatness of the landscape, as did occasional draws and arroyos. A whirlwind played to their right, then another danced to their left.

At noon, they ate the extra cold bread and meat that Jessie had prepared that morning in camp. They washed it down with tepid water, and didn't build a fire to perk coffee. They spoke a few words, but hadn't indulged in a real conversation since rising, even though they were riding side by side on the road.

Just before reaching Horsehead Crossing, Navarro halted and lifted himself in his saddle. His keen gaze stared at the area beyond them. "Lots of dust. Somebody's coming. Let's get out of sight. We don't want any trouble." He guided her into a ravine a good distance from the road and dismounted.

Jessie was surprised and pleased when he assisted her down, as she was a skilled rider. She watched him lead the horses into the deepest section and secure their reins to a scrub. He came back to where she awaited him and scrambled up the bank. He extended his left hand and pulled her up beside him. Their gazes touched for a moment as he steadied her, but they were pressed for time. They took their places where they could peer over short mesquites, crouching low near the edge until it was time to jump into the ravine to hide.

"It could be freight wagons, or soldiers, or a band of outlaws on the move," Navarro deduced. "Too much dust for one or two men. I'm not taking any chances with you."

"You think they saw us?"

"Nope. We were moving too slowly to create any signs at that distance."

"Is that why we've been traveling at this pace?"

"Yep. It isn't too hot for a faster one if we rested and watered the horses, but you can see a long way out here so it's best to be careful."

They watched the dust and movement get closer and closer. Men with extra horses rode steadily in their direction. Sounds of the travelers finally reached their alert ears. The mesquites were shorter in this area and they were a good distance from the road, but Navarro said, "Let's duck now."

He slipped over the rough edge, then helped her down beside him. They lay on their stomachs on the sloping bank. He kept her close, and his arm went over her back in a protective cover. "Don't talk or move when they reach us," he whispered. "Sound travels out here."

Jessie obeyed his gentle order. As the group neared, he gingerly slid farther down the bank and pulled her along with him. On his back, he pressed her head to his chest, and Jessie allowed the stimulating contact. Navarro remained motionless, and so did Jessie. She felt the strength of his embrace and arms. She felt the warmth of his comforting body. She heard his heart beating at a steady pace. She inhaled his manly odor. She was safe in his arms. She relaxed with her cheek against him and her arm over his stomach. She closed her eyes. He was a splendid and wild dream, and she longed to capture it, to make it real.

A lengthy time passed, and the group was long gone. Jessie was so calm and relaxed in his arms that Navarro wondered if she had fallen asleep. She felt wonderful cuddled in his embrace, and he hated to end it. During his eight years with his mother's Apache people, he had seen how important women were to men, though he hadn't learned that by the way his white father had treated Morning Tears. Although few women were given names or mourned at death, life often centered around them. The most successful man had many wives, and proved his worth by being able to support them. When he failed in a raid, the wives ignored him and taunted him, and he hung his head in shame. He redeemed himself by bringing home many goods and gifts for them. He strutted under their affection and praise, as if the most important thing in life was pleasing them, though it was never said.

Apache women preferred a man who was a good thief over a brave warrior. They wanted to be the second, third, or fourth wife of such a successful bandit. To be a man's only wife meant he was poor and there was more work for her to do. Since Apache women could choose their own mates, it was usually a man who already had other wives. They were selfish, greedy creatures who wanted a husband who could give them many trinkets and supplies through deceit or robbery. His bravery was only valued if the white soldiers were attacking. Navarro had never cared for those women. He had supported his mother in the village, but never sought a wife. No doubt none would have tended the horses he staked before her parents' tepee, the sign she accepted a proposal, because he was only concerned about becoming a good warrior and surviving the white onslaught, not becoming a clever thief.

Jessica Lane wasn't like that. She was strong, brave, honest, and hardworking. She admired courage and honor and warrior skills. She would want to be the one wife and partner of a man, not share him with others to lessen her chores. She didn't seem to care about trinkets and false faces. She never shamed a man for revealing a moment of weakness, as when he was shot.

He recalled what she had said about love, pride, and honor. Pride was important to him, but he knew little about love and honor. He had lived a dangerous and destructive life, merely existing for twenty-seven years. He had been broken in prison, but Jessie made him feel strong and unconquerable again. Her attitude made him feel worthwhile. He hadn't realized he possessed hungers for peace and love or that he needed anybody until he met her. He wanted her, but not just sexually. She touched him, moved him, inspired him to crave a new and different life. Others had made fresh starts at her ranch after bad pasts. Could he? How long would it last before the law swooped down like a vulture and devoured him? How would Jessie feel if she learned the truth about him, his mixed blood and criminal life?

Sweat increased over his body, and it wasn't because of the sun on his front or the warm earth at his back. *Shu,* she was one irresistible woman!

Jessie felt the tension enter Navarro's body. She heard his heartbeat increase. She noticed the change in his breathing. She felt the moisture on his shirt.

"They're gone," he finally said, sensing the danger of lying there longer. *Run, Navarro! Get clear of this powerful temptation before you're trapped.*

Jessie lifted her head, and their gazes locked. He saw and felt her body react the same way his was doing, except her cheeks flushed and her eyes softened and glowed. The desperado wondered if she realized how she was looking at him, how she affected him. He wondered if he was reading her right. If he was mistaken and made a move toward her . . .

# CHAPTER FIVE

Navarro wanted to kiss her, to hold her forever, to make her his; but such daring behavior could frighten her. He didn't want that; he wanted more time with Jessica Lane. To have it, he must earn it. If he tried to seduce her, she might think it was an unspoken price for the aid she so desperately needed. If she yielded to him, he didn't want it to be for that reason. He couldn't help but think that if she knew the truth about him, she wouldn't be looking at him with yearning in her blue gaze and she wouldn't be tempting him to steal the treasures she possessed. He could sate himself if she were another woman, a female for hire, but she wasn't. Jessie was a woman to love, not use.

Love? his flustered mind echoed. What did he know of that emotion? Very little. He couldn't start something, anything, with Jessica Lane because nothing could come of it, except anguish for both of them. Where could it lead? Nowhere. After spending days with her, he couldn't bring himself to hurt her. If not for his dark past, Navarro admitted with bitterness, he would go after her, wouldn't he? Yes. The strange answer flooded his mind. Here was a woman who knew how to love, to share, to hold on, to inspire self-worth. But his past did loom over him like dangerous storm clouds about to strike the land below with their cruel violence and undeserved destruction.

Jessie sensed the turmoil in Navarro. She read it in his worried gaze that he always seemed to try to keep impassive. Here was a troubled man, a man who didn't know his value and appeal, a man who bore resentment and scars from life's cruelty, a man in bitter conflict with himself and others. He was so confident and strong in some areas, and so weak and vulnerable in others. He must have known anguish and rejection many times in the past. Could he change? she wondered. Did he long to become different? Or was he so set in his ways that it was too late? Jessie wanted him, but it was too soon, if ever the time would be right with this tormented drifter.

If she enticed him, it could lead anywhere, nowhere. The time and place were wrong for seeking the truth of why they were drawn to each other, in both a physical and emotional way. If she did expose willingness, he could reject her, become angry at her wantonness, could run for cover far away. Also, he could think she wanted to surrender to him just to make certain he aided her cause. He already considered her self-sacrificing. She needed more time to get to know him, to get closer to him, to let him do the same with her.

"You think it's safe to leave now?" Jessie asked in a strained voice.

"Yep, the sooner the better."

Both stood and brushed off their dusty clothes. They went to the waiting horses and mounted. They wound their way through the dense mesquites and headed down the deserted road again.

They reached Horsehead Crossing. They crossed the wide and shallow Pecos River, journeyed to the Comanche River. Near it, the yuccas, mesquites, and cactus were joined by oaks and cottonwoods. Mesas lifted heavenward from the harsh terrain of rocks and light-colored sand. Fluffy clouds decorated the sky today. Ten miles above Fort Stockton, they followed a branch off the main river and found a safe and secluded campsite. They were stopping early this evening, but it was necessary. They didn't want to halt too near the post and town, and it would take too long to get miles beyond them. They dismounted and glanced around the lovely setting.

Navarro unsaddled the horses and tended them while Jessie collected scrubwood. After lighting a fire, the redhead went to the water to wash her face, hands, arms, and hot feet. It felt good to her to clean and cool her dusty parts. When she returned to the campfire, the handsome male had coffee perking and their meal in progress. Jessie was surprised and pleased by his participation in the chores tonight. He looked up as she approached. When she smiled and thanked him, he responded with a one-sided grin, as if he were only first learning to smile. Jessie took over the cooking, and soon they were eating a common trail meal of beans, fried meat, skillet bread, and coffee.

Little talk took place between them. When they finished, Navarro helped her wash the metal cups, plates, utensils, and cook pots. Supplies were put away for the night, and bedrolls were laid on areas swept clean with a brush limb. Each realized there were only two more hours of daylight. Each was aware of their strengthening attraction and of the night ahead.

As they both needed something to occupy their hands and minds, Jessie suggested, "How about a few hands of poker? I brought cards along for me and Big Ed, but we never got around to playing any games."

"You know how to play?"

"The boys taught me. It passes time when you're on the range guarding herds or while you're waiting for a mare to foal. We only play for fun—no gambling. I can use leaves for money, and you can use small stones. How about it?"

"Fine. A handful or certain number of stones and leaves?"

"Fifty each, so we can keep count."

"If you win, you want to know it, huh?"

Jessie laughed. "Don't you?" she teased.

"Yep."

They collected their "money" and sat down on Jessie's bedroll, facing each other. They heard the rippling and rushing of water as it passed rocks and twigs in the stream. The fire crackled and sent wisps of gray smoke heavenward. The odors of their meal left the area as an occasional breeze wafted through camp. The most noticeable smells were the dusty dryness of air belonging only to the desert and the smoke drifting upward from a dying blaze.

As Jessie shuffled the cards, Navarro pointed out the porcupine who had come to drink downstream from camp. The spiny, rotund creature took his fill and waddled off into the trees on the other bank, paying little attention to the couple. The paint and the sorrel were at ease, whinnying softly ever so often, their hooves making noise as they shifted about as they grazed and drank. It was a pleasant evening and tranquil setting.

After Navarro cut the deck, Jessie passed out five cards each, facedown. They studied their hands and plotted strategies. Bets were

made, and other cards replaced unwanted ones. Two rounds of
raises ensued before Navarro called her. Jessie grinned as she pulled
the winnings—leaves and pebbles—toward her with a hand of three
jacks against his pair of kings.

"You are good. Never trust a woman smarter than you are, I've
always heard."

"Then you have nothing to fear; it was pure luck of the draw.
I was going for a pair, but that third jack leapt into my greedy
grasp."

As Navarro shuffled the cards this time, he asked, "How big is
your ranch?" He hoped that talking would distract him from his
rising desires for her.

"Three hundred thousand acres. It's green land with rolling hills
and lovely trees. There are some mountainy regions, but mostly beyond our boundaries. We have the Calamity River coming from the
south, and the Alamito along our western side. Our grasslands are
some of the best in Texas. It's beautiful, Navarro."

After dealing their cards, he continued with, "How much stock
do you run?"

Jessie arranged her hand and decided which cards to replace.
"One hundred thousand head of cattle and horses. We had more,
but several periods of hard times thinned us out. We're rebuilding
and strengthening the herds now. The panic in '73 devastated many
ranchers. Papa was hurt by it, but not destroyed like many were."
Jessie opened, Navarro matched, and she exchanged three cards.

"What happened?" The desperado asked. He had been in prison
in '73 and hadn't heard about a panic. *Keep her talking and not tempting
you, man.*

"The railroads were competing heavily for business from ranchers. The market was so good for beef the season before that some
ranchers drove every head they could to Kansas stockyards: cows,
heifers, yearlings, and immature steers. I don't know how much you
know about ranching and breeding, but those are called stock cattle.
The best cattle to market are four-year-old steers, males castrated
as calves." Jessie raised Navarro's last wager. "Trying to get rich,
some ranchers flooded the market, but the buyers didn't want stock
cattle, just big and healthy steers, and few of them at that time.
Most of the regular buyers didn't even come to town that season.
Papa didn't have an advance contract from a packing house, army

post, or Indian reservation, and we arrived late, the end of September, because of rustlers on the trail."

Navarro checked his hand and raised Jessie's last bet. "What happened?"

"All the ranchers could do was hold the cattle there, fatten them in stockyards, and hope to sell them the next season. Or they could return home, if they could afford to pay for another cattle drive. Supplies, wages, losses, and incidentals can add up to an unaffordable price. So can using stockyards for a long time. Most of the men had to borrow from banks to survive and to feed their herds. Their loans were due in October. When the Panic started back East, it moved here fast. The banks couldn't loan them more money or extend their notes."

Jessie matched Navarro's last bet, but didn't raise it. "What made it worse was the terrible corn crop that year. There wasn't enough to feed and fatten such large herds over a long period of time. What corn there was, was priced high. On top of that, the season had been rainy, so the grass on open range was bad. Some men shipped cattle ahead with hopes of making sales once their herds reached the East; it didn't work and they took awful losses. The Cattlemen's Association said the losses amounted to over two million dollars."

As Navarro planned his next move, Jessie related, "A lot of cattle had to be sold off just for tallow and hides. Many ranchers and bankers lost big. News came that the easterners didn't need or want more cattle. Papa divided and sold our herd to small buyers because we had good steers. Prices were low, but we had no choice. It was too hard on the cattle to drive them back home, and too expensive. Better to earn a little than to spend or lose more. The buyers knew it and took advantage of everyone. Usually a mature steer weighs around twelve hundred fifty pounds and sells for about three cents a pound. Papa got ten dollars a head instead of thirty-five to forty. He was trying to raise money that year to buy more shorthorns and blooded bulls for better breeding."

When she stopped talking and checked her hand, Navarro called her.

As she laid down the cards—two sixes and two aces—for him to view, Jessie said, "In a way, we were luckier than most ranchers; at least we still had our stock cattle at home, and horses for army sales."

Navarro grinned as he spread out a straight of two, three, four, five, and six.

Jessie eyed the cards and teased, "You had my six. I needed it for a full house. That would have beaten a straight."

"I'll only help you beat Fletcher and his gang, not defeat me, woman."

"One last hand to break our tie?" she hinted.

"Yep. You deal. Don't cheat, 'cause I'm watching you close." As she shuffled, Navarro remarked, "That was smart of your father not to drive his whole herd to market to get rich quick."

Jessie worked with the cards again. Hoping Navarro would open up more if she did, she kept chatting. "Papa's taught me a lot about breeding and marketing to prepare me for the time I take over the ranch one day. He's had a hard time over the years. He's faced hardships and failures many times, but they've never broken him. He lost two sons and my mama, and that hurt him deeply. Jedidiah Lane is proud and tough, but I think you'll like him. He's determined to succeed with the ranch and to hold on whatever it takes. Don't be upset if he's standoffish at first. He hates for others to fight his battles for him, but it can't be helped this time. He's been there twenty-six years." Jessie dealt five cards each. "Just as things look bright for him, dark clouds move in. He almost failed another time in '68 to Spanish Fever. Sometimes people call it Texas Fever. It was a hard time."

"How so?" Navarro inquired, watching her closely. She was so beautiful and tempting, and their conversation wasn't distracting him like he'd wanted.

"A lot of Texas longhorns were sold and shipped back East that season. Nearly every shorthorn they came into contact with died. The eastern ranchers, feeders, and butchers went loco; some lost everything, and blamed longhorns and Texans. They tried to pass quarantines and laws against shipping longhorns out of our state. Railroads began refusing to ship our cattle. When we tried to drive them to markets, we weren't allowed to travel over certain lands or use ponds for drinking. People became afraid longhorns would spread the disease everywhere."

After the opening round of bets, unwanted cards were put aside and others taken. A slow series of raises followed as they talked.

Jessie continued her explanation. "You see, Spanish Fever rarely troubles or kills Texas-bred cattle. But if you mix the herds or let eastern cattle graze the same land behind longhorns, the other herds die fast. For a while, people were afraid to buy or eat Texas beef. The easterners hated longhorns and Texans. We couldn't ship or sell our steers, because Papa mostly had longhorns. We only survived ruin because of beef and horse contracts with western posts and Indian reservations. That's when Papa got into crossbreeding."

"What kind of crossbreeding?" he asked.

"Papa bought two Durham bulls. Shorthorns gain faster on corn and certain grains, but longhorns grow faster on grass. Crossbreeding high-grade bulls with female longhorns improves the bloodline, quality of meat, and sales. There's a good change in their color, shape, and size. Some of the best and largest steers are crossbreeds. If you don't know a steer's been crossbred, you have to look close and be smart about it to realize the half-breed has Texas blood of the mother."

The word "halfbreed" stung Navarro. To conceal his reaction, he asked, "If your bulls are so important, do you keep them guarded from Fletcher?"

"We have two Durhams, one Booth, and one black, hornless Galloway. Papa keeps them near the house. Luckily the crossbreed looks like a shorthorn, but he's not endangered by Spanish Fever, like his Texas mother isn't. Matt makes certain the boys keep an eye on the bulls. We can't afford to lose them."

"Who's Matt?" he probed, catching a new softness in her voice and expression.

"Our foreman, Mathew Cordell. He's a lot like you—quiet and serious," she explained at his surprised look. "You'll like him. Matt's easy to be around. He's been with us since I was a child. I call." She spread her hand: a flush of clubs.

Navarro exposed his cards one at a time: a full house of two fours and three queens. The last card revealed was the queen of hearts. As it touched the sleeping roll, his gaze locked with hers as if sending her a subtle message.

"You win again. That was fun, Navarro. We'll have to play again some time. It's almost dark so we'd better get some sleep. We have one more night and a day and a half on the trail."

"You restless to get home?"

Jessie couldn't tell him that the responsibilities of home seemed far away and almost unreal at this moment. How strange, she mused, that only Navarro and this setting seemed real. It was as if they had been together for a long time. She wished she could spend more time alone with him, but duties and dangers called to her from far away.

Navarro was aware of the past six days between them, and of what little time remained before they reached the ranch. He wanted to hold her tonight, as he had in the ravine. He yearned to feel their lips and breaths mingle, to have her bare flesh against his, to have her murmuring his name, to unite their bodies in sheer pleasure. He warned himself he should run fast from this impossible situation, but he couldn't, not until she was safe from Fletcher and his gunmen.

The cards were put away. The horses were checked. The fire was down to embers, creating a soft glow. Night birds and insects sent forth their tunes and cries. A frog went "plip" as it jumped from a rock into the stream. Limbs and leaves moved in a gentle breeze, creating shadows and shapes on the ground. Stars twinkled overhead as if dancing in place against a darkening backdrop. Jessie and Navarro claimed their bedrolls and remained silent.

Jessie heard her own breathing. Her eyes adjusted to the darkness. She glanced at the shape that she knew was Navarro lying on his side away from her and the fire's last glow. A coyote howled in the distance, but she didn't fear it. She asked herself what she wanted and needed in life, from life. What would her father say if she chose this mysterious stranger to share it with, to share the ranch Jed had created from sweat, blood, hardships, and toils? What if she wanted Navarro, but couldn't win him? What if her father rebelled at their union? What if her father was willing, but something stood between them?

Jessie wanted him to be with her, to stay at the ranch. She wanted him as a friend, a helper, a lover, a husband. She had known many men who worked on the ranch and those she'd met in town or on cattle drives. But this man reached her, touched her, awakened her as a woman as no other man ever had. This was the man for Jessica Lane, she decided. He wasn't perfect, but who was? This was a man to whom she could give her all, a man whose children she wanted to bear, a man whom she could love and labor side by side with for the rest of her life, a man worth fighting for. She envisioned him laughing, talking, and being with her. She saw his smile, the glow in his hazel eyes, the tension gone from his body and mind. Those images filled her head as she drifted off to sleep.

Navarro propped on his elbow and watched Jessie. Her breathing told him she was asleep. He knew she had been restless since the sensual episode in the ravine. His troubled past seemed so distant tonight, as it had since meeting Jessie. But it was real, and he shouldn't allow himself to forget that for even a moment. The threat would never disappear; he had escaped prison, killed a man, and stolen from others. How long did he have with her before he must be on the run again? How should he handle that insufficient time? If only he could have her for a while—even once would make the coming dangers easier to accept. It would be unbearable to never have anything good or special in his life. Didn't he, didn't everyone who had been cheated by life, deserve a few of those bright corners she had mentioned? Trouble was, he could get entrapped there. Was helping and being with Jessica Lane for a short time worth the risk of his freedom and his life? He must decide soon.

Navarro and Jessie awakened; their gazes met across the space which separated them. A twig broke, capturing their attention. Both glanced that way and saw a pronghorn at the stream with her young. Jessie smiled at the sight of mother and child. She hoped Navarro wouldn't want to kill them.

The desperado wasn't even tempted. He recalled how the Apaches often captured birds and animals to give to their children to torture. The women in particular enjoyed watching their children learn that skill. Mercy was a rare thing for some tribes to feel or show, especially to their worst enemies, the Mexicans and whites. That was another way in which his Apache blood was not strong. Killing for survival was natural and necessary, but torturing for sheer pleasure was not.

Navarro shook such thoughts from his head. He stood and flexed. "Up, sleepyhead," he told Jessie, who hadn't moved from her supine position. She was far too tempting lying there with her unbound locks flaming around her lovely face.

Jessie stretched and yawned. "I feel lazy today. It's been a long journey. As soon as we get home tomorrow, we'll be put to hard work immediately. I dread it, but I want it over with. We'll plan our strategy at the ranch."

Navarro thought she appeared just as reluctant to get on the move as he was and to end their private time together. He gathered wood and lit a fire while Jessie splashed water on her face, then brushed and braided her hair. As he made coffee, she cooked meat and bread.

Within twenty minutes, they had finished eating and washing the dishes. Jessie tossed the blanket over Ben's back. The saddle was thrown over it, then cinched in place. She secured her saddlebags behind the cantle, and tied her bedroll atop them. Her rifle was sheathed and her rope was hung over the stock. She filled two canteens and looped them over the horn, then tied the supply sack in place. "Ready," she told Navarro, and mounted.

They bypassed the town near Fort Stockton, and the army post. They would camp once more tonight. Jessie didn't want to get home late and send the edgy Navarro into a bunkhouse of curious strangers. Nor did she want to disturb weary hands turned in for the night. This would be their last night alone.

As dusk approached, Jessie was disappointed by how quiet and reserved Navarro had been all day. During their rest stops and midday meal, he had kept to himself once more, and that troubled her. Each time they made progress with their friendship, he halted it and backed off again. It was as if he feared something would happen to spoil their budding relationship. Yet he had opened up more than she had expected. She would back off and let him relax.

As they skirted a rolling hill, Jessie halted him. "Look," she said, pointing at two men who were cutting fences beyond them. "Don't let them see us."

They retreated to cover. "If we go around the other way, we can slip up on them through those trees. Fletcher's men," she added.

They almost succeeded, but Jessie was sighted at the last minute as she sneaked up on foot while moving from tree to tree behind Navarro, who was leading their attack. The villains drew their weapons and opened fire. Navarro shoved Jessie to the grassy earth. The desperado and redhead exchanged gunfire with the two men. One was wounded in the arm and the other in his leg. Navarro surged forward and got the drop on them. Jessie joined him.

Navarro ordered them to strip. When they were down to their longjohns, he told them to mount. After he was obeyed, Navarro tied them to their saddles and slapped their horses on the rumps to send them racing homeward. "That should give their boss a message. We could have taken them to the law, but it wouldn't do much to stop your trouble. They wouldn't betray Fletcher. He would have them killed, even in jail. It's best if we handle that landgrabber."

"I agree. Once they get home, Fletcher will know about you."

"Doesn't matter. He would have known soon anyway. We can expect more trouble from this incident; men don't take humiliation well. Let's get this repaired."

"How? we don't have tools or barbwire."

"We'll use our ropes to close the gap. You can send men out tomorrow to mend it right. All we need to do is keep your cattle in until then."

Jessie noticed how Navarro always said "you" and "your," never acknowledging her father. Maybe he considered the problem with Fletcher hers alone, and that was why he was helping. That was good, because it meant he cared about protecting her.

When the gap was closed with strung ropes, Navarro replaced his knife and remarked, "This is good grassland, Jessie."

"It's some of the best. It cures up easily for superior winter feed. It fattens our stock quickly. It's kin to buffalo grass, and it's very sturdy . . . How do you like this area? Isn't it beautiful?" Her eyes were dreamy as she gazed around them.

He looked over the verdant terrain and agreed. "Yep, I can see why you love it so much. I'm sure you're anxious to get home."

She was, and she wasn't. Navarro was standing too close to be ignored. Her fingers reached up and lifted a section of his black hair. "How's the wound?" It was still discolored and not fully healed, but it seemed to be doing nicely.

He didn't step back or push away her hand. "No more pain."

"That's good. If I forgot to tell you, thanks for saving me that day. If you hadn't shoved me down and caught that bullet, I'd be dead."

"If you'd left me there, *I'd* be dead, so we're even."

It would be dark in an hour, as there would be only a half-moon tonight. "There's a line shack nearby. We'll camp there, then ride in tomorrow. All right?"

"Sounds good to me."

They retrieved their horses and headed that way. Within thirty minutes, they were dismounting at the secluded cabin used during the winter and during fall roundups. No one was around, and no smoke from campfires could be seen. Jessie knew the men should be gathering cows in the south pastures or be at the bunkhouse many miles away. They were alone one last time.

While Navarro unsaddled and tended the horses, she went inside with their supplies. She closed the shutters and barred them to prevent any lanternlight from escaping, just in case someone was in the area and might see it, especially Fletcher's hirelings. Later, she would bolt the door. As the evening was cool, the cabin wouldn't get too stuffy.

Jessie used the iron stove to prepare their meal. As the ravenous travelers devoured the food at the small table, she said, "Fletcher's been undercutting our prices so he can steal army contracts from us. He doesn't need money, so he can afford a cheap price. I don't know how long we can sell for less or refuse to sell. Papa's been keeping the books a secret since last winter. I know he made some large purchases for those last two bulls, and we didn't have many four-year-olds to market last season. Don't worry about your salary; I know Papa will cover whatever you ask for payment," she added, knowing how her words must have sounded.

Navarro halted eating to respond, "Don't worry about what I'll charge, Jessie. That sorrel, saddle, and food are about all I'll need for a while. When I get ready to move on, I'll need a little cash for supplies on the trail. For now, the same as you pay your hands is fine."

Jessie was surprised by those words. "But you could earn a lot of money with your skills, Navarro. We wouldn't cheat you out of a fair deal."

"About the only use I have for money is eating and ammo and feed for my horse. I don't stay in hotels; I like to camp in the open."

"What about saving up for something special, like a ranch of your own?"

"Not interested in settling down."

"How long can you stay on the move, Navarro?"

"As long as I need to or want to. I've got nothing to hold me down to one place. I took this job because it sounded exciting, and I needed to rest a while."

"Don't you ever get tired of moving around?"

"It has its bad points. Shame is, the good ones never outweigh them."

"What if they do one day?"

"I doubt they ever will."

"If they did?" she persisted, their gazes locking and searching.

"Like you said before, how can anybody say what tomorrow holds?"

They completed their meal and cleared the table. "Why don't you relax with your coffee while I wash off outside? There's a windmill and a tank for the cattle."

Jessie left him sitting there in deep thought while she bathed in the vanishing light. She put on the one skirt and shirt she had brought with her in case she needed to dress as a lady during her mission. She unbound her hair and brushed the dark-red locks. When she went inside, Navarro stared at her before leaving to do the same after saying he wanted to look his best for his new job tomorrow.

He returned as she was about to braid her hair before turning in. He bolted the door and dropped his saddlebags to the floor, then approached the table where she was sitting. On impulse, he entreated, "Don't capture it, Jessie; leave it free. It's like a red river and my hands want to jump into it." Ensnared by her beauty and the heady moment, he stroked her silken hair.

Jessie closed her eyes and savored his gentle and unexpected touch. When he halted and stepped away, she stood and faced him. "Navarro . . ." She hesitated and lowered her head. She knew he could ride out of her life at any time and be lost forever. This was their last time for privacy. If she didn't let him know how she felt tonight, there might never be another chance. Without his knowing the truth, he might not be tempted to stay with her. He needed to learn he was loved, he was wanted, he was needed for more than the job she offered. He needed to see that he was special, that he had a place with her if he dared to claim it. She had to give him something only she could give: her love, herself, her trust. She wasn't sure what to do, but her mother had told her that things like this always took care of themselves. Something deep within her seemed to say, *It's now or never, Jessie,* and she couldn't resist that urging.

Navarro told himself to back off, that he shouldn't have approached her, but he couldn't find the strength or will to do so. He lifted her chin and looked into her eyes. "What is it, Jessie?" he asked. She seemed confused and apprehensive. Was she afraid to be here with him alone tonight? Did she want to ask him to go outside to camp? Should he have done so and not placed her in this embarrassing and uncomfortable predicament? "Do you want me to leave? Is that it?"

Jessie misunderstood. "Of course not. I need you."

"I meant, do you want me to camp outside tonight?"

She had known almost from the first moment she had met Navarro that he was the man for her. But she had realized during her days with him that he would need convincing. Jessie decided in a split second that before they risked their lives fighting Wilbur Fletcher, she wanted to taste love, his love. He was the only man who had stirred her emotions in this powerful way. Her mother had been taken from her father. Her grandfather had been taken from Gran. Jake could have ended her life in San Angelo. Josh could have slain Navarro on the trail. Both could die soon from Fletcher's bullets. Life could be so short and cruel. Before death claimed her, she must experience the joys and secrets of love. Once they were bound in hearts and bodies, surely he would stay at her side. Her love would be what won him over and what held him in her life. She had to prove to him that she was a risk worth taking, a dream worth capturing, just as he was to her. "No, don't leave," Jessie admitted.

"It's dangerous for me to stay around you tonight," he warned.

"I know."

A merciless battle waged within the desperado. His mind shouted for him to run. But as he looked at her, his heart begged him to stay. "Do you, Jessie?" he asked. "I haven't known many women, and none like you. The problem is, we may not have much time together. It isn't fair to let you believe we do. If we're killed or captured or your father decides not to hire me tomorrow, this could be our only night together. That isn't much to offer a good woman like you." Navarro realized she didn't know how true those words were. Time was a prize he couldn't grasp and hold very long; yet, he couldn't tell her why. He didn't want her to learn what a terrible thing he had done.

Jessie admired his honesty, but rashly believed she could change his mind later. "Isn't one night better than none?" she replied bravely.

"For me, yes. For you, is it? Don't answer too fast. Once a deed is done, you can't ever change it."

Jessie's gaze roamed his features. Yes, she concluded, her last statement was true. "I want more than one night from you, Navarro.

But if this is all you can give for now, so be it," she answered, her courage and resolve unfailing.

"Not just for now, Jessie, forever. Make sure you understand and accept that. I won't guide you down a false trail of pretty lies and broken promises like most men will to get what they want. You're too special for that."

"For as long and as much as you can share yourself with me, Navarro, I want you."

The desperado's heart pounded in desire and hesitation. If only he had met Jessie years ago when a life with her was possible. He had been cold and hard like a frozen landscape. She was a flaming sun that softened and melted his icy heart. If he let Jessie distract him and he stayed too long just to be near her, he could destroy himself. It would hurt them both when he had to leave, especially since he couldn't tell her why. Yet there was so little happiness in life, in his past and in his future, and none in his present if he didn't grasp this moment. Although he had little hope of surviving if he stopped running, wasn't this risk worth taking?

Jessie watched him battle with ghosts and worries that were trying to pull him away from her. A man like Navarro might never come along for her again. Having been raised as a son and heir, she was different from other women. It would take a special man, a strong one, to stand at her side. "This has nothing to do with you taking my job, Navarro. Whether you stay with me or leave for some reason, this is between us as a man and a woman."

Navarro made his choice, and hoped it wasn't the wrong one. "Even if you change your mind about surrendering to me tonight, I'll still work for you, Jessie. I've tried to hold back from you because that's best for us, but I can't any longer."

Jessie moved closer to him. "I've done the same during our journey. You're so different from other men I've known. None of them has made me feel this crazy way. If we die at Fletcher's hands, at least I'll have had you once."

Navarro pulled Jessie into his arms. No matter where his path led tomorrow, this was one night he would never forget. For a moment, he did nothing more than hold her, feel her against him, and tell himself this was meant to be. He lowered his head and kissed her. The contact was more potent than any whiskey he had consumed.

Jessie looped her arms around his neck and returned the ardent kiss. His embrace tightened and he moaned against her lips, revealing his great desire. She quivered at the force of their shared passions. Her body warmed swiftly and uncontrollably. Her pulse raced. She felt strange and wonderful all over. If she couldn't capture this dream, then she would enjoy it for one beautiful night.

Navarro was staggered by the stimulating way she was kissing and holding him. An intoxicating aura surrounded him, and his thoughts seemed to dance like grass in the wind. Her kisses and embraces were unlike those of the women he had paid to release him. His experiences with women were few and far between, but he felt that his sexual prowess would come alive with this unique beauty.

They shared many kisses that became deeper and more urgent. Navarro's lips trailed over the soft surface of Jessie's flushed face, then traveled down her throat and back again. He nestled his face against her hair and savored the feel of it on his cheek. His strong hands wandered up her back and drifted into those auburn locks, allowing her curls to tease over his fingers. He clasped her head to his chest and kissed the top of it. "Nothing in my life has ever felt as good as you in my arms."

Jessie heard his heart thumping, gaining speed with each minute he held her close. It was as if he wanted and needed her desperately but was trying to control himself and not rush their union. Her hands roamed his back and her fingers traced the strength dwelling there. His back, shoulders, and arms were taut and well muscled. Her fingers encountered defined ridges and ripples, like rolling hills and playful water. She was so happy and free that she feared her heart would burst with emotion.

Navarro meshed his mouth to hers as his quivering fingers unfastened the buttons on her shirt. He peeled it off her shoulders and arms, then dropped the blue garment to the floor. His fingers roamed her satiny flesh with slow and arousing movements. They slipped beneath the straps of her chemise and removed it with ease, as she had unlaced and unbuttoned it for him. His hands covered her breasts and reveled in their firm softness. Her nipples hardened into taut peaks as he caressed them while he kissed her with rising hunger.

Jessie was amazed and surprised by how stimulating his fingers felt at her breasts. She had expected his touch to feel good, but not this wonderful. She felt his hands releasing her skirt, and she clung to him to make certain he knew to continue. Assuming he didn't know how to loosen and remove her bloomers, Jessie released them and let them fall to her ankles. She was glad she hadn't put on her boots after her bath; she wouldn't have to part from him to discard them.

Navarro's hands ventured over the bare figure within his reach. She had a strong and agile body from years of hard work, but it was every inch a woman's body, an enticing woman's body. Her tanned skin had a rosy hue, and he felt no flaws on it. She was warm and stirring in his embrace. He wanted to feel her against his naked flesh. First, he had to put out the glowing lantern to conceal the secret on his back. He swept her into his arms and placed her on the bunk where her bedroll was spread. For a brief time, his gaze admired her beauty from head to foot. She made no attempt to cover her breasts or the reddish-brown hair between her thighs. She looked almost too beautiful to touch. He wanted to see her every minute they were making love, but what *she* saw could inspire dangerous questions. He doused the lantern, stripped, and joined her. Instantly her arms closed around him and her mouth fused with his, stealing all thoughts except those of her and this dream come true.

Jessie's fingers played in midnight hair as Navarro's lips adored her breasts. A curious tension gnawed at her, but the pleasures from his skilled mouth and hands were stronger. When he stroked her where no man had ever touched her before, Jessie moaned and squirmed in astonishment and delight. Having seen many animals breed before, she knew something of what to expect. There was no frightening mystery to be solved tonight. She knew what would soon take place, and she was eager for it to happen.

Navarro slipped atop Jessie. With gentleness, he checked to be sure she was ready for him. Then, with care and leisure, he guided his manhood to her welcoming portal. He rubbed against her several times to accustom her to his presence. When Jessie kissed him fiercely and arched toward him, Navarro worked himself within her. He noticed that she only stiffened slightly and inhaled sharply, then relaxed. She didn't cry or wince or retreat, and he was glad. When he was fully inside her, he waited a moment. He hoped he hadn't hurt her, as he had been told it could be rough for a woman on her first time. He knew Jessie hadn't been with a man before, and he was overwhelmed that she chose to give him a woman's most valuable gift.

It was hard for the half-breed to believe he could touch anyone— and especially a woman like Jessie—so deeply. People had always taken from him, never given to him or shared with him. Yet, all she wanted from him was *him.* She didn't care who or what he was. It stunned him that she wanted him so badly, that she liked him and trusted him, that she was honest and open and brave enough to claim what she desired.

The mild discomfort passed quickly for Jessie. Each time Navarro moved within her, it was sheer bliss. What a wonderful part of love this was, she decided dreamily. How beautiful and special to have their bodies joined as one, to have such powerful feelings racing through both of them, to discover such joy together. There was no way to fully share oneself with another except through lovemaking.

Their breaths mingled as their mouths worked as one. Their hearts pounded in unison. Their caresses teased and pleased at the same time. Their responses simultaneously thrilled and inspired. A bond was forged; she belonged to him and he belonged to her. Whatever happened in the future, nothing could take away the beauty and unity of this night.

Upward they climbed, seeking something Jessie could only wonder at. Skyward they urged themselves, growing breathless at the dizzying heights of their passion. And then together they reached a moment of ecstasy that made Jessie cry out with sheer pleasure. Navarro held her tightly, never wanting to let her go as they cuddled in sated tranquility.

"Jessie?" he finally murmured when his breathing was under control again.

"Yes?" she replied in the darkness.

"Are you . . . all right?"

Jessie smiled in joy. "More than all right, Navarro, the best." She heard him sigh in relief and felt him relax. She nestled into his beckoning embrace and rested her head on his shoulder. They were both damp from their exertions, but she didn't care. She liked the way his arms banded about her possessively and the way his fingers trailed over her moist flesh. She liked it even more when his hand grasped her chin and turned it to seal their lips. He seemed so happy and giving at this moment.

Jessie was right: Navarro had never felt better or freer than he did lying next to her and loving her. For tonight, he told himself, reality didn't exist, only this beautiful dream with Jessica Lane did. He closed his eyes.

As they drifted off to sleep, locked in each other's arms on the bunk, Jessie recalled the scars she had felt on his back during the heat of their passion. She had seen and felt Jimmy Joe's scars from beatings by his abusive father. She knew they were lash marks. She wondered who had dared to put them there. Someone had overpowered this strong and proud man, then whipped him brutally. Her mind was flooded with questions: Why? Where? When? Had Navarro killed him, or them? Did that cruel incident have anything to do with the obstacle between them? Did it have anything to do with his bitterness, wariness, and restlessness? Or were those feelings much older than the raised scars? They must have been the reason why he had undressed in the dark—not from modesty or a fear of alarming her with his nakedness. He hadn't wanted her to see them and question him. Jessie warned herself not to probe him about the scars or his past. That might drive him away. In time, hopefully he would trust her with the truth. If not . . .

CHAPTER SIX

Navarro awakened first and eased from Jessie's arms and the cozy bunk they had shared last night. The creak of the door only caused the redhead to sigh and roll to her side facing him. He slipped away to bathe and dress in privacy. When he finished, he sat in the open doorway to await her stirring. The troubled man leaned his dark head against the rough wood and worried about what Jessie would expect of him after their closeness.

She had said one night was enough for her, but would it be? Did he want her to feel that way? No. Would one night be enough to last him forever? How could it, when he craved her fiercely again this minute?

Navarro wanted so much more with her and from her, but that was impossible. What, he scoffed, did Navarro Breed have to offer Miss Jessica Lane? Nothing but a lot of heartache. On the run, he couldn't even offer himself, as if a half-breed bastard was anything for a woman like her to desire! He told himself that he should have kept his distance, done her job, taken his payment, and left. He shouldn't have allowed this complication to happen. He shouldn't have birthed false hopes in her or opened himself up for more torment. That's what deserting and losing her would be: utter torment.

Navarro glanced at the slumbering woman who had touched his heart and life as no other person ever had. *Shu,* she had his guts tied up in knots and his head dazed! He had never been one to think of the future. He had lived for the present, just surviving day to day, until Jessica Lane was thrown into his path.

The desperado told himself he was a fool, a silly dreamer on loco weed! Hadn't the Apaches who had partly reared him said never to go against overwhelming odds? Yes, his heart admitted, unless the prize was worth the dangers. Yet, he couldn't abduct her and flee to safety farther east. Even if Jessie was willing to give up her family and world to escape with him—which she surely wouldn't if she learned the grim truth about him—he couldn't allow her to do so. He wasn't the simple drifter she assumed him to be, and she would be endangered.

Jessie had him thinking and feeling and behaving crazy! Wife, home, family, love, and future—they hadn't entered his mind and tempted . . . no, *tormented* him before their paths crossed a week ago. Why, he demanded, did he crave those things now when it was too late? He would have to leave her soon, and in silence, but not until she was safe.

Through a fringe of thick lashes that were barely parted, Jessie observed the man in the doorway, as she had been doing since he sneaked from her side. She guessed he had crept from the bunk for the same reason he had made love in the dark: his scars. She had feigned sleep to give him time to dress and think, to accept this sudden change in his life. He looked so wracked by confusion and anguish, so vulnerable. Such feelings had to be new and hard for a man like him to accept.

Let him adjust on his own, Jess. No questions or pressures. Don't make him skittish or defensive. You don't want him to panic and run. Let him come to you when it's right for him.

Jessie stretched and made throaty noises to alert Navarro to her wakefulness. She sat up, holding a light blanket over her bare breasts. She smiled at him and said, "Good morning. I'm as sluggish as a desert tortoise today. You starving?"

Navarro stood and went to the potbelly stove. "Coffee will get you going, Boss Lady. I'll start our grub while you dress." He found her much too tantalizing there in the bunk and naked. Her soft flesh summoned him to caress it. Her lips beckoned him to kiss her. Her blue eyes called to him to rejoin her on the bunk. Her tumbling tresses of fire blazed their image inside his head. Her entire aura enticed him to claim what he had already won—her willingness for him to possess her. To take her again would give Jessie the wrong idea. No, his heart argued, the right one: that he had a weakness for her. He was relieved when she left to bathe and dress and ceased her pull on him.

When they sat down to eat the biscuits and gravy from the cabin's stores and to sip coffee, Jessie said, "In a few hours, no more dull trail food. Biscuit Hank is a good cook. The hands love his dishes. You'll have hot, delicious meals from now on. Sound good to you, Navarro?"

"Yep. What if your father's changed his mind about hiring help?"

Jessie assumed the man was trying to talk about anything except what had taken place between them last night. "He won't. We need you. I hope you'll like the ranch and everyone there."

"Feelings don't matter when you've got a nasty job to do."

"Friends matter, don't they?" she asked, the words slipping out of her mouth.

"Never had many. None I can think of these days."

"What about me? Aren't we friends?"

The look in her eyes compelled him to respond, "Yep. But it's strange, you being a woman and all."

A bright smile softened her limpid gaze and warmed her face. "You'll make friends with the hands, too. They're a good bunch. You'll see."

"I doubt they'll take to my kind, but don't worry about it."

"Don't sell yourself so cheap, Navarro."

"You count me too high, Jessie. I ain't worth much. Just a drifter."

"You're far more than that, Navarro. Maybe you'll change your mind about yourself while you're living and working with . . . us."

"Don't fool yourself, Jessie. Men like me don't change or settle down," he cautioned, and stole the smile from her face. He needed to prepare her for the inevitable and to prevent her from having hopes of anything permanent happening between them.

Jessie eyed him a moment, then shrugged as she reminded herself of her earlier decision. "Maybe, and maybe not. That has to be up to you."

"You're one stubborn, dreamy-eyed female. That can hurt you later."

Jessie laughed to ease her anxiety. "Papa and Matt would agree on the stubborn part. I prefer to think I'm steadfast. As for the other trait, I'm guilty. When a person wants something, they dream about it first. Then it takes hard work and persistence to make it come true. You can't give up until your fantasy is real. I dream of my family being safe, well, successful, and happy. I do all I can to make it happen. Wilbur Fletcher turned our beautiful life into a nightmare. I'm going to stop him. With your help and friendship."

"You have them, Jessie. But I don't want you getting hurt. You have to learn when to fight, when to compromise, and when to retreat."

Jessie knew his last statement had nothing to do with Fletcher, as Navarro would never back away from that villain. She let it pass unchallenged. "Getting hurt is a risk I have to take. If it gets bad, Navarro, *you* don't."

"Yes, I do. I've promised to help, and I will, no matter what."

"I thought you didn't make promises," she teased.

"Usually I don't, 'cause I don't hang around long enough to keep them."

Jessie forced herself to hold back asking why not. "That's fair and honest. Thanks. But I will understand if something entices you to leave our battleground." She stood and said, "We better get moving. I'm sure Papa is eager to see me home safe."

The house and other structures of the ranch came into view. Jessie saw Navarro tense and frown, then take a deep breath. "There she is, home," she announced.

Navarro saw a white house, a large barn, corrals, miles of fencing, an oblong bunkhouse, several smaller sheds, a chicken coop, and a large plowed area for a garden. He noticed cattle and men working a short distance from the neat settlement. Spring branding was clearly in progress. He counted nine hands.

As they approached the area, the sights, sounds, and smells of the task underway reached Jessie and Navarro. They rode to a corral near the barn and dismounted, then unsaddled their mounts and tossed the leather seats over the top rail. The sorrel and paint were placed in the corral for feeding and watering, as no currying down was needed after their leisurely ride this morning.

Jessie saw her wary companion check out his new surroundings, as if looking for signs of peril and a path of quick escape. When he asked what was in each direction, she told him, "Box L land for miles and hours, Fort Davis thirty miles northwest of us, Mexico several days southward, mountains and rugged hills to east and west—and Fletcher fifteen miles northeast. We don't get much company."

"What about the sheriffs and soldiers from Davis and Stockton?"

"We rarely see them unless we go into town for supplies. Let's find Papa and tell him I'm home. Follow me," she invited.

Jessie guided him through a gate and toward the men. The hands saw their boss's daughter coming and shouted greetings to her, all the while eyeing the man at her side. The stranger's walk, alert gaze, and strapped-down holsters told them who the new arrival was: Jessie's hired gunslinger. Tom almost hopped on his twisted foot, in such a rush to get to his sister.

The redhead hugged him and teased, "Did you miss your teacher much?"

His green eyes sparkled with joy as he revealed, "Pa's letting me help with the branding. I'm keeping the tallies," he added, referring to how the numbers and sexes of branded calves were recorded in a book.

"That's an important job for a thirteen-year-old boy. It's good that you're so smart in arithmetic and can handle it for Papa," she replied, fluffing his damp auburn hair. "You best get back to your post, Mister Thomas Lane, or you'll lose count and Papa will blame me. We'll talk during supper."

"Who's this?" the freckle-faced boy asked, squinting through dirty glasses to get a look at the man with Jessie.

"Navarro. He's the man I've hired to help us defeat Wilbur Fletcher. You can get to know him at supper. Back to work, young man; you're getting behind."

Tom obediently returned to his place, but kept glancing at the couple.

Jessie quickly introduced the ranch hands, each man nodding a welcome as his name was called: Rusty Jones with the irons, Big John Williams tending the fire, Miguel Ortega and Carlos Reeves as ropers, Jimmy Joe Sims and three others as two pairs of flankers, and Jefferson Clark as the marker. "Where's Matt and Papa?" she asked.

"Fletcher's been real nervy since you been gone, Jessie," Jimmy Joe replied before another could. "I hope Navarro is faster than a shootin' star with his guns."

As he labored, Rusty added, "We've done branded the new fillies and colts; weren't many of them. Best we can count, we got about fifteen thousand calves this year. The boss bred 'em real good last season. We got us four to six weeks' work to get it done. No wranglers came by to hire on, and Matt couldn't get any in town. It's Fletcher's doing. We think he's been buying off the seasonal help or scaring 'em off. Matt put nine of us on branding while the others ride fence and guard the herds. He and Jed are on the range now, but I don't know where. Lots of trouble while you been gone. Jed'll tell you at supper."

Anger flooded Jessie and danced within her blue eyes. "He'll pay," she vowed. "I'll tell Gran I'm home, then be back to help. Navarro, come with me," she said, thinking it best if he stuck with her for a while to avoid problems.

"Send Big Ed over after he's tended the horses. He's had his fun long enough. We saved some special work for him," Rusty teased.

The fire left Jessie's eyes. "Big Ed took a fall and broke his neck. I buried him outside San Angelo before I met up with Navarro. Rattler spooked his horse."

The men halted their tasks for a few moments of silence as that grim news settled in on them. "He was a good man. He'll be sorely missed," one said for all.

As they walked toward the house, Jessie told Navarro, "Our herd stays about the same size because spring calves replace the mature steers we sell off each fall. The heifers—those cows under three without calves—who come to age this summer, will be bred next season. Papa's working hard to improve our bloodlines. This time of year, the hands separate the cows with calves from the herds and bring them to the holding pens for branding. Once they get the Box L mark, they're turned loose to graze again. The best males are culled for breeding; the others are castrated to be raised as beeves. We have four graded bulls and about twenty good crossbreds."

"Sounds to me like ranching takes a lot of work and wits."

"It does. If we have about fifteen thousand calves, as Rusty said, it'll take them a month or more to finish the branding without help from seasonal wranglers. They can toss, brand, clip ear, and castrate a calf in about a minute. Working ten hours a day for six days, they can do about thirty-six hundred a week. But that's hard on the men. Papa usually gives them Sunday off, but without extra help, we have to work round the week because castration can't wait too long. You know the differences in cattle?" she asked, chatting to distract herself from her fury and from her worries about her father's safety out as he was with only four men.

"Nope. What are they?" Navarro aided her ruse.

"A calf is less than one year old, a yearling less than two, and a cow is a mature female. A heifer is under three years old and un-bred, a steer is a castrated male being raised for beef, and a bull is used only for breeding. We raise and breed all except the steers; those we sell at four years, unless we need money badly at three. Fletcher's brand is the Bar F. You read brands top to bottom and left to right. A short, horizontal line is called a bar. It's placed over the F for his mark."

They passed Biscuit Hank on his way from the food-storage shed to the chuckhouse. She halted. "Got you another mouth to feed. I want him treated real good, Hank, 'cause I need him to hang around until Fletcher is whipped."

With Jessie, the crusty cook didn't pretend his hearing was im-paired, as he did with the men. "I'll be jiggered! You *did* git yourself a hired gun." His merry eyes looked Navarro up and down. "Looks sharp as a knife to me, Jessie."

She was delighted by the compliment and reaction to her com-panion. "He is. He saved my skin three times before I could get him home."

"Sounds like you been havin' as much trouble as we'uns have. Yore pa's madder than a hornet with his nest under fire. That snake over yonder is strikin' ever few days. He knows we got our minds elsewhere, and he's cookin' up trouble."

"Like what, Hank?" she questioned in distress.

The thin-haired cook shifted the slab of salted meat to his other shoulder. He didn't want to reveal such dreadful things to Jessie so soon after her return. It was best to let his boss, her pa, tell her, espe-cially about old Buck. "I'll let Jed tell you when he rides in. It's a long and sorry tale, girl. I got to git vittles goin' for the boys. After a hard day, they quit work, starvin' and jawin'."

Jessie understood his reluctance. "That's fine, Hank."

"Yore grandma's been he'pin' me with the cookin' and washin' 'cause I been doin' the boys' chores in the bunkhouse. They ain't hardly had time to suck air."

"As soon as I speak with Gran, I'll help them. They look like they need somebody to give them a rest stop. I hate to have them work-ing on Sunday."

"Can't be he'ped, Jessie. Be seein' you later." He strode off in a rush.

Chickens clucked and scattered as the couple disturbed their scratchings on their way to the well-kept clapboard house. Eight posts lined the edge of the porch that traveled the length of it. Jessie and Navarro mounted the steps and entered a large sitting area with a fireplace on one wall.

As they walked through the homey room, Jessie pointed to their right and said, "Gran's room is on the front. Mary Louise and I share one on the back." Motioning to their left, she added, "Papa's room is there."

Straight ahead, they entered an oblong area where the kitchen and eating rooms were located. To the right was a bathing closet with a second door to the back porch. At the far end of the dining section, she told him those stairs led to Tom's attic room. Gran wasn't inside so Jessie led her companion toward the back door and outside onto the porch, where she heard noises.

Jessie sighted her grandmother and rushed to the well. She took the heavy bucket from the woman's stiff fingers and scolded in a soft tone, "You should let Mary Louise do this, Gran. You have enough trouble and pain with your hands without aggravating them. As soon as that part arrives, Papa can repair the pump and halt this chore."

With twinkling eyes and mirthful laughter, the woman returned Jessie's motherly concern. "I see you got back safe, child," she said. "I been worried plenty these past eleven days. So has your pa. And Matt, too." The older woman looked at the handsome stranger who, without a word, took the bucket from her granddaughter's hand and carried it inside. Martha's gnarled fingers grasped the railing as she pulled herself up the four steps to the porch.

Jessie knew this was one of the times when she didn't dare assist her aging grandmother, who was still proud and strong at seventy. "I'll tell Mary Louise to fill the kitchen barrel before I change to help the hands. Where is that lazy girl, Gran?"

"Gone," Martha replied, halting to catch her breath before explaining.

"Gone? Where? When? What happened this time?" Jessie asked in dismay.

"She was riling Jed about visiting her friends back East again. He wouldn't yield, but he didn't have time or spirit to be troubled, so he let her stay in town for a week. She'll be coming home next Sunday. She claimed she wanted to observe the schoolmarm to see if she wants to start teaching. Jed let her have her way this time. He dropped her off when he went for supplies Friday."

Jessie knew her father had complied to get his defiant daughter out of his hair during this hectic time, and she was angry that such action was necessary. She also knew that her sister had lied to get her way. "Mary Louise should be here helping you and the others, Gran, not playing in town. I don't know what we're going to do about her. Hank told me how hard all of you are working. You can get some rest now that I'm home. I'll tend the wash tomorrow. And I'll take care of the chickens, eggs, and milking. After I get you caught up with chores, me and Navarro are going to deal with Fletcher. We'll keep him and his men too busy to trouble Papa and the hands."

"This is Navarro?" Martha hinted, nodding at the dark-haired man who was leaning against the door jamb and holding a respectful silence.

"Where in blazes are my manners? Gran, this is Navarro; Navarro, my grandmother, Martha Lane, but everyone calls her Gran. You can, too." Jessie briefly explained about Big Ed and how she'd found Navarro. "You'll hear it all tonight, Gran."

"We owe you a big debt, son, for taking care of our Jessie. We couldn't do without her. She practically runs this place. Will, too, one day. I'll bake you a special pie for dessert tonight. You'll take supper with us?" she asked.

Jessie answered for him. "I thought so, Gran, so we can hear the news and make plans against Fletcher. Hank and the boys warned me it's bad news. With Big Ed gone, that leaves us with only twelve hands, Matt, and Hank. Blazes! How can we get branding and planting done without more help? Especially with Fletcher coming at us stronger and meaner than ever. Damn him!"

Martha inhaled sharply. "Jessica Lane! Watch your tongue, child. Your pa will be red in the face if he hears such words coming from you."

"I just get so mad, Gran, that they slip out. I'm sorry. I'll be careful."

"I know, child," Martha sympathized, patting Jessie's back.

"I'll get changed into some old clothes and boots, then fetch the water for you. I'll see you in a minute or two, Navarro. Wait here for me." Jessie left the room.

Martha Lane focused faded blue eyes on the quiet male whose height towered over her five-two frame. "Where are you from, son? What's your last name?"

Navarro straightened. "Colorado and Jones, ma'am," he lied.

"A man of few words like Matt," she teased.

"While Jessie changes, I'll fill that water barrel for you, ma'am," he said, then lifted two buckets and headed for the well with haste.

When Jessie returned to the kitchen, Gran remarked, "Your Navarro is short of talk, child, and a wary man, but I like him. Strikes me as a tough man who hides a gentle side. I can tell he's had a hard life; his eyes give it away."

Jessie glanced out the door at Navarro as he drew water from the well. "I'm sure he's had plenty of troubles, Gran, but he's a good man. He hasn't opened up much to me yet, but I hope he will. He seems so lonely, but doesn't seem to want anyone to know it. We'll talk about him later. He's coming, and I have to hurry." Jessie wanted to get away before her tone and gaze exposed her feelings and intimate behavior. She was glad her sister was gone for a while and relieved at not having to deal with the rebellious girl at this time.

"That's it, ma'am," Navarro said, placing the two buckets aside.

"Let's go," Jessie instructed, then led him outside. "Thanks for helping us. Do you mind hanging around me this afternoon while I work?"

"Nope. I'll help, too. Just tell me where I'm needed most."

"You don't have to, Navarro. This isn't what you were hired to do. I just thought you'd feel easier in strange surroundings around me."

Navarro's hazel gaze locked with her searching blue one. "I feel easier around you in any surroundings, Jessie. Just think of me as hired help and give the orders, Boss Lady." He grinned, then laughed.

Jessie liked the look and sound of both. She smiled. "Thanks. You're a mighty special man, Navarro. I hope Gran didn't intrude too much."

"Nope. She's a fine woman. I never knew either of my grandmothers, and only met one of my grandfathers. They're all dead now. I'm the only one of my family left." Navarro scowled and broke their gaze. He hadn't meant to reveal anything about himself, but Jessie had a curious way of culling out facts when he least expected it. "I told her I was from Colorado and that my last name's Jones. You might need that information with the boys later."

Jessie didn't think either claim was true, but she didn't challenge them. "Well, Navarro Jones of Colorado, let's get busy. It's going to be a long and hard afternoon. Know anything about branding?"

He was relieved by her acceptance of him and of what he was certain she knew were lies. "Nope, but I learn fast."

"Good, because we're shorthanded, as you heard."

Branding was a loud, dirty, dangerous, and fatiguing task. The odors of smoke, the sweat from men and horses, singed hair, manure, blood, and arid dust permeated the area. The air rang with the sounds of shouts, pounding hooves, bawling cattle, clanking irons, whirs of lariats, creaking of saddles and stirrups, and the hissing of hot iron to hide. Everyone sang herd songs and ballads to calm the cows and calves who were waiting impatiently to be separated for marking. Verses from "The Dying Ranger" and "Bonnie Black Bess" only partially settled down the cattle that were bunched tightly in the holding pens.

Miguel Ortega and Carlos Reeves, expert ropers, tossed their Mexican lariats around hind legs and dragged bellowing calves forward one at a time. Each man was skilled at cutting out calves and keeping up with the rapid schedule. Sombreros shaded their dark eyes, and chaps protected their legs from horn scrapes and chafing. During each day, they used several highly trained cutting horses, changing mounts when one tired. Carlos always said that geldings were best because they never had romancing the mares on their minds. Miguel teased him that he should know, since Carlos was the one who tamed and trained most of them.

Two sets of flankers were kept busy by the Mexican and half-Mexican vaqueros. One flanker from each pair seized the calf by its shoulder hide and flipped it to the ground, pinning it there by snug holds on its head and right foreleg. His partner, sitting on the ground, grasped the right hind leg with his hands, then pressed his boot against the lower one to prevent any movement. Today, Jimmy Joe Sims was paired up with three other men as flankers.

Big John Williams, their smithy, tended the fire. The black man kept the coals at the right heat and replaced the irons tossed aside after use. Rusty Jones, the ironman, made certain the tool was hot enough to leave its five-inch mark and a scab, but not hot enough to hurt the hide or blur the Box L mark. The bearded redhead applied light pressure and held the iron in place a moment.

While Rusty was doing his task on one end, Jefferson Clark worked as the marker on the other. The black man clipped the calf's ear to match that of all Lane cattle. He tossed the bloody piece into a pail to be counted and compared to the day's tally. The clip provided another means of identification in case a brand was altered or obliterated by rustlers and aided the ropers while cutting out unworked calves from the restless herd.

As soon as Rusty and Jefferson finished stamping and notching, the back flanker lifted the calf's upper leg—if it was a male—for castration. With skill and a razor-sharp knife, in about a minute, Jefferson split the sack, peeled out the testes, snipped the cord, tossed them into another pail, and stepped back to indicate he was finished. The area would drain, scab, and heal quickly. The calf was released to trot to its bawling mother.

Jessie relieved a flanker to rest and to get a drink or to be excused, then moved to the next weary and thirsty man. Navarro fetched water from the second well near the bunkhouse. He sharpened the knives that Jefferson tossed aside when dulled. He helped Miguel and Carlos by saddling and unsaddling their mounts while the two men took short breaks. He didn't know how to rope legs, or tend fires, or stamp, or clip ears. Within a short time, the men felt enough at ease to yell for his help whenever needed. Both Jessie and Navarro noticed how he was welcomed into the laboring group.

Navarro was too distracted by the flurry of activities and excitement to think about his past or to stay on his guard around strangers who were laughing and talking as they worked. Rusty even jested about them being kin because of the desperado's matching name, Jones. The fiery-haired ironman told them that Fletcher was in big trouble with two Joneses to battle. The desperado found himself relaxing and enjoying the work and genial company.

When Jessie and Navarro met at the water bucket to soothe their dry throats, he handed her the dipper and smiled through dusty features. Each used a bandanna to mop sweat and dirt from their faces. Their clothes and boots were a mess. They were weary but elated. His black hair was wet. Hers was braided and tucked beneath her hat to keep it as clean as possible. Her work clothes were faded and frayed, but his stolen ones were only a few months old.

"Supper and a hot bath are going to be wonderful," Jessie remarked. "But our bodies might refuse to move in the morning. You didn't realize what you were getting into, did you?"

"This wasn't the work I had in mind, but it isn't bad. You have a good place and hands, Jessie. I can see why you love it here."

"Then maybe we can entice you to stay around permanently." His smile faded, and she knew her words were a mistake. As if a joke, she added, "Surely you don't want us to do all this work alone. Trouble is, it never ceases. It's roundup and branding every spring, then roundup and cattle drive every fall. Not much adventure and excitement for a man with trail dust in his blood and on his boots."

"Sorry, Jessie, but that's true." He liked the way she seemed to catch her errors and correct them with genuine concern.

"Back to work for me. I'll take over Tom's place for a while." Jessie stepped around and over smelly piles of manure where flies buzzed. It was a familiar odor, so it didn't bother her too much. More flies buzzed around the discard pails of ear notches and testicles, attracted by the fragrance of blood. She shut out the noises of the area and concentrated on her tally after telling Tom to take a rest and praising him for doing a good job.

The freckle-faced redhead hobbled in Navarro's direction, dragging his twisted foot from fatigue. The boy was fascinated by the man he believed was a legendary gunslinger, paying no heed to the fact Jessie had denied it was so. While the stranger was talking with Miguel, Tom removed his glasses and cleaned them as best he could. "Need help, Mr. Jones?" he asked with eagerness when the Mexican returned to his roping.

"You can help me sharpen those knives for Jefferson."

"Are you gonna ride over to the Bar F and challenge Mr. Fletcher to a showdown?" the youth asked in a rush. "I'll bet you're real fast with those guns. I'll bet you gun him down with the first shot. He's real mean, Mr. Jones. I would handle it for Jessie and Pa if I was able," he murmured, frowning and slapping the thigh of his bad leg. He pushed his thick glasses back in place, as they had slipped down his greasy nose when he glanced at his filthy socked foot.

Navarro was moved by the boy. Though different from his own, Tom's problems clearly had a similar effect on his life and character. "Killing a bad man isn't always the best answer, Tom. Sometimes it's better to shame him and defeat him. Bloodshed usually leads to more bloodshed. A man has to prove he's stronger, wiser, and braver, or another troublemaker will take his place."

"How are you gonna defeat him?" Tom asked, intrigued.

"He's spooning out bad medicine to make us sick, so we'll do the same with him. When he's had enough, he'll back off."

"What if he don't?"

"We'll figure what to do when that time comes."

When Tom's glasses slipped again, the boy muttered as he shoved them back into place. Navarro bent over and retrieved something from the ground. He cut two lengths of rawhide from the long strip that had broken free from Miguel's saddle—thongs used for securing items to it. "Let me see your glasses for a minute." Tom handed them to the man, who tied a section of rawhide on each earpiece. He replaced the spectacles and knotted the rawhide ends behind the boy's head, then fluffed auburn hair over them. "There, that should keep them from falling again. Sweat and oil makes them slick on the nose. I knew a man once who did his like that to stop them from bothering him. Doesn't even show with hair over it."

Checking the snug fit with dirty fingers, Tom grinned and said, "Thanks, Mr. Jones. I never thought of it before. You're real smart."

"Like I said, Tom, there's always a way to solve a problem. Glad I could help."

"Some things can't be solved," Tom remarked with resentment. "I got this crazy foot that the doctors can't fix. I can't even hide it in a boot like you hid that strip with my hair so people won't stare and be mean about it. People laugh 'cause I'm clumsy. It ain't funny. They'd know if they had to live like this."

To be helpless and bitter were things Navarro understood. To be an outcast, to be stared at, to be mistreated, to be scorned and avoided—he knew about those, too. The desperado was surprised by the words that came from his own mouth and heart. "People are mean or curious when they don't understand something, Tom, or when they fear it. When you act ashamed, they think there's a just reason for it. I know it hurts to be different, to want something you can't have. Don't let it make you hard and bitter. Don't let it stop you from trying anything you want to do. It might be harder for you than others, but it's a challenge. Doesn't that make victory taste better?"

"You talk like Jessie. She's the only one before you to understand how I feel." Tom repeated what his older sister had told him before leaving to hire Navarro. "If Jessie says it and you say it, it must be true."

"You're lucky to have Jessie for a sister."

Tom brightened. "Yep, she's the best in the whole world. She loves me more than anyone. I don't know what I would do if anything happened to her. You won't let Mr. Fletcher hurt her, will you? He knows she's the one keeping Pa strong against him. I'm scared he'll try to get rid of her to make Pa sell. Don't tell them I told you. Pa would be mad."

"I won't tell anyone. Good friends have to trust each other."

"You'll be my good friend, too, like Jessie and Matt?"

"Yep, if you call me Navarro."

"Yes, sir, Navarro."

"Let's get busy, or the others will think we've quit for the day and start ribbing us." Navarro walked slowly to make sure the disabled Tom could keep up with his long strides. He saw Jessie send him a smile of gratitude, even though they had been out of earshot. It warmed him from head to foot.

Jessie knew something special was happening between Tom and her lover. Tom didn't take to many people, and she knew Navarro didn't, either. It was obvious Navarro had somehow won over her brother, and the other way around, too. She was overjoyed to see them striking up a friendship that hopefully would help both with their problems. What, she mused, a contradictory man he was! Her heart danced wildly and a hot flush raced over her body. If only things would work out for Navarro here, then perhaps he would stay with her.

"You missed two, Jessie," Jefferson whispered as he tugged at her arm.

The redhead blushed at her lapse of attention. "Sorry. It's been a long and tiring trip to San Angelo. I'll put Tom back on tally while I do a few chores before suppertime else I won't be able to get up or lift a fork. Tom! You take over here. I have to go. Navarro, I'll need your help."

Navarro followed her to the barn.

"The boys will be quitting in about thirty minutes. I thought you might want to get your bath and get changed into clean clothes while you still have privacy at the water shed. Some people don't like stripping in front of a bunch of strangers. So if you're shy, Navarro, you can be done and dressed before they finish. I have a few chores to do, then I've got to get scrubbed for supper. When you're done, come to the house. You can visit with me and Gran until Papa returns."

Jessie pointed the way to the overhang beside the chuckhouse where several wooden tubs were located. "You can fill one with the pipe from the well. Biscuit Hank already has water heating so you won't freeze. See the fire and kettle?"

"Yep, but don't you need me to do chores?"

"I can finish alone. If you want privacy, you'd better get to it," she said with a laugh. "You can claim any bunk that doesn't have possessions by it. See you soon." She left to place their saddles in the barn in case of rain, to toss hay to the horses corralled nearby, to pen up the chickens for the night, to do the evening milking, and to get her own grooming done.

Navarro wondered if Jessie had felt his scars and knew he was trying to hide them. Such a secret couldn't be kept long, so he would think about handling it soon . . .

Navarro bathed in a hurry, then dried his muscled body. He dressed in a rust-colored shirt, dark pants, and a leather vest. His feelings were in turmoil. He couldn't believe that he had been talking and joking and working with strangers since noon. No one had mistreated him. He had been accepted as if he were a seasonal hand returning for new work. Their reaction to him and his to them baffled him. Never had he been so at ease in a group. The ranch was beautiful, like Jessica Lane. Life here seemed wonderful for everyone concerned, despite their troubles. He saw why Jessie loved it and would die to protect it. He admitted he wanted to stay there to help these people and to enjoy life. He hated the thought of returning to a barren and lonely existence. Yet his tension was returning. One fence remained to be approached and jumped: Jedidiah Lane . . .

# CHAPTER SEVEN

Navarro sat in the dining area that adjoined the kitchen, where Martha and Jessie were completing the meal. He sipped coffee as he listened and observed, answered a question here and there, and just enjoyed the novelty of being included in this cozy moment in a real home with a good family. When Jessie came to set the table, Navarro asked if she needed any help.

Jessie smiled and shook her head. "But thanks."

"What work do you do, son?" Gran asked.

"A little of everything and anything. Haven't tried ranching before. This is new to me. Hard work."

"Have you handled many problems like ours?" the older woman inquired.

"None, ma'am."

"But he'll do fine, Gran," Jessie vowed. "He's fast, smart, and good."

"He must be, or you wouldn't be here to speak up for him."

"That's true," Jessie murmured, smiling at Navarro.

"Ma, I'm home," Jedidiah Lane shouted from the front door.

"In here, son," Martha replied, "with Jessie and her friend."

Jed entered the room, embraced the girl who ran into his open arms, and said, "Sure glad you're home safe, Jess."

"Papa, this is Navarro Jones. He's the man I've chosen to help us."

Jed walked forward to shake hands with the tall man. "Good to meet you, Navarro. The boys told me how you pitched in and helped today. I'm much obliged. They told me how you took care of my daughter, too. Can't tell you what that means to me. This girl is my heart and soul."

Navarro noticed how the man looked at his daughter, eyes filled with love and beaming with pride. A surge of envy shot through him. "Like I told your mother, I don't know much about ranching and cowpunching, but I'm willing to lend a hand where needed. Until I take on Fletcher."

Jed glanced Navarro. He wasn't what he'd expected in a gunslinger. Navarro seemed too kind and polite to be a hired killer. "I need to wash this dust off before supper. Then we'll talk. Matt's coming, Jessie, so set him a plate. I have plenty of news for you."

"I can't wait to hear it, Papa. The boys wouldn't give me a clue."

"That's good. No need to work it over twice. I'll be back shortly."

Jessie added a sixth place setting to the table. She smiled at Tom as he came down the stairs. "You look handsome tonight, Master Tom."

"You look beautiful, Jessie," he replied. "Don't she, Navarro?"

The desperado shifted from one foot to the other, then nodded. Jessie was wearing a blue cotton dress, and her hair was hanging free down her back. The wavy locks nearly reached her waist. The shorter curls framed her face and softened her bold features. The skirt swayed with her movements and captured his attention. There was no doubt tonight that Jed's "son" was a lovely woman.

"You act as if you've never seen me in a dress, Thomas Lane."

"Not much. I like your hair down. Ain't it pretty, Navarro?"

To her frustration, Jessie blushed again. "I always dress when we have company, young man. You stop putting Navarro in the fire with your questions. Besides, it's, 'isn't it pretty,' not 'ain't it pretty.' Your lessons are sorely lacking. I'll have you back to work at those books tomorrow."

"But I have to keep the tally. I'm doing a good job."

"Yes, you are, but studies are more important."

Navarro intruded before he thought about it. "He's needed out there, Jessie, with you being shorthanded. You and I have work to do. Who'll take his place?"

"Navarro's right, Jessie," Tom added, grinning at the man.

"Are you two plotting against me?" she teased.

Tom and Navarro exchanged feigned innocent looks and shook their heads. Tom laughed. Navarro shrugged and grinned.

"I see, two against one. You win this time, but you'll have to study twice as hard later. Agreed?"

"I promise."

"You promise what?" Jed asked as he returned.

Tom explained, then told how Navarro had fixed his glasses. Jed praised the gunslinger's ingenuity, then succumbed to Jessie's coaxing look. "The boys said you did work hard today, son. You're hired on until branding is over."

"Thanks, Pa. I'll do it good and right. You'll see."

Their other guest arrived. Jed introduced the two men. "Navarro Jones, Mathew Cordell. Matt was with me before the war. Then he came back when it was over. He's been foreman for ten years, but he's more like one of our family. I couldn't do without him, so follow his orders as if they were mine."

As they shook hands, Navarro studied the foreman. Matt was a few inches shorter than he was, and appeared to be in his midthirties. He was what women would call good-looking, with his brown hair and eyes and a neat mustache lining his upper lip. He realized how important this man was; he had heard his name many times from Jessie and the others.

"The boys broke you in hard before you could breathe."

"They worked me good today," Navarro responded.

Matt left the two men to walk to Jessie. He looked her over and smiled. "I can relax now; you're safe."

"I'll bet it's been quiet without me around to stir up things," she teased, and noticed how Matt's glowing eyes lingered on her. His gaze was soft and warm like melting chocolate, and she found his spellbound reaction to her flattering.

"Too quiet, Jessie, except where Fletcher's concerned."

"What's been going on?"

"Let's get seated first," Jed suggested.

Tom took his regular seat beside his sister. Jed and Martha did the same at the ends of the table. Matt and Navarro sat next to each other opposite Jessie and Tom.

The dishes were passed around and each person filled his plate. No one talked for a time as they prepared to devour the delicious meal of meat, home-canned vegetables, hot biscuits, and coffee.

"The boys told me about Big Ed. Sorry to get that news, Jess. What happened? And how did you meet Navarro?"

Jessie went over the highlights of those incidents. When she finished, with Jed's and Matt's eyes wide with fear, she added the news of the cut fence.

Jed's face flushed with anger. "We'll get it repaired tomorrow. He did the same on the east fence. We took care of it today. 'Course they rustled some cattle while the fence was down. We saw their tracks. That isn't the worst part, Jess."

"What is, Papa?" she asked reluctantly.

"We found Buck dead near the cut fence. That old dog must have sniffed trouble and tried to attack them."

Sadness and fury filled Jessie. "How cold and cruel can the man be, Papa?"

"While we were out during roundup, somebody sneaked over and killed some of the chickens. They were tied up along the corral posts. You see what we're up against, Navarro?"

"Seen any faces or horses you recognized?" he inquired.

"Nope. They're real careful-like. They're good about luring us away to do their mischief. I took your sister into town. She claimed it was to work with the schoolmarm, but I think she was getting scared after that chicken episode so near to home. It riles me to see them so cocky that they'll come so close to the house."

"Fletcher sounds like a determined man to me," Navarro commented.

"No more than I am, son." Jed flowed into the rippling story of how he settled this land and how he would never sell out to anyone.

"I can see why, sir. You have something special here."

"Why kind of work have you done before?" Matt asked. Jealousy chewed on him, because he caught an alarming undercurrent between the handsome stranger and his Jessie. He prayed he hadn't waited too long to let her know his feelings.

"Whatever job is available. No family or a place to call home, so I stay on the move. Nothing to hold me in one area very long. I like seeing new places. Came from Colorado, but spent most of my days north of there. Jessie told me you're into crossbreeding." He changed the subject from himself and his past.

"You said you don't know much about ranching?" Jed hinted.

"Nope, but it sounded interesting."

"If I can get Fletcher thwarted, I'll get back to it. Longhorns can take heat, thirst, and hunger; but they're leaner and tougher and stringier than purebreds. I've been mating mine with Durhams, Booths, and Galloways for a few years. As soon as I get more money, I aim to purchase me some Angus and Herefords to blend in. It costs a lot to buy them and have them shipped here."

"I'll see what we can do to stop Fletcher from interfering—."

"First," Jessie injected, "we have to catch up on chores. I'll help Gran with the washing, chickens, and milking tomorrow. That north fence needs restringing. It only has our ropes keeping the stock in."

"I'll help with it, Jessie, if Matt will show me what to do."

She smiled at him. "Thanks, Navarro. Then we'll go to work on Fletcher while the boys handle the branding."

"What if Tom shows me where Fletcher's place is on Tuesday? I'll keep him a safe distance away. That'll leave all the hands to keep to their chores, and you can help your grandmother. I need to study his layout, men, and schedule before we make any moves. Is that all right with you, sir?"

"Please, Pa, I can do it. I'll do everything Navarro says. I promise."

Jed mused for a time. "Tom doesn't do much riding. If you'll take care of him, he can go. That'll keep Jess and the boys busy here."

As Tom began to rush Navarro with questions about their impending adventure, Jessie told him, "Later, Tom. Let Navarro breathe and eat." Her brother obeyed, though she saw it was hard for him to do so.

As the meal continued, talk drifted into areas unfamiliar to Navarro. He was as careful as Jessie about concealing their true relationship. If Jed learned what had happened between them on the trail . . . Then there was Matt. The desperado noticed how the foreman subtly watched Jessie; he looked like a starving man picking up every crumb of talk that she dropped, feeding on each smile and gaze, drinking in every movement. He saw how easily Jessie smiled, laughed, and spoke with Mathew Cordell. They had known each other a long time. Matt would be here after he was forced to leave. Jealousy nipped at him like an angry dog on a stranger's heels. He listened to every word and observed each person. The longer he sat hearing about people, places, things, and times he didn't know about, the more restless and nervous he became and the more slowly the evening passed. He was feeling closed in, as he had in prison. He needed fresh air, movement.

Jessie glanced at Navarro every so often, but tried not to stare or to expose her warring emotions. It was hard being this close to him without touching him. If her father even suspected the truth of her behavior, he would order Navarro off his property. She had to give Jed time to get to know her love, time to accept him. And the same was true of Navarro and her family. Yet she sensed the anxiety building within the man across the table from her. She saw how straight and stiff he was in his chair. She saw how he toyed with his fork and how his gaze darted about from person to person. He was panicking.

Impulsively Jessie wriggled off her slipper and slid her bare foot across the floor. When it reached her love's booted foot, she stroked his leg with her toes. She pretended not to notice when Navarro reacted to her bold action. She brought her foot upward until it rested on his knee. His hand drifted into his lap and his fingers closed over it. Slowly and sensuously Navarro's thumb caressed the side. When her grandmother suggested they serve the dessert, Jessie hated to cease the action that seemed to relax both of them. She pulled her foot away and eased it into her slipper. "Gran made a special dessert for Navarro."

The dried-apple pie was warm and tasty. Its odor filled the room. Navarro thanked the older woman, and devoured two pieces.

"More?" Jessie offered.

"Too full. Best meal I've had all my life, ma'am."

"She's trying to teach me all her secrets, but I'm not a good student."

"You're good at everything," Matt replied with a grin. She looked so beautiful and feminine with her auburn locks flowing freely and her trim body clad in a dress. Her blue eyes laughed each time her lips did, and he hungered to make her kisses his dessert.

"You're just saying that because you practically raised me, Mathew Cordell."

"Did a fine job, too."

Jessie loved Matt as a brother. Tonight he looked extra nice and was most charming. She wondered how different his lovemaking and kisses would be from . . . She rushed a response. "Thank you, kind sir. Tom, it's bedtime. You've a busy day tomorrow."

"But I want to talk to Navarro."

"There's plenty of time for that, young man. He'll be here a long time."

"I hope he gets our trouble settled fast," Matt said, looking at Navarro.

"I'll try. I'll know more after Tom and me do our spying."

Jed stood, and so did Matt. Navarro followed their lead. As Jessie and Gran cleared the table, Tom mounted the steps.

"Let's head for the bunkhouse," Matt suggested to Navarro. "Good night, Jessie."

"Good night, Matt. See you tomorrow, Navarro," Jed said. "If you need anything, just tell Matt. We couldn't run things without him; he's like my adopted son."

"You sure it's all right if I use that sorrel, Mr. Lane?" Navarro asked.

"It's yours, son. Jessie gave him to you. It's hardly enough for saving my girl's life. We'll talk money tomorrow, if that suits you."

"Don't worry. I know you'll be a fair man. A drifter don't need much."

The two men left the house, and Jed went to his room. Jessie tried to get her grandmother to turn in while she did the dishes, but Gran wouldn't allow it.

From the corner of her eye, Martha watched her granddaughter as she remarked, "Your Navarro is mighty mysterious and restless, Jessie. I hardly learned a thing about him. Real closed-mouthed."

"He's a loner, Gran; they're like that. He spends most of his time on the trail by himself. He doesn't get much chance to talk or sit in one place long. Don't poke at him too hard before he gets used to us. It might scare him off."

"You wouldn't like that, would you?"

"Like *what?*" Jessie asked distractedly, her mind having drifted to the bunkhouse as she wondered how Navarro was mingling with the hands.

"Don't you think you've gotten too attached to a stranger too quickly?"

"What do you mean, Gran?" she asked as she stalled for time to think.

"Since when does Jess Lane blush? Or put on a pretty dress? Or wear her hair down? Or fly away on dreamy wings?"

"Stop teasing me, Gran. I do it every time we have company."

"Navarro isn't company. He's a hired gunslinger, a paid worker."

"He's more than . . . that," she finished hesitantly. "He saved my life, Gran. He's going to help us defeat our enemy, save our home and lives."

"What else is he going to do here, child? Steal the boss's daughter?"

"No."

"You sound sad about that."

"Maybe I am. I know it's impossible."

"Nothing is impossible for you, Jessica Lane, not when you want it."

"He is, Gran. The minute his task is done, he'll leave. I'm sure of it. Just as I'm certain there is nothing I can say or do to keep him here."

"You hardly know him, child. Is that what you really want?"

"For the first time in my life, Gran, I feel like a real woman. He tugs on me in a new way, and I like it. He makes me think about having my own home and family. Is that so terrible even though I haven't known him long?"

"No, but I don't think you should share this news with anyone, Jessie, not your pa, your sister, Tom, or even with Navarro himself. It's too soon."

Jessie had always been able to confide in and trust her grandmother. Yet there were things about Navarro that she couldn't reveal or discuss. Not yet anyway. "I know, Gran. Why tell them about something that will never happen? Don't worry about me. I'm a grown woman. I'll be fine. At least it's gotten me to thinking like I should at my age," she teased.

"The right man will come along for you one day, like my Thomas did for me."

"You're right, Gran. When he does, I'll know it." *I do know it, Gran, and it's Navarro, whoever and whatever he is.*

Jessie was up early to gather eggs and to release the hens from their noctural protective coop so they could scatter and scratch in freedom until dusk, except of course for those sitting on eggs. She tossed hay to the horses corralled nearby, including her cherished Ben who had been named after her grandfather Thomas Benjamin, as had her brother. She milked three cows that stayed in the pasture close to the barn. Usually she did those chores in the morning and her sister did them in the evening, when Jessie did ranch tasks while

Mary Louise did household ones with Gran. The redhead carried two pails of milk to Gran and one to the chuckhouse cook, along with a basket of eggs for the men's breakfast.

She placed both items on a table. "Morning, Hank. Smells good. I'll bet the boys' noses are sniffing the air already."

As Hank shoved another pan of biscuits into the oven, he responded, "Mornin', Jessie. The boys will be crawlin' outta their fleatraps anytime now. I'm 'bout to clank the ring. Don't let 'em trample you gettin' to it."

Jessie laughed. "I've learned to move fast at mealtime, Hank. I'll be helping Gran with the wash today. Tell the boys to leave their stuff on the bunkhouse porch and we'll do their laundry. I'm sure they're too busy to think about clean clothes, and we need them to stick to the branding. Everybody's chores will be twisted around for a while. If you need extra help, sing out. See you later. Want me to signal the hands as I leave?"

Biscuit Hank finished setting the tables. "Much obliged if you do. I'll get the milk and the coffee poured, and get these eggs to movin' in a pan."

Jessie approached the metal triangle that was suspended from the porch beam. She lifted the rod and clanged it against the three sides rapidly. Men came from beside the chuckhouse where the bathing area was located, hair damp and shirts sprinkled from washed faces and hands. She heard boots clattering on the bunkhouse porch as others hurried after yanking on clothes. She didn't see Navarro or Matt, and decided Matt must still be inside his private room at one end of the bunkhouse. Or perhaps he and Navarro were preparing to leave for their chore. Jessie waved and spoke to the Box L hands who passed her as she headed across the yard toward her home to enjoy her first meal of the day.

"Jessie, wait up!" a familiar voice called out and halted her.

She turned and smiled at Navarro. "I hope you fared well last night."

The desperado took in her snug jeans and green shirt that revealed a shapely figure. Her locks were braided, and the waist-grazing plait swung as she moved. The sections of hair she had cut in San Angelo for her disguise curled and framed her face in an enchanting manner. The colors of her fiery hair and rosy-gold complexion made her pale-blue eyes glow. They were large and expressive, and they shone with warmth this morning. He enjoyed just looking at her and being around her, but he wished he could pull her into his arms and kiss her. He cleared his tight throat to speak. "No problems. Most of the boys were turned in when me and Matt got back from supper. He says we'll ride out to mend that fence after we eat. Will you be all right here today?"

"Fine. I have plenty to do for Gran and the boys. The hands all took to you yesterday. So did Gran and Tom. He told me how kindly you treated him. Thanks, Navarro. You can't know what that meant to him, and to me."

"Yep, I do, Jessie, but don't ask why. He's a good boy. He just needs . . ."

"Needs what, Navarro?" she pressed when he fell silent and looked moody.

"Needs to be treated like everybody else. Not different. Not like a cripple in any way. Every time he's not allowed to do something, or at least try it, he sees more and more he's not whole. A boy's spirit can be crushed only so many times, Jessie, before it's destroyed. Pretty soon he won't care about trying. I'm glad your father is letting him ride with me, but . . ."

"Why did you stop again? You can tell me anything, Navarro."

He glanced at the ground. "Ain't really my business."

"If it can help Tom, please go on. It's between us. I promise."

Navarro's haunted childhood provoked him to intrude. "I think your father's doing it for the wrong reasons. If Tom suspects, it'll be worse than letting him go."

"Explain," she coaxed.

"He didn't want you and me out alone together, and he can't spare any of his hands. He's letting your brother go because Tom's the one least needed with the chores."

"I'm sorry to say I agree. You're very perceptive about people. Thanks for being honest and for trying to help. Anything you can do about Tom will be appreciated. You know, you're like an armadillo: beneath your hard shell, you're soft inside," she murmured, stroking his chest. When he looked disturbed by her touch and her words, she said, "Gran and I are washing today. Toss your clothes on the porch and we'll get them done for you. Don't argue," she teased when he started to protest. "We're doing it for all the boys while they're so busy."

"Navarro, grub's about gone! Let's eat and ride," Matt shouted, wanting to separate Jess and the gunslinger. He'd spent a sleepless night thinking about Navarro's pull on her.

Jessie smiled and waved to the foreman, who did the same to her. "Good morning, Matt. He's coming," she replied. "Sure you want to help?"

"Yep. We'll get things done, then work on Fletcher, if he lets us."

The hands returned to their seasonal schedule of breakfast, brand, dinner, short rest, brand, supper, and bed. Matt and Navarro rode northward. Tom kept the tally again. The other men rode range with Jed. Gran and Jessie did chores.

When it was nearing eight o'clock, Jessie built a fire under a kettle outside. While water heated, she gathered the men's clothes and linens, then sorted them. The redhead was glad there was no wind today to give them trouble with smoke in their eyes. She chipped soap off a homemade bar into the hot water and stirred it until melted, then drew water from the well and filled the rinse tubs, the task requiring more time and work with the pump broken.

Gran joined her. They scrubbed the clothes and linens on ribbed metal boards. The rinsed items were draped over sturdy cords that were strung tightly between posts, lower to the ground than usual because of Gran's short stature. Each time the water became too dirty or cool to do its job, Jessie fetched and heated more.

The task took the Lane women until three o'clock to complete, seven hours of sweaty toiling over the laundry tubs. Their muscles ached all over, and their hair was mussed, their arms and hands nearly raw. They were both soaked in spots from splashes. But more tasks awaited them. While Martha began the evening meal, Jessie used the soapy water to scrub the house and porch floors, then rinsed them using water from the other tubs. They would dry before dusk in the arid air. The tubs and kettle were dumped and stored. The dying fire was doused. The soap was returned to its place.

Jessie entered the kitchen and sighed wearily, but didn't complain about the hard labor. "Gran, I'll fill the water barrel, then get cleaned up while those clothes finish drying. I don't want you do anything more today than supper. I'll tend to the chickens and milking, then collect the laundry later."

Jessie thought the lines of fatigue and age on Martha's face looked deeper today. Though her grandmother had combed and rewound her white hair into a neat bun at the nape and put on a fresh dress, she could not conceal her exhaustion. Jessie wanted to take over preparing supper, but she knew Martha would not allow it.

Martha kneaded the dough for biscuits with sore hands. "Put some salve on those chafed hands after your bath, child. Is Navarro coming to supper again?"

"It wasn't mentioned. I don't know what time he and Matt will get home."

"Might be best if he sups with the hands. We don't want the others feeling jealous of a stranger getting favor. If he does come, bring Matt, too. If we make it look like we got business to discuss, the men won't take any offense."

Jessie heard the chow bell sing out while she was bathing. The bath felt so wonderful that she wanted to linger in it, but she didn't have time. She donned a paisley print dress, then brushed her hair. As she did so, she decided to keep it trimmed shorter around her face because it made her look more feminine. When all was straightened in her room and the water closet, she told her grandmother she was going outside to complete her chores, as dusk was near.

"Best hurry. Your pa's late. When he rides in, he'll be ready to eat."

"I won't dally, Gran," Jessie responded, merry laughter trailing her words.

As Jessie pulled the first piece of dry laundry from the cord, Matt joined her and asked, "Need a pair of extra hands? I'm sure you're bone-tired."

She glanced at the soft-spoken foreman and replied, "If you don't mind, I can use the help. I'm late with everything today. Papa isn't back yet, so supper is waiting on the stove. You and Navarro want to join us?"

"Just finished eating. You did good closing that gap with ropes."

Jessie placed folded pants on his extended arms. "It was Navarro's idea. How did you two get along?"

"He don't talk much."

Jessie laughed and teased, "Then it must have been a mighty quiet day out there." He was wearing clean clothes and his brown hair was combed. Even his mustache had been trimmed since his return. She looked into his chocolate gaze, and found it warm and searching. "Anything wrong, Matt?"

"How much do you know about this gunslinger?"

Jessie hoped the foreman didn't notice her startled reaction to his question. "He isn't a gunslinger, Matt, but he's as skilled as the best. I don't know his life history, but he strikes me as a good man. Was there a problem with him?"

"No, but there's something about him has me worried."

Jessie stopped her task to meet his troubled gaze. "Like what?"

"He ain't the kind to hang around a ranch."

"He's here because I hired him to do a job. Like lone eagles, even drifters have to light somewhere sometime to rest. Is it something he said or did?"

"No. I can't grasp it yet."

"When you do, come to me first, not Papa. I'm the one who chose him and hired him. If there's a problem, I want to handle it. All right?"

"Sure, Jessie. Just watch him close, will you?"

"Don't worry, Matt; I will."

The boss's daughter and the foreman carried several loads to the bunkhouse for the men to sort and claim. The hands thanked her. Navarro wasn't there.

Jessie closed the gate to the chicken coop and latched it. Night would engulf the landscape soon. She scanned the horizon for her father's approach but didn't sight him. Concern gnawed at her. Jessie halted at the structure where supplies, meats, and home-canned goods were stored for the Lanes and their men.

As she sealed the door to leave, Navarro said, "You been working hard."

Jessie turned to face him. "I wanted you and Matt to take supper with us when Papa returns, but he said you've already eaten."

"Hired hands don't eat with the boss much, do they?"

Jessie realized it was more of a statement than a question. "Not usually."

"I found my wash on my bunk. Thanks, Jessie."

"You're welcome." To keep him with her longer, she chatted about little things. "I was penning up the chickens and getting flour and rice for Gran. We're letting some sit over there in a separate coop to restock those Fletcher's men killed. We don't normally let this many keep their eggs for hatching, just enough to replace those we eat or the ones that stop laying with age."

"Owning and running a ranch involves a lot of work."

Jessie surmised he wasn't used to small talk but was seeking it to stay with her longer. That pleased her. "How did you and Matt get along today?"

Navarro glanced around while deciding what to say. Several hands were sitting on the bunkhouse porch as they talked and laughed, and one made music on a fiddle while Biscuit Hank blew on a harmonica. He knew Miguel, Carlos, and two others were inside playing cards. Although Matt stood in shadows near the barn, Navarro sensed the foreman's watchful gaze. It was obvious that Matt didn't trust him yet; but only because of the Texan's feelings for Jedidiah Lane's daughter. He had observed Jessie and Matt since his arrival. He wished he knew what their relationship was, but he dared not ask.

"Navarro?" she prodded as worry filled her.

The handsome man inhaled and met her gaze. "Sorry, Jessie. My mind drifted. I love this time of day. What did you ask me?"

The redhead didn't think he had forgotten her question. "Nothing. Here comes Papa. I'd best get inside and help Gran get our meal on the table. I'm tired."

"Will I see you before I leave in the morning?"

"I'll be up early, like every day. Good night."

" 'Night, Jessie."

While Jessie was doing the milking, her father and the foreman got Navarro and Tom on their way. She didn't like not seeing them off, and hoped Jed and Matt hadn't planned to exclude her. When her other morning chores were done, Jessie churned butter, ignoring her hands that still ached from yesterday. Later, as she heated the iron and pressed garments, Gran labored in the garden.

A stroll after supper brought strange revelations for Jessica Lane. After waving to her, Miguel and Carlos left the bunkhouse and walked to the corral. At twenty-seven and thirty-one, both men were good-looking and virile. Hard work had made their bodies strong and lithe. Miguel propped one foot against a post as his deft fingers toyed with a pistol. Carlos rested his buttocks against a horizonal rail; his cigarito sent smoke spirling upward as the half-Mexican drew on it, then exhaled. Their attire—pants, jackets, hand-tooled leather belts with silver buckles, ornately stitched boots, and Spanish spurs—revealed their roots.

An uneasy feeling washed over her as she saw them leave the others and halt in her path, decked in their finery. Usually the men washed after a dusty day and put on the clothes they would dress in the next day. Carlos and Miguel hadn't done that tonight. She had an odd feeling they were waiting for her arrival.

In the fading light before a three-quarter moon rose, Jessie smiled and joined them. "Don't you both look handsome tonight?" she remarked. "Are you expecting a wagon of fort laundresses to pass through?" she teased, referring to the women at army posts who saw to the soldiers' pleasures.

Carlos chuckled at her naughty innuendo. Miguel smiled, revealing the whitest and straightest teeth she had ever seen. Or maybe they only looked snowy in contrast to his black hair, dark eyes, and deep tan.

"You look pretty tonight, too, *amiga.* I like your hair cut that way."

"Thank you, Miguel." She related the story of why she had cut it.

"You are lucky he arrived to rescue you, *chica.* He seems a good *hombre.*"

"He is, Carlos. You know the Lanes only pick the best men for jobs."

"Gracias, chica. He is a strange one. Indian blood always makes Mexicans nervous. Our peoples have warred for many years with Apaches and Comanches."

"He told you he's part Indian?"

"He did not have to, *amiga,"* Miguel responded. "His looks speak of it."

"Does that bother you two?" Jessie inquired, holding her breath.

"Jamas, so release that air, *chica."*

She exhaled, and they all grinned. "What else do you know about him?"

Miguel repeated the same brief story that Navarro had told her family. Jessie didn't believe that tale, but she didn't challenge it. Nor did she tell the two men of her doubts. "Do you like him?"

"He has done well, *chica.* But he must relax for us to learn him," Carlos said.

"It will take time, *amiga,"* Miguel added. "He is a man with a shadow over his past. Such men keep a distance. He has known much trouble and pain."

"How do you know that, Miguel?"

"The scars on his back. When we washed last night, we saw them. He said an *hombre* was cheating at cards and he exposed him, then in a shoot-out, the cheater was killed. His brothers tracked Navarro and whipped him for hours. They left him for dead. But as you know, he did not feed the buzzards."

"He is not a man to be lashed," Carlos added. "It is certain he tracked those *hombres* and tasted revenge. A man such as Navarro Jones is always near danger. It runs in his blood as surely as restless dust fills his boots."

"Are you two saying I can't trust him?"

"He is part Indian, a man who lives with troubled spirits, a man who will kill to survive, a man who must be free or die. He has been hurt many times; this I see because I was like him long ago."

"Is that a yes or no, Miguel?"

"He will honor his word, but nothing more. He will fight to the death to do his job. Stay alert, *amiga.* He is a man to steal a woman's eye. He will not stay."

Jessie felt her heartbeat increase. "You did, Miguel. You said you were like him once. You changed. You stayed. What's the difference?"

"I had my revenge, my justice. I buried my past. Navarro has not. He is still searching for something, and I do not think he will ever find it. He is from two worlds, yet he fits in neither. He is the kind of man who destroys himself, and hurts anyone who comes too close to him. He is not bad and does not mean to harm those few he loves. It cannot be helped. He is a breed unto himself, *amiga.* He would not know how to survive if he changes. Do not try."

Wednesday moved at a steady pace for Jessie with morning chores and afternoon branding. By quitting time, she was exhausted. She bathed and dressed for the evening meal. Just as they began eating, Tom and Navarro returned. Gran reminded the excited boy to hold his story until after he washed up and sat down. Jessie was annoyed when her father told Navarro to return and give his report as soon as he ate supper. Jed also told him to bring Mathew Cordell along.

"We'll have cake and coffee while we talk," Jessie added.

After Navarro left to get cleaned up and eat, Jessie looked at her father and said, "That wasn't polite, Papa. We're eating, and you know the hands have finished. Hank probably has put away everything. He should have stayed."

"That isn't a good idea, Jess. I don't want a man like that getting too close to my family. Tom's already following him around and hanging on his every word. Tom, remember he's a wild gunslinger, not a man to pattern after."

"But, Pa—"

"Hush, boy. I know what I'm saying. I've seen his kind before. If we didn't need his skills, I wouldn't let him be here."

The tone in Jed's voice and the look in his eyes warned Jessie and Tom not to argue back, but both were disappointed and angry about their father's attitude. Tom stared at his plate, his joy and appetite gone. Jessie forced herself to eat to conceal her conflicting emotions.

Afterward, the room was quiet as no one tried to make conversation. Gran and Jessie cleared the table and washed the dishes. Jed remained in his place and sipped coffee. Tom was sent to his room to get ready for bed while the adults talked. The boy wanted to be included; he wanted to relate his stirring adventure. Jessie whispered to him that she would sneak up later to hear about it, which appeased Tom.

When the two men arrived, Jessie showed them to the table.

"Matt, would you like cake and coffee?" she asked.

Sitting to Jed's left, he replied, "Sure, Jessie. Gran cooks the best."

"Navarro?" she hinted.

Near the far end of the table, he answered, "Yes, Miss Jessie, I sure would like some."

When she served them, Navarro thanked her politely, and so did Matt. Jessie realized that Navarro was making a strong effort to show manners and correct behavior around the man who had been almost rude to him earlier. She hoped and prayed her father would not drive her love away.

"Fletcher's men were branding calves like your hands, Mr. Lane," Navarro related. "I saw about twenty men doing chores close to where he's settled. They were all unarmed, so they don't expect any trouble from us. I got a good look at Fletcher; Tom pointed him out to me from our hiding place. Couldn't hear what he said, but he didn't seem to be planning anything."

"How do you know that?" Matt asked.

"None of the men strapped on guns and rode in this direction. Didn't see anybody packing up supplies, either, planning to be on the range a while. Nice spread, but not like yours, sir. Fancy house with a walled yard like a hacienda. Two big barns. Not many longhorns in his herds. But he's got plenty of good horseflesh. Nothing with Box L brand that I saw. When the men changed shifts, I counted about five or six new faces from those doing branding. I didn't want to do too much riding around and risk being seen by men on the move. I got the layout of his ranch set in my head, and pretty much know his schedule. I'd say, from what I've learned here, he has about two more weeks of branding. That don't mean he won't pull some men to attack before he's done. From all Jessie's told me, he's to blame. But we can't act until Fletcher does. That is, if you want this handled like I think you do."

"How is that?" Jed asked, his stern gaze locked on Navarro.

The desperado shifted in his seat. "With as little trouble and bloodshed as possible. You want him defeated and stopped, but not killed. Whatever he's done, you're still a good man who hates to take the law into his own hands."

The room was silent as Jessie's father and the man she loved stared at each other. Finally Jed spoke. "You're right. I'm no murderer. I don't want him gunned down. He's been smart. No witnesses or proof to back my charges. He's got the sheriff and Army fooled. He claims rustlers are using these tricks to cover their thefts. Claims he's been having mischief over at his place, too. Says somebody might be trying to drive us both out of the area. He's a liar. Nobody's tried to buy my spread except him. What do you have in mind?"

"Me and Jessie decided to do to him whatever he does to you. He'll learn fast that your loss will be his loss. You willing to do it that way?"

"I don't hold to making innocents pay for the guilty's actions. I can't order no dogs and chickens slaughtered. We can't rustle any cattle, either. If we got caught, I'd be held accountable."

"I agree, sir. Why don't we wait for him to move, then make plans?"

The talk ended almost immediately, as all were tired and it was late. Jessie walked the men to the door, where she asked, "Did Hank give you any supper, Navarro? You got in late."

Matt answered for the reluctant man. "He didn't eat, Jessie. Hank was in the bunkhouse. Navarro washed up and changed."

"Don't worry over me, Jessie. I've missed plenty of meals before."

"You won't have to miss any here. I thought this might happen, so I held a plate for you in the warming oven. Wait here while I fetch it."

While he obeyed, Matt stayed with him. "She's a fine woman, Navarro."

"Yep, I can see she is." He thanked Jessie for the food when she returned and handed him a heaping plate. He left before his emotions ran wild over this good woman who always thought of others.

Jessie turned to find her father watching her. "Giving him food isn't the same as letting him join us, is it, Papa? We do need him strong and healthy."

"Sometimes you have too much heart, daughter."

"How can a person be too kind or too polite?"

"Good night, Jess" was his response.

"I'll go tuck in Tom."

Jed halted his departure to his room. "He's too old for that."

"I know, but I still enjoy it. He was so excited about his adventure, but he didn't get to share it with us. I don't want him to feel left out tonight."

"I was foolish to let him ride with that man. He could have been hurt. I would never forgive myself if anything more happened to him."

"You can't protect him forever, Papa. Victories can't be won unless challenges are confronted. If you have no victories and joys, what good is living? He has to try things to make him feel as close to normal as possible. Even if he gets hurt, he'll be happy. Let him grow, Papa. Let him take risks. Let him find his place in life. Let him know you're proud of him."

"Do I have to let him get hurt worse or killed to prove I love him? To let him be happy? I can't, Jess. Tom is different, and nothing can change that."

Jessie watched her father disappear into his room. She went upstairs to find her brother asleep. To let him know she had kept her word, she wrote a message on his chalkboard: "Navarro said you were a big help. Thanks. I love you. Jessie."

*   *   *

Just as breakfast was completed in the Lane home and bunk-house, one of the hands galloped to the barn. He leapt off his sweaty mount and raced to the warning bell. He rang it with all his might. When everyone rushed outside, he hinted between gasps for breath, "Trouble, Boss, nasty trouble."

 ## CHAPTER EIGHT

Jed, Matt, Jessie, and Navarro surveyed the horrid scene before them. Along the Calamity River in the southeast section of their ranch was a terrible sight. They rode in silence for a time, then dismounted. The ranch hand who had delivered the grim news had remained behind to rest and eat.

"Fletcher didn't prepare for this foul deed overnight. I thought you said you saw nothing unusual on his land!" Jed declared in an angry tone to Navarro.

As Jessie eyed the numerous dead coyotes that were strewn along both sides of the bank and tossed into the shallow water, she was shocked. "It looks as if they go for miles, Papa. It's an awful trick, but you know his motive. It's to terrify the stock and drive them away from water. His men must have hunted prairie wolves every night for days to get this many. He must have stored them somewhere in secret until he had enough to use for his vile mission. Navarro told you he didn't ride Fletcher's range. Even if he had, this task was done elsewhere. Then the bodies were hauled here. He couldn't have known about it to warn us."

"She's right, Jed," Matt added. "His hands must have been busy with branding, so Fletcher must have hired extra men to hunt them and bring them to his ranch."

"He could have hidden the bodies in the mountains, Papa."

"Some were trapped. Mangled legs." Navarro pointed out examples nearby.

Jessie looked at the wicked destruction of life. The coyote was smaller and built lighter than the wolf. The timid prairie wolf was misunderstood and slain by most men but was a creature that rarely preyed on stock or wild game. Although cunning and swift—the coyote fed on rodents, hares, and vegetable and meat carrion. What made Jessie even angrier were the pups and mix-breeds slain along with parents who mated for life. Coyotes readily bred with dogs, and offsprings were called coydogs. Pups, surely entire litters, of both had been killed without mercy. She knew that Fletcher's hirelings had done this cruel task at night, as the coyote was a nocturnal creature that lived in burrows during daylight.

Jessie glanced skyward in all directions. It appeared as if hundreds of vultures, the clue that had alerted their ranch hand to trouble, either were circling the lengthy area or landing to enjoy the enormous feast. Countless black dots were seen against the horizon, indicating more carrion-feeders were on the way, as if something had rung a supper bell near and wide to summon them here. "Papa, we have to get rid of these bodies fast so the buzzards will leave. Our stock won't come near this area with the stench of death and decay so heavy in the air. We don't have windmills in this area. The cattle and horses will scatter or sicken from lack of water before the air clears and they settle down."

Jed tried not to inhale the putrid odor surrounding him. A mixture of rage and depression overcame him. "I'll pull the men off branding and have them collect and bury these poor critters."

"Fletcher has only windmills for water supply," Navarro ventured. "Right?"

When Jessie nodded, he suggested, "Blow for blow. If we haul these coyotes over to his place and drop them around his windmills, his stock won't go near them. Fletcher did the killing; let him do the burying."

Jed looked at his daughter's hired man with new respect. He brightened as that tit-for-tat idea settled in and excited him. "You're clever, Navarro. We'll send him back his message."

Despite the distressing scene around her, Jessie smiled in pleasure.

Navarro went on. "Me, Matt, and two of the hands can wrap them in blankets or old canvas, then ride 'em over by packhorse after dark. Fletcher won't be expecting it so he shouldn't have any guards posted. When me and Tom were spying, he seemed too cocky and confident to be on alert."

"He'll be hopping mad tomorrow. He'll deny he's to blame for this outrage."

"The only way he can accuse us of returning them, Mr. Lane, is by revealing he knows where they came from. He'll keep silent."

"By Jove, you're right again! He can't say or do anything without exposing his guilt. We'll get revenge this time."

Jessie had held quiet while Navarro impressed her father with his keen wits. She spoke up to refute. "Justice, Papa, we'll get justice."

Jed's dark blue gaze fused with Jessie's light-blue one. Lines furrowed deeper on his face as he grinned. "This time, Jess," he said, "revenge and justice are in the same bucket. We'll make plans right now."

Jessie changed Navarro's suggestion. "Me, Matt, Navarro, Pete, and Smokey can gather the carcasses in piles while the other hands keep to the branding. We can use those old blankets in the shed that you used for Indian gifts long ago. Talbert, Roy, and Walt are flanking today with Jimmy Joe. Papa, that leaves you and Davy to check on the frightened herds. In case Fletcher's having us watched today, Matt, Pete, and Smokey can wrap and load the bodies after dark while me and Navarro haul them to Fletcher's windmills. The work will go fastest that way. We have to be finished by sunup tomorrow. You sure you don't mind helping with this nasty chore, Navarro?"

"I hired on to fight Fletcher and his tricks; this is one of them. But you don't need to help with a dirty job like this, Miss Jessie."

"I've done similar tasks before, when we had stock die of disease or were gorded during a stampede. You and I only need to deliver about ten to each windmill. The rest, all of us can haul to his south pasture and dump."

Jed, eager to repay and rile his foe, said, "Let's head back and get prepared."

At the house, Jessie dressed in well-worn clothes and located old gloves that could be discarded later. She grabbed a bottle of flowery cologne, then rushed back to the corral with the food Gran had packed for them. Water was taken along in canteens, since the river was befouled with rotting flesh. She noticed that Matt, Navarro, and two hands were ready to ride. Another hand was to bring the blankets and packhorses to them later as a precaution against Fletcher's possible spies. Jessie tossed Navarro some old pants and a shirt that she had taken from her father's work chest, aged garments saved to be used only once for tasks such as this one. "Use these so you won't ruin yours."

Navarro changed in the bunkhouse and returned. As Jed and Davy headed out to check on the stock and hands started branding near the corral, the four men with Jessie rode southeastward to the river.

The group approached the first bodies of coyotes, pups, and coy-dogs in various stages of decomposition. Jessie asked each man to pass her his bandanna before he folded and tied it over nose and mouth to shut out as much of the stench of death and decay as possible as they worked. She dotted the cologne on the triangular cloths and returned them before securing her own in place. The men thanked her. Even though Jessie rarely wore the cologne, Navarro and Matt were stirred by the womanly air that filled their nostrils.

"I'll put it in my saddlebag. Don't hesitate to use it," she told all of the men.

Each began to drag the animals into piles. Often, skittish vultures had to be scared off with loud shouts and waving arms. The persistent buzzards simply flew to another body farther away and ripped into it, as if devouring their first meal in weeks.

Jessie thought the vultures were ugly creatures, but they served a purpose as they rid the land of carcasses. Their weak feet were big, made for walking and grasping. Their strong beaks, skilled at tearing into hides and meat, made her cringe at the thought of lying weak and helpless while carrion-feeders circled overhead.

Jessie shuddered and cast that horrible vision from her head. She looked at the pitiful creatures she moved to the growing piles along the riverbank. Brush wolves hunted alone or in relays. Many times she had listened to their nightly serenades of mingled short yaps and mournful howls. Killing them was wrong, as they rarely harmed mankind and his possessions. Although their pelt colors varied, most were a grizzled buff with reddish legs and splashes. Their long fur was coarse, their bushy tails black-tipped. Their golden eyes were mostly closed in death.

As the group labored, the sun's heat and brilliance increased. The fetid odor worsened. Flies buzzed and gathered on the furry mounds and on uncollected bodies. They worked all day—sweat, blood, dust, loosened fur and flesh clinging to them and making their horrible task harder.

They halted and put a distance between them and the rank location to try to rest and to eat a light meal. Both were almost impossible. At dusk, the packhorses and blankets were delivered by Jed and Davy.

Jessie persuaded her weary father to return to the house to get some sleep for the tasks ahead tomorrow while she, their foreman, and two hands rested after their lengthy chore. It was getting cooler, but she resisted putting on her light wool jacket and ruining it. She glanced at the setting sun that was providing the last remains of daylight. Soon a full moon would rise from the east and give them enough light to work through the night.

"This was a vicious and evil deed; it shows how twisted Fletcher's mind is," Jessie remarked as reeking creatures were loaded on packhorses and tied down.

"Get the next load covered and ready," Navarro told Matt. "We'll return soon."

Jessie and Navarro rode for the nearest windmill on their enemy's land. They were cautious during their journey, but didn't sight any of Fletcher's men, not on that trip or any of the other ones. She decided that the confident man must have allowed all of his men to return to his bunkhouse that night.

The malodorous task continued far into the wee hours of the morning. The couple hauled and discarded coyote bodies around each windmill. Bar F stock nearby hurried away from the fearful odor of death. They hated to punish innocent creatures for their owner's wickedness, but it wouldn't be for long, just enough time for their foe to get the message that they wouldn't stand still for such repulsive acts. Wherever the task was done, Navarro let Jessie ride ahead while he lingered behind and used his Apache training to conceal their tracks. He had told them that using wagons was unwise, as wheel marks were harder to cover.

Many carcasses were hauled to the south pasture on Wilbur Fletcher's spread and piled there to be found in a few hours. While Matt and the others burned blankets and took the extra horses back to the corral, Jessie and Navarro made their last haul northward. The plan was to join them afterward at the ranch, which was closer to their last destination.

After covering their trail, Navarro joined Jessie at a group of trees near their boundary. He saw her leaning against the largest trunk, appearing so still as to be asleep on her feet. She didn't move as he approached. He dismounted and went to Jessie, whose eyes remained closed. His gaze scanned the woman who was also smelly, filthy, and exhausted.

Navarro tugged at her arm. "Let's go, Jessie," he said, "so you can get into bed. You worked hard; you need rest."

Jessie forced her eyes open, eyes that were red-streaked and puffy. She was barely able to move or stay awake. "Worked hard for a woman?" she teased.

Navarro smiled and countered, "For anybody."

Jessie yawned and stretched. "I should have told them we'd camp here. I dread that long ride home. Blazes, I'm sore and tired. I'm sure you are, too."

"If we don't get back, they'll worry and think we've been captured. I'll help you. You can ride double with me." Navarro held her arm with one hand and circled her waist with his other one. At his sorrel, he released his grasp. He gathered the reins of the packhorses and secured them to a rope, which he tied to his saddle. He rolled the stained blankets and their gloves into a bundle that was strapped to one horse, to be burned later. He mounted, then bent over to pull her up onto his lap. When she was settled in his arms, he led the horses away. Her Ben followed. "Take a siesta. I'll wake you when we near the house."

Jessie looked up at Navarro's handsome face. It felt wonderful to be in his arms. How she wished they were going home to bathe and sleep together. After this episode, surely her father thought more highly of Navarro. If not, soon Jedidiah Lane would be compelled to alter his low opinion.

Despite her sorry condition and fatigue, she savored being so close to her lover. She wished they were camping somewhere secluded and private, with no one waiting for their return. "Thanks for all you did today, Navarro. You've proven I was right about choosing you. Papa was most impressed. I'm glad, because he's too distracted to think clearly these days. He doesn't mean to be cold or rude; he just has so many worries."

"I know, Jessie. It's as bad as you told me, or worse. I'm worried, too. This Fletcher shows a crazy streak. Crazy plus mean is dangerous."

"Whatever he does, be careful. I don't want anything to happen to you."

"The same goes with you, woman."

Their gazes locked—searching, speaking, revealing, caressing.

Each moved toward the other, fusing their mouths in an urgent and needed kiss. Navarro stopped the horses and held Jessie as close as he could. The kiss drifted into others, each deepening and lengthening. This was a time in their lives when they needed each other for strength, help, and survival . . . and love.

Finally, each seemed to realize that they could not repeat the sensual experience they had enjoyed in the cabin six days ago, not here and now. But their attraction had grown stronger since they'd arrived at the Box L, and each knew it would grow even more during the days ahead. They would find a place to be together. That seemed to help them through this difficult moment when a union was impossible. Jessie smiled when Navarro kissed the tip of her nose, and both passed understanding to the other. Their journey home continued. Jessie fell asleep in Navarro's embrace. As the fugitive watched her slumbering peacefully, the feeling of tranquility left him.

The desperado tried to keep his yearning gaze and thoughts off the woman in his arms. If not for his criminal past, this was the woman he could spend his life with. The people here could change him for the better. They could give him peace and happiness. He wished there was a way he could obtain a new face so he could stay with Jessie forever. He wished they could keep riding, travel far away to where his past couldn't reach them. If he dared ask, would Jessie go with him? If she refused, was it worth it to seek a new beginning alone? If she agreed, what if his past did catch up with them? What would become of his love then, after she had sacrificed her home and family in Texas to be with him? He was taking too many risks to be with her now; he couldn't take more with her life at stake. He wanted Jessica Lane more than he had ever wanted anything, but . . . No, he decided, it was too dangerous and selfish. Once she was safe, their relationship must end.

When they neared the corral, it was almost sunup. Hands were stirring. Matt and Jed hurried to meet them. Her father had slept fitfully, worried about his daughter. Pete and Smokey had eaten and gone to bed. Mathew Cordell had awaited Jessie and Navarro's return.

Navarro walked the horses at a slow pace to avoid rousing Jessie. He motioned to the two men to talk softly. In a near whisper, Navarro asked, "Can I take her to her room, sir? She's exhausted. The job's finished, and our tracks are covered." The fugitive noticed the look of jealousy that gleamed in Matt's eyes.

Reluctant but helpless, Jed nodded permission.

Navarro left the other horses with the two watchful men and rode to the house. He dismounted with Jessie in his arms, and carried her into the house. Gran smiled and led him to Jessie's room. The older woman tossed a blanket over the clean covers so her granddaughter's dirty clothes would not soil them. Navarro laid Jessie down and removed her boots without awakening her. He glanced at Gran as she handed him a second blanket to place over her.

Jessie sighed and curled to her side, but remained asleep. She did not see Navarro nod to Martha Lane and depart to report to Jed. Navarro then ate and turned in until noon. As for the redhead, she slept until one o'clock.

Upon awakening, Jessie was told by her grandmother that Jed and Matt were riding the east boundary to check for trouble from their enemy. The older woman added that she had seen Navarro working in the branding pen with the hands. Before the women could say more, Tom came to the house on a break.

"Jessie, you're up! Navarro said you'd tell me about the coyotes. He's too busy to talk. Me, too. I'm keeping tally again. Pa said I was good at it."

Jessie related the grim tale of yesterday's and last night's labors. "I can't imagine what that wicked man will try next. Tell me about your adventure with Navarro. We haven't had a chance to hear about it, have we, Gran?"

The older woman coaxed, "Yes, Tom, what happened?"

The boy's eyes brightened. He told how he guided Navarro to the area and how they spied on Fletcher's settlement and men. "It was fun, Jessie. He don't treat me like others do. I hate when people pity me and stare at me. You know what he said? He said everybody can do something special. He said I just have to learn where my path is and ride it. I like him, Jessie. I hope he stays with us after the trouble is over."

Jessie thought it was best not to display her matching feelings before the watchful Gran. "It would be nice, Tom, but I doubt it," she said lightly. "Drifters don't like to settle down in one place long. He's not a cowhand. Once this trouble is over, there'll be nothing to keep him here."

Tom frowned, then asked, "You think the trouble will last a long time?"

"I hope not," Gran answered. "We have work to do."

"Speaking of work, you and I better get busy, Tom. I'll help with the branding until Papa and Matt return. I'll quit in time to help with supper, Gran."

Jessie and her brother walked to the noisy and dusty area. Navarro turned the tally task back over to Tom. The redhead eyed the weary flankers. "Navarro, think you can do Walt's job while I take Jimmy Joe's?" she asked.

Jimmy Joe glanced at the redhead and grinned. "You been lazin' around long enough, huh?"

"I deserved a nap, Jimmy Joe, after working day and night straight through. Maybe you're as tough as me and don't need relieving," she teased in return.

"You know I can't show up the boss's daughter. Take my seat fast."

Jimmy Joe let the bawling calf loose and jumped to his feet. "I need a good stretchin'. My arms and legs are tighter'n strung barbwire. Thanks."

"Want to try it, Navarro?" she asked again.

"I've been watching a lot. I think I can do it. I'll willing to try."

Carlos Reeves dragged a calf over to them with a rope around its hindleg. He grinned as the dark-haired man grabbed it by the neck hide and struggled until it was flipped to its side on the ground. "Pin his head with a knee across his neck. Grab his foreleg and bend it back. He won't be able to move if you hold tight."

Navarro followed the instructions. He watched Jessie seize the right hindleg and stretch it backward, then grip it firmly. Her right boot propped against the knee joint of the calf's lower leg and held it motionless. Rusty stamped the creature with the Box L brand, while Jefferson Clark notched its ear.

"Girl!" Jessie shouted to the black marker and to the tally keeper.

The next time Navarro took a calf from Miguel, he had clearly mastered the task. Jessie shouted over the noise, "Boy!" When the "ironman" moved, Jessie leapt up, placed her left heel against the calf's bottom leg, straddled its body with her right leg, and lifted the animal's top limb. Jefferson deftly castrated the male. Jessie released her grip and stepped aside, then Navarro did the same. The calf trotted to its bellowing mother, who nuzzled his bloody ear.

"I can't believe how strong and skilled you are, Jessie."

"For a female, Navarro?" she jested.

"This time, yep, for a woman." He looked at the brander and

asked, "Is there anything she can't do as good as the best man, Rusty?"

"Nope. She can even use hot irons as good as me."

Jefferson chuckled and added, "She kin do my job, but she ain't as fast."

"Your job is my least liked chore, Jefferson. I'm glad you're good at it and never sick. I don't like paining any critter. But you boys are wrong. I can't do everything. I can't take over for Carlos. The last time I tried to tame a half-broken horse, he almost busted my arm and leg. Did get my nose. I'll leave that dangerous chore to the best broncbuster in Texas. Right, Carlos?"

The half-Mexican grinned. *"Acaso, chica."*

"Perhaps, nothing," she retorted with a merry laugh.

Miguel dragged a calf to them as the other roper returned to the herd.

"Miguel there is the best roper in Texas. He can lasso any part of a critter, even a lowered tail. I can rope heads, but I'm not very good at legs."

"That is because you do not practice, *amiga.* No need when you have me."

"You see, Navarro, I have talented help. I only learn enough to take over in a bind. I have to know a little about everything. How else can I give the right orders? If a woman's gonna be owner and boss, she best know what she's saying."

"Jessie does," Rusty remarked. "She couldn't know or do better if she was Jed's son. You never catch her sleeping on her elbow when she rides herd."

"I don't dare, Rusty. You'd ride by, knock it loose, and send me falling. He always sneaks up on unseasoned wranglers and teaches them a lesson the first week. One's head snapped so hard that I thought his neck was broken."

"That's 'cause he was six feet under in sleep. A man that deep won't hear or see nothing. He never napped on my shift again."

When Jimmy Joe and Walt returned, Jessie said, "I have to get washed up and help Gran with supper. You boys need anything else before I go?"

Everyone shook their heads "no" so Jessie added, "Navarro, you didn't hire on for this kind of work so you can knock off whenever you're ready."

"You're shorthanded so I'll help them finish today. Tomorrow I want to ride out and see how Fletcher is taking our challenge."

"I'll go with you. I'm sure he's furious and plotting something new."

Jessie took care of her other chores, then bathed and changed into a skirt and blouse. She went to the kitchen and assisted her grandmother with the meal.

When Jed and Matt returned, she was told they hadn't seen or heard anything from Fletcher or his hirelings. That made Jessie suspicious and worried, but all she could do was wait.

On Saturday, the bad news arrived before Jessie and Navarro went riding: Fletcher's men had destroyed a windmill in the area most lacking in water supply.

Jed's face flushed with new anger. "Just like us, he hit at a windmill. I can't keep stock from drifting into that area without posting men there, and I hate to pull any hands off branding. With no water around, the stock will be too far from the river and other windmills before they're thirsty. They'll start stampeding in a search for it, or get too weak to make it to another source. We'll have to repair that windmill today and move the stock to water."

"Wait, Papa. We have to get those calves branded so we can turn them and their mothers loose to graze. Big John can work on the repairs while Navarro and I stand guard for him. You and four of the boys can round up the scattered stock and get them to water. You should check other windmills and for cut fences. Matt can team up with Roy as flankers with Jimmy Joe and Walt. Hank can tend the branding coals, and Gran can cook extra for the boys. It shouldn't take but a day or two, if the damage isn't bad. Big John already has part of the job done; that's the windmill we were going to replace soon," she reminded him. Jessie had seen how upset her father was, and had taken control of the situation to give him time to clear his head.

"I forgot. It's that old one in the southwest area. We'll get supplies loaded in a wagon, then you three can head out. Be real careful-like, Jess. I don't trust Fletcher. He might have men waiting around to prevent repairs."

"Navarro and I can handle them, Papa. Don't worry."

Nails, hammers, saws, sharpeners, wood, hole diggers, food and water supplies, bedrolls, weapons, and new windmill parts were loaded on a wagon. Big John Williams, who usually tended the windmills by checking and oiling and repairing them, climbed aboard and flicked the reins. Jessie and Navarro mounted their horses and rode one on each side of the wagon. They headed south-westward.

Several hours later, they arrived at the scene of Fletcher's latest attack. Big John examined the damage while Navarro scouted the nearby area. Jessie waited for the large black man to give his opinion.

"Deys chopped 'er laigs an' head good, Miss Jessie. 'Er gears ain't bad. Shaft an' pump looks to be all right. I kin replace dem broken blades an' tail. I'll be needin' yore he'p wif dem busted laigs."

"Let's get unloaded and get to it, Big John. Just tell me what to do."

When Navarro returned and reported sighting no threat nearby, he helped Jessie and Big John get prepared for the task ahead.

As they labored, Jessie told him, "These are made specially for areas like this one. Would you believe a New Englander invented them? I'll bet he'd never even seen this kind of rugged countryside. Thank goodness we have plenty of wind. Ever since they came about in '54, they've helped open up dry areas out here." She explained how the windmills worked: the gears at the top were run by windpower on the eighteen blades, causing the mechanism in a box to force the shaft up and down to pump water. The liquid poured into a pond or large trough. The tail controlled the direction of the wheel, keeping its face into the wind. During rainy spells or to avoid pumping too much water on brisk days, the tail was folded to halt its work, as a wise man never risked wasting his precious water supply.

While Navarro assisted Big John, Jessie stood guard with her Winchester in her hands. She glanced at the two men as they cleared the four holes of old posts and debris, then placed the lower section that John had constructed in them. A second section was added, then a third. The loud sound of hammers against nails rang out across the quiet landscape, accompanied by the noise of sawing wood. John positioned the small platform and secured it to the tower. A temporary post was hauled up the ladder to aid with lifting the multivaned wheel. Navarro joined John on the platform to help with that task.

Jessie observed with apprehension as the two labored on the small surface so high above the hard ground. Windmills were twenty to thirty feet tall and she sighed in relief when Navarro climbed down in safety. She saw her love use a rope to pull the remaining parts and tools up to John. Soon the new tail was attached. Gears were oiled. The shaft and pump were checked again. As the last rays of daylight vanished, John turned the crank at the base to put the tail to work. The broad piece moved with the breeze. The wheel faced windward, and turned. After a few creaking sounds, the speed increased. The shaft moved up and down, and water poured into the trough. Jessie, John, and Navarro cheered.

It was too late to return home. While the men loaded the wagon to leave at dawn and placed bedrolls on the ground, Jessie prepared them a meal of fried meat, scrambled eggs, red-eye gravy, and warmed biscuits from Gran. The campfire glowed and crackled. Smoke drifted skyward. The smell of aromatic coffee teased their nostrils as a full moon shone overhead.

As they ate, Jessie said, "It's so quiet tonight, too quiet. I doubt there's a coyote left in the area. Those he didn't have killed have fled in fear. The pronghorns took off, too. Haven't seen one all day. Papa should have the stock back in this area by midmorning. What next, I wonder?"

"He's a bad 'un, Miss Jessie. I dun seed his kind afore."

Jessie knew he was referring to his days of slavery. "I know, Big John."

When they finished and all chores were completed, Jessie asked, "Navarro, would you like to take a walk? I need to relax before I turn in or I won't sleep any."

Big John went to his bedroll and lay down. "See ya in the mawnin'."

"Good night, Big John."

" 'Night, John."

" 'Night, Miss Jessie, Navarro."

Jessie and Navarro strolled for a time, the moon lighting their path. Mesquites, small oaks, and yuccas grew in the area. They didn't go far in case trouble arose for their slumbering companion in camp.

Navarro noticed how the moonlight played on Jessie's red hair and brought out its fiery soul. He saw the shadows it created on her features. He was tense. He knew he wanted this woman, but he wasn't sure what to say or do. He craved her closeness, but feared an overture would mislead her. It wasn't right to keep pulling her toward him when he must eventually leave. To make love with her implied she was important to him, which she was—but important enough to compel him to remain here, which was impossible.

"You're a good worker, Navarro," she commented to start a conversation. "You've done about everything but use your guns for hire."

"That'll come in due time, Jessie. Fletcher is riding a steady course. He's getting bolder and meaner all the time, just like you said. Trouble is, we still don't have proof he's behind all this. We have to catch him with dirty hands. I have a plan," he said, then went on to explain it . . .

"That's very clever, Navarro. We'll try it Monday night."

"I hope you'll stay at the house. There'll be shooting."

She halted and looked at him as he did the same. "Afraid I'll get hurt?"

"Don't want you to take that chance."

"I must. This is my home and family in danger. One day when you and Papa are gone, I might have to defend them again. Now's the time to learn self-defense from the best. Unless you've decided you love it here and want to stay."

Navarro put a little distance between them and turned away from her. He stood with his boots planted apart and his hands on his hips, staring into the shadows as he considered his answer. He heard Jessie approach him, felt her closeness. "It's a good place, Jessie, but not for a man like me."

"You still have to leave, Navarro?" she asked in a soft voice. "Why?"

"Because of me. I got my reasons. Don't ask me to explain."

"Can't I give you any good reasons to stay?"

"I wish you could, but my answer's the same. I can't."

"You understand what I'm offering, don't you?"

"I don't think you understand it's not possible."

"You can have me, a home here, whatever you want."

It was the hardest thing he had ever done to say, "Even if your father said yes, and he wouldn't, I can't."

Anguish knifed her heart. She had spoken too soon, been too bold. "I'm sorry I was so brazen. I didn't mean to corner you. I was just hoping you had come to feel the same way about me that I feel about you. I won't embarrass you again. Your friendship means a lot to me. Please don't get upset and leave. I'll behave myself, I promise."

Navarro turned to look at her. "This is hard for me, Jessie. I do want you and need you. I just can't give you what you need. You're the settling-down kind, and I'm not. If I let you think I can be per- suaded to stay, that would be wrong. You'd get hurt when I left. You need a man raised like you, a rancher, somebody who can share a home and family with you. I won't lie just to have you for a while. I like you too much for that. I can't stay any more than you can jump on Ben and leave with me tonight. You can't become a drifter and I can't become a rancher. We're too different."

"If I would become a drifter, would you ask me to leave with you?"

Navarro's heart was pounding. "I shouldn't answer that, Jessie. It could hurt both of us."

"Hurt me because you wouldn't ask or wouldn't take me along?" she pressed.

"Wouldn't ask," he replied, then saw tears glimmer in her eyes. "Wouldn't ask because you might say yes, and that would be a big mistake for you."

"What about for *you*, Navarro?" She had to know.

"What kind of man would I be if I let you sacrifice everything for a wild life with me? If you rode off with the likes of me, your father would never let you return. I know what this ranch and your family mean to you. You're willing to die for them! I'm not a match for them, Jessie. Don't be blinded by desire for me."

"If I didn't have a home and family, would you take me with you?"

"Yes, Jessie. I would ask you to go, and I would try to make you agree."

Jessie was elated, but confused. "You want me enough to take me with you, but still you can't stay to have me?"

"It's not that I don't want you enough, woman."

"Then what is it?"

"It wouldn't work for me to stay or for you to go. You've always lived here and had loved ones. Your life has been happy, safe, set- tled. Mine hasn't. You're asking me to fit into your life. I have to be free and on the move to be happy, Jessie. If I was crazy enough to accept, it would destroy both of us one day."

"But won't losing each other do the same thing?"

"It will hurt us but not kill us. When I leave, forget me."

"Why don't you tell me to stop breathing, too? That's as easy."

Navarro turned and walked away again. "Damn," he swore softly. He couldn't tell everything. If she didn't despise him afterward, she would try to help him by endangering herself, and him. There was no road open for them. It was rash and cruel to think he could clear one.

Jessie stepped before him. It was obvious that something was eating at him. He wanted her, but something had him convinced it wouldn't work. She must persuade him it could. "All right, we have no future, but we do have a present. Can't we share it as long as possible?"

"It's too little to offer a woman like you, Jessie."

"It's more than I have, Navarro. Isn't it more than you have, too?"

"To have you for only one day is worth any risk I'm taking."

That confession, his choice of words, intrigued and touched her. Somehow she had to discover what or who stood between them. Until then . . . Jessie leaned against his hard body and put her arms around his neck. She drew his head downward as she raised on her tiptoes to taste his kiss.

Navarro groaned as his arms banded her pliant body. His lips savored her sweet ones as his fingers slipped into her silky hair. He felt as hot as one of those branding irons in the smoldering coals.

Jessie tried to cling to him when he released her. "Don't pull away, Navarro. I'm yours by choice."

He had to struggle to retain his strength and will. That inner battle made his voice husky with emotion. "Then do as I say, Jessie. Not here. Not now. John could awaken. Fletcher's men could attack. Your father could arrive."

Those reasons to halt this passionate moment were real. "When? Where? How?" she probed, yearning for him. "My time with you is so short."

"If your father guessed the truth about us, he would hate me, but he'd try to force me to marry you to save your honor. When I refused, and I would have to, Jessie, he'd kill me. You know what that violence would do to you and your family. Don't tempt me to hurt you or them. Help me be strong for now. We have to be careful. Soon, I promise. We'll have plenty of time together. Alone," he added.

"You're the boss," she conceded. Yet she wished she could have him one more time before her beautiful sister returned home tomorrow. She dreaded to think what would happen when Mary Louise discovered this handsome man within her greedy reach.

CHAPTER NINE

As Jessie and Navarro dismounted, Mary Louise met them at the barn. Jessie looked at her younger sister, who was wearing a new and very pretty dress. Her blond hair flowed down her back like a river of soft sunlight. Her sapphire eyes were examining Navarro from head to foot, and Jessica felt a surge of irritation.

"I assume this is Navarro Jones, our new hand?" Mary Louise asked coyly.

"That's right," Jessie responded. "Navarro, this is my baby sister, Mary Louise. Did you learn anything in town, little sister?"

"Enough to know I was right in not becoming a schoolmarm. They work dreadfully hard and long hours and hardly earn enough to survive. No, teaching is not for me. What did you two do last night?"

"The same as everyone—slept after a hard day of work. Are your chores done? From that fancy dress, I assume you've been lazing around as usual. Is Papa back yet?"

"No," Mary Louise answered, her gaze still on Navarro.

"Then I would get my chores done before he returns. You left at a terrible time. Everyone's been doubling up to cover for you."

"Don't be so bossy, Jessica. I had a long and tiring ride."

"So did we, but the work isn't done yet."

"Don't mind my older sister, Navarro; she's a slave driver. Don't let her work you too hard for what little she's paying you. Gran and Tom told me all about you. How long will you be with us?"

"Long enough to settle the trouble. Then I'll be on my way." Navarro sensed the tension between the sisters. "Jessie, I'll take the horses and tend them. We'll see what your father has to say when he returns."

Jessie was delighted that Navarro didn't seem enchanted by her exquisite sister. "I'll find you when I finish in the house," she told him, then smiled.

Navarro smiled back, then nodded at Mary Louise and left.

Mary Louise's gaze followed him. "If I had known we had a man like that working here, I would have returned home sooner."

"And let Papa discover you lied to stay in town to enjoy yourself while we worked our hands raw?" Jessie scoffed.

Mary Louise's dark-blue gaze settled on her sister's light one. "Don't be a prude in men's britches, Jessica Lane. You know I had to lie to get away. If I could have, I would have stayed longer. I can't believe Father let you stay out all night with a stallion like that."

"We weren't alone; Big John was with us. We were working hard."

"On the windmill or on each other?"

"Mary Louise Lane! Whatever did they teach you at that boarding school?"

"I learned what real men are for. Have *you*, big sister?"

"You are a lazy, conceited, spoiled, naughty girl."

"I'm a woman, Jessica. Are you?"

"You surely came home in a foul mood. What ails you now?"

"Being back, of course. I did enjoy myself in town. It was pleasant to get away from this smelly place and this silly war you and Father have started."

"It isn't silly. Didn't Gran and Tom tell you what happened while you were gone?"

"Oh, yes, your ridiculous charges about Mr. Fletcher. You're wrong about him, Jessica. He couldn't have done those awful things. He was in town. I saw him there several times. He's quite charming and handsome, as well as rich."

"Fletcher was in town this week?"

"That's correct. I first glimpsed him on Thursday. He was still there when I left this morning. I wonder how he managed to be in two places at the same time."

"He doesn't have to be at his ranch for his hirelings to carry out his bloody orders."

"Do hired hands normally make plans and carry them out without obtaining their boss's permission? After you dumped those dead beasts on his land, who made the decision to attack our windmill? Mr. Fletcher was in town that night. If he's as intelligent as you and Father think, why would he give someone else that authority? I believe you're mistaken."

"I believe you're loco. He's to blame; mark my words, sister."

"I believe you and Father are going to get into serious trouble over this error. What is the law going to do when Mr. Fletcher makes charges against you two?"

"For what?"

"After what you did, Jessica, there must be a hundred things, starting with trespassing!"

"He'll have to prove it first. He can't. Surely you wouldn't betray us just so we'll be jailed and you can escape your miserable existence here?" Jessie said sarcastically. "You *are* desperate to flee, aren't you?"

"That's a cold and cruel thing to say."

"That's what *you've* been lately—cold and cruel to everyone. If you hate it here so much, perhaps you would be happier somewhere else."

Astonishment claimed Mary Louise's expression. "You want me to leave home? Why? So you can work on that handsome drifter? Are you afraid I'll outshine you, big sister? If I want him, rest assured I can get him."

"The sun would cease to rise first. He's a loner."

"Does a loner normally hang around so many people for so long?"

"When he's getting paid well for a job, yes."

"What is he earning, Jessica? Since we don't have enough money to hire help for Gran or enough for me to take a trip back East, it can't be much. If not money, what is holding Mr. Jones here? How intriguing . . ."

Jessie watched her sister through narrowed eyes. She feared Mary Louise intended to practice her wiles on Navarro. Mary Louise would never become serious about a man like Navarro; he didn't have enough money, breeding, and power to suit the girl. Yet her sister was not above playing with him, flirting with him just to have fun.

"Oh, yes, I almost forgot; Captain Graham wants those horses he contracted delivered tomorrow. He said if we couldn't supply them, Mr. Fletcher can. You have until noon Tuesday to get them to the fort."

"A day-and-a-half notice? That isn't fair. How can we round them up and herd them to the fort in such a short time?"

"You always get a job done when you want to, Jessica."

The redhead stared at her sister. "How did you get home? Papa was sending someone after you tomorrow."

"Mr. Fletcher offered me a ride."

Shocked, Jessie demanded, *"What?"*

"Come now, Jessica, your hearing hasn't gone bad yet."

"What if he had kidnapped you and harmed you? He's an evil man. He's our enemy. He's trying to destroy us. Papa will be furious."

"Everyone, including Sheriff Cooper, saw us leave together so I was perfectly safe. Father should be proud of my courage. I tried to charm our neighbor to learn all I could from him."

"What did you learn? Nothing! He isn't fool enough to expose anything to Jedidiah Lane's daughter. He probably was amused by your silly attempts to trick him." Jessie realized her sister had contradicted what she'd said earlier about Fletcher being in town when she left. She listened and waited for the girl to entrap herself.

"If amusement was what he felt, my foolish sister, I know nothing about men. He seems much too intelligent and well bred to do the horrible deeds of which you and Father accuse him. Besides, he's considering a move to Dallas."

"Don't be a fool, Mary Louise! He's not going anywhere. If he were, he wouldn't be trying to buy our ranch or run us off it. Don't you go near him again. That's an order."

"You aren't my parent, Jessica."

"If you disobey, you'll wish I were. When Papa hears about what you did, I don't want to be within a mile of the house."

Mary Louise laughed. "Maybe he'll send me back East to get me away from that dangerous wolf," she jested.

"What in blazes is wrong with you! Don't play with a hot iron like him. You may think you know all about lassoing men, but you know nothing about one like Fletcher. Before you know what's happened, he'll have you tossed on your back with his filthy brand on you just to hurt Papa. If you're so smart, sister, you'll see through his attempt to use you."

"A woman can be duped and used only if she allows it to happen."

"You aren't that naive, Mary Louise. But I'm afraid you are that cocky. Don't get anyone hurt trying to protect you from that beast."

"You underestimate me, Jessica."

"No, Mary Louise, I don't. You get in the house, get changed, and do your chores. I have to see Matt about those horses."

The blonde whirled gracefully and headed for the house. Jessie doubted she would obey her orders. There was something about her sister today, something that alarmed her. But Jessie didn't have time to worry about it now.

Matt took all the men who weren't needed on branding, including Navarro, to round up the horses to fill the army contract. They couldn't afford to lose it or to allow their enemy to get his foot in that valuable door. Jessie remained at the ranch to help with branding and to do her other chores. Jed had suggested she stay, and she hoped she wasn't misreading his motive for doing so. It would take the men all afternoon to gather the small herd and they would camp on the range, but she had done that many times in the past.

Mary Louise penned up the chickens, milked the cows, and helped Gran with the preparation of their evening meal. The redhead suspected her cooperation had to do with her sister's confession, which would most likely come during or after supper. And it did. When their father discovered Mary Louise's presence on the ranch, the girl claimed a friend had brought her home and that she would explain everything to him later in private.

After they had eaten and the dishes were being cleared, Mary Louise asked to speak with her father in the parlor. The two left the dining area. As the dishes were washed and dried and put away, Jessie and Gran could hear the talk in the next room. They were stunned as Mary Louise revealed her shocking actions to her father, but vowed good intentions as her motive.

Jed exploded with anger. "What in tarnation! Are you crazy, girl?"

"I thought you would be pleased, Father," she scoffed, "if I could learn something useful from our enemy. He would never suspect a girl of spying on him. When men are relaxed or distracted, they drop hints about things. I'm clever enough to pick up on those slips. It was worth a try, wasn't it?"

Jed was so furious that his responding tone was sarcastic. "Did Fletcher make any mistakes? No, but he saw and heard my daughter acting like she has no wits under her fancy hat! How could a Lane be so foolish and shameful?"

Mary Louise frowned. "I can't do anything right in your eyes, can I, Father? Sometimes I think the only child you love is Jessica. You keep me here like a prisoner just to punish me. That's mean and unfair. If I had the money, I'd leave tomorrow and you'd be rid of me. I could have a wonderful life back East, meet the right man to marry, and be happy. I can't do those things here."

Jed worked hard to control his temper. "You're unhappy because you're defiant, lazy, and disrespectful."

"Only because I'm forced to be that way to stand up for myself. If Mother were still alive, she'd make you face the truth. Let me go, Father. Please."

"Not until you straighten yourself out, girl, if you can. I'm scared it's too late; I'm scared you're ruined for good. And that's a bloody shame, Mary Louise."

"You mean I'll be straightened out when I start looking, acting, and working like a man as Jessica does. Even if I did that to please you, you wouldn't let me leave any more then than you'll let Jessica leave now and have a life of her own. She isn't your son, Father. You've ruined her by treating her like one. What man would want a rough and ill-mannered tomboy for a wife?"

Before he could prevent it, Jed's hand lifted and slapped the hateful girl. The blow sounded loudly in the quiet room, causing the startled Jessie and Gran to jump in the kitchen. "Don't you ever talk about your sister like that again! I wish you were only half the woman she is! If you keep up this way, girl, everybody around here will see you get a strapping every day. I'm warning you, Mary Louise, you've tried my patience too long. I never thought to see the day when I struck one of my children in anger. See what you've done to me."

The blonde rubbed her stinging cheek and glared at her father. "One day you'll be sorry for what you've done to me." She stormed from the room and slammed the door.

Jessie and Gran exchanged worried looks.

The older woman embraced her elder granddaughter. "Pay no

mind to her, child," she soothed. "She's just rattling on to get her way. She's going to be trouble around here, just like that drifter is."

"Navarro is nothing like Mary Louise, Gran. I'll see to Papa." Jessie found him sitting on the edge of a chair with his hands over his face. "Papa . . .?" she began hesitantly.

His expression exposed anguish as he lifted his head to meet her sympathetic gaze. "I hit her, Jess; I struck one of my own children in rage. Worse, it felt good. That girl will be the death of me. If I let her run off like she is, she'll be in all kinds of trouble. I'm tempted to do it to teach her a lesson, but your ma would cry in her grave. It's a battle of wills now, and I have to win."

"I know, Papa, and I'm sorry." Jessie couldn't blame Mary Louise's cruel words on the heat of anger, because she believed her sister meant them.

Breakfast passed in strained silence at the Lane table. As soon as his food was consumed, Jed left to begin his chores and orders. Tom returned to his job as tally keeper. Jessie helped with the branding. Mary Louise didn't apologize to anyone this morning. Yet she must have taken her father's whipping threat seriously, for she did all of her chores without being prodded, did them right and without complaint, but in cold silence.

The men returned with the herd by noon. Matt and two hands left immediately to get them to Fort Davis before their Tuesday deadline.

"Some of us better ride fence, Papa," Jessie suggested. "Fletcher knows the hands will be spread out with chores so he'll think it's a good time to attack. I'll go with Navarro if that's all right with you. I've been flanking all morning so I can use a break. You want to come along?"

Jedidiah Lane was still stinging from Mary Louise's words and feelings last night and was distracted by the problems surrounding him. "I'll stay here and see how I can help the boys, Jess. You and Navarro be careful-like. Keep an eye on those bulls. We'd be out of luck without them. See you at supper."

While Jessie was speaking with her father and preparing to leave, Tom told Navarro what had happened in the house last night. Navarro promised not to break his confidence with anyone, including Jessie.

As they checked out several areas and clustered herds, neither Jessie nor Navarro mentioned the spiteful incident with Mary Louise. They talked little, as both seemed caught up in their own troubled thoughts. As dusk approached, they returned to the corral. While unsaddling their mounts, Matt and the two hands rode in, with one wounded. Davy was assisted down and carried to the bunkhouse for Hank to doctor him.

Matt explained how they were attacked, the horses rustled, and Davy shot. "They were waiting to ambush us, Jed. We were penned down for two hours while the others got a head start. No need to try and track them in the dark; they're long gone by now. Besides, we can't spare the hands to go after them."

"You boys are safe; that's all that matters tonight. There's no way we can gather more horses and get them to the fort on time. I'm sure Fletcher is on the road with replacements. That troop will be mounted and gone before we arrive."

"Davy took one in the wing, but he'll be fine in a few days. Bullet passed clean through and didn't do much damage, just a lot of bleeding."

"You sure we can't track and overtake them?" Navarro asked.

"They headed straight for the border. With the lead they had, they'd be in Mexico before we could catch up. Those were strong horses; they can run 'em fast."

Mary Louise joined them, and Jessie suspected it was only because she wanted to be around Navarro. The blonde spoke to the men and behaved politely for a change as she listened to the grim news. Her hair traveled down her back like shimmering gold. Her sapphire eyes matched the color of her fashionable dress and matching slippers. Jimmy Joe's and Miguel's gazes lingered on her.

"Did you tell Fletcher about the horses being sent to Fort Davis?" Jed asked.

"I didn't have to, Father. There were many people around the boarding house when Captain Graham gave me that message for you. Everyone heard it."

"It was Fletcher; I'm sure of it," Jed murmured.

"Why don't you send someone to the fort to see if he drove horses there?" Mary Louise suggested in a cultured voice. "If he did, that means he had to know yours would be stolen. Certainly that would be a clue to his guilt, Father. If he didn't take advantage of the rustling, he didn't know about it."

"But, Papa," Jessie injected. "He won't try to make a sale in our place. He's too clever to expose himself in such a simple way. That means we can use Navarro's plan tonight. Fletcher will expect us to guess he won't fill the contract. He'll expect us to gather more horses in the morning to drive over and explain our delay. That troop can't leave without new mounts. What he'll do is rustle the horses in the west pasture to stop us. If we set a trap for his men like Navarro suggested, we'll get them. Then we'll have our proof for the law."

"You're right, Jess. He'll think that we'll try again tomorrow, not tonight."

"We should get moving, Mr. Lane, before his men reach that area."

"You boys heard Navarro; let's grab some supplies and get riding."

Nothing happened all night. Their anxiety made it a long one, and a lack of campfires made it chilly. The hands took shifts sleeping and watching the group of excellent horses. At dawn, they headed for the corral with the stock.

By the time they arrived, Navarro suspected why Fletcher hadn't fallen into their trap. "He's more cunning than I realized, Mr. Lane. He guessed we set a trap for him. He probably laughed all night thinking about us sitting out there getting tired and aggravated. I think I know what he's up to now. He believes we'll expect him to make another strike on the trail today so we'll send nearly all our hands as guards. That will leave the cattle unprotected. That's where he wants to strike. He doesn't want a small herd of horses; he wants a large herd of steers. That loss will hurt you most. I say you send only a few men with the horses; we'll set another trap for him with the rest. What do you think, sir?"

"Tarnation! You've got a good head, Navarro; you think like he does. That's what the snake is up to, I'm sure of it. Matt, take two men and get these horses to Captain Graham. Tell Sheriff Cooper what happened on the trail and here last night. Tell him to expect some prisoners tomorrow."

"I wouldn't do that, sir," Navarro advised. "Not unless you trust this lawman completely. If he's being paid by Fletcher not to help you, he could warn him and ruin our plan."

The older man scratched his graying auburn head. "Toby Cooper seems an honest man, but you could be right again. We'll surprise him and Fletcher with our success. You seem to know what to do, so I'm putting you in charge here."

The desperado nodded. "We should get the steers gathered into one area—a place with plenty of trees and hills for good hiding places. We don't want any saddled horses or guards in sight to give us away so I hope all or most of you can ride bareback when the time comes to chase them. If he has anyone spy on the house today, he'll think the boys stopped branding to take those horses to the fort so that shouldn't look suspicious. Tom, Gran, and Hank should work in the garden or keep to their chores to show some life around the house. Jessie should ride with us; she's an expert shot. We don't know how many rustlers he'll send so we best use every one we can." Navarro knew he hadn't mentioned the blonde standing nearby, but she was Jed's problem.

"Everybody get your supplies and weapons ready," Navarro instructed the watchful hands. "We need to get moving and concealed before he strikes again. I don't expect him to come at us until dusk or tonight, so it'll be a long wait again. But that'll give us time to get ready for 'em."

"What do you want me to do to help, Father?"

Jed glanced at the blonde in surprise. "Your chores will be nice, Mary Louise."

"I'll tend Jessica's, too, while she's gone."

"Thank you," Jessie told her, wondering what the girl was trying to pull. She was up to something; of that, the redhead was certain.

The hidden men stayed on silent and motionless alert all day. At mealtimes, they munched on cold biscuits stuffed with ham and washed them down with water from canteens. Their horses grazed nearby, ready to be mounted for the pursuit. Navarro had arranged them in a semicircle, with the herd flanked by a lengthy pointed top hill. With Matt and two hands gone, Hank at the ranch, and Davy in the bunkhouse wounded, that left Jessie, Jed, Navarro, and nine hands to face Fletcher.

It was only an hour past dusk when the action began. Masked riders galloped toward the gathered steers, passing between the Box L watchers. Fifteen men entered the attack area, making the odds fairly even. At a signal from Navarro, the Box L hands opened fire on the rustlers. The startled bandits reined up mounts, some so fast that the animals nearly tripped.

Firing back, the villains rushed for cover or escape. It was obvious to the bandits that they had ridden into a clever trap, but there were gaps between the Box L hands and many of the rustlers fled without injury. A few were wounded, but kept riding homeward. Some were trapped as the Box L hands jumped on their horses and closed the holes in their defense line. Two rustlers were killed and two were captured.

Navarro took control of the prisoners while the hands hurried off to settle down the frightened stock. He glanced at Jed and Jessie and remarked, "Their horses don't carry a brand; that's smart. But we know who you boys work for: Wilbur Fletcher." As he yanked off their masks, he taunted, "Didn't he tell you that rustling is a hanging offense? I don't recognize any of them. Jed, Jessie, do you?"

None of the three did, which struck Navarro as odd since he had spied on Fletcher's ranch, and the Lanes had lived near Fletcher for years. The same was true when the hands returned; no one recognized these strangers.

"This your first job for Fletcher?" Navarro questioned. "He hire more men?"

"Who's this Fletcher?" one surly man scoffed. "We been ridin' fur days from Mexico. We only wanted to cut out one steer to carve an' eat. We're starvin'. No call to shoot my friends. I'll pay you, an' we can ride on, mister."

"The only place you're riding is to jail," Jed informed the two cutthroats. "You'll be sorry you hired on with Fletcher to ruin me."

"You're talkin' crazy, old man. We don't work fur nobody in these parts."

"We'll see who's crazy when you're swinging from a rope."

The villain's eyes grew colder and narrower. "No hungry man will hang fur goin' after a little meat when he offered to pay fur it."

"If you aren't cattle thieves, why the masks?"

"Keeps dust outta yore nose when yore ridin'."

"Yep, grass stirs up a lot of that," Navarro said wryly.

"Papa, we need to move fast. We'll get these men and bodies on the way to the sheriff before Fletcher's men report back to him.

You'd better guard the house good tonight. He may attack to get our evidence."

"You going, Jess?"

"One of us needs to tell our side to Sheriff Cooper. I think you're needed here more than me to give orders. We should meet up with Matt and the boys on the trail. By now they're camped somewhere on their way back home. If we don't hook up tonight, we'll probably join them tomorrow. Don't worry, Papa. Navarro and I can take care of ourselves on the trail. We've had practice."

"I don't like you two riding alone. Fletcher's men might come after you."

"He'll expect us to take his boys back to the ranch tonight, then haul them to the sheriff tomorrow. If he attacks anywhere, it'll be at home. You need all the hands there with you. Navarro and I can manage two bound men and two bodies."

"I suppose you're right. But don't take any chances, Jess."

"We won't, Papa. We'll turn them in, make a report, then come home. If we meet up with Matt, I'll keep him with us and send the other hands home."

"What about supplies?" Jed fretted.

"We'll take what's left from here. We'll make do."

Navarro had held silent. His heart had been pounding in anticipation of being alone with Jessie on the way back, until she mentioned they'd probably have company. "I'll take care of her, sir. You have my word of honor."

As Jessie prepared to leave, Jed told him, "Remember your word, son, 'cause I won't forget it. That girl's my life, so guard her good."

Navarro was a little unnerved by the man's subtle threat. "I will, sir."

Jessie and Navarro reached the town of Fort Davis at dawn. Their journey had been slow and cautious over the hilly and mountainous terrain. They headed for Sheriff Cooper's office and awaited his arrival.

The tall and lanky lawman didn't join them till seven. His gaze swept over the two scowling prisoners sprawled on his porch and the two bodies tied over horses at the hitching post. "More trouble, Miss Lane?"

"Plenty, Sheriff Cooper. We caught these rustlers red-handed."

She explained their successful trap, then remarked, "Wilbur Fletcher's men."

"How do you know that?"

"We know."

"I can charge them and hold them for the judge next week, but where's your proof they work for Mr. Fletcher and he's behind your trouble?"

"He's to blame, Sheriff. Take my word on it."

"I wish I could, Miss Lane, but the law says I need evidence to arrest a man."

"You mean you still won't investigate him?"

"I can ride over to his place and ask questions. But if he's guilty, he won't confess. You men got anything to say?" he asked the sullen culprits.

"We're innocent, Sheriff. We wuz just ridin' along an' they attacked us. Accused us of bein' rustlers an' brung us here."

"He's lying! They were masked and trying to steal our herd! I have twelve witnesses who'll back up my word this time."

"That's enough proof for me to hold them." He checked the dead men, then rejoined Jessie and the quiet stranger at her side. "Don't know any of them. No brands on those horses to tie them to Mr. Fletcher. Haven't seen you around, either," the lawman remarked to Navarro.

The deceptively calm fugitive extended his right hand and responded, "Navarro Jones, Sheriff. Hired on with the Lanes three weeks past. From Colorado."

"We lost Big Ed in an accident, and Davy was shot Monday." Jessie interrupted, eager to take the sheriff's attention away from Navarro. "None of the regular seasonal wranglers returned to sign on for spring roundup and branding, and no new ones came by, either. We're short of men, and we can't get our work done with them attacking us. We think Fletcher's behind it. Have you seen any of his men talking with wranglers in town?"

"Nope, but it's mighty curious none of them came around for jobs like usual. What about you?" he asked the desperado.

"I hired him in San Angelo," Jessie replied. "We were there on business. Did Matt report what happened Monday?"

"Yes, before he left last night. He was anxious to get back to the ranch so he didn't stay the night. Like he said, no need to spend time tracking those men and horses. You must have missed him and the boys on the trail in."

"We took a different way in case Fletcher's gang tried to overtake and ambush us to set these two free before they talked. Do you know if Matt reached the fort in time to save our sale?"

"Yes. Capt'n Graham and a troop are riding your way tomorrow. Matt convinced them to have a slow look around. I plan to ride along and do the same. I'd like to get this trouble settled as much as you would."

"You'll stand a better chance if Fletcher doesn't know you're coming and lays low." Jessie knew it was best not to mention the coyote incident.

"What if Mr. Fletcher isn't behind it, Miss Lane? None of his hands have been seen. Nothing suspicious points to him."

"Because he hires strangers like these two and uses unmarked horses."

"We'll see what we can learn. The Army doesn't like anyone messing with their deliveries. That troop couldn't pull out until they got fresh mounts. Start tampering with the Army's schedule and they get riled. With both of us on the lookout, maybe we'll get somewhere. I know you got a long list of charges against somebody, but to be honest, I ain't convinced it's Mr. Fletcher. Why don't you rest up today and travel with us tomorrow?"

"That sounds good. We're tired and hungry. We left straight from the range after a long day. We didn't want their gang to have time to report and cut us off on the trail. What time in the morning?"

"About seven."

"What about them?" she asked, motioning to the prisoners.

"My deputy will guard them. The others go to the undertaker."

After a hot meal and baths, Navarro joined Jessie in her room. She was wearing a half-buttoned shirt and a light blanket was wrapped around her hips and legs. "Did we miss Matt on purpose?" he asked.

Jessie glanced at him and replied, "Yes, so we could be alone on our way back. Now that we're staying here today, we don't have to worry about the sheriff and soldiers being with us on the way home."

"You think they'll find anything? If Fletcher makes a mistake with them around, this trouble can be over in a few days. Then I can be on my way."

"I was afraid you'd feel that way. You don't mind remaining here with me until tomorrow, do you? Is that being too forward?"

Navarro went to her. "No, Jessie, I'm glad we'll have today alone. You think anyone will come to visit you?"

"No. Sheriff Cooper knows we rode all night and plan to nap. Can we . . . be together?" she asked boldly.

Navarro's hands cupped her uplifted face. He gazed into her eyes. She could be lost to him sooner than he had imagined now that the authorities were getting involved. He prayed there wasn't a wanted poster out on him and, if there was, that Cooper didn't have one in his office. The lawman hadn't seemed overly interested in him. "Yes, Jessie. I want you," he said at last.

Their lips fused in a soulful kiss that revealed their longing. Jessie's arms encircled his body as Navarro trailed kisses over her cheeks, nose, eyes, and mouth. It was as if he wanted to taste every inch of her face. He nestled her head against his chest and untied her hair ribbon to loosen her braid. With leisurely gentleness, his fingers worked to separate the wavy strands and spread her tresses around her shoulders.

He looked down at her. The red mane enhanced her complexion and made her eyes glow. "I want you so much, Jessie."

Her hand lifted to caress his cheek, then trailed several fingers over his full mouth. "I want you, too," she murmured. She fluffed the midnight hair over his left forehead, then traced the prominent bone structure under his brows, on his cheeks, along his jawline, and over his chin. Her fingers wandered across the hollows of his cheeks. "You're so handsome, Navarro. I can't think clearly when I'm so close to you. I want to kiss you a million times and that wouldn't be enough. I want our bodies touching with nothing between us. I want to feel the same way I did that night in the line shack." Jessie unbuttoned his shirt, parted the material, and looked at his smooth and muscular chest. She spread kisses over the heated skin, then caressed the firm flesh with her cheek. As they kissed with rising urgency, she removed her own shirt and pressed her naked chest to his, causing both to groan in fierce desire.

Navarro's hands trembled as they stroked Jessie's enticing frame. She was so soft, yet so firm. He pulled away only long enough for her to peel off his shirt.

"I'll wait for you in bed," she murmured against his mouth. Then she flung aside the covers and lay down, her gaze beckoning him to hurry.

Navarro quickly removed his pants and boots and joined her, pulling her into his arms. "Jessie . . . Jessie . . . Jessie . . ." He whispered her name over and over as his lips and hands explored her tingling flesh.

Navarro's touch made Jessie writhe with desire, and she eagerly caressed his strong, lean body until he was as frenzied with passion as she was. At last they could restrain themselves no longer, and as their bodies united as one, they savored love's delights. Afterward, sated and and sleepy, they cuddled together, and slept in each other's embrace.

It was past two in the afternoon when they awakened. Navarro had shifted to his right side, and Jessie was curled against him on hers. Her left arm lay over his waist, and her hand was held in his.

Jessie eyed the numerous scars on Navarro's broad back. She pulled her hand free of his light grasp and felt the ridges. He had endured terrible agony. She shuddered at the thought of her love receiving such a violent lashing. She kissed the ridged skin as if to remove any lingering pain and hugged him.

Navarro shifted to his other side to face her. She rolled to her back. Tears were in her eyes. As one escaped, his right forefinger captured it before the moisture slid into her tousled hair. He read such concern and confusion in her gaze, yet she never asked about the scars. She wanted to, but knew she shouldn't. "The man who did it is dead, Jessie. You know what I told the boys happened?" When she nodded, he continued. "I thought they'd mention it to you. Did they tell your father?"

"I don't know. Miguel and Carlos told me while you and Tom were spying at Fletcher's."

"But you already knew about my scars."

"Yes, I felt them that night in the line shack. I've seen Jimmy Joe's, so I knew what they were. I'm sorry someone made you suffer like that."

"I didn't want anyone to see them, but I knew I couldn't keep them a secret at the ranch. They're ugly, and they spark questions I don't like to answer."

"If you ever want to tell me the truth, Navarro, you can trust me. If not, I understand."

"That's one of the best things about you, Jessie; you know when to step back to let a man breathe easier. Thanks."

"It seems we're good for each other, Navarro. We sense what the other needs most. We strengthen each other's weaknesses. We fill the lonely holes and brighten the dark corners of the other's life. That's rare."

"Nobody has ever been this close to me before. It's scary, but it feels good."

"I've had plenty of people close to me, but none like you, Navarro. I hate to lose you and what you bring to me."

"I know, Jessie, but it has to be that way. If I could change it so I could stay, I would."

"I know that's true, Navarro, but it still hurts for something so special to end. If you ever change your mind, will you come back to me?"

"The things that hold us apart won't ever change, Jessie. There's no hope."

"Never?"

"Never," he mumbled, then inhaled deeply.

Jessie squeezed her eyes closed and took a deep breath, too. When she opened them, she said, "I'll let you go if I must, Navarro, but not until I've tried everything to keep you."

"Don't, Jessie," he urged. "There's nothing you can do. False hopes bring nothing but pain; I know from experience."

"Then love me while you can." She pulled his head down and kissed him.

By six-thirty the next morning, Jessie and Navarro were ready to leave town. They had made love, eaten supper, made love again, then slept all night in Jessie's room. At dawn, Navarro had sneaked away to take care of a chore and to rumple his unused bed. They had met downstairs for breakfast, then headed for the sheriff's office.

Toby Cooper looked up when they entered the jailhouse. He tossed papers aside and revealed, "I have bad news, Miss Lane."

Jessie's eyes filled with fear. "Is it my family? Did Fletcher attack there last night to get back his men? Was anyone hurt?"

 # CHAPTER
TEN

"Settle down, Miss Lane," the lawman coaxed. "That isn't it. Those rustlers you brought in are gone. And so are those bodies from the undertaker's office."

"You let Fletcher have them back? Why? I have witnesses this time."

"I haven't seen Mr. Fletcher or any of his men. My deputy was hit over the head when he peeked outside to check out a noise. He didn't see who done it. I found him out on the floor this morning. He's at doc's getting patched up. I looked around . . . but nothing. I'm sorry, Miss Lane. I never expected anyone to attempt a jailbreak here. Mighty daring of them."

"I should have guarded them last night," Navarro said grimly. "I should have known their boss wouldn't risk having them talk. When you check Fletcher's ranch, look for unbranded horses and wounded men. We winged several more who got away."

"Don't blame yourself, Navarro," Jessie told him. "We were tired. We've been working hard for so long." She told the sheriff about the windmill incident and fence cuttings, as well as the slayings of their dog and hens. "Rustlers and thieves don't do things like that, Sheriff Cooper. Fletcher wants to buy us out or scare us off our land. We won't leave."

"Mr. Fletcher was just in town," the sheriff said. "Then, he sent word in on Monday. He filed a report saying those same things had happened at his place. He accused the Lanes of being responsible. I told him, like I told you and your pa, we need proof."

"That lying snake!" she scoffed. "He can't get proof because we're innocent. We can't get it because he's clever. What else did he tell you?"

"About lots of dead coyotes being dropped on his land and around his windmills."

"We'd never do such a brutal thing. Besides, we don't have time to plot against Fletcher. We're trying to get our branding done without extra help. If Fletcher will stop attacking us, we can. But he won't."

"We'll try to get this mess cleared up soon. I don't want no range war between you two. We need to get to the fort. Capt'n Graham will be ready to leave a little past seven. We'll get to the bottom of this."

They reached home around four o'clock. After Jessie related the bad news about the jailbreak, Sheriff Cooper and Captain Graham talked with Jed about the situation between the two ranches. The lawman and soldiers intended to ride over the Lane spread for a few days, then head for Fletcher's to do the same. Though Jed and Jessie told them it was a waste of time, that Fletcher's gang would only lay low until they left, the troop split into four units and rode off in different directions.

As she watched them leave, Jessie said, "Fletcher broke his men out of jail before they could betray him. Those two are long gone and those bodies are well hidden by now, Papa. The authorities wouldn't be here if Fletcher hadn't made those crazy charges against us. We're under more suspicion than he is! At least the sheriff and those soldiers will keep him quiet and on his land for a while. With them on our range, we can put everyone on branding until Sunday. We'd best take advantage of this break. That snake will be crawling again next week."

Thursday through Sunday passed in a flurry of noisy, smelly, dusty, exhausting work. The herd of cows and calves in the holding pens were dwindling down, but not fast enough to relax Jed and Jessie. The hands labored hard and long hours from dawn to dusk.

At quitting time, they splashed off, ate, and fell into their bunks. Yet Navarro found the time to teach Tom how to throw and use a knife, despite Jed's mute disapproval when he learned of it.

Jessie observed her brother and Navarro as their friendship grew stronger, and came to love the mysterious drifter more and more. She watched him with the hands, and she was delighted to see him fitting in better every day. Dreamy-eyed hope filled her. Although it was difficult being around him and keeping their secret, she did, and so did he.

Nevertheless, Mary Louise was suspicious and envious and watchful of the couple who spent so much time together. Martha saw the glow and felt the change in her elder granddaughter, but said nothing to anyone. All noticed how Tom was budding like a flower in spring, and knew Navarro was responsible. But Jed worried over how Jessie and Tom would react when the drifter left them behind.

Jed insisted everyone take Sunday off after the necessary chores were done. There was no guessing when they would be able to rest again. As usual, most of the hands met at the front porch to hear Jed read from the Bible and to sing a few hymnals, as there was no church close enough to attend.

Navarro leaned his back against the end post and gazed toward the large barn across the clearing. He dared not look at Jessie. She looked beautiful today in a blue dress and with her unbound hair shining in the sun. Their day in town consumed his thoughts. He wished his life could be that way all the time . . .

As the ranch service ended, the sheriff and soldiers stopped by to say they were leaving the Lane spread—having found nothing—to visit Fletcher's.

"Join us for ring toss, *amigo?*" Miguel asked Navarro.

"Later. I have something to do first, a surprise for someone."

Tom was disappointed that he couldn't accompany Navarro, but Navarro said he would understand why not this afternoon.

With Big John Williams, Navarro headed for the smithy shed, a structure that sat away from the barn in case of sparks that might cause a fire.

Jessie worked with Tom on his neglected lessons, while Jed pored over his books and visited with the men. Gran rested, and Mary Louise wrote more letters.

Jessie and Tom left the house when Big John summoned them to the smithy. She watched Navarro help her curious brother sit on top of a wooden barrel.

Navarro removed Tom's right shoe and the soiled sock on his left foot. "Close your eyes and don't cheat," he told the boy. Navarro worked a knee-high Apache moccasin onto the right foot, over-lapped the soft material near the ankle and calf, then laced the side ties. He worked the other one on to Tom's clubfoot, then secured it. He had made them in this style so the leather shoes would go on the boy's twisted foot, and made them alike so they would not draw attention. Navarro helped the boy to the ground. "You can look now." As Tom eyed the moccasins, he said, "They're strong enough to protect against rocks, cactus, and thornbushes. You can walk or ride anywhere and not get hurt. I padded the left one to make it more level with the other for easier walking."

Tom moved about with less effort and discomfort. He beamed with delight. "Thanks, Navarro! How did you make 'em?"

"I measured your feet not long ago, remember?" The boy nodded. "When we were getting those Indian blankets to wrap the coyotes in, I saw a tanned buffalo hide and leather shirt the Apaches had given your father. They gave me this idea. Jessie said I could have them, but she didn't know why. I cut them to size. Then John helped me make the holes with a saddle tool, and we both stitched them. Buffalo hide makes a stronger sole than rawhide. Holding the stuffing in while we closed the seam was the hardest part. We're making you a second pair for when these need washing or you get 'em wet from rain."

Tom walked again, grinning and laughing. "This is easier, Jessie. My calf don't strain like with the sock. It don't show as much, ei-ther. I got shoes on like everybody else!" The boy went to Navarro and hugged him around the waist. With misty eyes and a choked voice, he said, "People won't stare at me now, Navarro."

Jessie saw that Tom's reaction touched Navarro deeply. Yet, the gunslinger obviously didn't know how to respond. His hazel gaze darted about nervously until, at last, he patted the boy's back and said, "You're welcome, Tom. But I didn't do all the work. John helped a lot."

Tom smiled at the black man and said, "Thanks, Big John."

"You be mighty welcome, Tom."

"I wanna show Pa and Matt." The excited youth hurried to do so, his head and shoulders high with pride and joy. John tagged along to watch.

Jessie's eyes were filled with happiness. "You're one special man, Navarro, but I knew that from the beginning. Thanks."

"It wasn't much, Jessie—just moccasins. Soft leather can be put on easier than a hard shoe or boot. Now he won't feel so different."

"Like you do, Navarro?"

"I guess, but my flaws can't be covered up like his can."

"I don't believe you have as many as you think."

"But the ones I have are bad, real bad. Leave it, Jessie," he entreated. "Let's go before someone wonders what's keeping us here so long."

Within an hour, everyone heard Tom's good news and saw him strut around. Mary Louise and Gran came to check on the commotion.

"They're Apache," Jed remarked.

"Yes, sir. I met an old man on the trail who made and sold them at forts and reservations. I watched him for hours in camp, even helped a little. I remembered how he'd done it. Hope you don't mind."

"No, 'course not. You made Tom real happy. I've had lots of dealings with Apaches. They can be sly and mean if you don't trick 'em into a truce real fast."

"Deceit's about all they know and use, sir," Navarro replied, not wanting to give Jessie's father any clues about his past. He saw Martha watching him closely again, and wondered why.

Gran thanked Navarro and she enthused over the moccasins, his cunning, and his generosity.

"He's making me another pair, Gran," Tom revealed, "for when you wash these or rain wets 'em. You can't hardly tell I got a bad foot."

"You're very clever and helpful, Navarro," Mary Louise murmured. "I'm amazed by how many talents you possess. We're fortunate Jessica found you for us."

Jessie glanced at her sister. Mary Louise had been on her best behavior since her quarrel with their father last Sunday. The smartly dressed blonde was walking, talking, and acting like a well-bred and well-educated lady. Somehow Jessie didn't trust the girl; a person couldn't change so in only a week.

"Thank you, Miss Lane," Navarro replied. "I'll join the boys for a game now."

Jed, Matt, Mary Louise, and Gran watched as Navarro walked away, and Jessie watched all five with great interest. She suspected that none of them wanted to like or accept Navarro. She wondered at their reluctance.

With the law gone, Matt assigned several men to ride guard around the ranch that night. As the hands left, Matt joined the men, who were tossing metal rings around posts fifteen feet apart. Others played cards, made or listened to music on the bunkhouse porch, or did rope tricks to entertain their friends.

At ten, Roy returned to the bunkhouse to roust Biscuit Hank for doctoring. Roy was in terrible pain with four broken fingers. While Hank tried to straighten and bind Roy's injured hand with Matt's help, Navarro fetched Jed. Jessie heard the noise and went to investigate.

In the bunkhouse, Roy claimed, "I fell, Boss, and bent 'em back. They snapped like twigs. I won't be no good for a long time—if this hand ever heals right. I'm heading for my uncle's ranch in San Antonio at first light. Davy's fine, so I won't trouble you with caring for me. You got enough work on your hands."

Roy took more swallows from the whiskey bottle that Hank urged on him for dulling the agony. The man grimaced. "Sorry, Boss. It was a crazy accident."

Jessie and Jed exchanged glances. "You sure it was an accident?" Jed asked.

Roy looked scared and nervous as he vowed, "It was, Boss."

"You've been with me for years, Roy. I've never known you to be careless."

Roy drank again and groaned in pain as Matt helped Hank set the breaks as best they could.

"You need a real doc for this mess," Hank remarked.

"They got two in San Antonio. My aunt can tend me good. I cain't work like this. No need for me to hang around and be more trouble."

"It's three hundred miles. You need doctorin' afore that," Hank protested.

"I'll go to Stockton and hitch a ride. Be easier than horseback. Won't cost much." Roy spoke without convincing the others.

"Mighty anxious to leave," Matt said. "Speak the truth, man."

The strong liquor took effect and Roy snapped, "You would be, too, if—"

"Who did this?" Matt insisted, interrupting. "We been friends a long time. You owe us the truth. A fall don't tear a shirt like that."

"He'll find out and they'll kill me next time. I hafta leave."

"Who?" Jessie entreated. "We'll protect you, Roy. Tell us, please."

"I cain't, Miss Jessie."

"Yes you can," she urged in a soothing tone.

Roy shuddered in anguish and fear. "I don't know. I swear it. That gang just called him 'Boss.' They broke my fingers so I cain't work. They said if I wasn't gone tomorrow, they'd git me. They got a spy here. That's how they know to do ever'thing. He'll tell 'em I talked. They'll ambush me."

"Spy? Who?" the redhead asked.

"Don't know, Miss Jessie. One of our hands is working for him. Maybe they scared him into doing it. They're real mean. There's lots of 'em. We cain't stop 'em. We'll all get killed. Sell out, Jed, or yore family could be next. If you tell the boys what I said, that spy will talk and they'll be gunning for me. I hafta quit and ride out, Jed. I hafta."

"Let him go, Papa. But you have to promise to come back to work when this trouble is over. Deal, Roy?"

"I will. Just don't say what I tol' you."

"We won't," Jed said to calm the shaking man.

When Roy finished the whiskey and was put to bed, Matt asked, "You believe we have a spy here?"

"No, 'course not. They were just scaring Roy off. I can't let him stay like that. Fletcher could get to him again and use him against us. Once a man breaks, he can't be trusted again. We won't tell the boys what happened until he's gone. That leaves us with thirteen men, me, and Jess. Anybody else you think can be scared off, Matt?"

"No, sir. Roy was the weakest and had been with us the shortest time. If any strangers or old hands come by, we shouldn't hire them."

"Why?" Jed questioned.

"Maybe Fletcher's gotten to them. Too risky."

"I have another plan, Mr. Lane, if you want to strike blow for blow."

Monday night beneath a waning crescent moon, the group Navarro had selected met at the corral. "Carlos, did you pick the darkest and best-trained horses for our raid?"

"Sí, amigo, the best."

Navarro eyed the men in dark clothes and hats that would help them blend into the night. "Any of you wearing anything that might make noise?" The men all replied they weren't, as ordered. "I know you boys can ride bareback. We don't want anything to make sound and we don't want to be seen. The moon's on our side tonight, but we have to be careful. We can't allow any of us to be captured and turned over to the sheriff or Army. Anybody who makes a mistake or gets surprised takes the blame for the whole thing."

They all concurred. "Carlos, you ride with Jimmy Joe. Matt, you go with Miguel. Jessie will be with me. That'll split up our best shots and best riders. Keep your partner in sight. If you have to leave him behind to protect the Lanes and the rest of our group, be brave and do it. Just like we planned, dynamite the tops. Big John said that'll hurt him the most. If it breaks those windmills' fingers, good. If not, we'll settle for taking off their heads. Fletcher'll have to put lots of hands on them for repairs. That'll repay him and give us time to work."

"Where did you get this dynamite?" Matt inquired.

"At the fort while me and Jessie were waiting on the troops to get ready to leave. I got to talking to one of the soldiers and he showed me around. When the guard turned his back in the magazine, I stuffed three sticks in my shirt. I wish we had more. You have the time down?" They all said yes. "We need them to blow together. That'll cause confusion. Cut fences on your way back—but hurry. No chances. Me and Jessie will fire his south shed as we leave. As soon as you're back, curry your horse and release him, then get in the bunkhouse. If Fletcher rushes over, we want it to look like a regular night. We'll be going now, sir," Navarro told Jed.

"You boys be real careful-like," Jed warned. "Navarro, you take care of Jess for me. I don't like her going on this job. It's dangerous."

"I'll be fine, Papa. Navarro needs the best shots and riders in case of trouble."

Jessie noted the time on her father's pocketwatch. They hadn't seen anything but stock since they reached their enemy's land. Navarro climbed the windmill and tied the dynamite to the gear box on the wheel. At two o'clock, she told him to light the long fuse. He struck a safety match and did so, then scampered down to leap on his horse. They galloped for distance from the impending blast. It shook the night like thunder and lightning during a bad storm.

Watchful for approaching men, they rode to a pasture shed and set it ablaze. Again, they galloped away toward safety, and for home this time. On Lane land, Jessie halted her mount and called out for Navarro to do the same.

"What's wrong? Did you hear or see something?"

"No, but I need a kiss," she replied, edging her horse closer to his.

"We have to hurry," he responded, but released the animal's mane to lean over and cup Jessie's face between his hands. He kissed her with tenderness that rapidly turned into raging desire. He groaned as he leaned away. "We have to ride."

"I know, but I needed you for a moment. We have so little time alone."

"I wish that weren't so, but it is, Jessie, and it'll be that way for good."

"Please stop reminding me that I'll lose you, Navarro," she beseeched him.

"If I don't, you'll ignore it. I've come to know you well, woman."

"Yes, you have, better than anyone. You sure you can get along without me after you leave?" she asked, trying to keep her tone teasing and light.

"It'll be hard, but I have to learn, don't I?"

Jessie knew he didn't expect or want an answer, so she responded, "Yep. Just as long as I know it'll be as difficult on you as it'll be on me. Let's get home, partner." She nudged her mount and galloped off to give him that breathing space he always needed when she got too close.

*   *   *

Tuesday morning, Wilbur Fletcher arrived to see Jedidiah Lane. Mary Louise entertained their neighbor until Jed and Jessie reached the house. Martha had gone to fetch them and warn them of their enemy's presence. They found the man sitting in their parlor and sipping coffee as if he were an invited guest!

"What do you want here?" Jessie asked. "You're not welcome on Lane land."

"How dare you enter my home!" Jed added in a cold tone. "Mary Louise, you know better than to invite this rattlesnake inside. If you have anything to say to me, Fletcher, come outside. I don't want you fouling my home with your evil stench. But since we have nothing to discuss, just ride off the same way you came."

"And don't come back," Jessie finished.

Fletcher, looking annoyingly unruffled, set down his cup and rose. "You're a hard man to deal with, Jed. There's no need to be impolite or hostile. We *are* neighbors."

Jed walked outside in a hurry as he tried to master his raging temper. At the porch, he turned on the man and said, "You've never been a good neighbor. You crave my land, but you won't ever get your dirty hands on it. Never."

"I made you a fair offer. You're getting too old to manage such a large spread. Your son can't take over for you, and surely you don't expect these young ladies to do so. What kind of father are you to work them so hard and to keep such beauties secluded way out here? With my offer, you could have a good life in town. You're making Miss Jessie as hard and stubborn as you are."

"Jess can manage this spread as well as I can. And she will when I'm gone."

"She's a woman, Jed, a beautiful woman. She shouldn't have to shoulder such a burden because of your pride and selfishness. She should be married with children of her own. You're making that choice impossible for her. As for Miss Mary Louise, she's much too educated and ravishing to be trapped in a wilderness. And that son of yours, he could receive treatments for his problems in a big city."

Jed was furious. His face flushed and his sturdy body stiffened with barely leashed emotion. "Don't go telling me how to run my family matters! You don't even have a wife and children, so what do you know about them? Nothing! I never understood why you settled here in what you call a wilderness. Why don't you give up and move on? You've got plenty of money to buy a good spread somewhere else, near those big cities you like. You can't grow here with me in your path so you're wasting your time waiting and talking."

"Expansion is precisely why I want to purchase the Box L. You have the best grazing land and water supply in the southwestern area. I'll even raise my offer. Name a fair price and we can settle our business today."

"We have no business with you, Fletcher," Jessie remarked.

"Give it up, 'cause I'll never sell out, especially to the likes of you."

The brown-eyed man responded in a calm voice, "If you keep attacking me, Jed, you'll lose. You'll find yourself in prison very soon. Then what will happen to your family and property? I know you dumped those coyotes on me. You're also to blame for dynamiting three of my windmills last night. I've sent word to the sheriff about your crazy doings. He should be returning to question you this week. You've gone mad, Jed, and I'm sorry to see that happen. You have this insane idea I'm your enemy, but I'm not. I freely admit I want your spread badly, but I wouldn't do the things you've accused me of doing to get it. I don't have to resort to such vile actions. You'll lose this ranch all by yourself through your criminal deeds. When you step too far, I'll be there to buy this spread, and you'll be the loser."

Jed looked as if the man's words alarmed him, but still he claimed, "I don't know anything about coyotes and windmills, Fletcher. If you aren't behind all this trouble I'm having, maybe that ghostly gang you mentioned is harassing both of us. I'm a God-fearing, hardworking man. I don't fight unless I'm forced to."

"Don't be sarcastic, Jed, and don't lie. You're boxing yourself in with these undeserved attacks on me. I want to get this land legally and fairly."

"When would I have time to attack you? We're busy with branding. We're shorthanded, but you know all about that. If you send your hirelings over here again to kill my critters, or do damage, or scare off any more hands, you'll be sorry. Plenty sorry," Jessie's father added with renewed courage and coldness.

Without raising his voice, Fletcher said, "Don't threaten me. I'm getting as mad as *you* claim to be. I've been patient waiting for you to work this craziness out of your head or for the sheriff to capture the real culprits. Neither has happened. The only change in our situation is that it's getting worse. The next Box L hand I see on my place will be shot for trespassing."

"If you murder any of my men, you'll hang. Toby Cooper and Captain Graham know us, have for years; they'd know you shot an innocent man. We both know everything you've done to me. I've been lying back too long while you challenged me. It's fighting time. You'll get everything you deserve," Jed warned.

Fletcher reacted to that threat by narrowing his dark eyes for a moment, then forced himself to relax again. He brushed some flicks of dust off his well-made suit from Dallas. He glanced at his neatly trimmed nails. "I'm sorry you feel that way, Jed, and that you're being so stubborn and unreasonable. When you finally give up because you go broke or someone gets hurt, my offer won't be as good as it is now. I sincerely wish we could work this out without more hostility."

"Why do you really want this ranch?" Jessie inquired.

Fletcher's eyes roamed her head to foot. "I told you why, Miss Jessie."

Beneath his brown gaze, Jessie felt she must look a mess. Mary Louise was right; he was handsome, virile, and well mannered. He was a smooth and clever charmer! "I don't think so," she refuted. "There are too many other places you can go and settle. If you want our land this badly, there must be a better reason than greed for water and grass. If you keep pressing us, the truth will come out. I wonder how that will affect the law's reactions."

Fletcher smiled, and his aristocratic features softened. His dark hair was combed from his tanned face. His hairline receded slightly at his temples to form a brown widow's peak in the middle. His brows were thick, his nose straight, and his mouth full. She had never paid much attention to his looks before; now she realized how appealing they were. If she didn't know the truth, she would think she was crazy to suspect such a dashing and polite man of attacking them in such horrible ways!

"You're a surprising and refreshing woman, Miss Jessie. You'll make some lucky man a very strong, intelligent, and dependable wife."

Jed didn't like the way his enemy was eyeing his daughters. "I should have claimed all the land up to the mountains; then you couldn't have moved in and started trouble. I only needed three hundred thousand acres, and I never thought anyone would claim land without water and much grass. 'Course with your wealth, you can afford to build plenty of windmills. Tell me, Fletcher; why did you box yourself in like that? You don't belong in a place like this."

"I saw this area and fell in love with it, as you did. I planned to live here a while, then move back East. I decided it would be easy to sell later for a nice profit if I created a nice spread. But the longer I remained, the more attached I became to my ranch. I decided I wanted to make it the biggest and best in this area. This is where I want to spend my life, so I'm staying."

"You're a big-city man. Your being here don't make sense, like Jessie said."

Fletcher glanced from Jed to Jessie, eyed her once more, then looked back at her father. "I don't need to explain myself to you or to anybody. When I want something, I get it, because I have the money and wits to do so. Eventually all of this will be Bar F land. The sooner you face that reality, Jed, the better for all of us. I don't want to ruin you to win, so don't force me to break you. You know I can undercut every deal you try to make. I can hire every seasonal wrangler who comes to this area and let them sit on my bunkhouse porch. How will you get your cattle to market then? I can purchase the supply stores in both towns, then refuse to sell goods to you or price them so high you'll go broke or wanting. There are plenty of ways to change your mind without violence. I'm a rich and powerful man. I'm smart and I'm determined. I don't need to resort to the sort of vile tactics you're using and accusing *me* of using. I won't tolerate them any longer. Attack me again, and it will be war between us. I don't have a family to worry about protecting, and I do have more men working for me. Think twice before challenging me again."

"You're about as innocent as the devil is about tempting Eve!" Jed retorted. "Sheriff Cooper and Captain Graham are keeping an eye on this area. You'll make a slip soon and be unmasked. We'll see how much your money matters then."

"They can't unmask me if I'm innocent. If I were you, I'd look for whomever my real enemy is and go after him. Somebody wants you out of here worse than I do. I'd ask myself who and why. Goodbye, Miss Jessie. Good-bye, Miss Mary Louise," he said, smiling and tipping his hat to the blonde standing in the doorway observing them. "I do hope you fine ladies will enlighten your father as to the error of his ways before this matter is out of control."

Jessie watched their neighbor ride away in a sturdy buckboard. He was joined beyond the house by three men who took guard positions on both sides and behind their boss. Fletcher traveled at a leisurely pace, his departure creating little dust. Jessie saw him constantly look from right to left as he surveyed the land he craved. "It's working, Papa; we have him plenty worried. If he weren't nervous, he wouldn't have come here to threaten us."

"How can a man look and sound so innocent and be so dang guilty!" Jed stormed. "No wonder they all believe him. He's like Lucifer, Jess; he can fool you if you aren't sharp-eyed and careful."

After Jed walked away, Mary Louise joined her thoughtful sister. "He's a real man, Jessica. How can you and Father suspect him of such wickedness? I was horribly embarrassed when Father was so rude to him."

"If you had to clean up after his evil deeds like we have, little sister, he wouldn't look so good to you!" she snapped. "I guess you realize now he lied about moving to Dallas!"

"What's biting your backside?" Mary Louise asked with a frown.

"Secretive men," Jessie replied, then hurried back to her chores.

Jessie told Navarro about their talk with Fletcher. "The liar!" she concluded.

"What if he *is* telling the truth, Jessie? What if somebody is trying to force out both of you? We don't have any proof it's him. He's only our best suspect."

Jessie stared at him. "Don't you start that nonsense, too. Mary Louise is convinced it isn't him. That smooth talker even has Papa questioning himself."

"The next time he comes around, I want to meet him and size him up. A man gives away a lot in his voice and gaze. Sometimes there are clues in his words if you listen close."

"That hasn't worked for me where you're concerned. But it has with Fletcher. I'm positive he's guilty, Navarro. I would never go against him if I weren't."

"I'll take your word and keep working on him for you."

Miguel called for Navarro to come give him a hand. Jessie watched her love walk away. She didn't know how long she could hold him here. He certainly did not intend to become a ranch hand.

Her emotions were in a maelstrom. If they left Fletcher alone or only responded blow for blow, Navarro would have little but hard ranch work to occupy him. If they attacked continuously and won, Navarro would leave. Either way, she couldn't keep him very long.

Wednesday, things got worse. Scout and fifty steers were shot. "Scout was a trained longhorn who led our cattle to market," Jessie explained to Navarro. "He kept the herd calm, moving, and under control. He'll be a big loss. We'll have to get the others skinned. Some will have to be cut up and buried. We can't save this much meat or get it into town to sell."

"It's a good trail, Mr. Lane," Navarro told Jed. "I'll follow it while it's fresh. They didn't even try to conceal it. That's strange."

"I'll go with you," Jessie said.

Navarro shook his head. "You have too much work to do. I'll go alone."

"There could be trouble," she argued. "It might be an ambush. I'm—"

"All the more reason not to go, Jess," Jed interrupted.

"We can't let Navarro take such a risk for us, Papa."

"I'll be careful, Jessie."

Navarro reported back at dusk. "The trail led to Fletcher's land, but he had men riding fence so I had to turn back. By now they've destroyed it."

"I can't go blow for blow this time. I don't murder innocent critters to get even. We can't rustle his herd, either. That's too dangerous. Let me think a while."

Sheriff Toby Cooper arrived Thursday to question them about the windmills and fire. The lanky lawman looked distressed to be suspecting the Lanes.

"Where would we get dynamite?" Jed scoffed. "That's crazy! And we wouldn't start a fire, either. It could spread to my land. Ever seen a prairie fire? You can't stop one. I think Fletcher did those things so he could point a finger at me and away from himself. That rich bastard can afford to replace them all a thousand times without feeling a pinch in his pocket. If I wanted to hurt him, I'd shoot the bastard!"

"Don't do that, Jed, or I'll have to arrest you. I'm riding over there. I'll see what he has to say."

"Ask him about Scout and my steers!"

Cooper returned Friday afternoon. "All of his men swear they're innocent, Jed. I checked that trail you mentioned, but it headed south about a mile on his land, then vanished. Did your men happen to notice those horses weren't shoed?"

"They were shoed with iron, Sheriff," Navarro corrected. "I followed them to the boundary, but his men were all around so I had to turn back."

"Not what I saw. I think we got renegades in the area again."

"Somebody changed them to fool you. It's not Indians."

Toby Cooper eyed the stranger whose looks said he was part Indian. "That would be hard. I used to track for the cavalry. If anybody rubbed out the old tracks and made new ones, it didn't show. That takes real talent."

Navarro shrugged. "All I know is what I saw and trailed: shoe prints."

"We all saw them, Sheriff. They were shod horses. Did you check his barns for unbranded mounts?" Jessie inquired.

"Yep. None there. No strangers or extra men around. No wounded ones, either."

"Because he's hiding them somewhere. He's real smart, Sheriff."

"I don't know, Jed. A lawman can't follow a trail that isn't there. I'll be coming around more. I don't want you two killing off each other. Mind if I stay the night? It's late for striking out."

"You can bunk with the boys, and take supper with us in the house. We have to get back to work. Make yourself at home. Look around all you like."

Saturday, three men dug fresh pits in the spring-softened ground. Then others helped move the Lanes' and their hand's outhouses to new locations. The dirt was used to fill the old holes, and another task was completed.

For days, Mary Louise had been doing her chores and helping

Gran in the garden without complaints, to everyone's surprise and pleasure. Yet Jessie couldn't forget her sister's hateful words several weeks ago.

Nothing terrible happened until Tuesday, six days after the cattle killings. It was dusk when billowing smoke was sighted and checked on by one of the hands riding range. Pete hurried to the house and rang the bell. "Fire! Fire in the hay shed!" he shouted as the clanking alarm sounded louder than his voice.

The men responded quickly. Barrels were loaded on rapidly hitched wagons, then filled from the well. The storage shed, where stock gathered in the winter to be fed, was three miles from the house. Last year's hay was dry, and it burned with ease and speed. The main concern was to contain the blaze. Everyone went to battle the fire except Gran, Tom, Mary Louise, and Jessie. The redhead stayed behind and inside the locked house to stand guard over the family with her Winchester. All peered out windows.

Jessica saw clouds of thick smoke rising and expanding against a darkening blue horizon. She knew the fire was a large one, but rolling hills obscured any sight of red flames. She frowned as the words "blow by blow" came to mind. This was twice Fletcher had used their strategy against them. She assumed it was only to terrorize them, since more hay could be grown this summer or purchased in town for any winter needs.

Agonized bawls and frightened "moo-ooo's" caught her ear. Her gaze darted to the barn that was slightly right to the front of their home. She knew her sister had milked the three cows, who stayed near the barn at night. Jessie sensed something was wrong. "Get my pistol and lock the door behind me," She told Gran. "I have to check on them. Don't come out for any reason."

"Don't go out there, child. The men are gone."

"Maybe they were lured away for a reason, Gran."

"That's why you shouldn't go out there alone."

"They could be firing the barn and bunkhouse, Gran. Or killing the bulls."

"What if lots of men are out there, Jessie?"

"I'll fire shots and scare them off, then ring the bell if we have trouble back here. Don't worry; I'll be careful. I'll sneak out the back way and work around."

Gran locked the door behind her. Jessie peered around the corner of the house. It was almost dark, and the waxing moon would give little light. The animal's cries compelled her forward. She made it to the bunkhouse without a problem and, hearing nothing inside, continued on to the chuckhouse. She eased around it and saw movement in the enclosed, small pasture where the milk cows stayed at night.

Jessie knew the dark shadow was not a Box L hand. Her squinted eyes searched for more movement, but could detect none. The cows had ropes around their necks that were tied to posts, holding them captive. One stamped and shifted and bawled. Another wriggled and cried out.

Jessie fired over the cow's backs several times. When she heard running in the other direction, she raced around the barn and past the smithy to cut off and hopefully capture one of Fletcher's men for the sheriff. But the villain had a head start and less obstacles than she did, and got away. He leapt on his horse behind a shed and galloped away. Jessie fired more shots at him, but despite her skill, he moved too fast and was too far away to wound or kill.

"Jessie!" Gran called from the front door. "You all right?"

"Fine, Gran! He's gone! I'll check on the cows!" She assumed the large bulls were safe. No shot had been fired from the man who surely couldn't get close enough to the powerful beasts to harm them in silence. She reached the crazed cows and tried to calm them as she did during her morning milking chore. The animals looked wild-eyed and they stomped their hooves and bawled. She couldn't see much in the darkness and through the fence.

Jessie propped her rifle against a post and fetched a lantern from the chuckhouse. She wriggled through the fence, then moved with caution closer to the nervous creatures. She held the lantern high to examine them, singing and talking softly. She fell silent. Her free hand clamped over her mouth, and she feared she would lose her supper. Disbelief and fury assailed her. With tears in her eyes and a lump in her throat, she checked all three cows. She couldn't help but sigh in relief that she had saved one from torment.

Gran and Tom headed to join her where a lantern revealed her location. "What is it?" they both kept asking the stunned girl.

"Go back!" she suddenly shouted, as if coming out of a trance.

"What's wrong?" they persisted, halting their steps.

"I . . . have to shoot two of them. Fletcher's bastard sliced off their teats! Get in the house. You don't need to see this. Hurry!" she ordered the shocked people who hadn't moved. She didn't want the cows to linger in agony.

On the way to the house, Gran rang the alarm bell that carried sound for miles. She hoped the men could hear it over the commotion of the fire and would respond quickly. She hurried Tom inside and closed the door.

Jessie took careful aim and shot the first cow, then the second. They hit the ground with heavy thuds. It was one of the hardest things she had ever done; the cows had almost been like pets. She calmed the last one and led it into the barn, confining it there. She cleaned the mess as best she could. Later, she wouldn't recall wiping blood on her clothes.

The dazed redhead called Ben and he came running to his mistress. She leapt on his back and galloped to the gate to the adjoining pasture. She bent over, unlatched it, flung it wide, and rode inside. She rounded up the protesting bulls and herded them close to the barn and house. She turned Ben loose nearby, then trudged to the dead bodies and bright lantern.

Riders came in, dismounted, and, sighting the lantern, hurried to her. Jessie didn't realize tears were slipping down her flushed cheeks.

Matt rushed to the woman he loved, scrutinizing her. "Are you hurt?" he asked. "There's blood on you, Jessie. What happened?"

She gazed into his concerned eyes and uttered in torment, "He cut off their teats, Matt; the bastard mutilated our milk cows. The fire was a trick to lure you men away. I had to shoot them. I got the bulls near the barn. They're safe."

Matt pulled Jessie's head against his chest as she wept. His hand behind it kept it there, as did his arm around her shoulder. "Don't cry, Jessie. It's over."

Jessie cried in his consoling embrace.

"I'm sorry, Jessie. We should have left guards here. We'll never leave you and the house unprotected again," he vowed, stroking her unbraided locks.

"Por Dios," Carlos murmured as he held up the lantern and the men examined the grim scene. "What devil would do such a thing? The man is *demente!"*

"Where is the third one?" Miguel asked, glancing around the area.

Jessie lifted her head, wiped at her eyes and cheeks, and replied, "In the barn. I heard the commotion and came to investigate."

"That was dangerous, *amiga.*"

"I know, but something was wrong. I spooked him before he got to her, thank God. He got away. I wish I had killed him!"

"Don't worry, *chica,* we'll make him pay."

"How, Carlos? He's too clever and mean."

"We'll get him, Jessie," Navarro vowed from nearby. He wanted to hold her and comfort her as the foreman was doing, but he held his jealousy in check. "We won't be fooled again. I promise."

"Thanks, Navarro. Where are Papa and the others?" she asked, afraid to look at or move toward her love. She needed his embrace, but couldn't have it.

"They stayed behind to make sure all sparks were doused. I think he needed time to settle down. We heard the bell on our way in. We got here as fast as we could, but not quick enough," Matt told her.

"This was over when Gran rang the alarm."

The others arrived and the horrid tale was repeated. Jed stared at the dead animals. Despair flooded him, knowing it could just as easily be his family lying there instead of cows. This brutality knifed at his heart. "Maybe I should sell Fletcher some land with water, that section from his place to the Calamity, to stop this trouble. Less land is better than none."

"No, Papa! Navarro and I will stop him. You'll see."

"The trouble's gotten worse since Navarro came and we started fighting back. Tarnation, Jess, that could be you and Ma lying there!"

"But it isn't. He's running scared, Papa. We can't give up now. Not ever!"

"I'm the one scared, Jess, not Fletcher. It's real bad now. No man likes being broken, but I have to think of my family."

"He won't break us, Papa. We can't let him win. We won't be pushed out of our home and off our land. *Our* land, Papa. He has no right to it. We stand and win, or we stand and die as fighters. We're Lanes, and Lanes don't back down."

"She's right, Jed," Matt agreed, placing his arm across the back of her waist.

Navarro spoke up. "Even if he breaks you, sir, he won't be satisfied. You've resisted and attacked him. He'll probably take back his offer or lower it. He'll be expecting us to retaliate, so he'll have guards posted. We need to wait a while, then attack again."

"Every time we do, he does worse," Jed argued.

"If you back down now, sir, he'll win. Jessie's right; he's worried and desperate. He can't keep attacking forever. He knows we'll be on guard, too."

"I'll do it your way for a while, Jess. But if it gets worse, I'm making a deal with him so I can protect my family."

"He won't deal, Papa. He wants it all. If you suggest a deal, he'll know you're weakening. Then it *will* get worse, far worse. Are you ready and willing to give up everything we've built here to a man like him? Can you grovel before that bastard and ask him to take away your heart and soul, your life, Papa? Can you leave Mama, your two sons, your papa here with that filthy vermin? Can you let all the blood, sweat, tears, and hard work end this way? Can you, Papa? If so, tell me now. But I'll stand against him alone if you say yes. I won't let him get away with all he's done and take our land, too. I won't."

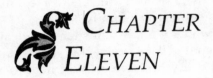# CHAPTER
ELEVEN

Jessie's words and intense emotions had the desired effect on Jed Lane. He hung his head in shame and dismay. "You're right, Jess. I'm not thinking clearly. I've never been a coward, until now. I just can't stand to lose any more of my family. We have to keep guards posted around here from now on. You go on into the house. Me and the boys will take care of this mess."

Jessie embraced her father. "You've never been a quitter, Papa. I knew you were only upset. I didn't mean to speak so rudely, but I had to clear your head. It will be hard to fight Fletcher, but we'll win; I know we will," she said with heart-felt confidence. "Don't get discouraged. Good night, Papa, boys, Matt, Navarro. I'll see you all in the morning. We can make decisions tomorrow when we're all rested." Jessie left.

As the men worked, Navarro contemplated what he had learned tonight. Jed was not as hard or cold as he had believed. Navarro knew the agony of being broken, and he had had only himself to consider and defend. He now knew how love could control a man's actions. Jessie had made him believe in himself, in the future, and in love. She had become his world, his soul, his golden dream. But she had entered his life when it was too late to save him. If only he could share everything with her. She was the proof love existed, that life was worth living.

Dare he, the fugitive wondered, stay and put a claim on her, then see if Jed would accept their decision? No, the law would never forget about his crimes. He had been sentenced to twenty years for a gold robbery and he had killed a man to escape what they called "justice," then robbed others to survive. What did it matter if he were innocent of the original charge? He was guilty of many others. If Fletcher discovered the truth about him, he could be used as a weapon against these good people. He had to take that risk for a while longer, as he couldn't leave them defenseless. He was ensnared in a bottomless trap and there was no way out for him, ever. And no matter what it took, he couldn't pull Jessie in with him to perish.

"Gran told me what happened," Mary Louise said. "I'm sure Wilbur wouldn't do such a horrible thing."

Jessie was exhausted and tense. "What did you do, complain to *Wilbur* about your chores so he lessened them by destroying our milk cows? Instead of siding with him, why don't you use your charms and talents to get him to stop attacking us?"

"Jessica Lane, that's mean and untrue!"

"Maybe so. I'm tired and upset. I'm going to bed. Don't jump on me tonight, little sister, because I'm not in the mood to be nice."

On Wednesday, Navarro suggested that he and Jessie sneak over to Fletcher's ranch to inflict damage there. "Fletcher thinks we'll be on alert and scared to strike at him again. But if I have him figured right, he'll have his men on patrol just in case he's mistaken. That means his settlement will be vulnerable. We can strike at his critters without harming them." He revealed his daring plan.

Jessie grinned. "You're so clever. We can't sit around waiting for him to hit us again. We won't tell Papa or the others so they won't try to stop us or worry. We'll sneak out after dark and slip over there."

She explained how.

Jessie and Navarro rode to the boundary between Lane and Fletcher land. He cut the top strand of barbwire so their horses could jump over without risking injury. Afterward, he tied a strip of rawhide to the sharp end and secured the gap so it wouldn't be noticed by anyone riding fence tonight. They made their way to the area where Fletcher had built his many structures. It was fortunate for them that their enemy had spaced their targets away from his home and bunkhouse. Too, there were trees to aid their secrecy.

The redhead and the desperado left their mounts a safe distance from the bunkhouse. With care, they sneaked to the first object of their mission. The pigs were rousted from sleep and urged toward the open gate, but their grunts weren't loud enough to endanger the couple. As if enjoying their freedom, the rotund creatures trotted off in several directions. By morning they would be scattered far and wide. The chickens weren't as cooperative; many clucked in panic at the intrusion. Navarro hurried them along by tossing a lantern into the roosting shed. The dry wood caught fire.

"Let's make tracks, woman," he ordered.

The couple rushed to the cover of the first tree, then slipped to the next and next until they were back to their horses. Commotion filled the area left behind. They mounted and walked their horses to prevent noisy galloping that would give away their location. Soon they picked up their pace and rode for home.

They didn't even make it to the cut fence before they heard riders coming. They halted and concealed themselves behind a group of trees. The men rushed past them, responding to the alarm bell that was ringing near Fletcher's home. When the men were out of sight, Jessie and Navarro returned to Lane land. With the barbwire he had dropped nearby, he rapidly repaired the damaged section, having learned how from Matt weeks ago.

They rode for thirty minutes before deciding it was safe to stop and talk.

"That was fun," Jessie remarked amidst laughter. "I can see his men trying to capture those hens and pigs. He'll be steaming like hot coffee."

"If we're lucky he'll pull men in to guard his house and barns tomorrow night. We'll cut a few fences and scatter his herd. I'm glad his ranch isn't as big as yours or there'd be too much land for us to cover. Fletcher should figure that we'll strike near his settlement again. He should think we'll believe that he expects us to hit a new target—his land—but we'll go after the same one again."

"What if he reasons like you, Navarro, and guards his fences and herds?"

"From what you've told me about him, he's too vain to think we're as clever as him. He doesn't realize how smart we are yet, but he'll figure it out soon. Right now, by trying to outwit us, he'll out-wit himself."

"You're clever, Navarro. If you weren't here, I'd do exactly what he'd reason we'd do: hit the house again, expecting him to be on the range."

"That's why you hired me, so I'm only doing my job, Miss Lane." His tone altered as he remarked, "You were real upset last night. Are you all right now?"

"What he did to those cows threw me like a wild mustang. Killing is one thing, but mutilating is an atrocity beyond words. I needed you to hold me so badly."

"Matt did a good job of comforting you," he said before thinking.

"Jealous?" she teased, then reached over to caress his cheek.

"Yep," he admitted to her surprise, "but I have no right to be."

"You're right. You have no reason to be. Matt is like an older brother to me. He half raised me. We've been good friends for years. He's one of the nicest, most honest, and sincere people I know. He would do anything for a friend."

"I don't think he sees you as a little sister or only a close friend. I've watched him watching you, Jessie. Don't you realize he's in love with you?"

Jessie's eyes widened with surprise. "Mary Louise hinted at it several times, but I didn't believe her. I hope he's not, Navarro. I wouldn't want him hurt. He's never tried to romance me."

"A man doesn't go after what he doesn't think he can win, Jessie."

"Does that mean you knew I was leaning in your direction, cow-poke?"

"We both felt the pull between us. It was too strong to fight. If I hadn't gotten your signals, I wouldn't have made a move toward you."

"That's why I sent them, so you would have the courage to come after me."

"But I shouldn't have. A person shouldn't offer what he can't give."

"You've given everything you offered. You made certain I understood your position before I surrendered. You haven't misled me, Navarro. You've been clear and honest from the beginning. I appreciate and respect that."

Clear, but not totally honest, my love, his mind refuted, and guilt plagued him. "Only because a woman like you deserves to know where I stand."

"A woman like me only finds a man like you once in her life, Navarro. I wasn't about to lose what little time I could have with you."

"I wish it could be more, Jessie, honestly I do."

His tone and gaze touched her deep inside. "I know."

He pulled his eyes from her lovely face and said abruptly, "We have to get back. Fletcher's men might be on the move. We don't want to be discovered out here alone by either side. If we can't sneak back, what will you tell Jed?"

"The truth, that we outfoxed our enemy tonight. Since you'll be leaving when this is over, I don't think it's wise to tell Papa—or anyone—about us."

"I hate to make you be deceitful for me."

"People do what they have to do, Navarro. Right now you're more important to me than being fully honest with my father and family. It's strange, but I don't feel very guilty about it. Does that change your high opinion of me?"

"Nothing could ever change my high opinion of you, Jessica Lane. You don't know what you've given me and brought into my life."

"I know what you've done for me. Do I get a kiss before we leave?"

Navarro lifted her from her horse and placed her across his legs. He caressed her face, then hugged her with longing. His mouth covered hers.

For several minutes they kissed, caressed, and embraced. Bittersweet feelings surged through them. Their bond was powerful; their future was impossible. He knew it, and she suspected it. Yet they couldn't resist each other for as long as fate allowed them to remain together.

Navarro replaced her on her horse, then smiled sadly at the woman who had stolen his heart, who offered a beautiful dream that he could never capture. "Let's go before we get into more trouble."

At the ranch, the fugitive felt Mathew Cordell's gaze on him from the foreman's private room at the end of the bunkhouse. None of the other men along the two rows of bunks moved or spoke, and the desperado knew he hadn't disturbed any of them with his comings and goings. He was glad Matt didn't come out and question his behavior, but he would tell him of this night's work tomorrow to prevent trouble and suspicion, just as Jessie would tell her father. No doubt, Jed would be upset.

At first, Jed was angry, then he calmed himself. He was proud of his daughter's courage and wits. Yet he didn't like the time she was spending alone with the gunslinging drifter. He recalled what Roy had said about a spy, but he reasoned it couldn't be Navarro Jones. Surely no hireling of Fletcher's would destroy his boss's property, even if the villain could easily replace it. Still, that was a good way to win their trust . . .

When Jed mentioned that fear to Jessie, she gaped at him in disbelief and disappointment. "Surely you don't think such a terrible thing, Papa. Look how he's helped us. Besides, I found him and hired him in San Angelo. We met by accident, and he didn't know who I was."

"What if he was trailing you and watching you all along, Jess? What if that's why he stepped in and rescued you. To win your confidence."

"You're wrong, Papa. Navarro is a good man—different, but good and kind. Please don't mention your doubts to him or the boys. If they started treating him strangely, he could leave before he helps us finish this job. We need him, Papa."

"Promise me you'll be very careful around him. He worries me, and Matt, too."

Jessie knew why both men were concerned about her friendship with the handsome stranger. She cautioned herself to keep their relationship a secret. It wouldn't do for either Matt or Jed to guess the truth. Her respectable father would insist they wed, and a bitter confrontation would ruin everything. Another woman might force the issue with hopes it would be resolved in her favor. But Jessie had been around men long enough to learn you never backed one into a corner. If Navarro stayed or returned, it had to be his decision. "I know what I'm doing, Papa. Don't worry. I'll be on guard."

That night, to dispel Jed and Matt's suspicions, Navarro took Carlos and Miguel along with Jessie and him. The four cut fences along Fletcher's southern boundary and stampeded cattle from the man's property. Navarro had guessed right: Fletcher had his settlement guarded heavily, and no one was on the range to halt their actions.

*   *   *

On Friday, Jessie, Tom, and two hands went to the town of Fort Davis to purchase more barbwire and search for another milk cow. One wasn't enough to supply the Box L with milk and butter.

The group was almost home on Saturday when they were attacked by two men. They were going slow up a steep grade when shots rang out from behind rocks. Jessie saw Smokey fall off the seat to the ground and lie still. Pete fell back into the wagon where she and Tom were sitting, a bullet wound to his chest. The laboring horses stopped when the reins went slack, as did the cow tied behind the wagon.

Jessie grabbed her rifle, but no more shots were heard. She knew the general area from which the others had come, and she watched it closely for signs of movement. Navarro and Matt prodded their horses past them and toward the gunmen's location. While they waited, Jessie checked on Pete and kept Tom down. The cunning Navarro had been prepared for this, as he and Matt had been trailing them the entire time. But the assault had come too quickly to prevent Smokey from being killed and Pete from being wounded.

Matt joined them and said, "I'll get you home. Navarro's gone after them."

"Alone?" Jessie asked, looking frightened. "I'll take your horse and—"

"No, Jessie. He can handle two men. You work on Pete in the wagon while I drive home. If more men are lying in wait ahead, I'll need your guns."

"You're right, Matt." While the foreman recovered Smokey's body and tied it to his horse, Jessie tore Pete's shirt and bound his wound as best she could to staunch the bleeding. But her mind was riding with her love on the vengeance trail.

At the ranch, Hank removed the bullet and bandaged Pete's shoulder. Smokey was buried in a short ceremony. That left them with twelve hands, and one of those wouldn't be able to work for weeks.

When Navarro returned later, he reported that he had slain the two men who had attacked them. "I cut Fletcher's north fence, sent the horses galloping home with their bodies tied to their saddles, and rode here. I figured, since the horses were unbranded, it wasn't much good to save them for the sheriff. He couldn't prove they were Fletcher's men, but your enemy will get our message."

"Fletcher and his boys would only say they didn't know them," Jessie said.

"No way to tie them to Fletcher, sir. I figured it would be better to let him know that if he attacks us, we'll attack them. If some of his boys start getting killed, maybe it'll worry the others. So far, they've been safe from harm. It's time they learn it's dangerous to work for Fletcher."

"I hate killing, Navarro, but you did right. Leastwise, we know they were guilty and deserved to die. We got Smokey buried, and Pete will be healed in a few weeks. I'm glad you and Matt trailed my daughter and son. If not for that, they could be dead now, too."

"I don't think Fletcher will hurt your family, sir. He's trying to scare off your hands. He expects that to change your mind."

"Jessie's convinced me we have to keep fighting and holding on. Actions like these only tell me she's right. I'm sure that snake would double cross me if I said I'd take his last offer. He can't be trusted."

"At least Fletcher's out four men, sir—the two we killed in that trap and these two today. We're lucky we've only lost one to death and one to fear. I'll try to make sure you don't lose any more, Mr. Lane."

"Thanks, Navarro. Roy said he'd send a letter when he reached San Antonio. I can't blame him for leaving; his hand might never heal right. It ain't his land to fight and die over. Maybe when he's safe, he'll send evidence back to the sheriff about what really happened that night."

"Don't count on it, Papa; he was scared." Jessie sighed. "Smokey has a sister in Brownwood; we should write to her about his death and send her his belongings."

"Will you do it for me, Jess?" Jed asked wearily.

"Sure, Papa, tonight," she replied gently. As everyone was parting, she sent Navarro a smile that said, I'm glad you're back safe.

The month of April ended with a party to celebrate the completion of spring branding and no trouble from Fletcher for two weeks. During their respite, the hands and family had worked hard and fast catching up with chores with everyone doing more than his or her share. The cows and calves were back to grazing on the range, the garden was growing, and a big crop was anticipated. Soon fresh vegetables would replace canned and dried ones.

The part for the well had arrived, and Big John had repaired the pump to the house. Pete's shoulder had almost healed, and he was back doing light chores. The level of anger and frustration on the Box L had subsided during this peaceful reprieve.

After quitting time each day, Navarro had worked with the hands to teach them tricks to use during fistfights, how to shoot better, and how to set ambushes. Tom had followed him around and devoured every word and action. But Jessie feared her love was preparing the men for his departure.

When the hands played a practical joke on Navarro, it revealed to her how they felt about him. From what Jessie could see, Navarro appeared happy and relaxed at the ranch. She had seen him laughing and joking with the men. He had spent six weeks on their land— seven including the time alone with her—and Jessie wondered how much longer he could be persuaded to stay.

As Jessie chatted with Navarro at the party, she said, "I'm relieved the boys' joke didn't upset you. It shows how much they accept you. I'm glad you've earned their respect and friendship. You deserve them, Navarro. You've worked hard for us and taken risks beyond what we're paying you for."

"It's a good thing you told me beforehand about their tricks. I would have thought they were making a fool of me and trying to get rid of me." He nodded a greeting to Miguel, then continued. "Whew, that was the hottest chili I've had! When they all kept eating, I didn't want to hurt Hank's feelings. It took a bucket of water to cool my mouth and throat. My belly burned for hours."

Miguel had approached the two in the middle of Navarro's accounting of the story, decked in Mexican finery again this evening. "We didn't expect it to take so long for you to catch on to us, *amigo.* I was about to warn you when I saw smoke coming out your nose and ears, and your eyes were watering. You'll get used to us. We're good *hombres.*"

"Yes, you are," Jessie agreed with a bright smile.

"Me and Carlos want to know if you will teach us to use the bow and knife as you have taught Jessie and Tom."

"Sure, Miguel. I thought we might need silent weapons when Fletcher goes on the warpath again. One job I had in Arizona called for silence, and I used them then," he remarked, then wished he hadn't made that slip. "Since you two are Mexican and have had trouble in the past with Apaches, I wasn't sure if you'd want to work with Indian weapons."

"We have no problem with using them, *amigo.*"

Mary Louise had joined them, too. "Would you like to dance, Navarro?" she asked. "The men are making merry music. There's no need to waste it."

Navarro looked uncomfortable at the invitation and the girl's sensual smile. "Sorry, Miss Lane, but I don't dance, never have."

The blonde grasped his muscled arm and tugged on it encouragingly. "I'll be delighted to teach you. It's very easy and lots of fun."

"He said no, Mary Louise," Jessie told her sister, "so don't pull at him. Miguel loves to kick up his heels, so ask *him.*"

Miguel placed his hand on his hip and cocked his elbow at the blonde as he said, "I would be honored to share a dance with you, my lovely señorita."

Jessie saw the girl's look which said, 'My superior manners prevent me from refusing before others.' She watched her sister rest her fingers on the Mexican's arm and walk away with him.

Gran took Miguel's and Mary Louise's place with them. "You two having fun?"

"It's wonderful, Gran. You cooked so much delicious food. The boys are really enjoying themselves." They were eating barbecued beef, dried peas, roasted corn canned from last year's crop, and a mixture of tomatoes with okra. Jed was even serving a little wine and whiskey.

"The men deserve a treat, Jessie. They've worked so hard. Why aren't you dancing?"

"Navarro doesn't dance, Gran."

"Then I'll keep him company while you toss up your skirts. I know how much you like to dance, child. Go on," the older woman urged.

Jessie felt she had to go dance or her grandmother would wonder why she didn't. She excused herself from Navarro, approached the others, and asked Jimmy Joe to be her partner. The sandy-haired twenty-year-old was delighted. Afterward, friend after friend— Matt twice—claimed her hand for the next dances.

As they observed the merriment, the white-haired woman remarked to Navarro, "She's a fine girl."

"Yes, ma'am, she is," he concurred as he watched her do the Texas two step.

"I don't know what we'd do without her if she ever left."

"Why should Jessie ever leave home, Mrs. Lane?" he asked, pretending not to understand what the older woman was hinting at.

"Jessie's twenty-four. Women her age often take off to build their own homes. My son depends on her so much; we all do. Jessie's our strength and pride."

"From what I've seen, she doesn't have a sweetheart, so I wouldn't worry."

"How much longer will you be with us, Navarro?"

"Until this trouble is settled. If it doesn't take too much longer, that is. I get restless when I corral my horse and body in the same place for more than a few weeks. I like to keep on the move. When I accepted Jessie's offer, I didn't think it would take so long to help her win."

"You think Fletcher has given up his fight? You've dealt him some hard blows, and he's been quiet for two weeks."

"He's just biding his time and waiting for us to relax and drop our guard, ma'am. He hasn't backed down for good. A man like him don't give up his dream."

"Very few people do, Navarro, until they realize it's futile."

They chatted about ranching, breeding, branding, and the hands for a while, as Navarro continued to keep an eye on Jessie.

Jessie noticed Navarro was looking tense. She went to him and grasped his hand. Laughing, she said, "It's time you learned to dance, Mr. Jones." She practically dragged him away from her grandmother to the dance area where Mary Louise was moving around the circle with Carlos, and hands were partnered up with each other. All were laughing and talking—having fun.

Before they reached the group, Jessie whispered, "Sorry, but it's the only way I could rescue you, and I need to touch you or scream. I'm much too bold for my own good at times, but you're too handsome to resist."

"I can't dance, Jessie. I'll look stupid and embarrass both of us."

"Just watch what I do. Stand beside me," she instructed, and placed him to her left. She laid her open hand on her right shoulder and said, "Take my right hand in yours," which he did. She extended her left before his waist and said, "Grab this one, too," which he also did. "Now we step with our right foot, then flick our left foot toward our right knee like this," she said, and demonstrated the movements. "Three times. Pause. Repeat. Move with the music. Now, step, step, and switch sides." She continued the lesson, moving to his left. "Step, step, and switch back. Then, go again. That's all there is to it. Over and over. By the time the dance ends, you'll have it down for the next time. That's right," she encouraged. "You learn fast, Mr. Jones."

Navarro was stiff and reluctant at first, but he obeyed because it felt so good to hold her hands and touch her body. Each time she passed before him, her fragrance—the same one she had dotted on his bandanna during the coyote incident—teased his senses. Her flaming tresses played against his chest and sometimes tickled his chin. Her laughter warmed his ears, and her smile enflamed his heart. Her hands were calloused from hard work like a man's, but she was as gentle and refined as any woman could be. She could help any man become the best that was in him to be, including him if she was given the chance. He always felt so good, so special, so worthwhile around her. Soon, he was thinking about Jessie so much that he was dancing without difficulty. He was even dipping and swaying at the right times. "I felt foolish at first, but it isn't so bad," he finally admitted.

Jessie glanced up at him with a radiant smile. "You should try new things every so often so you won't miss so much fun in life."

He murmured near her ear, "New things are only fun if I do them with you, Jessie. You make me feel brave and daring. And you don't make me feel silly."

"That's why you should stick around me for keeps. We'd have a wonderful life together. I know there's plenty you can teach me. It's more fun learning with someone you . . . Sorry," she murmured when he tensed and faltered. "It slipped out. I won't say any more."

The music halted and Jed announced, "I'm afraid that's all, boys. It's late."

Jessie was bubbling with happiness and energy with Navarro beside her. "We were just getting started, Papa. Just a few more. Please," she coaxed.

"We begin a new week tomorrow, Jess. We all need our rest."

"But we've worked so hard lately. This is our first party in ages."

In a gentle voice, he urged, "No more arguing for tonight, and we'll have a bigger party after we defeat Fletcher. Is that a bargain?"

Jessie decided her father was nervous about her being so close to Navarro and was halting the evening's festivities to end their contact. "All right, Papa," she said obediently and smiled at him.

As Mary Louise passed Navarro, she murmured, "I thought you didn't dance."

"Jessie's stubborn," Navarro answered. "She wouldn't let me say no about learning."

In a seductive tone, she replied, "Next time, I'll be as persistent as my older sister." With a swish of her full skirt, she pranced toward the house.

"Mary Louise!" Jed called. "Help Ma and Jess with the cleanup back here."

The blonde turned and smiled. "Sorry, Father. I'm coming."

As the girl and Jed carried things into the kitchen, Mary Louise remarked, "I'm surprised that drifter has stayed around so long, Father. He seems to forget his place at times. Men like that think they can latch on to a wealthy lady and raise their stations in life. I don't like him being so friendly with me and Jessica. After all, he isn't one of the regular ranch hands. I hope Jessica isn't becoming too fond of him. He seems so rough and secretive, don't you think?"

Jed gave her a hard look. "What do you mean, girl?"

"Oh, Father," she murmured. "You know how Jessica is. She's so kind-hearted. I fear she doesn't see the danger in such men. She always wants to help everyone improve. I hope such goodness and generosity don't get her into trouble with Navarro Jones. There's something so very strange and frightening about him. I know you all like him, but I fear I don't trust him. He makes me nervous the way he watches me and Jessica."

"Should I say something to him?"

"Oh, no, Father. He would deny he meant anything bad, and perhaps he doesn't. I don't want to cause more trouble. I've been so bad of late, and I'm really trying to change. It's just that my life here is so different from what I was accustomed to back East. I realize I've been petulant and selfish. I'm sorry for giving you a bad time. I'll try to do better; you'll see."

Martha Lane overheard them and wondered what her youngest granddaughter was up to with her pretty lies, but she kept the curious conversation to herself.

*   *   *

Wilbur Fletcher visited them again Sunday afternoon. This time, he stood on the porch chatting with Mary Louise while Gran fetched Jessie and Jed. When the two arrived, both frowning, he said, "I thought you would want to know that two dead men were left on my property recently. I turned the bodies over to the sheriff so he can try to discover who they are. Do you know anything about them, Jed? They were put through a cut in my north fence."

"We haven't seen any strangers around here since your man butchered my milk cows and set fire to my hay shed."

"Is that why you had your men release my chickens and hogs and fire my coop? This retaliation for things I haven't done is old, Jed, old and tiring. If we work together, we might solve this mystery and put an end to our troubles."

"How would we do that, Fletcher?" Jed asked in a sarcastic tone.

"Join our men into small groups and let them ride both ranges. That way, you and I will know for certain the other isn't behind anything that happens."

"Get my men separate and alone so you can kill them or try to scare them off like you did to Roy, Smokey, Davy, and Pete?" he scoffed.

"If you've lost four men, I'm sorry. It sounds as if you can use my help."

"You haven't lost any hands to accidents like I have?" Jed hinted for a slip.

"No, I still have all twenty-five, strong and healthy."

"Why do you need so many hands for such a small spread?" Jessie asked, aware Navarro was standing nearby sizing up the enemy.

"So I'll be well protected during times of trouble, Miss Jessie, and so I'll be covered if no seasonal help comes around—like this year."

"Yeah, that was strange, wasn't it?" Jed said in the same accusatory tone.

"If you'd bothered to check around as I did, Jed, you'd have learned all of the ranchers in our area had the same problem. Perhaps this section is too hard to reach for them to keep heading our way each spring and fall."

"Covering your tracks in every direction, aren't you?"

"You're a stubborn and foolish man, Jed. I didn't prevent any wranglers from coming here, and I haven't harmed any of your men or animals. When are you going to see the truth and accept it?"

"I already have, Fletcher. You won't win. I'll fight as long as you do."

Wilbur shook his brown head and scowled. "But I'm not fighting you, Jed, not yet."

"We've had enough of your lies," Jessie said angrily. "You'll make a slip soon and we'll catch it. You're going to pay for all the evil you've done to us. I swear it."

Fletcher eyed her intently, then frowned. "I hope you aren't the one putting these crazy ideas into your father's head, Miss Jessie. I wouldn't want you to be responsible for getting innocent people hurt or even killed."

"The only crazy person around here is you, Mr. Fletcher. Papa doesn't need me to point out the truth to him. But I would fight you even if he yielded, which he won't. This is Lane land, and it will remain Lane land until we all die."

"I beg you, Miss Jessie, don't encourage his misconceptions. I'm innocent. Someday I'll expect apologies from both of you. Good-bye."

Jessie watched their enemy climb into his buggy. Another man was waiting for him, a well-dressed gentleman who had a pad on his knees and was writing or sketching upon it. She wondered who the stranger was. She didn't like the way he kept glancing at Navarro as he worked.

After Fletcher left, Mary Louise remarked, "He certainly knows how to control his temper, doesn't he? I'm certain he was furious inside. What do you think he'll do?" she asked them.

"I can't imagine. Nothing seems too brutal and daring for him."

"Father, if you believe he's truly that dangerous, why are you resisting his offer? What if he kills us all to get what you think he wants?"

"That's a risk we have to take, girl. This is our home. We can't give up."

Monday morning, May first, Jed and Matt left for Fort Stockton for a few days to set up cattle and horse sales for the fall roundup. Jed left Jessie in charge of the ranch, but asked her to avoid as much trouble as possible until their return.

While they were away, Jessie couldn't seem to get a few minutes alone with Navarro because someone always interrupted them. She began to feel as if her father had left orders to keep them apart! Then she scolded herself for being so suspicious of everyone.

She returned to Tom's daily lessons, but it seemed difficult for him to concentrate. He wanted to finish quickly so he could join Navarro and the hands, as he was allowed to ride with them on many occasions. The clever moccasin that Navarro had made for Tom gave him confidence and a more level walk, and Navarro had fixed the boy's left stirrup so his bad foot wouldn't slip through it. Tom also tied his glasses in place every day as Navarro had shown him weeks ago. The youth had come to think of Jessie and Navarro as his best friends, and that pleased her. Yet she worried about how Tom would react when Navarro had to go.

On Wednesday, Jessie had a quarrel with her sister. Mary Louise accused her and Navarro of creating more trouble and danger than they prevented.

"If you two hadn't done all those terrible things to Mr. Fletcher, he wouldn't be so mad at us. You have no proof he's to blame, Jessica. Have you ever considered you and Father might be wrong? What if he is innocent?"

"He isn't."

"How do you know?" the blonde persisted.

"I know."

"How? Wanting to buy our ranch just isn't convincing enough."

"It is for us."

"Why?"

Jessie glared at her sister. "Darn it, Mary Louise! It's just a feeling. By now we've all learned to trust our instincts."

Mary Louise moved before her again when she turned away. "Feelings and instincts can be wrong. What if you're battling the wrong enemy?"

Jessie tossed aside the laundry she was folding. "We aren't."

"Prove it to me. Show me any shred of evidence, any clue," she challenged.

The redhead picked up a shirt again. "I can't. He's too clever."

"Or he's innocent."

Thursday, her father and the foreman returned with shocking news. Jessie was furious when she heard what had happened.

"Not one contract, Papa? He blocked all sales? How can he do that?"

"He undercut every price I made, Jess. Read the telegrams for yourself. I can't sell for the same or less than the deal he's offering them. That would be giving away my steers. We'll have to wait until fall, herd them to market and hope for the best."

"But he doesn't have that many mature steers, Papa. How can he fill those contracts?" she asked in confusion and dismay.

"It's my guess he's buying out some of the other ranchers. He's paying top dollar and keeping them from having to make the cattle drive. He can afford to do that, Jess, but we can't. What's worse is if he stops us from getting to market on time or floods it before we get there. I don't know what to do," he admitted.

"Go to the Cattleman's Association, Papa."

"I wired them, Jess. He's already taken that precaution. He's made charges against us that have to be investigated and cleared before I can join and get their help. They won't meet again until after fall roundup; that's too late to do us any good. We'll need money by fall, Jess, and I'm doubtful I can raise it."

"The bank will see us through, Papa. We have good collateral."

"I'm afraid not, Jess. I already tried them. Fletcher has big deposits in both banks. He's threatened to withdraw and get his friends to do the same if they loan us money. That snake has thought of everything!"

"He can't do that, Papa! Surely it can't be legal."

"He has done it, Jess. He has blocked every path."

"Then we'll find a new one."

"I hope so. We have plenty of everything but cash and credit. We can't make it without one or the other. Fletcher was in town, watching and gloating."

"He was there?"

"Yep, like he knew I would be. Maybe we do have a traitor here."

That remark surprised her. "I doubt it, but I'll ask Navarro if any of the men acted strange or vanished for a while."

"Don't ask him, Jessie; ask Miguel."

"Navarro can be trusted, Papa; I'd stake my life on it."

"We have, Jess, many times."

"And we haven't been wrong."

"He's been getting us to attack Fletcher, not just defend ourselves. What if Fletcher's trick to win is using our retaliation to get us into trouble with the law? Navarro could make sure we're trapped and exposed one night. When he was over here, Fletcher said we'd defeat ourselves. Maybe that was a slip."

"He could hurt us only if he works for Fletcher, Papa, and he doesn't!"

"You've become mighty defensive of him, Jess. You spend more time with him than with your old friends here. Are you letting that drifter charm you?"

"Papa! I'm not a foolish young girl."

"No, you're quite a beautiful woman, Jessica."

He so rarely called her by her full name, Jessie almost shot back, *So, you've finally noticed I'm not a son!* She calmed herself and said, "If you're worried about my friendship with Navarro, don't be. He's leaving when this is over."

"Are you sure?" he asked, sounding hopeful.

"Positive, Papa. He's been very clear about it from the start. He only agreed to work for us for a while. It's taking longer than he planned, but I convinced him to stay on until the conflict is resolved. The only reason he's remained is because everyone's been so nice to him. If you and Matt start throwing around doubts about him, I'm sure he'll pull out. You know how much help he's been. We need him. With the branding over, we can concentrate more on Fletcher."

From the corner of her eye, Jessie saw Mary Louise standing in the doorway to their bedroom. A curious chill passed over her. She shrugged and dismissed it, then returned to her talk with her father.

On Saturday, Mary Louise caught Navarro in the barn alone. "We have to talk," she told him. "Something terrible has happened. Father will be furious about what I'm planning to do. He talked to Jessica last night about you. I think it's big trouble. We can't talk here. Don't let anyone see you, but follow me after I leave." She took a horse and headed away from the corral.

Navarro was intrigued and worried. He couldn't march to the house and ask to see Jessie alone, not with Jed there. He slipped away. When he caught up with Mary Louise, he dismounted and joined her. "What's wrong with Jessie?"

"She's standing between us" came the shocking reply.

"What?" he asked, looking and feeling baffled.

"You don't notice me with her around. Ever since I came home and met you, my head's been spinning. I become hot and weak all over when I'm near you. I want you, Navarro. I know it's bold and wicked, but I do." She fondled his chest as she entreated, "Kiss me before I die of hunger."

Navarro grasped her hands and tried to push her away. "No, Miss Lane. I—"

"Yes, Navarro," she persisted as she rubbed herself against him.

When she tried to pull down his head to kiss him, he scolded, "Behave, girl, or your father will whip both of us. I thought you said—"

"Not if he doesn't know about us. I won't tell. If he finds out and intrudes, something could happen to him." She sent him a sultry smile. "If you get rid of Father, Jessica will have to sell out and split the money with me. It'll give us plenty to start a new life together somewhere. If Jessica refuses, you can take care of her, too. Please, Navarro, my love, let's run away together."

The desperado was stunned. All he wanted to do was put distance between himself and this greedy creature. "Get mounted, girl. This isn't a game."

"Far from it, my handsome drifter. This is your chance to win both me and plenty of money. I'm yours for the taking. All we need is money to make our dream come true. You can blame Mr. Fletcher for Father's death."

The fugitive gaped at the blonde. "Either you don't know what you're saying, or this is a trick or a cruel joke. I don't want to take you, Miss Lane, or hurt Jed. Forget this happened. Let's go."

Mary Louise grabbed his shirt and yanked on it, causing it to rip. "I'm more beautiful and desirable than my spinster sister! I'm offering you two treasures. I'm more of a woman than she'll ever be. We're rebels at heart, Navarro; we're perfectly suited to each other. We can escape together."

Navarro couldn't believe he hadn't seen this coming. Mary Louise must have been planning this for days. "No, we aren't matched at all, Miss Lane. You shouldn't behave this way."

"We *are* alike," she argued, pouting and glaring.

"No," he stated in a firm tone to discourage her.

As Mary Louise shrieked, "Yes, we are, damn you!," she scratched his cheek.

Navarro backed away and stared at the raging beauty with the flashing blue eyes. She was nothing like her older sister, nothing. He rubbed his stinging cheek and saw blood on his fingers. "Why did you do that?" he demanded.

Mary Louise settled down and frowned. "I lost my temper. I'm sorry," she murmured as she lowered her head. "It's just that I've been craving you so long and so much that it's driving me crazy. Are you sure you don't want me, Navarro?"

He tried to be kind and polite as Jessie had taught him. "I'm sorry, but no."

Mary Louise waited a moment, then said, "A woman can't force a man to desire her. I was certain you'd feel the same way I do. I was mistaken. Give me a minute to calm myself, then we'll head home. I won't trouble you again. About Father and Jessica, I was only testing your loyalty and honor. I don't want them hurt."

Navarro watched the girl retreat behind a row of bushes. He wiped his injured cheek, and wondered how to explain it to everyone. He couldn't tell Jessie or Jed or the others what the girl had offered; it was too cruel, too shocking. He straightened his shirt, noticing several buttons were missing. He wondered if he should escort Mary Louise home or just leave her there. As he paced and waited, he heard a curious sound, like another rip, then a harsh slap!

Mary Louise returned with mussed hair, ripped and dirty dress, and scratches on her neck. She muttered peevishly, "I'm so clumsy today. I fell and made a mess of myself. My dress is ruined." The blonde mounted her pinto, grabbed the sorrel's reins, and raced from the scene with both horses.

Navarro was taken off guard and she was already too distant to halt her. He was befuddled and vexed. *What in . . .* Dread filled the wide-eyed man and stiffened his tall frame. His heart pounded. He ran after the vindictive girl who had taken his mount. He suspected she would drop its reins soon, if he was right about what she intended to do. He was; he found the animal grazing over the next hill. Winded from his run, he leapt on his sorrel and raced after Mary Louise. He couldn't overtake her in time.

As she neared the barn, the blonde screamed for help. Men came running to her aid. She fell off the horse into Matt's arms, sobbing and looking terrified. "Don't let him near me!" she shrieked and clutched at Matt as Navarro approached. "He tried to attack me! Navarro ambushed me and tried to rape me," she accused, then snuggled her face against the foreman's protective shoulder.

# CHAPTER TWELVE

Mathew Cordell's astonished gaze locked on Navarro's angry expression. The foreman saw his torn shirt and bleeding scratches. Matt looked at Mary Louise's disheveled injured condition. He was perplexed and disappointed, as were the other hands.

"You've been one of us for months, Navarro," Matt said. "I can't believe you would do something terrible like this."

"I didn't, Matt; *she* did. Miss Lane asked me to escort her riding. When we halted, she got too friendly. I tried to discourage her, but she went wild and attacked me. Then she messed herself up like that and hightailed for home to get me into trouble. She even ran my horse over a mile so I couldn't stop her. I never touched her."

Jed and Jessie arrived during Navarro's denial and shocking accusation. The hands—who had been around the "drifter" for only seven weeks, but around their boss's daughter for years—didn't know what to say or believe. They knew the girl was defiant and unhappy, but they couldn't imagine anyone lying about such a serious thing. Jessie was stunned speechless for a time, fearing the outcome of what she was certain was her sister's spiteful mischief.

"That's a lie, you heartless beast!" Mary Louise raged. "You trailed me and waylaid me. I would never entice a saddletramp like you! Surely you don't expect everyone to believe I injured myself. Look at us; we're both wearing the evidence of your guilt."

Navarro's gaze narrowed and hardened at the destructive and wicked girl. "You know I never tried to—"

"Hush, both of you!" Jed stormed. "Girl, tell me what happened."

Mary Louise dabbed at fake tears. She repeated her wild tale. "I'm sorry, Father. He caught up with me and wanted to talk. I didn't realize he could be this dangerous. I know I've been terrible lately, but I'm not to blame for this trouble. Honestly I'm not," she vowed, her blue gaze widening in an attempt to appear truthful. "You know I've never liked or trusted him, so why would I entice him?"

Jed glared at Mary Louise who looked so like his dead Alice at that moment, then at Navarro, who was a threat to his family. "What did you do to her?" he asked. "I never expected something like this from you."

"I swear I didn't harm her, sir."

"Then how do you explain all this?" Jed argued, pointing to the "evidence."

Navarro related his side of the story, except for the blonde's idea about killing Jed and Jessie. He knew they would never believe that evil part, and it would cause them to doubt his other words. He finished with, "When she took off like this, I guessed what she had in mind. I raced after her to reason with her——."

"He's lying, Father! He——"

Irate, Jed thundered, "Silence, girl! Let me handle this. This is crazy, Navarro. Why would Mary Louise hurt herself to frame you?"

"I don't know, sir, but I'm innocent." Those words echoed through the fugitive's mind from a day long past when he had used them after being accused and arrested for that gold robbery. No one had believed him then, and he had been brutally and unjustly punished; he could tell that was going to happen again today. If not for Jessie and the changes she had wrought in him, he would curse them and leave without another word! "I'm innocent," he repeated, but knew it was futile. Fury and bitterness flooded him as he watched and listened.

Jed waved everyone to silence as he considered this matter. He had seen his oldest and favorite daughter, his helpmate, responding more and more to this drifter every day. There was no way he could allow Jessie to get tangled up with a saddlebum like Navarro Jones. This was the perfect excuse to get rid of him before the gunslinger won Jessie's heart. Jed knew how much he loved and needed Jessie, how much his mother and son needed her. "I've heard enough of this sorry affair. I have to fire you, Navarro. You can't stay. In addition to this new trouble, for all I know, you could be on Fletcher's payroll. Roy said we have a spy in our midst; that could be you."

Navarro was incensed. "That isn't true, sir. I'm loyal to the Lanes."

"I don't know what really happened out there. You've been a big help to us, but I have to let you go to keep peace around here."

"What about Fletcher, Mr. Lane?"

"We'll take care of him."

"Can you do it alone, sir? What about your family? They're in danger. I wouldn't touch your daughter; I swear it. Tell them the truth, Miss Lane."

"I did," the blonde vowed.

Jed exhaled loudly. "Even if it was a misunderstanding or a rash mistake, it's best for you to leave, Navarro. I can't take your side against my own daughter. I have enough trouble without adding you and her to it. Get packed and ride out."

"No, Papa!" Jessie shouted. "I know Navarro and he wouldn't do anything like this. It's Mary Louise's fault; punish her, but not him. We need Navarro, Papa."

"Are you calling me—your own sister—a liar?" Mary Louise shrieked.

Jessie glared at the devious girl. "I'm saying you're wrong, that's all."

"If you—"

"Silence, girl," Jed ordered a second time to prevent a hateful reply before the others. "Leave, Navarro, before there's more trouble. Be glad I have doubts about what happened and gratitude for all you've done or I would have the boys tie you to the corral so I could whip you good to defend my daughter's honor. Get riding, son, before I change my mind," he warned.

At that familiar threat, rage filled the desperado's mind, and it stiffened his body. It glittered ominously in his brownish-green eyes and tightened his jawline. *Framed again!* He was tempted to reveal how much the girl hated Jed and Jessie, but those incredible words would cause a fight for certain, and he couldn't lick this many men at the same time. No man, he vowed, would ever lash him again! Besides, Mary Louise was to blame, not the others, so why hurt them? He was fired, he told himself, so he had no choice but to leave.

All his life he'd been used, betrayed, and then discarded. Yet, after all this time here, he had thought these people were different. Only his sweet and brave Jessie believed him and had stood up for him. Yet, he admitted, he couldn't expect the other hired hands to go against their boss and friend for someone who was almost a stranger. His only regrets were how this would hurt Jessie and Tom. He dared not look at his love. "I'm innocent; one day, you'll learn that the hard way, sir." He stalked to the bunkhouse to pack, telling himself he should be grateful for an excuse to desert Jessie without having to explain the truth. But somehow, he wasn't.

"You can't do this, Papa! It isn't fair or right. He's innocent."

"Don't become disrespectful like your sister, Jess. I have to do what I think is best for all of us. Mary Louise, go to the house and get cleaned up. And do your chores without any back talk."

"Yes, Father," she replied, and hurried to obey.

"Let him stay until morning, Papa," Jessie implored, "so you'll have time to calm down and think clearly. We need his help."

"I can handle Fletcher from now on. I've been dodging my duty or letting others do it for me too long. This is *my* ranch and family. *I'll* defend them. You boys get back to work. Sorry you had to witness such a disgrace."

The concerned foreman and men also obeyed their distraught boss.

Gran, who had positioned herself and Tom on the front porch, urged the youth to go inside until everything was settled.

Tom protested, as he wanted to go to his friend's defense. "It ain't fair, Gran. He's innocent. He wouldn't hurt nobody here."

"You can't help him, Tom; your pa has spoken. Don't argue with him."

"But Navarro's my friend, Gran. At least let me go tell him good-bye."

"Your pa won't like that. And you don't want to make leaving harder on Navarro. He knows how you feel. Come inside."

Mary Louise reached the porch. All exchanged glances. She frowned at the suspicions she read on their faces. "I can see you two believe him over me!"

"You're mean, Mary Louise, a liar!" Tom accused, hurt and angry.

"I'm glad he's leaving. That drifter is no good; he's trouble."

The youth's florid complexion became rosier. His weak eyes squinted. "He is not! I hope Pa beats you for lying! If I was big enough, *I* would."

Mary Louise pinched his arm, and he jerked and yelled. "You only like him because he's pampered you like a baby. He can't change you to normal, Tom. Nobody can. Forget that road trash and being something you aren't."

Ignoring her aches, Gran straightened herself to her full five foot two. "Mary Louise! Hush your mouth, girl, or I'll tell Jed to whip you."

"Does everybody hate me and doubt me? I can't wait to leave here! My friends back East never treated me this horrible way." She ran into the house.

At the corral, Jessie was still reasoning with her father. "What's wrong, Papa? This isn't like you. He was working hard and fitting in well here. You shamed him and hurt him."

"Better to hurt a stranger than us, Jess."

"Is it, Papa? Cruelty backlashes. I'm going to see him before he leaves."

"Don't, Jess!" he said in a sharp tone.

Her blue eyes glistened with defiance. "Sorry, Papa, this is one time I can't obey. I brought him here. I gave him hope for friendship and peace. If you're going to steal them away, I have to let him know I'm sorry and I don't agree with you."

Navarro stalked past them with his saddlebags slung over one shoulder, his bedroll under his arm, a sack of supplies from Hank in one hand, and his rifle in the other. His holsters were strapped to muscled thighs, and his hat was low on his forehead as if to conceal his bitter gaze. He didn't look at or speak to either Jed or Jessie. The desperado packed his possessions and mounted. Off he rode at a fast pace, fearing he had seen Jessica Lane for the last time.

Jessie ran to the horse Mary Louise had used and swung into the saddle. She ignored her father's shouts as she pursued her lover. When she neared him, she yelled, "Navarro! Wait up!"

Navarro reined in, but didn't look back. He sat stiff in his saddle. When Jessie reached him, edged close, and finally faced him, he kept his gaze ahead. "What is it, Miss Lane?" he asked, his tone intentionally icy and his manner forbidding. It was time to go. 'Coldness would make it easier for both of them to part.

Tears moistened Jessie's light blue eyes. "You didn't say good-bye."

"Was there any need to? I came here leaving, like I do every place," he responded.

"I'm sorry Papa humiliated you and hurt you, Navarro. It wasn't right, and I told him so. He felt he had no choice but to defend her, even though the little witch doesn't deserve it. Mary Louise is miserable; she hates this place and wants to leave, but Papa won't let her. I wish he would. No, I wish he had long ago; then this wouldn't have happened to us. When Papa calms down, he'll be sorry and be ashamed of himself for treating you so badly. I believe you're innocent, Navarro, because I know you."

"Do you, Jess?" he asked, finally meeting her misty gaze.

The redhead realized that the two men she loved most now called her Jess. She didn't ask Navarro why he had decided to call her that today. "I don't know much about you, Navarro, but I know what kind of man you are. She lied to cause trouble."

"Are you certain?" he challenged, causing her to grimace.

"Please don't try to hurt me to make this parting easier, Navarro. We have so little time left, and I have some things to say. Even if I didn't know you and my sister, evidence doesn't lie. You're left-handed; those scratches, the rips in her dress, and that slap mark were on the wrong side for you to have inflicted them. I was going to challenge her about her so-called evidence, but tempers were too hot for reasoning. Papa usually listens to me, but not today. He's a good man, Navarro, but all his troubles are changing him. Don't think too harshly of him. He has a large burden on his shoulders. He doesn't want any of us to see how scared he is. Papa's fifty-four and he's worked hard, but he has health problems. Sometimes I see him rubbing his aching hands like Gran does. Sometimes I've seen him so stiff in the legs and back after sitting a long time that he can hardly get up from a chair or get off his horse. I've noticed a lot of little things that he tries to hide. I love him, Navarro, but he's wrong this time. Please camp nearby while I reason with him and try to force the truth from Mary Louise. I'm sure Papa will apologize soon and rehire you. Please give us time and patience."

Navarro wanted to warn Jessie about her sister's evil, but he couldn't bring himself to hurt her more than she was hurting now. Nor could he tell the redhead that he suspected Jed had believed him and had used the incident to separate them. To expose Jed's motives would cause pain and trouble, and wouldn't make it possible for him to win the woman he loved. Jessie had taught him to think of someone other than himself and of something other than his troubles. "No, Jess, he won't change his mind or apologize. A proud and stubborn man never backs down once he takes a stand. His conscience might plague him a while, but that's all. I told you in the beginning I couldn't stay long. I let you convince me to change my mind. It's best if I move on now."

"It's not best for us, Navarro," she refuted.

"Branding and planting are over, Jess. The men can concentrate on fighting Fletcher. I've taught them plenty of tricks they can use. Also, the sheriff and Army are involved now. Promise me you'll hang back out of danger. You've been a good friend, and I don't want you hurt, ever."

"I didn't mean best for the ranch or my family," Jessie clarified. "I meant for us, you and me. We've been far more than friends, Navarro. I don't want to lose you, especially like this. I love you."

That confession staggered him. He had longed to earn and deserve her love. Those were the sweetest words he had ever heard. He wanted to yank her into his possessive embrace, kiss her, hug her, then ride away with her in his arms and keep her forever. There was a heaviness in his heart as he had to say, "Don't, Jess. I'm not worth your love. I'm no good for anybody, not even for myself. There's so much you don't know about me, and I can't tell you. Don't love me, or you'll get hurt."

That was not the response Jessie wanted. "I can't help it; I love you. I need you. Stay here and marry me." He was leaving; she had to be bold. She saw his shocked reaction to her proposal, and she hurried on. "Papa can't stop us. I'm twenty-four. He'll have to accept my wishes or risk losing me if we were forced to leave together. I'll even convince him to send Mary Louise back East so we can all have peace. I can make you happy; let me prove it. Stay, Navarro. Make your home and peace with me," she entreated.

Here it was at last: Navarro's dream was there for the taking. How, he wondered, could she give up everything for him? That meant she loved him more than anything in her life, as he loved her. That was incredible, overwhelming, strengthening. He had to be just as self-sacrificing for once in his miserable life. "I wish I could, Jess, but I can't marry you or take you with me. I can't stay, either. The longer we're together, the worse it will be for us to part. We're too different, and you don't even realize how much. It wouldn't work, *tsine.*" For a moment, he slipped back into his Apache days and called her *love.*

"Do I mean nothing or so little to you that it isn't worth a try?"

Her expression and words seared his heart. Maybe he should tell her the whole black truth and turn her against him. Someday, he would. "That isn't it, Jess. There's too much in my past standing between us."

"What? Any problem can be resolved, Navarro. Let me help. What we have is real; it's special. Don't make us lose it."

"It's too late for me, Jess. Too late for us. I've told you that all along."

"It's never too late, my love. What haunts you so painfully?"

Navarro told himself she was only in love with the man she thought he was. She didn't know he was a murderer, a thief, a half-breed, a bastard, the son of a cold-blooded outlaw and hostile Apache, a wanted man fleeing prison and the hangman's noose, a man who could destroy her and her world. He couldn't risk letting her or anyone discover his many secrets. He couldn't risk involving her in such danger. If he confessed the love that filled his heart to overflowing, she would fight even harder to win him, and he couldn't allow that.

It would be better, he decided painfully, to let her hurt a little now than to hurt a lot when his dark past engulfed and destroyed them. He couldn't let her watch him be captured and hanged. He had to be strong and unyielding for both their sakes. "You're a special woman, Jessica Lane. What you're offering is a valuable gift, but not one I can accept. Mine isn't a life I can share. I have to move on; that's what I need. You've had all I can share. I have nothing more I can give. You must believe me and accept that truth. I swear it."

"Why, Navarro? At least give me an explanation."

"Not everyone has the same needs and dreams, Jess. I'm a loner, a drifter, an adventurer. I can't become a rancher, a husband, a father. Not now, not ever. If I could, you'd be the woman standing beside me. I swear it."

Jessie sensed a terrible struggle within him. She was positive he wanted her, wanted to stay, wanted the life she was offering. Something wouldn't, couldn't, let him surrender—not yet. She had to keep him with her until she could unmask and destroy his demons. "Couldn't you hang around for just a little while longer? I'm sure Fletcher is about to make his big and final move. When he does, our war will be over one way or another. Please, only a few more weeks. Afterward, if you haven't changed your mind, I won't beg you to stay; I promise."

"I'll think about it. If you don't hear from me soon, you'll know I'm gone, for good. Before I leave, I want you and Tom to know I didn't attack your sister."

"We know. This is all because of me. Mary Louise is a mixed-up girl, Navarro. She has been ever since she returned from the East. She wants to hurt me because she thinks Papa favors me over her and Tom. She doesn't know what a burden it is to be his 'son' and heir. She probably realized how I feel about you, so she struck at you to hurt me. She's angry because I won't persuade Papa to let her leave home. There have been so many harsh words and feelings between them lately. For a while today, I almost hated her for being so vindictive and deceitful. It's awful to feel that way about your own sister, and I do feel sorry for her and I try to understand her side, but she makes it so difficult. Moving back East isn't as simple as she thinks. Besides, she is too immature and reckless to be on her own. I've talked and talked, but nothing seems to help. I'm sorry you were the target of her revenge against me. Please, Navarro, stay nearby until I can work out this situation. If Wilbur Fletcher learns you're gone, he'll attack with a fury. You're the only thing that's stayed his hand."

"If I hung around, your father would think I was up to no good. It's best if I leave. If he's worrying about me, he can't keep his mind on Fletcher. And that's dangerous for all of you."

Time, not pressure, is what you need, my love. Time to see what I mean to you. "If you don't return, always remember me. And if you ever need anything, you know where to find me. Anything, Navarro, no matter what Papa says."

"What I need and want, neither the white nor Indian God can give me."

He sounded so hopeless, so sad. "Nothing's impossible, Navarro."

"Some things are, Jess, some things are. Go home, and watch your back. Enemies can strike from where you least expect them. Be alert for that spy Roy mentioned in case it wasn't a lie. I think and hope Fletcher is going after the ranch in a different way now, by ruining you financially, and I can't help there. He's smart enough to know he can't keep attacking or the law will get him."

"He won't give up. Greedy, evil men like him never do."

"I hope you're wrong. Good-bye, Jess. Thanks for being a bright corner in my life. I won't forget you. Tell Gran, Tom, and the boys good-bye for me. And tell 'em I'm sorry about this trouble. Be safe and happy."

"How can I if you leave? At least kiss me and hold me a last time."

"I can't; Matt's coming to safeguard you. Good-bye, Jess. Forget me!" he ordered, then galloped away before he lost the strength and will to do so.

Jessie watched her lover's departure until Matt joined her. She looked at the steadfast foreman she had known nearly all of her life. They had spent most of their lives together, except for the few years when he was off at war. When the Yankees attacked, he had felt compelled to protect and aid his family in Georgia. They were all gone now, except for one brother whom Matt rarely saw or heard from. She was glad he remained quiet while she collected herself. Matt always seemed to grasp her feelings and knew how to respond to them. Whenever she felt trapped by her life, he was the one person who could lift her spirits. It wasn't so much what the sedate foreman said; it was his cheerful smile, his comforting gaze, his gentle touch that made her feel better. She couldn't imagine living and working without faithful Matt nearby.

She sighed deeply and said, "If ever a man needed and deserved understanding and acceptance, it's Navarro. I don't know what happened in his past, Matt, but he's had a hard and lonely existence. There's so much good inside him, but he's afraid to let it run free and risk being hurt worse. I'm sorry Mary Louise caused more trouble and heartache for him; I think he's suffered more than his share." Jessie looked at the foreman. "She lied, Matt. I don't know why, but my sister lied."

Matt grasped her hand and squeezed it. "There's nothing you can do about either one, Jessie" came his gentle response.

"I know, but it makes me so angry. We need him. He knows how to deal with men like Fletcher. He's the one who made all the plans and taught us how to use caution. When Fletcher hears that he's gone . . ."

"We'll have to face him ourselves. I won't let anything happen to you, Jessie."

"You've been a good friend for a long time, Matt. I really trust you and depend on you. It'll be up to us to keep Papa strong and not let Fletcher win."

"I would do anything for you, Jessie. Whatever you need or want, just ask me."

What she wanted and needed, only Navarro could give.

"What about Navarro's pay? That's why I rode out. Jed gave it to me."

"I'm surprised Papa thought about that. I guess he didn't want Navarro to have a reason to return. He told me once he didn't need very much. Maybe last month's pay will be enough to see him to his next job."

"Did he say where he was heading?"

"No."

"Do you think he'll come back?"

"I doubt it. Papa was pretty cruel. Let's get back to the house. I want to talk to that dishonest sister of mine."

In a feigned tone of concern, Jessie asked, "What happened out there, Mary Louise?"

"I don't want to go over it again. It was horrible."

"I'm sure you didn't give all the details in front of Papa and the hands. Tell me everything, little sister. I found him and hired him. I feel responsible."

"I'm still too upset to repeat it. Perhaps later, another day."

"I'm going to be more upset than you are if you don't explain," Jessie persisted. "Did you flirt with him and things got out of control?"

"Heavens, no! All right!" she snapped. "He followed me on his horse. While I was strolling, he joined me. He wanted to know what you and Father thought about him. I asked why. He said he wanted to court me if Father and I didn't mind. Of course I was shocked and alarmed. I told him I didn't get friendly with hired help. He became angry, as if I had insulted him. He said he was as good as any man and he would prove it. He said no woman had ever resisted him or denied him his wishes. He grabbed me and kissed me. When I jerked my head back, he seized me by the throat to pull it forward again. That's when I got these scratches." She touched the ones on her neck.

"I warned him Father would kill him for hurting me, but he laughed. It was such a cold and cruel sound, Jessica. He said Father was a weak fool who would never challenge an expert gunslinger like him. I panicked. When I tried to run, he grabbed me and tore my dress. He forced another kiss on me, and I feared I would retch. He touched me . . ." The blonde put her hand over her left breast as she explained. "He fondled it as if it belonged to him."

When Jessie remained silent, the girl continued. "I clawed him and cursed him. That's when he slapped me." She rubbed her left cheek. "He got off balance while we were tussling, and I grabbed his shirt and pushed him to the ground. I ran to my horse and escaped before he could get up and catch me. It was frightening. I'm glad he's gone."

"There's something I don't understand," Jessie murmured.

"What is that?"

"How does a left-handed man scratch, tear a dress, and slap a woman facing him on the left side?" As she asked her question, Jessie demonstrated her points with her left hand.

Mary Louise backed away and stared at the redhead.

"If I use my left hand, as Navarro would have, you're rubbing the wrong side, little sister. On the other hand, if a right-handed person did such damage to him or herself, it would be on the left, as yours is. How strange."

Mary Louise glared at her. "What is your point, Jessica?"

"You're far too smart for me to have to explain. Did you stop to think how dangerous a man like Navarro Jones can be when crossed? I think not. Nor did you stop to think how furious Papa will be when he learns the truth. Not to mention what the men will think about such a destructive little liar."

"How dare you accuse me of making up something like this!"

"I dare because I know you and I know Navarro. I dare because we needed him in this war against Fletcher. I dare because you were cruel and spiteful. If you don't tell Papa the truth, I will. It will be simple for you to claim you were mischievously naughty, then afraid to tell the truth."

"Are you mad? They would never believe such a wild tale!"

"I think they already do. The only reason the men held silent was because you're Jed's daughter. The only reason Papa did was because your looks remind him so of Mama and that clouds his brain. Once their minds clear, who do you think they'll believe? You or me? The longer you hold to this story, the harder it will be to correct it."

"They'll believe me because it's obvious Navarro has you blinded!"

"Perhaps to you, but not to them," Jessie refuted.

"So that's why he . . ."

Jessie laughed. "Refused you, little sister, and it stung?"

"What's between you two?"

"Something you would never understand: respect and friendship."

"Is that all?" the girl asked with a sneer.

"If it were, what you claimed might have been true weeks ago. I would keep the windows and doors locked and never be alone, little sister. Navarro Jones isn't a man to wrong." With that intimidating warning, Jessie left the room with her sister gaping at her back and wringing her hands.

On Sunday, Jessie refused to go onto the front porch for the Bible reading and hymnals. Her absence was noted by everyone.

When Jed scolded her later, his daughter replied, "You read about love, charity, and forgiveness, Papa, but you didn't practice them yesterday. Why do I need to listen to meaningless words? Either Mary Louise was wrong or she was lying, and you knew it, or suspected it. Else you would have beaten him like you threatened. Navarro's left-handed, and that sure doesn't fit with Mary Louise's supposed injuries. You didn't have to fire Navarro. We could have kept them apart. If not, you can send her back East so we can have peace here again."

"Jess! You'd choose that saddletramp over your blood kin?"

"That *saddletramp* has been more loyal and helpful in a few weeks than Mary Louise has since she returned. Besides, that wasn't my point. She's determined to leave home. I think she created this situation to force your hand. I, for one, am tired of fighting with her. If she wants to ruin her life by striking out on her own, let her do so. Perhaps bad luck will teach her more than any of our words and deeds can. I can't abide a liar!"

"Even if she did lie, Jess, she has to stay home with us because she needs our help and influence. Under that circumstance, he couldn't stay. And you know the boys would always wonder if he could be trusted. How could we fight if we didn't all pull together?"

"Why didn't you ask them how they felt?"

"Do you think they would have sided with a gunslinging drifter over their boss's daughter?" he reasoned.

Jessie ran the men through her mind. "No, I guess they wouldn't, especially with you leaning in her favor. They're too loyal to the Lanes."

"Forget him and this nasty episode, Jess."

"With Navarro gone, I may not have to, Papa, because we might all be dead soon. I don't want to discuss it anymore."

Jed watched Jessie stalked from the house, and was about to go after her.

Gran halted him. "Let her be, son. They were good friends. They went through a lot together. She liked him and trusted him. She can't believe he's guilty."

Jed saw Jessie cross the yard, saddle Ben, and ride away. "Do you think he did it, Ma?" he asked his mother.

The white-haired woman looked at the troubled man and replied, "No, son."

Jed frowned. "Don't matter much now, does it?"

"I hope not."

"You think she's going to go to him?"

"No, son; he's gone. But I think you're going to wish he weren't for two reasons: Jessie, and Wilbur Fletcher. You should be grateful to that boy."

"For all the help he's been to us on the ranch and with Fletcher?"

"For that, and for not asking Jessie to leave with him. If he had, I think she might have gone. Don't look surprised, son. Haven't you noticed how she's changed since meeting him? She may dress and work like a man, but she surely isn't one. I think Navarro's the first man to make her realize she's a woman."

"Then I'm glad he's gone. That would have meant big trouble."

"Jessie deserves a life of her own, Jed."

"Not with a saddletramp like that! She's too good for him."

"That's her decision, son. If he ever comes back, don't force Jessie to choose between him and us. It's better for him to stay than for her to go."

Jed looked worried. "You think he'll return and cause trouble?"

"No. Something terrible is driving that boy to keep moving. It's a shame. I've watched him for nearly two months. He has a lot of good in him, but a lot of pain to cut out. If things were different, he could have been perfect for our Jessie."

Jed fretted for a minute. "Mary Louise, get out here!" he stormed. When she hurried to him, he demanded, "I'll ask you one last time, is he guilty?"

Her sapphire-blue eyes took on their most innocent expression. "Yes, Father; I swear it on Mother's grave. Jessica is enchanted by him, so she can't see the awful truth. He's much too dangerous for me to frame. If you had allowed him to remain here, he would have been after both of us to get at your ranch. You did the right thing, Father, to protect me and Jessica."

"If you're lying, girl, God help you—and us."

Wilbur Fletcher visited them again on Monday. This time, he offered to buy all or only part of the Box L Ranch. Jed and Jessie refused the offer.

"You can't defeat us by blocking my sales and loans and association membership," Jed said. "Nothing you do will change our minds."

"I told you, I have not nor do I need to use violence to win our conflict. These were my first moves against you, all legal, but not my last. If you can't get sales or loans, how can you hold on, Jed? You can't."

"No Lane has given up in the past, and I won't be the first. Get off my land!"

"He just wants to get stronger and to make us weaker," Jessie told her father after his departure. "He wouldn't be satisfied with a parcel of our land and water. He'll try to freeze us out little by little."

On Tuesday, Fletcher apparently replied with cut fences and rustled steers in the southeast pasture. A gang of masked bandits ran off the two Lane hands riding herd and raced the stolen cattle toward their southern boundary.

"I told you so, Papa," Jessie told Jed. "He's at it again because he knows Navarro is gone. Mark my words: it'll get worse and worse. Come on, Matt. Let's see where they're headed."

When they reached the boundary, they found more fences had been cut to allow for the villains' escape. Jessie glared at the trampled ground, then searched the horizon. "They're long gone, Matt. They're running the cattle fast and hard. They don't care about injuries or weight losses. This wasn't about selling good stock over the border. We could track them, but we'd probably ride into an ambush. I'm sure they're smart enough to let guards hang back until they cross the river."

"Best I can figure, they took about a thousand head. Running them like that won't give 'em much profit. It's just harassment. I'll rope up this gap like you and Navarro did. I'll send boys back with wire to repair it properly."

Jessie dismounted and handed the foreman her rope. She watched him as he worked, his eyes squinting against the bright sunlight. He looked especially handsome today in his light-blue-and-faded-red checked shirt. That and a dark-blue bandanna enhanced his deep tan. Brown hair peeked-from beneath his tan hat. He had a strong, appealing face. He was so different from Navarro. His expressions and manner were easygoing while Navarro's were usually intense. When Mathew Cordell smiled, he did it with his eyes and mouth and face, and smiling came easy for him. Something seemed different about him today, though, and Jessie suddenly realized what it was. "You shaved off your mustache!"

Matt glanced at her and grinned. He removed his hat to mop the sweat with his shirt-sleeve. His brown hair was mussed, giving it a wind-ruffled look. Sections fell across his forehead and teased at his wide brows. She noticed how white and straight his teeth were, and how the creases deepened around his mouth and eyes. "It looks wonderful. No need to hide a handsome face like yours."

The foreman chuckled. "You've been teasing me since your first pigtail."

"That was so long ago, Matt. The years have been good for all of us until now. I don't know what we would do without you and the boys."

"Don't worry, Jessie. I'll do all I can to take Navarro's place." The foreman knew she didn't realize the full extent of his words. He wanted this chance to prove himself to Jessie. He wanted to show her he was as brave and smart as that drifter who had so impressed and charmed her.

"No man is as unselfish or honest, or loyal as you are, Matt."

He looked surprised that she had praised him instead of Navarro. Jessie smiled at him. Matt was all those things and more. "You're my partner now."

"I would die defending you, Jessie. You and your family," he added.

The warmth of his smile and mood relaxed Jessie. "You're my best friend, Matt. I know that's strange coming from a girl, but it's true."

Matt secured the last rope in place, then looked at the beautiful redhead. "You're no longer a girl, Jessie; you're a woman, a mighty pretty one."

Jessie laughed and jested, "I didn't know any of you boys ever noticed."

"Pants, boots, guns, and a braid stuffed under your hat don't hide it anymore, Jessie. You've grown up into a really fine woman. I'm proud of you."

"Thanks, Matt. That means a lot coming from you."

The foreman mounted. "Let's head in before they worry about us."

Wednesday morning, Jessie, Matt, and the hands mounted up soon after dawn to ride fence. Tom was given permission to accompany them for a while. Before they broke into groups to check each direction and the scattered stock, a blast came from the eastern section. Everyone glanced that way, then looked around as more explosions sounded from the west and south.

"What was that?" Jed shouted.

All scanned the horizon and listened. The thundering and tramping of thousands of hooves soon reached their ears. Dust clouds rose in all three areas and soon merged into one enormous billowing of flying dirt and grass. It wasn't long before they felt the ground trembling and heard snorts and bawls. Dynamite had spooked the clustered herds around their property and was sending the charging and terrified animals straight toward the settlement. Soon the frantic creatures were in sight. Stock of many sizes, ages, and colors made straight toward them. Longhorns had their heads lowered, and piercing horns aimed at targets in their paths. They dashed at full speed and headlong toward the shocked people, racing wildly and powerfully over everything in their path: bushes, grass, and rocks.

Matt took command in a second. "Let's go head 'em off!"

The foreman, Jessie, Jed, and the men galloped to control the stampeding steers and horses. All knew they had to join the mad rush and ride along the outer edge of the stampede. It would take brave and skilled riding to prevent the stock from trampling anything and anybody in their path, and the herd could be injured or ruined if not checked swiftly. During such a panic, limbs could be broken, horns snapped off, animals gored, and weight lost. Sometimes stock would speed for miles before halting or being halted. The noise of the horde rapidly became deafening and ominous as it closed the distance between men, fence, and beasts.

The men reached the herd and dashed alongside, trying to capture the animals' attention, with familiar voices and songs. Yelling and singing at the top of their lungs, they separated into point, swing, and flank positions, and worked to string out the bunched animals. They were skilled at this task, as cattle often stampeded during drives to market. Sometimes a storm set them off—or thirst, or rustlers, or predators. Or steers with panic habits; those had to be killed or sold to prevent spreading the perilous trait.

In the excitement, Tom kneed his horse and rode to help the men protect his family and property. Gran yelled for him to stop and return but couldn't be heard over the thunderous commotion.

Mary Louise grabbed her arm and shouted, "Let's get into the house before they trample the fence and us, Gran!" She almost dragged the protesting woman from the scene. Both knew what damage the charging beasts could cause.

Jessie's eyes and cheeks stung from the dirt and debris being kicked into her face. Dust choked her, but she kept riding and singing and shouting. Animals nearby were being hooked by long and sharp horns or tripped by entangled hooves. There was no time to think of anything except her task and safety.

Matt spied Tom riding ahead. Suddenly the boy, unskilled at riding and stampedes, was thrown from his horse as it panicked and reared, tossing him to the ground in the path of the charging herd. Matt spurred his mount into a swift run toward the awkward youth who was getting up as quickly as he could. His horse had galloped away, leaving the disabled boy in great peril. Tom began to run clumsily toward the barn, but there was no way he could outdistance the thundering hooves and deadly horns coming at him. Matt reached him, bent over, extended his hand, and yanked the boy over his legs. The foreman guided his horse to the left of the horde just before it trampled the earth where Tom had fallen.

The riders turned the lead steers to the right and began to create a wide circle, turning them into the center of the herd. They kept the tactic up as they gradually tightened the circle. "Milling" was hazardous to the herd so they tried to calm them as rapidly as possible to avoid any more injuries and deaths. When all the animals were traveling in the circle, they gradually slowed their pace. The singing of a hymnal by all finally quieted them.

Matt helped Tom to a seat behind him, and the shaking lad wrapped his arms snugly around his rescuer's waist. Matt told the men, "Water and feed 'em here until they're well rested and calmed. We'll take 'em back to pasture later. Sing 'em a pretty ballad, boys, 'cause they're still nervous. I want guards posted today and tonight. I don't want anything like this happening again."

Jed looked at his son and asked, "What are you doing here, Tom?"

"He took a little spill so I let him ride with me," Matt answered for the boy. "He's a mighty brave one, Jed. Tom, why don't you help the boys sing to the herd? You got a good voice. You can keep Jimmy Joe company." He helped Tom to the wrangler's horse.

The auburn-haired youth smiled at the foreman in gratitude for saving his life and for trying to ward off his father's anger. "Thanks, Matt."

"Help the boys settle 'em good."

"I will. It's all right, ain't it, Pa?"

"Go along, but be careful—and don't get in their way."

As Matt, Jessie, and Jed rode toward the barn, Jed asked, "What happened?"

Matt explained, then said, "He's just eager to help and be like us, Jed. Don't be too hard on him. He has to learn and grow. He won't be a kid much longer."

"He could have gotten you or one of the boys killed trying to save him from his recklessness. I don't want him riding anymore."

"I don't think that's a good idea, Jed. Those moccasins and the stirrup Navarro made for him have given Tom courage and confidence. He needs plenty of both. Life is hard and mean sometimes. We won't always be around to help him or protect him. He's got to learn to take care of himself. With lessons and practice, he'll get better. I'll work with him if you don't mind."

Jessie was glad Matt had been around and was close enough to them to speak his mind. She knew he was right about Tom, and she hoped her father would agree.

Jed took a deep breath and released it with a hiss. "You're right, Matt. Lord knows I would take away that boy's infirmities if I could. I don't want him hurt more, but I suppose he needs to learn to stand on his own."

After her father left them, Jessie met Matt's gaze and said, "You and I have a job to do tonight, partner."

# CHAPTER THIRTEEN

Jessie and Matt skirted the southern boundary of Wilbur Fletcher's land, as most of it lay northeast of the Lane ranch. Wearing dark clothes and riding dark horses, they traveled for hours beneath the crescent moon. Their target—a herd of fine horses—was kept near the eastern side where Fletcher's best grazing land was located.

When they reached the point where the fence angled northward, they followed it at a safe distance. Jessie hoped Fletcher wouldn't think of placing guards in that area. They reached their destination and halted, slipping off their mounts to check their surroundings for sights or sounds of danger. Hearing none, they proceeded to the fence with Matt holding Jessie's hand and guiding their way. It was a strong and reassuring gesture that caused her to lock her fingers around his.

There, in near darkness, Matt grasped Jessie's arm and stopped her from going farther. "Let me check it out first," he whispered. "Wait here."

Jessie sensed that he needed to prove himself to both of them, so she obeyed his soft command. She watched him maneuver through the strands of barbwire that she spread with her gloved hands and boot. Soon, shadows engulfed him. The redhead strained to hear every sound, ready to go to his aid if necessary. Time passed, and she grew worried. Matt was such an important part of her life and she couldn't imagine losing him. If he got killed helping her, she would never forgive herself. She implored God to protect him.

Jessie knew they were taking a big risk, but Fletcher had to be punished. With Navarro gone, she had to take control of the campaign against Fletcher. They couldn't sit back and await their enemy's next strike or simply keep retaliating blow for blow. For now, she didn't know what else they could do.

Matt reached her and talked over the fence. "All clear. No guards around. The herd is still grazing over there. Let's hurry. Stand back while I cut a big gap. You know horses are scared of wire and will balk around it."

Jessie stepped away for Matt to cut several sections. When one end was released, each strand of wire whipped back toward the next imprisoning post. Jessie knew those razor-sharp barbs could tear bad holes in flesh and clothes, so she gave them plenty of room to dance in their freedom. Afterward, she helped Matt gather and toss them aside. With pieces torn from her father's old Indian blankets, Jessie snagged them on a few of the prickly knots to conceal their guilt. She scattered about beads from a broken Apache necklace. "There . . . that should confuse them, especially with us riding unshod horses. Big John will shoe them first thing in the morning. Shouldn't be any trouble for the Indians. All the Apaches and Comanches are gone from this area, except for a few renegades to the west." Before they mounted, she said, "I'm glad you're safe."

"Weren't worried about an old hand like me, were you?"

"Yes, but you aren't old. You only have ten years on me."

"Eleven afore too long," he amended.

They prodded their mounts into the pasture and rode to the horses. They herded the animals to the gap without any problem. Using ropes and whistles and encouraging words, they moved along at a steady pace. Once they were clear of Fletcher's property, they ran the herd faster. They traveled for over an hour toward the east. When they were certain the noise couldn't be heard by their enemy, they fired shots into the air to spook the herd onward. They knew the animals would run for a long time, then locate the grass and water ahead.

"He'll be mighty angry when his men find them missing tomorrow." Matt said grimly. "My pa always told us boys never to make a dangerous man angry, but you have no choice in times like these. It'll take 'em a while, but they should be able to recover all or most of them. Let's get home before light shows our faces."

"Thanks, Matt."

"For what? Tweren't much."

"For saving Tom's life and for helping me tonight."

"Knowing you, Jessie, you would have come alone if I had re-fused."

"Yes, I would have. But I'm glad you agreed. I feel safer with you here."

"I'm not as good with my guns and wits as Navarro, but I'd give my last breath protecting you."

"I know you would; that's why you mean so much to me. Home it is."

Jessie and Matt reached home just as dawn was lighting the land-scape and hinting at a beautiful day. They were exhausted yet elated by their easy success. The smithy joined them at the forge as they dismounted.

"Good morning, Big John. Shoe them as quick as you can. I don't want Fletcher finding unshod horses on Lane land. Thanks for the help."

The black man smiled broadly and revealed snowy teeth. "Yes-sum, Miss Jessie. I'll git a fire het up and have dem hawses ironed afore vittals."

"You can eat first," she encouraged.

"No'm, Miss Jessie. I wants 'em dun afore dat bad man rides over."

"Matt will tell Biscuit Hank to keep a special plate hot and ready for you."

The smithy started his task as he hummed a spiritual song.

"You get some sleep, Jessie. We can tend the chores today."

"You do the same, Matt, at least until noon."

"I don't want to be abed when Fletcher gallops over here."

"He won't, not today. Those clues will fool him for a while. He'll wait to see how that rustling Tuesday and the stampede yesterday affect us. If I've got him figured right, he'll give us a week to watch and worry. Besides, he probably thinks we've sent for the sheriff and soldiers again, so he'll be careful. No need to report to them; Cooper and Graham can't help us."

*   *   *

Jessie was right: Wilbur Fletcher didn't appear until the next Thursday. When he did, it was on horseback and accompanied by Sheriff Toby Cooper. It was five o'clock, and the hands were changing shifts or tending chores. Big John Williams was finishing in the smithy. Biscuit Hank had fed one group of men and nearly had the second serving ready. Miguel, Carlos, Jefferson Clark, and others were unsaddling their horses after riding fence and herd all day. Jimmy Joe, Rusty Jones, and a few others were riding out to take their places as night sentries. Mary Louise was milking the cows. Tom was in the house with Gran who was cooking the evening meal and Matt, Jed, and Jessie were talking near the barn.

Father and daughter walked to where the sheriff, Fletcher, and two men hitched their reins to the corral. Matt and the others gathered around, too.

The lanky lawman looked at the Lanes and their hands. "Jed, boys, I have to ask you a few questions. Mr. Fletcher has made some accusations against you."

"About what this time?" Jessie asked with a disgusted sneer.

"Robbery" came the reply Jed, Jessie, and Matt didn't expect.

"Robbery? Of what?" Jessie inquired in a sarcastic tone.

"His payroll and bank withdrawal. His men were killed and robbed yesterday on the way home from the bank."

Jessie eyed Fletcher, then the sheriff. "You think we did it?"

"The tracks led here, Miss Jessie."

"That's impossible. Fletcher probably hid his money and is trying to frame us for a crime that never happened. How are we supposed to know about his money and travels?"

"You took it because I kept you from getting those sales and loans," the other rancher accused. "You said you'd find another way to survive. It won't be on my money, Jed. Turn it over and I'll have Toby drop the charges."

"We don't have your payroll. We don't steal or murder. None of my men have been off this ranch for a long time. I'll swear that on the Holy Bible."

"You'd swear anything to get back at me and for fifty thousand dollars!"

"Fifty thousand dollars," Jessie murmured, wide-eyed. This was the first time she had seen Fletcher lose his temper. If the theft was for real, she could understand why. "Isn't that a bit much for a small ranch payroll? Something is funny here, Sheriff."

The man glared at the redhead. "I ordered a new bull and stud. They're arriving this week. The man wanted cash."

"Then I'd say he's the only one who knew you'd be withdrawing so much."

"She has a point, Mr. Fletcher."

"She's wrong. The seller wouldn't know when I'd withdraw the cash."

"Neither would we, especially since we didn't know about the purchases."

"If you'll check my account, Sheriff, you'll see I don't have his money."

"No man would be fool enough to deposit stolen money, Jed. You need cash."

"I got plenty until I make my fall sales."

"How?" Fletcher scoffed.

"There are plenty of markets west of here—forts, reservations, mining towns."

Jessie wished her father hadn't mentioned their prospects. Now Fletcher would try to block them, too. She saw the man's brow lift in interest.

"What about that drifter you hired to fight me?"

"He's been gone almost two weeks."

"Why did he leave?" Fletcher asked.

"We had a private disagreement. I fired him. If he was still around, we would have seen him while riding range. We haven't."

"I want my money, Jed."

Mary Louise had ceased her task and joined the group. "We don't have it, Wil— Mr. Fletcher. That drifter left weeks ago as Father said, and none of the other men have left the ranch. We had a terrible stampede here, and my little brother was almost killed. My grandmother and I were in the middle of it, too. The men have been staying close to protect us. I swear this is all true."

Fletcher smiled at the blonde. "I'm sorry to appear so upset, Miss Mary Louise, but it is a great deal of money to lose. I'm relieved none of you were injured during that stampede."

"It would suit you fine if we'd all been killed," Jessie retorted. To the sheriff, she said, "We didn't contact you, sir, because we didn't think you could do anything about it. Dynamite was set off in all directions, and the herds were sent charging toward here. We barely stopped them before they reached the barn."

"Dynamite, you say?"

"Yes, sir."

"Sounds like the same man, or men, who blasted Mr. Fletcher's windmills. I'll check around to see who's been purchasing it."

"I doubt you'll find anything. Fletcher here probably had his hirelings steal it."

"You've a bad tongue on you, Jedidiah Lane."

"Better a bad tongue than a black heart and mind."

"This quarreling won't help matters. It's time we leave. I'll come back when I learn something, Jed."

"*If* you learn something," Jessie corrected the sheriff. "Mr. Fletcher is very clever and determined; but so are we."

That night in her bed, Jessie wondered if Navarro had robbed Fletcher before traveling on. Surely if he was still around, he would have contacted her by now. Torment filled her—the anguish of not knowing where or who he was or the true reason he had deserted her. But she could not bring herself to regret loving him. Navarro had brought her a wild, passionate, and reckless love just when she needed it most. He had made her realize it was time to think of love, marriage, home, and children. If the past few months were all she would ever have of him, now she knew what her life was missing. He had taught her it was time to think of her desires, and the future. She had done her duties and responsibilities for others; it was time to do them for herself.

How, she didn't know yet. Navarro's loss was too fresh and painful. Too, someday he might return to her . . . or for her. Yet, she admitted, there was little hope for that. All he had needed to say was *Wait for me, I love you, I have to leave for a vital reason,* or anything like that. But he had held silent. Whatever had driven him away, he had kept secret. He had accepted her job, done it as long as permitted, and ridden off saying he couldn't ever come back.

Should she, Jessie wondered, allow herself to hope and dream? Could Navarro kill the ghosts that haunted him? Tears slipped from her eyes into her hair as she sensed that whatever stood between them was too strong to forget.

*   *   *

On Saturday night, the sounds of gunfire, breaking glass, and galloping horses shattered the slumber of all on the Lane ranch. Men rushed from the bunkhouse, yanking on clothes and carrying weapons. But it was over; the danger had passed.

Matt and the other hands hurried to the house to see if anyone was hurt. Jed opened the door and shouted they were fine. The men continued on to join him on the porch.

"Damn that bastard! I told him we didn't take his money!"

Gran, Tom, Jessie, and Mary Louise came outside to listen.

The shaking blonde shrieked, "You'll get us all killed, Father, if you don't sell out! Even if it is Mr. Fletcher, we can't win."

"Hush, girl, we aren't backing down now or ever."

"They weren't trying to kill us, little sister. All the bullets were aimed for the tops of the windows. None of us is that tall."

"They still fired at us!" the girl argued. "Go after the sheriff."

"That won't do any good."

"Then send our men after them."

"And let them lure us away like before for a worse reason? We can't trail them at night, and their tracks will be covered by morning."

"I'll post guards around the place," Matt said.

"That's about all we can do," Jed agreed. "Whoever goes on duty, be real careful-like. Jessie might be right about them trying to get us to race after them so they can double back and attack again. Light plenty of lanterns; let them know we're on alert. If he's got men out there watching, the others won't return tonight."

"Tomorrow we can patch the windows until we can get new panes next week," Matt suggested. "It hasn't rained in a long time, but a storm could break any day now."

Jed gazed skyward and remarked, "Weather's been odd this spring. Been too warm and dry for this time of year, and getting hotter every day. The mills and rivers are dropping low. Keep your eye alert, Matt. After that dynamite stunt, a violent thunderstorm could set off another stampede. After all this rustling and the last panic and the shootings, I've lost nigh onto ten thousand head. That's near a three-hundred-thousand-dollar loss at market time, and that bastard is fuming over a mere fifty thousand! We also need to keep the garden watered so we won't lose our crop. I surely hope it rains soon. If it don't we'll be in a bind as tight as Fletcher's."

*   *   *

Sunday night, under a lessening full moon, Jessie and Matt waited until the wee hours of the morning before retaliating. From rifle range and different sides of the house, they rapidly shot out windows in Fletcher's home. Matt rushed to join Jessie at the assigned place.

They mounted and galloped toward safety. Men rushed to pursue them. Before long, they noticed a fiery streak like a shooting star.

Jessie's heart pounded and her blue eyes widened. "It's a flaming arrow! The bastard is signaling somebody ahead of us! He must have taken the idea from that Indian ruse we pulled. We have to hurry before we're cut off."

"They're trying to trap us between forces. Let's head south and return from that way. If we get separated, keep riding southward until it's safe."

"If I slow you or get wounded, don't stop, Matt."

"I'd never leave you behind."

"You must. The law will go easier on a distraught and emotional woman than on you. Promise me you'll obey. It's an order from your boss!"

To settle her down, Matt promised, but he knew he would never obey. He guided them southward to skirt Fletcher's ambush. "They'll head for the ranch to see who's missing. We can't waste time."

As dawn approached, they rode hard and fast. The terrain was a blend of grasslands and rolling hills. The ranch was in the midst of a series of little valleys full of trees and hillocks that was set inside a large valley surrounded by ridges and mountains that were no trouble to cross. Southward and northward were tabletop mesas and more desertlike territory. The flatlands were often dotted by amaranth: roundish green scrubs that broke free of their roots in fall, dried to prickly balls, and tumbled across the landscape forever like restless ghosts. This area was usually tranquil and fragrant; the many wildflowers made it seem as though a special garden had bloomed amidst the harsh surroundings as a gift from heaven. But now the lack of rain had left its mark, mainly in the wilting grass.

As they neared the ranch, they saw Wilbur Fletcher and a band of men nearing the settled area. "Let's sneak in the back of the barn," Jessie whispered. "I have an idea."

It was light now, so they had to be cautious. At the last gate, they unsaddled their horses and let them go free, away from the corral their foe was certain to check for sweaty mounts. They tossed their gear over the fence and hoped they wouldn't be noticed at that distance, as bridles and saddles had been needed for a swift getaway pace. If checked, the damp undersides would expose their recent use.

As the family and hands hurried out to see what the neighbor wanted this early, they slipped to the barn and entered by the back door, then bolted it from the inside. They sneaked to the front door and listened to the talk outside. They peeked through cracks at the hirelings who checked the home and bunkhouse.

"How dare you!" Jed thundered. "Sheriff Cooper will hear of this outrage!"

"Don't fight me on this, Jed!" Fletcher shouted. "I don't want to get tough, but I have to know who's missing. I see all of your men except your foreman. And where is that fiery daughter of yours? Two people attacked me hours ago. They couldn't have beaten us here. I had guards posted along our boundaries. Seems you're caught red-handed this time. What's it worth for me not to have them charged and imprisoned? It's dealing time, Jed; you've lost our battle."

Jessie sensed what was coming and prepared them while Fletcher ranted at her father. She pressed a finger to her lips for silence, then smiled. Matt watched with intrigue as she loosened his shirt from his pants and mussed his brown hair. She unbraided her own, tousled it, and tossed pieces of hay on both their heads and clothes. They exchanged grins.

Jessie opened the barn door and looked outside. The creaking of it caused all eyes to rivet in that direction. Looking as if caught during wanton play, she glanced at her father and shrugged. As she pulled straw from her auburn tresses, she said, "We're in here, Papa. We were . . . talking and haying the cows. We started tussling like children. You know how Matt and I are at times."

As she pushed open the door, Matt was brushing off himself and trying to gain control of his wayward emotions. The intimate illusion she had created was arousing, and he wished it were more than a deception. He hurriedly tucked in his shirt as if he thought no one was noting his action. He jammed his hat over uncombed hair with its telltale gleams of hay. "What's wrong, Boss?" he asked, knowing Jed would grasp their ruse and not be angry. Matt assumed Jed's uneasy demeanor was part of their ploy to mislead Fletcher.

"Mighty early to be cleaning the barn," Jed remarked with a feigned scowl, playing along with their clever stunt. He liked the way they looked and worked together, and was annoyed he hadn't pushed a closer relationship sooner. He didn't know why he hadn't realized before that Matt was perfect for Jessie and the ranch, and the foreman would keep her mind off that drifter should he return.

Jessie saw a curious twinkle in her father's eyes. "Papa, we—"

"Later, Jess. We have other business to handle." Jed turned to his foe and charged, "I know you only came here to see how we took your shooting party Saturday night. You can't trick me by claiming we shot up your home last night. If anybody did, you can see it wasn't us. Get off my property and don't come back. No more offers, 'cause they're useless. And if you ever send your men over here to shoot at my house again, I'll kill you, you sorry bastard."

Fletcher looked confused before he could conceal his surprise. "If everyone's here, it must be that drifter again. You lied about him leaving."

Mary Louise, wearing a pretty dress as usual, vowed, "He's really gone, sir. He tried to ravish me, so Father fired him over two weeks ago."

"The beast," Fletcher murmured, then looked her over as if checking for damage. "Maybe he's the one who's attacking both of us."

"You said shots came from two directions," Carlos reminded him.

"Perhaps he's hired a partner for profit against me and revenge against you."

"That is farfetched, *hombre,*" Miguel scoffed.

"You can see we're all here," Jed told him, "and you can tell none have been gone. Unlike you, we have no unbranded horses or strangers around. As you said, it must be somebody after both of us. We better watch our backs."

"I don't know how, Jed, but I'm sure you're behind the robbery, rustling, and the shooting."

"A third charge now? All you gotta do is send for the sheriff and prove it."

Fletcher's scowl deepened. "I handle my own affairs."

"Is that why you came over with him the other day?" Jessie taunted. "And why you have twenty-five men on payroll for a small ranch? Do you pay them to watch you do your own dirty work? I doubt it, Fletcher."

"You've inherited your father's nature, Miss Jessie, but you won't inherit this ranch. Before long, it will be mine," he warned. "Let's go, men!"

After they rode away, Jessie whooped with delight and hugged Matt. She could not resist planting a kiss on his cheek. "We did it, Matt."

The others, all except Mary Louise, understood the interchange and grinned or chuckled. As the couple hugged and others praised them, she caught on to their ruse. "Congratulations, Jessica; you two fooled them."

"He's too cocky, so he thinks we aren't as smart as him," Jessie said. "And just wait until he tastes our next sour trick. Right, Matt?"

"What is that?" the blonde inquired.

"I don't know. Matt and I haven't made it up yet, but it will be a bitter one." Jessie looked at the nodding foreman, sent him a conspiratorial smile, and squeezed his hand. She felt him return the meaningful gesture with a firm grip.

Monday night, Jed invited Matt to have dinner with them. During the meal, the foreman mentioned that the two men he had sent after the new windowpanes would return tomorrow so the panes could be replaced on Wednesday. They discussed the unusually dry weather once more. Matt told them the irrigation troughs from the well behind the house to the garden would prevent any loss of that crop.

When Mary Louise asked what their next plans against Fletcher were, Jessie replied, "We don't know yet. We have to be careful and sly, because he's on watch now. We have to come up with ways to discourage him. If he sees it's going to be an impossible battle, maybe he'll leave this area. There are plenty of good locations nearer to Fort Davis or on the high plains west of us. I'd like to see him leave Texas altogether."

"If he's guilty, Jessica, he's going to become more and more dangerous. If you two push him too far, those bullets might strike lower next time. I'm scared."

Gran patted her hand and said, "We all are, girl, but we can't let him win."

"If any or all of us are hurt or killed, will your victory be worth it, Father?"

"No Lane has ever been a coward, girl."

"Isn't it better to be a live coward than a dead hero?"

"For some people, it might, little sister, but not for us."

After the meal, Jessie and Matt took a walk. "This may sound awful, Matt," the redhead told him, "but I don't want our plans talked about around Mary Louise. There's something about the way she's acting about Fletcher that makes me nervous. I know she can't be warning him, because there's no opportunity. But I don't like her attitude. It might just suit her fine for him to run us off our land."

Matt grasped Jessie's hand as they strolled. It felt wonderful to touch her, to be with her, and to feel her voice covering him like a warm blanket on a cold night. He halted and placed his hands on her shoulders. Moonlight reflected in her blue eyes as she returned his steady gaze. "I've been here long enough to speak my mind to you and Jed. Even if it hurts, you two expect me to be honest. We're good friends, Jessie, so I'll tell you what has me worried. Have you stopped to wonder what Fletcher and Mary Louise talk about whenever he comes over? She would have time to pass along a few hints if she had a mind to aid him. I've noticed he's been coming around a lot lately."

Jessie reflected on their neighbor's many recent visits. Her sister was alone with the man on most of those occasions. On the few that privacy had been prevented, Mary Louise had spoken openly to their enemy in front of all. The redhead recalled what her sister had said after the robbery and window shooting when Fletcher rushed over, and realized there could have been hidden messages in her words. "I know how devious she can be, Matt, but surely we're wrong to suspect her. If only she weren't so desperate and determined to leave home, I wouldn't have these doubts about her. I do know for certain that she framed Navarro to get rid of him. But did she do it to help Fletcher or to weaken us into giving up?"

"I don't know. I hope we're wrong, Jessie, but watch out for her."

As she had done many times in the past, the redhead wrapped her arms around Matt's waist and rested her head against his chest. Especially tonight, she needed the strength and comfort from her longtime friend. "I'm glad I have you to talk to, Matt. I can trust you with anything."

Matt's hands traveled to her back, then drifted into her hair. She smelled so enticing, and her mood was so mellow now. He enjoyed holding her and sharing anything with her. He wished she realized how much he loved and wanted her, and wished that she felt the same. He knew it was too soon to expose his feelings, that Navarro was still between them. His voice was strained with emotion as he replied, "You can, Jessie; I swear it on my life and honor."

She heard the affection in his tone and felt the arousing effect of their contact. It warmed but worried her. Despite her longtime relationship with Matt and Navarro's desertion, to enjoy Matt's embrace made her feel traitorous to her missing lover. She knew she must pull away. "We'll talk again tomorrow while we're riding range. Good night, Matt."

As the shifts were changing the next morning, gunfire from the northern pasture captured their attention. Matt assigned guards to the house while he and other hands rode to check out the peril. Anticipating more dead steers, Jed and Jessie went along. After a few miles, they saw and heard nothing.

Jessie yelled at them to halt. "It's a trick, Papa! Let's get back home!" She turned Ben and galloped for the house with the men strung out behind her.

Rapid shots told her she was right, and she prodded the paint to a faster pace. The guards at the house had been ordered not to be drawn away from their protective posts for any reason, and they had obeyed.

As Jessie and the others thundered into the yard, Davy shouted, "That way! Something's up!" He pointed toward the eastern pasture closest to the settlement.

The riders headed in that direction. When they reached the villain's targets, it was a horrid sight. The four prize bulls were lying dead on the ground. Jed hurriedly dismounted and approached the huge bodies. He dropped to his knees and stared at them. Tears slipped down his cheeks as his hand stroked the expensive Durham. He balled his fist and shook it in the air as he cursed Wilbur Fletcher.

Jessie took command. "Rusty, see to Papa. Matt, Carlos, Miguel, Jimmy Joe, ride with me. We're going to catch those bastards and kill them." The angle of the bullets revealed the direction from which the shots had come. The five took off southward.

They rode for hours on the fresh trail, but couldn't sight the culprits.

"We'll never catch them!" Matt finally yelled. "They'll keep running as long as we're chasing them!" After the group halted, he suggested, "We better head back before dark."

Jessie glanced southward once more. She knew the foreman was right; those men would continue on into Mexico if necessary to keep from exposing their boss. She lifted her face skyward, closed her eyes, and took a deep breath. As she exhaled, she lowered it and looked at Matt. "I've never been one to believe in violence, but we have no choice now. I don't know if Fletcher was robbed of his stock payment or if it was a lie to frame us, but he hinted about bulls, then murdered ours. If it's dead bulls he wants, then he'll get them."

"That is dangerous, *chica*," Carlos told her. "He will be expecting you."

"I'm learning fast from him, Carlos. Some of you will lure his guards away while Matt and I return his foul deed."

"What will your *padre* say, *amiga?*"

"I don't know, Miguel, but it has to be done. We must meet every challenge Fletcher makes. If we don't he'll win."

"She's right, boys. We can't let this go unpunished."

"Thanks, Matt. We'll make plans back home. I'll come to the chuckhouse after supper," she said, and knew the foreman caught the reason for her caution.

"What do you mean he's gone to confront Fletcher?" Jessie asked Rusty.

"He took off right after you did. He ordered me to take care of the bulls. He has two of the boys with him. I've never seen Jed like that."

It was nearing dusk and they were tired, but Jessie said, "I'm going after him. Papa's in danger. Fletcher will kill him, then claim it was self-defense."

The group hadn't reached the boundary when they intercepted Jed, Walt, and Talbert. They all reined in to talk.

"Why didn't you wait for us, Papa? That was reckless. Fletcher's men could have cut you down and claimed you attacked them."

The weary, dispirited man responded in a strained voice, "I told the bastard I would poison my water, burn my lands, and kill all the stock before I would let him take my life away. I told him I'm hiring as many gunslingers as he has and lining my borders with armed men. We'll shoot any man or horse belonging to him that comes near my place."

Jessie saw that he was too exhausted and depressed to keep his fury at full level. She hated seeing her father like this. But she had enough energy and fury to make up for what Jed had lost today. "What did he say?"

"Didn't bother him at all, Jess. He claims he'll outwait us. Said I would never harm my land. Said I can't afford to keep that many men on payroll long."

"It was easy because he knows it's true, Papa. You could never cut the heart from this land, and we can't afford the high price of gunslingers." Jessie's mind raced to Navarro. She wished he were there to lead them. They needed his wits and skills. Her father was losing hope and courage. Yet, as she had for weeks, she pushed him from her thoughts.

"Let's go home, Papa. You need to rest."

They reached the ranch after dark, a three-quarter moon lighting their way. The others came to greet them and to hear the news. Matt repeated it as Carlos and Miguel took Jed and Jessie's horses to tend. The redhead led her father to the house and handed him a glass of whiskey to settle his nerves.

"What happened this time?" Mary Louise asked.

"I'm sure Wilbur will tell you the next time he sees you. Leave Papa alone tonight. It's been a hard day. I'll help Gran get supper on the table. You come, too," Jessie ordered her sister, not wanting to leave her father to the girl's lack of mercy while his spirits were low.

"Father looks terrible. Tell me what happened," she persisted.

Jessie grasped the blonde's arm and pulled her into the kitchen where she revealed the news, which didn't seem to disturb her at all. "We're lucky Fletcher didn't use their visit as an excuse to kill Papa."

"Don't you think that's odd since you claim he wants to be rid of all of us? It would have been a perfect solution . . . for a guilty man."

Jessie glared at her sister. "He had a reason. A man like him doesn't do anything without a selfish reason." As the words left her lips, similar ones from Navarro the day they met sounded inside her head. She closed her eyes and prayed, *Please come back to us, my love. Wherever you are, hear me and return.*

"Jessica, are you all right?" Mary Louise asked. "You look pale and shaky."

"I'm just tired and angry. Let's eat and get to bed." What she didn't say was that she had a terrible feeling something worse was about to happen.

Big John put in the new panes on Wednesday, and Mary Louise washed them afterward. The hands did their chores in silence, as if some gloom hung over them and the ranch. The day was hot and oppressive, so most blamed the weather for their crazy moods.

While Jessie and Matt were checking on stock, a disheartened Jed rode to the family graveyard—located a little over a mile from the house on a lovely spot near a chapparel—to visit his wife. Alice, their two sons, and his father were buried there. The aging rancher was frightened for the survival of his remaining family. He didn't know if he should risk their lives by holding on here. If he could get Fletcher alone without his many guards, he knew he would kill the man and end this madness. But other matters troubled him, too: Mary Louise's hatred and defiance, Tom's disabilities and his sullenness since Navarro's departure, and the longing for the gunslinger's return that Jessie was trying to hide. He felt guilty over separating her from Navarro. He sank to his knees beside his wife's grave, buried his hands in his face, and prayed for the answers to his problems.

Late in the day, as Jessie was walking toward the house, Matt caught up with her and grasped her hand. Jessie halted and looked at him. Something in his expression told her there was trouble. "What is it, Matt?"

"I'll go with you. I want . . . to see Jed."

Jessie knew the men had told Matt to tag along for a reason, and she realized the hands had acted odd upon their return. Her heart pounded, as she knew something was wrong. She jerked her hand free and ran into the house. Jessie rushed to the kitchen, then glanced into the dining room. She paled and trembled. Her hand covered her mouth and moisture sprang to her eyes. "No," she murmured in anguish, and the tears escaped rapidly down her cheeks.

Matt's arm banded her shoulder. "I'm sorry, Jessie. The boys told me he was . . . dead. I didn't want you to come in here and face this alone."

Jessie left his embrace to walk to the long table where her father's body lay. Her grandmother was lovingly bathing her son to prepare him for burial. Dazed, the white-haired woman sang a hymnal as she worked, as if oblivious to her granddaughter's presence. Jessie's eyes touched the wound in his chest. She knew from experience it was from a knife blade. "What happened?"

Martha Lane continued her chore as if she hadn't heard the girl's words. Jessie looked at her and knew it was best not to press her for answers at this time. "Tom! Mary Louise!" she shouted.

Both came to the kitchen from their rooms. Tom gaped at the sight and buried his face against Jessie's chest and sobbed. Jessie clutched him to her and comforted him.

Mary Louise glanced at her father and remarked, "He killed himself."

Jessie's tears and soothing words halted, and she stared at her sister. Anger flooded her. "How dare you say such a thing, you wicked girl!"

Mary Louise backed away a few steps, looking as if she expected her sister to attack her. "I'm the one who found him, Jessica. I rode to the graveyard to speak with Father about my leaving here. I'm frightened, Jessica. He was lying across Mother's grave. There was a knife in his heart, and he was holding the handle."

"Only because he was trying to pull it out when he died, fool! He was murdered! Fletcher did it. I'll kill him. I swear, I'll kill him!"

"I didn't see anyone there, Jessica. Father's face was still wet with tears. He couldn't have been dead long. If anyone else did it, I would have seen him."

"If you did, you wouldn't tattle! You'd do anything to get away!"

"I know you're upset, Jessica, but don't attack me like this. Even though we didn't get along, he was my father, too."

"I can see how your heart is bleeding over his loss," Jessie scoffed, as the girl didn't appear the least bothered by their parent's death . . . his murder.

"We'll get him buried quickly, then contact Mr. Fletcher about accepting his offer. The sooner we leave here, the better for all of us."

Jessie's light blue eyes enlarged with astonishment. Anger such as she had never felt before consumed her. "You're crazy! I would never sell to that bastard."

"You have no choice. Father is dead. We can't stay here. Be reasonable. I've already started packing. We should move into town tomorrow after the funeral. From there, we can decide where to settle. If you don't want to try it back East, Dallas or San Antonio would be nice."

Jessie stiffened, and she clenched her jaw over and over. "This ranch is mine now, little sister. Go if you wish, but get out of my sight before I punish you as Papa should have!"

"You don't inherit everything, Jessica! Tom and I get something. I want my part so I can leave this awful place. When can you give it to me?"

Matt grabbed the girl's arm and almost shoved her into the parlor. He closed the door to the kitchen and said, "Leave them be! Let them mourn in peace."

"You aren't a member of this family!" she snapped. "Get out of our home!"

Matt had never been tempted to slap a woman until tonight. He had to struggle to control his temper. "I won't let you torment them with your selfishness, girl. If you love your family, settle down."

"So you can walk in and take over Father's place?" Mary Louise sneered.

"I'm responsible for them. I won't let you hurt them more than they're hurting already. How can you be so cruel at a time like this?"

"This is Father's fault. He knew he was going to lose, so he took his life."

"Jed Lane didn't kill himself."

"It looks that way to me. If we don't clear out, we'll be killed, too."

"You just said he killed himself." He pointed out her contradiction.

"He did, but he let this trouble push him to it. Jessica can't run this ranch."

"Yes she can."

"With your help, Mathew Cordell? I know you want her—and the ranch. I won't allow you or anyone to steal what belongs to me."

"Nothing belongs to you, Mary Louise. Jed left it to Jessie."

"She's not an only child, Matt. I have rights, too."

"Do you?" he challenged.

"I'm sure a lawyer will see it my way," she threatened.

"I doubt it. Jed made certain his will was legal. I was with him. He knew you would try to cause trouble when he died so he fixed it so you can't. If I were you, Miss Lane, I would behave myself before Jessie kicks you out with nothing. According to the law, she can do just that."

"You would be delighted to help her do it, wouldn't you?"

"Yep, I would. You've been nothing but heartache to your family since you returned home. You lied about Navarro Jones, and we all know it."

"I should think you would be glad I got rid of him. It opened the door for you to pursue my sister. With him around, you wouldn't stand a chance of winning her."

"Winning a woman through deceit and pain wouldn't be worth much to a real man. If I were you, I'd be scared. Navarro Jones isn't a man to double cross. You better hope he doesn't return now that Jed is gone. Jessie would never make him leave again. A cold and hard gunslinger can find ways of punishing a person without killing him . . . or her. You *did* lie about him, didn't you?"

Mary Louise looked frightened for a time. "Think what you will. I'm packing, because we'll be leaving soon. You'll see," she murmured, then went to her room.

Matt returned to the dining room, where Jessie was helping her grandmother prepare Jed's body. He went to the grieving women and asked how he could help.

"We're almost through here, Matt," Jessie said softly. "Ask Big John to prepare a coffin. We'll bury Papa tomorrow. After this, Fletcher should lay off a while. He'll expect me to panic and sell, so he'll bide his time for a week or so. Can you take care of the ranch for the next few days? I'll have a lot to do."

"Anything you need, Jessie, just ask me or the boys. Jed was a good friend and a good boss. We'll all miss him."

Jessie tried not to cry again, but her heart was aching. She told herself she had to be strong for her brother and grandmother. Death was no stranger to her; she had lost her mother in '70 and her grandfather years before that agonizing day. It was difficult for those left behind to go on without their loved ones. She still missed them, and always would. She knew that time and love and hard work were balms for the heart, but even they didn't help much during the first months. "I put Tom to bed. He's so upset. He and Papa loved each other, but there was always a distance between them. I hope you can spend time with him over the coming weeks. You're his best friend, and it will help him adjust."

"I will, Jessie. What else do you need tonight?"

"You did the most important thing by getting my sister out of here. How can anyone be so cold?"

"I don't know, Jessie. She has problems. If she troubles you again, just call me. I'll take her into town to get her away from here if need be."

"Thanks, Matt. I don't know what we would do without you."

The men had worked hard since receiving the grim news. The coffin was completed and brought to the house. Matt and Rusty helped place the body inside the box in the parlor. They closed but did not nail the coffin.

Tom had finally fallen asleep. Gran was mourning in her room. Mary Louise was plotting in hers. Matt held Jessie in his arms at the front door and comforted her. The men were quiet as the death of Jedidiah Lane settled in on them.

Jessie climbed into her parents' bed, as she could not sleep in the same room with her unfeeling sister. She wept over her father's loss, and the guilt she felt over it. The road before her would be hard; she prayed she had the courage and wits to travel it. She swore revenge on Wilbur Fletcher. She ached for her love's return and comfort.

Where are you, Navarro? I need you. I love you. Please, God, send him back to me.

Yet she remembered his parting words. He had claimed it was too late for them, but wouldn't explain why. He had said that if she didn't hear from him soon, that meant he was gone "for good." He had ridden off shouting, "Forget me!" But how could she stop loving, wanting, and remembering him? It was as if cruel Fate had stolen the two men she loved and needed most.

Jessie rested her head against Matt's strong shoulder. Now she allowed the tears she had kept pent up during the brief ceremony for her family's sake to flow. Long funerals were hard on loved ones, so Jessie had made her father's short.

Gran had taken Tom back to the house in the wagon. Mary Louise had come and gone with them, and had kept her wicked mouth shut today. The men had replaced the earth around the grave and returned to their tasks. Jessie had remained at the gravesite to mourn in privacy, and the foreman had stayed with her.

Matt stroked her unbound hair. He let her grieve in silence. There was little anyone could say or do to bring real comfort during a time like this.

When Jessie mastered her tears and wiped her eyes, she murmured, "It's all my fault, Matt. I should have seen this coming. I knew Fletcher was evil, but I didn't believe he would go this far."

"You're not to blame, Jessie."

She looked up into his gentle eyes and refuted, "Yes, I am. I was the one who kept spurring Papa on. It was my idea to hire Navarro and to attack Fletcher. If I hadn't challenged him, maybe he wouldn't have responded this way."

"What Jed did and said after his bulls were killed is what set Fletcher off."

"But I kept pushing Papa to hold out and to fight back. If I hadn't he might have given in; then he'd still be alive. It wasn't worth his life, Matt."

"Jed needed your courage and wits to keep him strong, Jessie. He depended on you. If he had yielded to Fletcher, he would never have been the same again. What is a man without his pride and honor? Jed was too proud and honest to give up his existence. What's left if we throw away our dreams when the going gets hard or dangerous?"

"But I can't let anyone else get hurt."

"You can't back down now, Jessie," Matt argued. "If good men give in to bad ones, they get stronger and bolder with everyone. Soon, they rule everything. If you surrender, Jessie, the fighting and Jed's death were for nothing. Jed would want you to hold out."

"But what if it's Gran or Tom next—or both? How can I stop him, Matt? Nothing we've done has slowed him. I'm the head of the family now. I must think of their safety and happiness, like I prevented Papa from doing."

"You're thinking through grief, Jessie. You'd be sorry and angry you sold out. It would be too late to expose Fletcher and punish him. At least wait a while before you make any decision. The boys and I will protect you and the others. From now on, we stay armed and on guard every minute."

Jessie glanced at her father's final resting place. She reflected on all he had endured to create this beautiful and prosperous spread. She looked at her surroundings and thought of all her years on the range. This was her home. This was Lane land. She loved it. No one had the right to take it from them. With Mathew Cordell and the hands behind her, she could continue her battle to save it. Matt was right; that is what Jedidiah Lane would want.

Her gaze went to the fresh mound once more. "I didn't get to tell him good-bye or tell him how much I love him. It isn't fair, Matt."

"He knew. He knows, Jessie."

Fury filled her. "I want to know whose knife that was in his heart. It wasn't Papa's. I've never seen one like it. He didn't take his own life."

"It wasn't marked so I don't know how we can discover its owner. We didn't find any tracks, either. Somebody clever concealed them. This is why Fletcher didn't attack Jed on his land; he wanted his body found here and looking like he killed himself."

"Let's get back so I can check on Tom and Gran."

Matt mounted and pulled Jessie up before him, as she was wearing a dress and couldn't ride behind. She laid her head against his chest once more and wrapped her arms around his waist. Matt was so comforting, and she needed his warmth and tenderness. She never stopped to think how contact with her affected him.

Matt glanced down at the woman in his arms. He wished she could stay there forever. He loved her and wanted her with every ounce of strength and emotion he possessed. When her anguish subsided, he would confess his love with the hope she could come to return it one day.

On Monday, Jessie wrote a letter to the Cattlemen's Association and asked for membership as the new owner of the Box L Ranch. She explained their troubles and accused Wilbur Fletcher of being responsible. She told them if they were men of honor and conscience, they would not allow Fletcher to prevent her inclusion in the association or be influenced by his money and status.

She and the hands were kept busy getting stock to water, as several windmills were running low and so was the Calamity River. They had never seen this area so hot and dry this time of year, and they were concerned.

Since Jed's loss, everyone had been quiet and sad. The men hadn't played any practical jokes on each other since that grim day last week. When music was played at the bunkhouse, it was soulful tunes that reflected the men's moods. Yet none of them doubted Jessica Lane's ability to run the ranch, and none quit.

That night, Matt, Carlos, Miguel, and Jimmy Joe sneaked to the adjoining ranch and slit the throats of Fletcher's prized bulls and studs. The ranch hands were accustomed to deft and swift slaughter of beast and fowl; they did their task with merciful quickness and skill that didn't cause the animals to suffer. It was a difficult course to take, but they all agreed with Navarro's blow-for-blow strategy to discourage their enemy. Matt didn't tell Jessie about their action until it was over, as he didn't want her to endanger herself by riding with them.

As she talked with him Tuesday morning, she was astonished to learn of their deed, and knew it had been done with compassionate speed. "That was a brave and generous thing to do, Matt. Thanks. No doubt Fletcher will be rushing over today with hot accusations. I'm ready for him."

But Fletcher didn't appear, and Jessie wondered why not. She also wondered why her sister was doing more than her share of chores without protest. Gran and Tom seemed to be adjusting slowly to the tragedy, but all of them were quiet and tense. Jessie blamed part of it on the inexplicable heat that blazed down on heads and land, greedily sucking the life from water and grass.

As she lay in her father's bed, having moved into his room, Jessie thought, *Wouldn't it be crazy if nature beat us both, Mr. Fletcher? If a drought is in the making, neither of us will have anything of value to sell.*

Dread and alarm attacked Jessie. *Please, God, we've had more than our share of danger and torment. Don't send more burdens to us. Let us find peace and happiness again. We miss Papa so much. Expose his killer. Punish Fletcher for his evil. You're a good and just God, so how can you allow this to happen to us? I want Navarro; I need him. Please guide him back to me. If you can't, then protect him and give him freedom from his torment. I've tried to understand and accept these troubles and losses, but it's so hard to face them alone. I've tried not to become bitter and hard. Please answer our prayers before I do. Protect Matt and the boys. Help Gran and Tom not to suffer so much. As for Mary Louise, Lord, I don't know what to say about her. I know she's the one who found Papa, but she couldn't hate him enough to kill him. I suppose it's wicked of me to have such awful suspicions, but I can't help but mistrust her. Help me in the days to come to do my best for everyone here.*

Wednesday, Fletcher arrived in the company of two men and Sheriff Toby Cooper. His gaze was narrow and hard. His aura was cold and threatening.

Jessie met them and glared at the man responsible for her father's death. "What do you want? Haven't you done enough to us? Get off my land!"

Fletcher scowled at her and the men who gathered around the redhead. "I came to see Jed. My bulls and studs were slaughtered Monday night. I know who did it. Toby is here to investigate. You'll all hang for this outrage."

"Investigate all you like, Sheriff, but not with him here! My father is dead. He was murdered last Wednesday. This ranch is mine now. I'm warning you before witnesses, Fletcher—if you or any of your hirelings ever step foot on Lane land again, I'll take it as a challenge and attack. And I'll kill you, you murdering bastard! You have no reason or right to be here. This ranch isn't for sale; it will never be for sale. Get out and don't come back or you're a dead man!"

CHAPTER FOURTEEN

The sheriff had left yesterday without searching the Box L Ranch or questioning the hands further. As if in grudging acknowledgment of the Lanes' grief, so had Wilbur Fletcher.

Miguel returned from his shift of riding range. He approached Jessie and Matt at the corral. He pushed his sombrero to his back, then rested his hands on his pistols. "Bad news, *amiga:* I saw your sister giving a letter to one of Fletcher's *hombres* riding fence. I hung back. They did not see me."

Jessie looked stunned, then angry. "At least she can't warn him about our plans—because she doesn't know 'em! Let's keep her ignorant. Tell the boys to watch her and report anything suspicious to me or Matt. She's been near perfect lately. She knows better than to give me open trouble before she can get her greedy hands on escape money. I know what she's waiting and watching for—me to fail. She thinks I'll give up soon, sell out, and move. She's wrong."

"She probably wrote Fletcher telling him to be patient while she works on you," the foreman suggested. "He won't. We have to guard the house and barns, and that'll spread us thin on the range. He's done so many things, I can't guess what'll come next. What we need are more men for chores and guards."

"Matt's right, Miguel," she told the Mexican vaquero. "I'll send you or Carlos into town next week to see if any honest ones are for hire. Perhaps we can use my sister's treachery to our advantage with a trap for her new friend."

Jessie scanned the sky and frowned. "This heat is getting terrible. Matt, we should cut the grass in the east pasture before it wilts and dies. We need to have hay on hand if this works into a drought. Tell Big John to check the reaper. It hasn't been used in a long time. Once we get it cut, it'll be safe while it dries. Maybe we can hire more men before we need to gather and bind it."

"If Miguel finds help, they can work on a new storage shed while it's curing on the ground. We'll need to hay again later with our stores burned. If winter's as crazy as spring, no feed could ruin you."

"Let's not take any chances with this. I'll have to prove to everyone that I can run this spread. As soon as I get settled with Fletcher, we'll need to locate new bulls for breeding season. It's going to be a rough year without Papa. I'll need help until I can do it all."

"You don't have to do it all yourself, Jessie. That's what me and the boys are for. Just 'cause you can't do or know a few things doesn't mean you can't run this spread as good or better than your father did. Are you forgetting you gave half and sometimes most of the orders? You were right there with us day and night. You're smart and brave and quick. You were Jed's right hand. Have faith in yourself, boss lady; you can do it."

She had needed those kind words. "Thanks, Matt. I hope so."

Matt gently stroked her cheek. "I know so, Jessie."

"So do I, *amiga.* You will not fail."

She sent them a radiant smile of affection and gratitude. "I'm lucky to have you boys. I don't know how I would survive without any of you."

"What you did yesterday, Jessica, was like a slap to Mr. Fletcher's face. I wrote him a letter of apology and delivered it to one of his men today."

As if that were news to her, Jessie shrieked, "You apologized to the man who murdered our father and is trying to destroy us!"

"If he is guilty, don't you think it's wise to be nice to him?"

"I'd rather cozy up with a rattlesnake!"

"That would be safer, if he's guilty. A snakebite can be treated; death can't. Don't you care about what happens to us—Gran, Tom, and me?"

"Of course I do! But if you say, *if he's guilty* one more time, I'll smack you!"

"Listen to me, big sister: if he's behind all this as you believe, one of us needs to think clearly to deal with him. At least my letter might get us extra time before our enemy strikes again. You need that time to clear your head, Jessica. You can't go around provoking dangerous men. We'll all be killed. Wasn't Father's death enough tragedy for this family? Give up this fight before it's too late for all of us. Please, I urge you to reconsider his fair offer. If you keep attacking him, he might withdraw it, or you might get into trouble with the law. If you go to jail, what then?"

"I haven't been attacking him lately. We didn't steal his payroll or rustle his horses or slaughter his animals. We *did* shoot out his windows, but he did it to us first. Either he lied about those other things or somebody else is after him."

"Who would that be?" Mary Louise asked, and looked worried.

"How should I know? An evil man like Fletcher must have lots of enemies. You can't go around hurting and destroying people without making plenty."

"You think it's that Navarro?"

Jessie glanced at her sister's pale face and wide sapphire eyes. "Worried about him returning to get you for framing him, hmm? It would serve you right for lying."

"I didn't lie! If he hurts me, it will be your fault, Jessica. You brought him here. I'm not to blame for him misinterpreting my good manners."

"If you hadn't been out riding alone, it wouldn't have happened. It was stupid to leave the ranch with all this trouble we're having. One would think you don't consider yourself in any peril from your *friend* Wilbur."

"I don't, because I don't believe any of us are in jeopardy from him. But I *do* believe somebody is after us. A woman can't run this big ranch, Jessica."

The redhead realized her sister was contradicting herself. If Mary Louise didn't believe it was Fletcher, then, she would have been in peril from "somebody" during her ride—unless she had invited along an unsuspecting escort. She didn't point out those slips in anticipation of more. "Have you forgotten you're talking to Jed's 'son'? I've helped run this ranch for years. I know as much as Papa did."

"Do you, Jessica? You haven't had as many years to learn as Father did. And do you think cattlemen will work with a female, especially a young one?"

"They surely will," Martha Lane said from the doorway.

Both women looked at their grandmother. Her lined face and blue eyes appeared calmer today, as did her voice when she said, "Jessie won't have no trouble with any men. They like her and trust her. They'll do business with Jess Lane." Her white hair was in a neat bun at the back of her head and her cotton dress was clean and crisply ironed. Gran dried her gnarled fingers on her apron and joined them. "The good Lord put us all on this earth for a purpose. Jessie's is to take over her pa's place. She's more than capable of running it and prospering because she loves this land like my son did. She has her pa's pride and strength. It's time for you to settle down, Mary Louise. You've been too hard on everyone since you came back, especially on your pa and Jessie. I don't know what spoiled you back East, but you have to cleanse that stain from your soul. Jessie has a lot on her shoulders these days, and we have to pull together."

"What we need to do is leave, Gran," the blonde argued. "It's dangerous for us here with Father gone."

"It was dangerous afore he died, girl, but he didn't give up. Jessie can't either. A Lane was the first man on this land, and a Lane must be the last."

"When Jessica marries, Gran, it won't be Lane anymore. *If* she marries. Because if she keeps up like this, she'll never find a husband. She'll die a spinster, dressing as a man and working as one. I don't want that for me."

"I'll make a deal with you, little sister: behave yourself until this matter is settled, and I'll give you money from our next stock sale and let you go where you please. It'll be enough to support you until you can find a job—or a husband. I can't afford more than that because I have to replace the shed and the bulls, and I have other repairs to make. The more Fletcher costs me, the less I'll have to give you for your escape. If you have any influence over him, get him to back off until you're away safely."

"You'll let me move back East?"

"If that's what you want so badly, yes. You've been ripping at the guts of this family too long. If letting you strike out on your own is the answer to finding peace here again, then go and be happy somewhere else. You certainly haven't been here."

Mary Louise licked her heart-shaped lips. "How much money?"

Jessie controlled her mixture of vexation and joy. "I don't know yet. It depends on how many markets I can find and how much stock I can get to them. Mostly, it depends on Fletcher not preventing my sales and drives."

Eagerness was in her voice as the blonde asked, "When?"

"As soon as possible. I'll work on it next week."

"You promise?"

Jessie made a large X over her heart. "I swear it on my life and honor."

"Then I accept your bargain, big sister."

The two women stared at each other as different and matching emotions filled them.

Captain Graham and a troop of soldiers stopped by near dusk. "We were chasing renegades west of here, so I thought we'd stop by to see how you're doing. Toby told me about Jed's death. I'm real sorry, Miss Jessie. He was a good man. You had any more trouble since then?"

"None yet, but Fletcher will be at us again soon. He won't give up. Why don't you camp here for the night? It might give us another day of reprieve. Some of your men can find bunks with the boys, and the others can use the barn. I'll tell Hank to prepare you a good supper."

"That's real kind of you, Miss Jessie. If there's any—"

"Fire!" Davy shouted as he galloped toward them. "South pasture's ablaze!"

Panic shot through Jessie. "We have to get it out fast. The wind's blowing in this direction. As dry as the grass and mesquites are, it'll spread fast. You know what to do, boys. Let's go."

"We'll help," Captain Graham said. "Tell us what to do."

"Leave some of your men here as guards. Fletcher's skilled at luring us away with trouble so he can attack here. Get everything ready, boys. There isn't much water down that way with this dry spell."

They saw the billowing smoke and leaps of red dancers long before they reached the scene. Range fires were hazardous, as they engulfed anything and everything in their path: stock, structures, fences, and people. They could travel swifter than a speedy landslide and sometimes prevent riders or stock from escaping. The blaze was greedy as it feasted on the nourishing landscape. Where the mesquites were dense, fire created a wall of flames. It licked at wilted vegetation and consumed it, then jumped to its next meal. They knew, if it got worse, it would be impossible to control.

Matt and Jessie shouted orders to the soldiers who joined her hands to battle the roaring blaze. Where it had passed, smoldering wood and blackened land was left behind. Hot air blasted across their faces and bodies. Smoke hindered vision and breathing. This could turn her land into ashes, and Jessie wondered why Fletcher would damage the property he craved.

Horses with plows were used to furrow breaks to prevent the fire's spread. Men labored to groove the endangered area as quickly as possible, and worked to calm the horses that were balking in fear. Between the rows, others set control blazes to battle fire with fire.

Jessie and Matt rode around the waving ocean of flames to see how large and fast it was. Men tossed shovels of smothering dirt or buckets of water from barrels on wagons onto the fiercest sections. Trees and bushes had to be allowed to burn because it was too hot to get close enough to chop them down. Two men drove back and forth between the blaze and the nearest windmill. It took a long time to fill the barrels, as the water table was low.

Jessie was frantic as she watched and listened to the ravaging monster at work. The men couldn't seem to gain control of the surging blaze. Before a break could be finished in one area, the freedom-seeking flames were leaping in another direction as if trying to outsmart and outrun them. The main tasks were stopping the spread northward toward the settlement and westward toward the clustering, terrified stock. The Calamity River—which would protect Fletcher's land from his mischief despite its lowered level—was southeast. Yet they all knew that the farther south one traveled, the hotter and drier the terrain. If the fire got into that area, there was no telling how fast and far it would journey.

Jessie heard the crackling and popping of dry bush and limbs as they fell prey to this vicious predator. She and Matt dismounted and grabbed shovels. They worked with the others to slow its progress. She coughed and sneezed as smoke wafted into her nose and mouth. She yanked off her bandanna and tied it over them, but it didn't make breathing any easier in the searing heat. Her eyes stung and teared; she constantly blinked to clear and soothe them. She knew Ben, her faithful paint, would not panic and leave her in danger in case she had to escape the surging flames. She was grateful the soldiers had arrived in time to help.

Dusk closed in around them, but they didn't need light to see their task. Flames brightened the darkening sky like a million lanterns. Men shouted over the noise of the job at hand, and horses whinnied and pawed the ground in fright. Suddenly a loud crash was heard.

Jessie halted and looked up. It came again, louder and longer. It sounded like tin being shaken violently or the roaring of a cannon in the distance. The heavens bellowed again, then sent lightning zigzagging across it. "A storm!" she shouted, "Hurry, God, with the rain; we need it desperately."

Matt checked the ominous sky. "It's moving in fast, Jessie, without warning. I just hope bolts don't strike and set off more blazes."

"Don't even say that, Matt," she murmured in horror.

The crashing of thunder increased. The wind picked up. More jagged flashes of light flickered across the sky. The noise bammed and echoed across the land. The air seemed to vibrate from it. The volume grew louder and closer. Wisps of dark-auburn hair blew into Jessie's eyes, and she pushed them aside. One boom caused her to jump and gasp. As if sensing their peril, the flames raced to consume as much terrain as possible before nature called a halt.

The arid land seemed to pop and crackle from the heat of the weather and that of the fire. The tension in the air was palpable. The rumbling moved closer and louder. The lightning grew in frequency and length. The wind was brisk, but sultry. Drops of rain began to splatter on them and on the parched and blackened ground. Within minutes, the heavens opened and sent down a deluge of water. Flames sizzled and smoked in protest. Some areas hissed like venomous snakes or furious cats. Blazes died. Quickly soaked, the exhausted and filthy people halted their labors to let nature control itself.

"Pass the word along," Matt shouted. "Gather the equipment and animals. Let's head back. This storm is going to be a bad one. Careful with those tools; we don't want them drawing down lightning. Let's get to cover."

Rain came down in a furious rush. It created black mud that spattered their sooty boots and pants. They were drenched, but shouting joyously in relief. The drops came down so heavy and hard that they could hardly see, even though hats shielded their eyes from the streaming liquid. It didn't help that darkness—now that the fire was snuffed—surrounded them and no moon was in sight. They hurried to collect their tools and get back to shelter.

"Shouldn't be any more trouble tonight, not with this storm raging," Matt remarked as they mounted. "I'll get some of the boys to check on the stock. We don't want this storm setting off another stampede."

"Will you take care of our guests, Matt? Make sure they get cleaned up and fed good. All I want is hot coffee, a long bath, and a cozy bed."

"Everything's fine, Gran. The storm put it out. The Lord gave us plenty of help tonight with those soldiers and rain." As thunder and lightning ripped and roared over the house, Jessie took a deep breath. "It's a bad one."

"Usually is after being so hot and dry this long. You all right, Jessie?"

The redhead hugged her grandmother and smiled, then realized how filthy she was. "I got you dirty, Gran; sorry. I'm doing fine. This will perk up everything and refill our water supply. I was getting worried."

"I know, child, but the good Lord always steps in when we need Him most. We'll make it, Jessie; you'll see. You couldn't have a better man at your side than Matt. He'll help take care of us and the ranch."

Jessie smiled again. "We're lucky he came back after the war. He's the best foreman and friend we could have. You go on to bed. It's late, and I know you're tired. Hank said you helped him cook supper for all the men. Thanks."

"I saved you a plate. It's in the warming oven."

"Sounds good, but I need a bath first. I have to get this smoke and soot out of my hair before I turn in."

"I figured you would. There's water heating and a fire going in Jed's room so you can dry your hair before bed. A nip of whiskey to relax you wouldn't hurt, either."

Jessie laughed. "I had the same idea. I'll get cleaned up, then eat and dry my hair before I sneak a nip. Don't worry about this dirt I'm tracking in; I'll mop it up later."

Jessie kissed Gran's cheek and watched her enter the room across from Mary Louise's. The blonde hadn't come out to check on the fire and its results, and Jessie knew her sister was curled in her bed dreaming of her departure. Mary Louise was a sound sleeper, so the redhead didn't doubt she was slumbering peacefully. Yet, she wanted to check on her brother.

Jessie slipped up the stairs and peeked into his room. Tom had left a lantern low to chase away the darkness. "You asleep?" she whispered.

"Nope. Is it done?" he questioned as he sat up.

Jessie explained what had taken place. "You get to sleep and we'll talk more in the morning. I'm drop-dead tired. I'll hug you tomorrow; if I did now, I'd get you filthy, too. I can't wait to scrub all the dirt off. Good night, Tom."

"Jessie, you think Fletcher will try to kill you too? He knows that me, Gran, and Mary Louise couldn't hold out against him but that you could."

Jessie gazed at his freckled face of concern. His green eyes were squinted to see her better without his glasses. Having removed her soiled gloves, she ruffled his wine-colored hair and coaxed, "Don't worry about me, Tom. Matt and the other men will protect me. We're on guard better now."

The youth hugged her around the waist and nestled his cheek against her stomach. "I wish Navarro was here. He'd kill him for us."

Jessie returned the hug and kissed the top of his head. "So do I, Tom."

The boy looked up at her and asked, "Why did he have to leave?"

"Papa fired him and ordered him off the place, Tom. It was a mistake, but Papa thought he was doing what was best for all of us."

"It was wrong. Mary Louise is bad. She lied. Navarro was my friend."

"I know, Tom, but bad things happen sometimes. You must be brave and strong. Soon we'll defeat Fletcher, and everything will be good again."

"I miss him, Jessie."

She didn't know if he meant their father or Navarro or both. "Me, too, Tom. I'll let you in on a little secret," she whispered, then told him about her bargain with Mary Louise. "I hate for her to leave, but she isn't happy here."

"I'm not sorry. She makes everybody unhappy."

"One day you'll understand her better. She has problems, too, problems inside that we can't see. When she gets them straightened out, she'll be a good person again."

"I hope she don't come back until she's well."

"She won't; I'm sure of it. Now, get to sleep, young man. I love you."

"I love you, too, Jessie. I'll pray like Gran says for you to be safe."

"I can use all the prayers you can send up, Tom. We all can. Good night."

Jessie took a bath in the water closet off the kitchen and washed her hair. She dried herself off and donned a soft nightgown. She nibbled at the food Gran had left for her, then put it aside. She wasn't really hungry. She poured a small glass of her father's finest whiskey and took it to her new room, where she tossed a comforter on the floor before a glowing fire, glad the heat outside had lessened as the storm forced cooling windows shut. She brushed her wet tresses and sipped the fiery liquid. Tom's mention of Navarro had seared her heart as the flames had seared her land.

Jessie remembered she had left her drenched and smelly clothes on the floor in the water closet. She took a candle and went to toss them on the back porch. She unlocked and opened the outside door and dropped them there. Before she could close it, Navarro appeared before her. She did not cry out, but she did almost drop the candle in surprise. Light flickered over his dripping face and soaked garments. She blinked to check her vision.

They stared at each other until a bolt of lightning and clap of thunder startled them back to reality.

Jessie smiled and murmured, "You're home." She went into his arms and sealed her mouth to his. She didn't care that her gown was getting wet. Her heart raced in joy and her body flamed with desire. Another crack of thunder and flash of brilliant light parted them. "Come inside."

He shook his head. "Your father will be furious, Jess."

"He's dead. He was murdered last week." Her eyes filled with tears at the sympathy on his face, but she cut him off before he could speak. "I'm staying in his room now. Let's talk there. So much has happened." She grasped his hand, and they sneaked inside. Jessie locked the bedroom door and turned to let her senses absorb his presence.

She placed the candle on a stand and went into his arms again. "I've missed you so much. I was afraid you'd never come back. It's been weeks."

As he held her, he asked softly, "What happened to your father, Jess?"

She related everything that had taken place since his departure, and felt him tense with anger. By the time she finished, her emotions were running so high that she was crying softly in his embrace. "I needed you so much."

The desperado stroked her damp hair and cuddled her in his arms. "I'm here now, *tsine*. I won't let him hurt you again. I'll kill him this time."

Jessie looked up at him. "Where have you been? I didn't know where or how to reach you."

Navarro's hand pushed her wet hair off her face. "I've been spying on Fletcher's men. I watched them rustle those steers a few days after the trouble with your sister, then followed them to the border. There's a sort of way station across the river. Men were waiting there to take the cattle and drive them on into Mexico. I trailed the others back to Fletcher's ranch and saw him meeting with them. He's guilty all right. I can identify everyone involved, but I can't go to the sheriff. He wouldn't believe me without proof." He took a deep breath. "I got close enough to hear what they were saying. Fletcher was expecting a big payroll delivery the next day, so I ambushed his men and took it off their hands. I buried it just north of your ranch." He described the location in detail.

"If you ever need money, it'll be there. I can't get caught with it. After I robbed his men, I figured it was best to lay low about a week. I wanted to contact you, Jessie, but I knew your father would be furious if I showed my face again. When it was safe, I went back to Fletcher's for more spying. Nothing appeared to be going on, so I headed to town for supplies and ammo while it was quiet. I have to stay ready to pull out after I get him. I rested up at that line shack, then came here to tell you good-bye before I kill him and leave for good."

Jessie went over what had happened after the robbery in greater detail. She tried to ignore what he'd said about leaving. "You can stay as long as you like, Navarro. The ranch is mine now."

He didn't respond to her offer. "When I got here, I saw soldiers standing guard and knew something was wrong. I hung back until everybody rode in and got settled, then put my horse in the far corral where it wouldn't be noticed. My saddle's over the fence. I've been hiding under the back porch until things quieted down in here so I could tap on your window and get your attention. But when I was peeking in the kitchen window to see if anyone was still up, I saw you coming with the candle. I was afraid you'd see a shadow and scream."

"I'll give Mary Louise some of Fletcher's money so she can leave and you can stay," Jessie suggested. "She's afraid you'll return and get her for framing you. She'll be overjoyed to take the money and run."

"That isn't why I can't stay, Jess. I have to get rid of Fletcher and get on the road again. This battle is getting too hot and drawing too much attention."

Attention from whom? she wondered. "I want you to stay and marry me, Navarro. Not to help me with Fletcher, but because I love you and need you."

His face mirrored the agony that attacked him. "I wish I could, Jess, but you don't really know me. I'm a half-breed bastard, a real one. My name is Navarro Breed, if a bastard can use his father's last name. My father was a cold-blooded outlaw, a white man. My mother was Apache. They're both dead. His band was called the Breed gang. They terrorized the Arizona and New Mexico territories for years. My mother worked at a fort washing clothes and cooking for soldiers. When several of them tried to rape her, Carl rescued her and killed them. But he had a selfish motive; he wanted her, and she became his squaw. Morning Tears was beautiful, so he kept her a long time. I wish he hadn't," he said with bitterness.

"From the time I was born until I was six, we lived on the run between jobs they pulled. Or we hung around dirty and wild towns near forts while the men drank and gambled and fought until the money was gone. When I was seven, Carl needed to lay low for a while, so he bought a sutler store at Fort Craig. That was a pretty good time in my life. At least we had a house if not a home. I had food, clothes, safety. I got to attend school and escape into books, like Tom does. But the children were as cruel to a half-breed bastard as they are to someone like Tom, and so were the grownups. But I learned a lot about the white world, and I learned fast. I figured getting head-smart would help me escape my father someday. Years later, Carl was recognized and we had to go on the run again. It was worse than before. He was meaner that time because he had liked his easy life. He never cared about me, but Morning Tears wouldn't let him leave me behind. I would have been better off if they had."

Navarro walked to the hearth and squatted. He gazed into the dying fire. "I helped her tend the horses, cook, wash clothes, clean up after those bastards, and wait on them like a slave. They picked on me all the time—pinching, shoving, and smacking—and called me crude names. They loved calling me 'half-Breed' for the son of 'The Breed,' as the law called him. Carl thought it was funny, thought it would give me backbone and meanness. I never wanted to be like them. I hated them and I hated my father. Sometimes I even hated my mother for being so weak. She endured anything he did to her. When she worked herself into losing her beauty and shape, he started sharing her with his men and treating her worse. Sometimes I tried to defend her or get her to defend herself, but all it got me was a bad licking with a belt. Finally she got the courage to take me and escape to her people—or maybe she was just more afraid of staying. I was twelve. That's when I learned she was the daughter of a famous thief in her tribe. They welcomed her back, because she brought along the loot from Carl's last hold-up. The Apaches do whatever is in their best interest, and they needed money to buy supplies and weapons. Until I was twenty, I lived and trained as an Apache warrior.

"I was a skilled warrior, but they wanted a cunning thief more. My Apache name is Tl'ee K'us; it means Night Cloud. My mother chose it to help me fit in, but I never did. They believe in pure blood, and I didn't have it. I was a loner, an outcast. I supported my mother, but she was ashamed of me. When soldiers attacked the camp, most were killed or taken to a reservation. I escaped and drifted on my own for three years. I worked my way through Colorado, the Dakota Territory, Wyoming, and New Mexico area, but people were the same everywhere. Nobody wanted a half-breed drifter around. I saw deceit and hatred on both sides, more than I saw good on either. While I was resting at one of my father's old hideouts, he showed up."

His eyes hardened and chilled and his body grew taut. "I hated him. I wanted to prove I was a better man, that he couldn't match my new skills. Maybe deep inside I even wanted to have a showdown with him. I could have outdrawn him and his men. I practiced all the time to be the best. Nobody was ever going to use me or hurt me again. The men knew I was faster, so they left me alone. I rode with his gang for a while, until I realized how stupid I was being. Six months later, I was gone and he was dead. I can't say I was or ever will be sorry about that."

Navarro put his hands on Jessie's shoulders and looked into her eyes. "You showed me different, Jess. You showed me goodness, kindness, and honesty. You took away part of the bitterness and anguish I've kept inside for years. You taught me I wasn't worthless. You accepted me for what I am, or what you thought I was. You wanted to bring out the good you believed I had in me. You eased my loneliness and filled my emptiness. You never believed I could be bad. You trusted me. You made me laugh and feel happy. If I hadn't met you, I would be colder, harder, and meaner by now. I'd be that unfeeling gunslinger you mistook me for in San Angelo. You've done all of that for me, but it doesn't change who and what I am. I have devils inside me, so I have to keep moving or they'll eat me alive. I've lived in torment, Jess, and I can't let it do to you what it's done to me. If I stayed, it would. I couldn't stand to see you gobbled up by demons, too."

"I can help free you, Navarro," she promised, hugging him tightly.

"No, Jess, you can't; nobody can. I haven't told you all of it. Before I leave, I will. I owe you the truth and more, but answers are the best I can give."

"I don't care what you've been or done. I know the inside of you, Navarro. Whenever you free yourself, I'll be waiting for your return."

"Don't tie yourself to a burning post, Jess. Your father is gone. Make a new life for yourself. Don't wait for me to come back," he pleaded.

"I understand how you've suffered, Navarro. But miracles happen. Several happened tonight: the soldiers arrived, the rain came, and you returned. Don't give up hope. But I won't pull at you. Just be my friend, and partner . . . and lover until you must go."

"How can you want me after all I just told you?"

"You had no control over your birth or the things that happened to you as a child. The things you did later were because you were hurting and bitter. Whatever you haven't told me yet—I know that's why you can't allow yourself to break free. Most of all, I love you."

Jessie unbuttoned Navarro's wet shirt, freed it from his pants, and peeled it off his broad shoulders. She unfastened his gunbelt and laid it aside. She stood, pulled her gown over her head, and dropped it. Extending a hand to him, she beckoned, "Come to bed, my love. We have so little time left together."

The fugitive took her hand and obeyed. He could not resist the magic and power of her very essence. He let her guide him to the bed, where she lay down. Navarro removed his boots and struggled out of his wet pants, then joined her. He watched the candlelight flicker over her face and body. Her auburn tresses were spread over the pillow. Her skin was soft and rosy bronze. Her gaze seemed a darker blue in the shadows, and it enticed him to do more than stare at her.

"You're so beautiful, Jess." He lowered his head to kiss the tip of her nose, then trailed his lips across her face and down her throat. His quivering fingers traveled over her receptive terrain, and he explored it as never before. He wanted to visit every inch of her ravishing landscape. He wanted to let her know which path he was taking, the way he couldn't in this life. His mouth and hands journeyed over firm mounds and silky valleys and sweet ridges until she trembled with urgency for him to seek his way home.

Jessie's hands wandered over his smooth chest and strong shoulders. They roved his scarred back and taut buttocks. She sent her fingers to play in his damp midnight hair. She pressed his head to her neck and shivered with delight as his lips lavished kisses there. She felt the hard muscles bunched in his arms and across his back. He was a treasure worth fighting for. She grasped his head and guided his searching mouth to hers. She took and gave and shared numerous kisses until she was breathless.

Navarro entered her to brand her as his own, if only for this night. He looked into her lovely face.

Jessie's fingers traced the lines of his brows as she savored the love and desire she saw mirrored in his hazel eyes. She knew with all her being that he loved her and wanted her. Her fingers began a circular trek, memorizing his features: across his left cheek, along his jawline, past his chin, up the other cheek, along his brow, down his nose, and to his full mouth where they teased his lips. His movements were tantalizing and bittersweet. She was torn between wanting to claim the sweet ecstasy that awaited them at the end of this long-awaited journey and wanting their passionate ride to continue forever.

Soon there was no choice in the matter. Their desires ran wild and free. Their kisses and caresses were urgent, demanding, thrilling. Their bodies worked as one; their hearts beat in unison; their spirits soared to heaven together. Ripple after ripple of wondrous sensation washed over them. They didn't even notice the storm outside for love's storm that raged within them, and they savored every moment—every sight, sound, taste, and touch—of each other before resting in each other's arms.

"I love you, Navarro Breed, and I want to share a future with you. Can't you see now that nothing in your past matters to me. Nothing you can ever say will change how much I love you and need you."

"It will, Jess; believe me, it will. Soon, I'll tell you the rest and you'll understand how impossible our situation is."

When Jessie awakened the next morning, Navarro was gone. She knew he had intended to sneak out before dawn so he wouldn't be caught in her room. Yet it would have been so wonderful waking up in his protective and loving arms. She was eager to hear what else he had to tell her; yet she dreaded the truth. She didn't want to think about why he felt he had to go. In all honesty, it didn't matter to her. Whatever he had done or whoever he had been in the past was over. Navarro had changed. He had wanted and needed to do so and he had, but still he vowed it was too late. Something deep within her said it was the truth.

Jessie left the bed and put on her clothes. She donned a lovely dress and left her hair unbound the way Navarro liked it. She glanced out the window and wondered where he was. The rain had stopped, and the day promised to be beautiful. She made her bed, straightened her room, and went to the kitchen.

No one was up in the house yet. She knew they were all tired. As quietly as possible, she slipped out the door. Jessie saw Navarro standing at the corral with Matt, Carlos, and Miguel. She went to join the men. They looked at her as she approached. Matt's gaze lingered the longest on her glowing face.

"Navarro, you're back," she said to him. "It's good to see you. Have the boys told you what's been happening here?"

"Yes, and I told them where I've been." He repeated his tale as if it were the first she had heard of it.

"Thank you, Navarro. We can use your help. Things have been so bad here."

"I'm sorry about your father, Jess. He was a good man."

"Yes, he was. Papa would want me to go on, and I will."

Captain Graham approached and talked for a while. After the officer promised more help if needed, Jessie watched him depart for the fort with his troops.

She noticed how the men easily accepted Navarro's return and were delighted by his success during his absence. She realized none of them believed Mary Louise's accusations, and she was glad. Still, she saw that worried look back in Matt's eyes. Qualms about her wanton secrets nipped at her.

"We're riding back to the fire site to check on the damage," the foreman said. "Navarro's going with us. You want to come along?"

To ease Matt's concern, Jessie smiled and said, "I'll stay here. I have a lot to do. I'm sure Fletcher will stand back to see how that fire scare affects me. If he had men spying on us while we were battling that blaze, he knows soldiers are here. He shouldn't try anything with them around. Hopefully he doesn't know they're gone. Make sure he doesn't get within sighting range of the house. How is the stock faring?"

"No trouble. Some of the boys stayed with them until the storm was over. We'll graze them in other areas until that section grows back."

Jessie made certain she didn't send Navarro too many glances or treat him too special before the foreman and ranch hands. After the men rode off, she returned to the house and joined Gran, Tom, and her sullen sister for breakfast.

Mary Louise finished in a rush, then said she would leave to get her chores done.

Jessie observed her hasty retreat and asked, "Think she's about to slide backward again, Gran? She was awfully chilly this morning."

"She's been strange since she woke up. I think you're right about letting her leave soon. It will be good for all of us to have some peace."

"Me, too," Tom concurred.

"I have a surprise for you, little brother: Navarro is back. He's out with the boys on the range. You can see him later today." She told them what Navarro had been up to. "I didn't want to start a quarrel with Mary Louise until I could tell you two first."

It was only minutes after that news that the blonde rushed into the eating area and shouted, "Why didn't you tell me that gunslinger is back? "You know he hates me! He'll try to hurt me! He can't stay!" Mary Louise shrieked, her sapphire eyes filled with panic as she wrung her hands.

"Why don't you apologize and beg his forgiveness?" Jessie suggested.

The girl scowled in anger. "He wouldn't believe me!"

"Make up a good story to explain your wickedness. You're skilled at that."

"This isn't amusing, Jessica! He's dangerous. Why did he return? How could you hire him again?"

Jessie began her plan. "Navarro's been working secretly for us, little sister."

"Doing what, pray tell?" she scoffed.

"You don't need to worry your pretty head with dangerous business. Just keep to the bargain we made and you'll be gone soon."

"Not soon enough to please me!"

"Navarro won't harm you. He's a good man."

"I don't trust him!"

"Well, I do, and that's what counts around here."

On Saturday, Jessie and most of the hands rode fence and guarded herds. Navarro stayed with Miguel and Carlos, and Matt stuck close to Jessie. Even the bubbly Tom was allowed to ride that morning and he didn't leave Navarro's side. Mary Louise remained out of sight as much as possible. Gran observed everyone with keen eyes.

Tom had just returned to the settlement when trouble struck. Masked riders galloped into the yard and fired in all directions to force everyone to take cover while they did their evil tasks. The irrigation troughs from the well to the garden were roped and torn apart. The wooden V's were dragged and broken, then discarded. Other raiders raced their horses through the garden, trampling and unearthing the tender shoots and vines. They whooped and laughed as they worked to destroy the ranch's food supply.

Gran grabbed a rifle and shot at the villains, wounding one. The men returned the old woman's gunfire, and Gran was forced to take cover. But Tom didn't. He grabbed another rifle and sneaked to the front porch to shoot around the corner. The wounded attacker sent bullets flying in the boy's direction, and one caught Tom in the shoulder. As the merry band galloped away, Gran hurried to check on her grandson, but Mary Louise stayed hidden in her room.

When Jessie and the others returned home, they found Gran and Hank working on a pale and bleeding Tom. The bullet had been removed, and they were bandaging the boy. They explained what happened. Matt and the hands went to check on the damage.

Jessie hovered over her brother and told him how brave he was. Navarro offered encouraging words to both. The redhead saw how nervous her grandmother was, and she finally told her hysterical sister to get out of the room.

"Me and one of the boys should track them pronto," Navarro said.

Matt entered as he was making that suggestion and said, "I'll go with you."

"I'm done here," Hank told them. "I'll get some supplies ready."

Jessie looked at the two special men in her life. "I'm sending Gran, Tom, and Mary Louise into town where they'll be safe until we can settle this for good. Fletcher is getting bolder. He thinks that he can win now that Papa's gone."

Navarro and Matt vowed to stop him, then left together.

Early Sunday morning, the wagon was ready for the trip into town. Tom and Gran were made as comfortable as possible in the rear, with the boy's head in his grandmother's lap and a pillow at her back. Mary Louise sat up front with Davy, while Miguel and Jimmy Joe—excellent shots—rode along as guards.

Jessie kissed Tom and Gran and begged them not to worry. She told her sullen sister good-bye, then waved as the party left. She turned to the remaining men and said, "Let's see what we can do about repairing those troughs and saving the garden. I don't know when Matt and Navarro will return. Rusty and Carlos, you two stand guard. Everybody keep your rifles and pistols handy."

The ground wasn't as muddy as they expected, since the dry earth had sucked up most of the rain. Big John and Jefferson Clark repaired or replaced the troughs. Hank and Jessie worked in the damp soil to replant any seedlings that weren't damaged too badly; they filled in with seeds where plants were beyond recovery. They all knew how important the crop was for fresh vegetables in the summer and fall, then canned or dried ones during the winter and spring. A shortage would be costly or ruinous.

The remaining three men—Talbert, Walt, and Pete—rode range to watch the herd. Jessie had ordered them to return home if more trouble struck. She didn't want them taking chances against greater odds. Stock could be replaced, but men's lives could not. She prayed Fletcher had done enough damage for one week.

Miguel, Jimmy Joe, and Davy returned on Monday. Jessie's family was safe in town. The sheriff had come along, but there was nothing he could do without proof. But Toby Cooper pitched in and helped them that afternoon, then spent the night.

The lawman hadn't left before Navarro and Matt returned on Tuesday. The two men had trailed the raiders farther and farther south until they guessed the band was heading across the Mexican border to lay low for a while. They decided it was best for them to return before another band made the next attack.

Jessie was relieved to see both Navarro and Matt back safely and told them they had made a wise choice. Guards were positioned around the ranch, and the work continued as everyone waited tensely for their foe's next move.

Wednesday evening at dusk, Toby Cooper returned with a letter from Jessie's grandmother. She read it, then looked at Navarro and Matt. "Mary Louise married the bastard," she cried with growing fury. "My sister married Wilbur Fletcher! She's coming home tomorrow to get her things and move over there. It's time for our plan. Sheriff Cooper, if you'll agree, our war can end this week. Listen to what we say; then help us get the evidence you need."

CHAPTER
FIFTEEN

Jessie watched her sister as she packed her belongings. "How could you do this, Mary Louise? You know what kind of man he is."

"Yes, I do. He's rich, educated, handsome, and powerful. And he's most virile," she added with a sly smile. "I told you I was leaving soon. When Wilbur proposed, I jumped at his offer. He'll give me the wonderful life I deserve."

"What will you do when he kills all your family to get this ranch through you?"

"Don't be ridiculous, Jessica. Wilbur is tired of all this bickering and troubles. As soon as he finds a buyer for his ranch, we're moving back East. He has family there and several businesses. I'll have the life I've always wanted."

"He told you he's leaving?"

"Yes, and that's why I married him, among other things."

"You should only marry for love, little sister."

"Oh, I did."

"Love for the wrong things, Mary Louise. You've betrayed us, and maybe gotten us killed. Fletcher is only using you, you little fool."

The blonde's eyes revealed her hateful emotions. "What would you know about love? I have my dream now, so don't try to spoil it. Besides, you can't. If I were you, I'd start looking for a husband. But I hope you don't have eyes for that saddletramp. He won't be around very long. Remember that man who came here one day with

Wilbur? He's an artist. He sketched Navarro Jones's face. Wilbur is having him checked out in every nearby state and territory. We know he's in trouble somewhere. As soon as someone recognizes him, he'll be gone or in prison. You can't share this ranch with a man like him!"

Jessie concealed her distress. "Why would you two think Navarro's in trouble with the law?"

"Wilbur can size up a man better than you two can. He had detectives searching for clues about that mysterious, no-good drifter, but he stopped them when I told him Navarro left. When he discovered the trash had returned, he put them back on the job. It won't be long before somebody shows great interest in your meddling gunslinger. I told Wilbur I had heard him mention Arizona, so he's sending one of his detectives there. I also told him how you two have been attacking him. You were right about me framing Navarro. I knew he was trouble and I was trying to get rid of him."

"You told him about us, and he's letting the matter drop? No way, little sister. How could you put nooses around our necks?"

"My loyalty is to my husband. I decided if I told him the truth, then let you know I had, you'd stop all this foolishness. Besides, Wilbur *isn't* behind it. I asked him not to make charges against you, and he's agreed to please me."

"It doesn't matter what you told him," Jessie insisted. "He can't prove anything against us. The law will think you're lying to help your husband. You wouldn't make a valuable witness against us. Who would believe a traitor and liar like you? No one. You're a bigger and greedier fool than I imagined."

The girl's dark-blue eyes sparkled with anger as she said coldly, "I told you, Jessica: he's letting it all drop and we're moving back East."

"Good, because he can't hurt us anymore. I'm hiring more men next week to ride fence and serve as guards. They'll have orders to shoot any man who trespasses on Lane property. While he was gone, Navarro contacted a man who'll loan me the money I need to repair all the damages your husband has done. He's a very rich gold-miner, and the man owed Navarro a big favor. I'm going into town tomorrow, then I'm meeting him on Saturday to pick up the loan. Navarro also worked out several deals with fort reservations to buy steers until my fall sale. I'm signing contracts in two weeks. Fletcher won't be a threat to me after Saturday. I'll have plenty of money to fight him with and to make this spread the best in the area. The miner is loaning me lots of cash against my fall roundup. I'll have enough money to buy out Fletcher so the next owner won't cause me trouble. We'll be back Saturday night. We're having a big party to celebrate. You'll understand why I can't invite you, *Mrs. Fletcher.''*

"It sounds as if we've both gotten lucky this time, sister dear. I wonder who you'll choose to share that wonderful life with," Mary Louise murmured in a taunting tone.

"Make sure you send me your address and I'll let you know."

Jessie, Navarro, and Matt rode into the town at Fort Davis on Friday. They took a different route and used great caution along the way. As soon as they arrived, they met with Toby Cooper to go over their daring plan. They were pleased to learn the sheriff was willing to assist them.

Since her love's return, Jessie had been unable to find more time alone with him. Tonight was no different, with Mathew Cordell in the room next to hers. She had been willing to chance exposure, but Navarro refused to risk tarnishing her name. What the desperado didn't tell the redhead was that he suspected the foreman was watching them especially closely because of Matt's love for Jessie and his determination to protect her from harm.

Saturday at noon, Jessie and her friends met with a stranger at the hotel, a man whom Toby Cooper had enlisted to aid their ruse. After a short time, she left with Navarro and Matt at her side, both carrying heavy saddlebags. The three mounted and headed for the trail back to the Box L Ranch. They rode in alert silence for half an hour before trouble struck.

At the sound of gunfire and pounding hooves behind them, Matt glanced over his shoulder, then shouted, "Get in front of us, Jessie! Ride hard and fast! We'll guard you! Go, woman!" he yelled when she hesitated. He wished she wasn't with them, but she had insisted on participating in this trap. Matt breathed a bit easier as she obeyed his last words with speed and skill.

Navarro and the worried foreman drew their weapons and, twisting in their saddles, exchanged shots with the gang pursuing them.

Dodging and returning bullets, the three galloped toward the hidden posse of Sheriff Cooper, several deputized men, and a troop of soldiers under Captain Graham. The gang rapidly closed in on them from behind, and all realized they would not make it to help. They and the lawmen had guessed that Fletcher would make his move at least an hour from town. It was evident to Navarro and Matt that it was too perilous not to seek cover and take a defensive stand, as Jessie's life was at stake.

"Take cover, Jess!" Navarro shouted. "We can't outrun them!"

Over the commotion, the redhead heard her lover's command. She slowed and guided her paint into a dense, rocky area, then dismounted. Jessie grabbed her rifle and concealed herself. Soon, the two men joined her.

"Stay down," Matt instructed. "Hopefully the posse will get worried soon and come looking for us. Don't take any chances before help arrives."

The foreman and the gunslinger prepared to defend the woman they loved. Both knew they would sacrifice their lives if need be to save hers, a frightening fact Jessie was aware of too.

Jessie witnessed Matt and Navarro's love and concern for her. She knew she was fortunate to have two men who cared so deeply about her. She didn't want either to come to harm, so she disobeyed to help them fight. She prayed assistance would come quickly, as they were greatly outnumbered.

Navarro and Matt told her to stay down, but she replied, "We need all the firepower we have. Don't worry about me, just think about them."

There wasn't time to argue with the determined female or to be distracted, so the men yielded to her resolve. All saw Wilbur Fletcher and his gang dismount and take cover a good distance from their location. In a loud voice they could hear, their enemy gave orders to his hirelings, who began to work their way closer to the pinned-down group. Men slipped around rocks in several directions.

"They're trying to encircle us and fence us in. They'll tighten our noose fast."

Jessie glanced at Matt, and he was eyeing her as if death was on their horizon. She sent him a smile full of confidence and undisguised affection. He returned it, then focused on the danger surrounding them.

"Take no risks, Jess." Navarro's voice broke into her troubled thoughts.

The redhead sent her love a radiant smile and nodded. "We'll be fine, you two. Surely the others will head our way soon."

"I hope so," Navarro murmured as he picked off another foe.

No one talked as the three faced different directions to protect each other. They heard Fletcher's voice increase in volume and agitation as his men were gunned down one by one. The desperate man worked his way closer to their place of concealment.

Jessie, Matt, and Navarro were unharmed so far, but it was looking bad to all three as more gunmen closed in on them from all sides. Fletcher and his men became more daring but used the protective terrain wisely. Jessie and her men knew there was no way to flee; they were trapped. If their ammunition gave out before the posse came to check on them and join the battle, they were all three dead, and the trio knew it.

"You shouldn't be here, Jessie."

"Yes, I should, Matt. He's after my ranch. He killed my father."

"Matt's right, Jess; we should have handled this danger."

"Don't lose hope, you two," she scolded in a softened tone.

Jessie was right; the large posse arrived with stealth and strength. A fierce gun battle erupted, one in their favor for a change. Their attackers panicked.

Determined not to be caught riding with his vicious hirelings, Wilbur Fletcher fought like a wild man. The gang knew they were exposed and outgunned; they struggled to escape. None made it. The bloody conflict—so long and costly to the Lanes—ended fast, with Wilbur Fletcher lying lifeless in the dirt, and those who survived surrendering their weapons.

As the lawmen and others gathered around the fallen bodies and captives, Jessie made a sweeping gesture and remarked, "There's your proof, Sheriff Cooper. I told you he was behind everything. I'm so glad you believed me and helped set this trap."

Toby Cooper looked at the ground and shifted 'uneasily. "I wanted it over with, Miss Lane," he admitted. "It was hard to believe Wilbur Fletcher could do such things. In all honesty, I expected to unmask somebody else here. You're lucky he decided to ride with them today. Strangers on unbranded horses would still have left questions about their boss's identity."

"There still is an unanswered question," Jessie murmured. "Why did he really want our land? I think it had to do with more than grass and water or expansion."

"I guess we'll never know," Matt commented, looking at their dead enemy.

Jessie nodded agreement. "Everyone all right?" she inquired.

"Only a few minor injuries on our side," Cooper replied. "We'll load these bodies, gather the prisoners, and head back to town. It's over, Miss Lane."

"It would have been over for us, too, if all of you hadn't agreed to help and arrived in the nick of time to save us. Thanks," she said, as she glanced around at the posse and smiled at them. "You can call on us for help anytime you need it."

They chatted as the men carried out the sheriff's orders. Then the lawmen and soldiers took the bodies and captives back to town and to close the lengthy case.

As soon as the posse departed, Jessie hugged and kissed the cheek of her foreman, then her lover. "Thanks, you two. You saved my life, my family, and my home. I couldn't have won this war without you. It's time to start learning how to move onward without Papa."

"You'll do fine, Jessie. You're smart and strong."

"Thanks, Matt, but I'll need you beside me every step of the way." She wanted him to know that Navarro would not push him out of her life and his home.

Navarro witnessed the easy rapport between Jessie Lane and Mathew Cordell; they appeared closer than upon his arrival in March. Envy surged through him as he thought about leaving his love behind with Matt. The foreman would probably stay with her forever.

"Anything wrong, Navarro?" Jessie asked, worried by his strained silence.

"Just tired and tense. We best ride for the ranch. We'll be lucky if we make it before nightfall. I'm happy this trap worked and you're safe. Looks as if my job's done around these parts."

Matt didn't want his rival's forlorn expression to work favorably on Jessie, so he said, "It's good you left Gran and Tom in town until everything is settled and Tom's stronger. Doc said he's healing fine, and doesn't have any permanent damage. That boy doesn't need more trouble in his life."

"Let's ride for home." Jessie said with a sigh. "We can finish talking there. I'm sure the boys are eager to see we made it out alive and well."

*   *   *

At the ranch, Jessie gave her hands the good news and the next day off, except for necessary chores that wouldn't take long. She asked Navarro and Matt to ride with her to Fletcher's home tomorrow to give the news about Fletcher to her sister. Navarro made a suggestion that surprised Jessie and pleased Matt: make the offer she had mentioned to Mary Louise on Thursday. He explained how to do it.

Jessie wished she could find time alone with her love, as she sensed the moment of parting had arrived. But the foreman must have sensed it, too, and stuck to the loner like a stubborn burr to a saddleblanket.

"I'm afraid I have bad news for you, Mary Louise. You were mistaken about your husband and, because of it, you're a widow now. I knew you would tell Fletcher about my loan, stock contracts, and new hands. I also knew he would try to stop them. He's already tried to kill our little brother and I knew he would come after me, too, so his wife could inherit the land he craved. He never intended to sell and move. He lied to you, or you lied to me." Jessie told Mary Louise all about the successful and fatal trap. "He's dead, and the trouble is over."

"You tricked me! You used me!" the shocked female shouted.

"That's right, little traitor. The sheriff and Army believed me, too; that's why they agreed to help expose him. He refused to surrender, so it's his fault he's dead. As for his widow, everyone knows what a treacherous girl you are. I also know now why you were so afraid of Navarro's return. You feared he would tell us how you tried to get him to kill Papa, and me, too, if necessary. How wicked you are! I can't imagine that Lane blood flows in your veins."

"It was only a trick to test his loyalty!" Mary Louise said huffily. "You know I would never hire anyone to kill my own family."

"You sided with Fletcher. How long have you been working with him?"

She glared at Jessie. "I haven't been. I'll admit I tried to pass clues to him, but that's all. I was terrified. I wanted the trouble over before we were hurt or dead. I can't help it if I fell under his spell and married him."

"I can see how grieved you are," Jessie scoffed. "Now, both Lane women are in the cattle business. Yet I fear you don't know enough to survive very long. Even with a good foreman, if you can find a man who'll work for a vile creature like you, you'll lose it all within a year. That's justice, Mary Louise."

"You're mean and cruel, Jessica. I can't stay here alone with these strangers. I don't know who I can trust among the hands. They could rape me and kill me and rob me after you leave. I have to go home with you until I can find a buyer and sell out, then move back East as planned."

"Would you like me to buy this place?" Jessie asked, "There are one hundred thousand acres, about thirty thousand head of stock, this house, and other structures. I'll offer you forty thousand dollars in cash; the balance will come in five-thousand-dollar payments every year until eighty thousand is paid, sooner if I can afford it."

"It's worth more. That isn't even a dollar an acre, and nothing for the cattle and buildings. I want more and I want the entire sale price now."

"But it'll save you the time and effort of searching for another buyer," Jessie countered. "There's no telling how long that will take. Not many men can afford a higher price or will want land dependent upon windmills for water and without room for expansion. The land isn't that good, Mary Louise; I only want it so another Fletcher can't move in and harass me. As for the stock, they'll replace those Fletcher rustled from us, so why should I buy them? Anyway, you don't have that many ready for market; most have years to mature. I'll have to pay men to tend them, feed them in winter and fattening pens at market, and hire drovers to drive them there. And you're forgetting you must be a rich widow now. What about those holdings Fletcher had back East? They must be worth a fortune, so why bleed your own family after all they've suffered from that man? I would imagine he also has a large account at the bank in town."

Jessie saw a glitter in the girl's sapphire eyes and could almost hear her avaricious mind racing in a lucrative direction. "You should be rich beyond your wildest dreams, Widow Fletcher. No matter— it's all I can afford. Forty thousand now and five thousand every year for eight years is a lot of money for support. If you invest it or buy a shop, it will earn you plenty to add to the rest. Are you forgetting I need to rebuild everything *your* husband destroyed? Breeding bulls don't come cheap; neither do sheds and windmills, or barbwire for all the fences he's cut. I'll have to hire seasonal wranglers for the fall roundup and pay for the cattle drive to Dodge. That's expensive and will take months. I know you're anxious to get back East and live in luxury. Maybe your widow's inheritance will sate your cravings for wealth, or you can find another rich husband to lasso back there. Take it or leave it. Let me know when you decide."

Mary Louise halted her sister's departure by yelling, "Wait! Let me think."

Jessie realized it was the hint about Wilbur's holdings back East that had swung the talk in her favor. "Well?" she prodded after the girl paced and mused a while.

"Where did you get so much cash? Is it from the robbery weeks ago?"

"I told you about the loan from Navarro's friend. Your husband and his gang were killed before they could steal it. I borrowed fifty thousand, but I have to keep ten to run the ranch with until fall roundup. It wasn't a gift, so I'll have to repay it." *Why shouldn't I use the bastard's money to buy his land?* Jessie mentally scoffed. *He owes me far more for all he did to us. With stock sales, I can come up with the other forty over eight years. The stock will be worth that much. It's perfect.*

"Are you sure you can come up with the payments? What if you don't succeed with the ranch? I'll be out forty thousand dollars."

"Even if I didn't, isn't forty thousand a lot to earn from such a brief marriage? Besides, you have the remainder of his wealth. Perhaps even a fancy mansion back there."

"I don't trust you, Jessica. You'll try to cheat me just to be mean."

"You know I wouldn't do that. I'll send for our lawyer tomorrow to draw up a legal contract. We can sign it Tuesday in his office. I can pay you; then, you can leave. There's a stage east on Thursday. You can be waiting for it. The sooner you lay claim to your husband's estate, the better. You don't want greedy relatives hearing about his death and rushing in to confiscate your treasures."

Mary Louise didn't think twice before seizing the golden opportunity. "That sounds fine. Let me gather a few things and we can go home."

"You *are* home, Mrs. Fletcher. But I'll leave Matt here to guard you. I want him to check over the remaining men and my new property. If you've forgotten, there are chores to be done here, too. I'll send a few men over tomorrow to stay here until the deal is closed. You'll be fine. You always are."

"What about Gran and Tom? I have to tell them good-bye."

"You did, when you deserted our family to marry our enemy. When Fletcher rode out with his gang, you could have sent word to the boys at the ranch to meet us on the trail to warn us, but you didn't. However, you can say what you like to them after our meeting. Gran and Tom are still in town. Surely you recall that our little brother was almost murdered a week ago. I'm going to fetch them Tuesday. We'll close our deal and go our separate paths. Besides, you need to stay here and pack for your long journey."

"You sure it's safe for me and Matt?"

"Yes, or I wouldn't let him remain behind. Fletcher's gang was different from his hired hands. Perhaps I'll keep some of them. I'll leave that up to my foreman. As soon as the deal's closed, we'll tear down the fence between us."

"You hate me, don't you?"

"No, Mary Louise. You're my sister, but I'm disappointed and angry with you. All you think or care about is yourself. One day you'll be sorry. You've caused us all a lot of pain, and I don't want you around us right now. Lord knows I wish it were different, but it isn't. You have what you wanted, so be happy."

The girl tossed her blonde hair over her shoulder. "I most assuredly will, Jessica. When I'm settled back East, I'll let you know where to send my payments."

"I'm certain you will."

"Tell Matt he can sleep in one of the other bedrooms."

"If you'll promise not to try to frame him like you did Navarro."

The girl frowned. "Whatever would I want with Mathew Cordell?"

"Since Fletcher's the kind of man who appeals to you, I can understand you wouldn't be interested in Matt. He's much too good for a cold and greedy woman like you."

"Don't provoke me into changing my mind, Jessica," she threatened.

"You won't, because it'll keep you here. But I'm warning you, little sister, if you don't sign those papers Tuesday, the deal is off *permanently*. Challenge me on this, and you'll pay heavily. I swear I'll let you flounder and fail to teach you the biggest lesson of your miserable life."

Jessie left the beautifully appointed room of the hacienda-style home. She walked through the walled yard and joined Navarro and Fletcher. "She took the offer. Are you sure you want me to have the money, Navarro?"

"Yes. You deserve it. Fletcher cost your family more. I'll go after it and see you two back at the ranch. My job's over, so I'll be leaving afterward."

Jessie rushed on to conceal her reaction to his words. "I told Mary Louise Matt would stay here tonight." She related the talk with her sister. "Do you mind, Matt? I don't want her coming home, but she *is* my sister. You think it's safe for you to stay here with their boss dead?"

"Navarro and I have looked the place and the men over good. It's all fine, Jessie."

"I'll have Davy and Rusty come over first thing in the morning. You tell the men what to do. Decide which ones you want to keep on, if any."

"I won't let you down, Jessie," the foreman vowed.

"I know, Matt. Thanks." Jessie turned to her lover who seemed to be pretending he wasn't watching her. She sensed how much he hated to leave her and end their relationship, yet she also sensed that he was anxious to depart as quickly as possible. She wished she knew why. "You sure you need to fetch the money tonight?"

Navarro glanced at the horizon and inhaled. "Yep," he replied. "I'll see both of you at the ranch tomorrow. I'll tell everybody good-bye, then ride out." Before Jessie could protest, the fugitive mounted and galloped away.

Matt was pleased that Navarro was still determined to leave, but he couldn't understand why the gunslinger would go. The foreman was certain the other man loved his life at the Box L, as well as Jessica Lane. He couldn't imagine why Navarro would rather return to lonely drifting and gunfighting instead of remaining with a woman who would no doubt marry him, bear his children, and make him a successful rancher and happy man. Something terrible had to be eating at Navarro and pushing him ever onward in search of peace.

To lessen her sadness, Matt coaxed, "Don't worry, Jessie; he'll be fine. Men like Navarro Jones know how to take care of themselves."

"I know, Matt, but he could have a good life here."

"Settling down isn't what he wants or needs, Jessie." He caressed her cheek as he urged, "Don't try to change his mind about leaving; it will hurt both of you. Part as friends; that's what he needs most from all of us right now. If he ever gets wandering out of his blood, he might return," he suggested, hoping Jessie would let the drifter go, and give him time to win her. He couldn't with Navarro present.

"You're right, as usual, Matt. I'll keep quiet. Thanks for the advice."

Matt smiled at Jessie and bid her farewell, glad Navarro would be gone soon.

It was nearing dawn when Navarro returned and placed the money in Jessie's hand. He had ridden all night to accomplish his mission. He looked tired and dejected. "I kept a little to see me to my next job somewhere far away. Your trouble's over, Jess. I have to leave now and I won't be coming back."

Jessie had slept little and her eyes were dark with worry. "Do you really have to go? I need you."

The desperado stared at the floor, then looked at her. "No, Jess, you don't. You're just tired and scared. Your father is gone and the ranch is yours now. In a couple of days, Fletcher's spread will be yours, too. You'll do fine. One day you'll meet a good man and marry him. Forget me, Jess; I'm nothing but trouble."

"How can I forget you? I love you. Please stay. I can make you happy. You can't keep drifting forever. I know you love me and want me, too. Don't be so stubborn and proud. Make your home and peace here with me, with *us* all. Please."

"Don't make it harder for us to part, Jess. I'll never forget what you've done for me. I took this job as a hiding and resting place, but I got too involved with you. I lost my head for a while. We can't settle down together. When your head clears after I'm gone, you'll know this is for the best."

"Will I, Navarro? You're the first man to make me want to be more than Jedidiah Lane's 'son.' You're a special man. How can anyone take your place in my heart and life?"

"Don't *you* be stubborn and spoil things for yourself, Jess. I hope I'm not the last man to make you glad you're a woman, a strong and beautiful and giving woman. Don't ruin the rest of your life because of me. I was wrong to let you believe this could last. I'm sorry I hurt you. If you remember anything about me, remember how well we worked together, what good friends we were."

"*Were*, Navarro?"

"It's past now, Jess, and the past can't be changed. I should know."

"I don't believe you. You said before you wouldn't say anything rather than lie. Now you're trying to pretend nothing important happened between us. That isn't true, and we both know it. I'll wait for you to change your mind. You can't run forever. When you realize that, I'll be here."

"Don't wait, Jess. I won't be back—ever. I can't. I'm a condemned man."

"What do you mean? You said you would explain everything before you left."

Navarro squeezed his eyes shut and inhaled deeply. "I dread this, Jess, but you have to know the dirty truth. I'm wanted for gold robbery, murder, and theft. I didn't commit the robbery, but I was arrested and imprisoned for it. The last time I was with my father, his gang stole a shipment of gold. I was at his hideout packing to leave when the law surrounded the place and attacked. Carl and his men were killed, but I was only wounded. I was tried and sentenced. I told them I wasn't guilty, but they didn't believe me. I spent two and a half years in a brutal prison in Arizona." He told her about the cruelties and deprivations he had endured, and how he had gotten the scars on his back. "I had seventeen and a half years to go. I couldn't take any more. I escaped into the desert one day, but was so weak that they recaptured me. Prison was even worse than the first time. I escaped again last November, but I had to kill the guard beating me. I set a false trail to Colorado, stole that horse and saddle and supplies, and rode this way. I was out four months when I met you. I figured the law was heading in the other direction and I needed rest, so I took your job. I only meant to stay for a little while."

Her hand grasped his. "But you're innocent. You had no choice."

He squeezed it and released it. "The law doesn't see it that way. You hang for murder, Jess. The longer I stay here, the tighter I feel that noose closing around my neck. I have to leave or all of you are in danger. If the law came here, you'd be charged with helping me. I can't do that to you or Tom or Gran. Fletcher sent out those sketches and detectives. Men could be on my trail this minute. If

I'm caught, you'd have to watch me hang. You could lose everything you've fought for because of me. It isn't worth the risk, Jess. None of you would be safe with me around. Think about Tom and Gran, Jess, not about us. Besides, I was raised a wild Apache half-breed. I have trail dust in my boots and blood. I'm not the settling-down kind." He had to discourage her. He could never endanger her and the others just so he could enjoy his dream for a short while. He was angry and bitter. He didn't want to lose her and the life she was offering, but he had no choice. If only he hadn't killed that guard, he might have been able to give himself up, serve his time, and return to her a free man. Maybe he could have straightened out his mess then, but now it was too late. "It's ride or die, Jess. I have to move on."

"I could sell out and we could go with you," Jessie suggested. "Surely there's someplace where we'd all be safe and happy."

"No, Jess. This is your home; you can't give up now. I don't want you all living like I'm forced to live. You and your family and the boys are the only friends I've ever had. Don't ask me to endanger them. You've taught me how precious life is and how good it could be if I didn't have this black cloud over my head. You made me open up and feel things I never have before. They broke me in prison, Jessie, but you gave me back my confidence. You made me care about *how* I survived. I'll try to stay out of trouble and danger from now on. It's been good here, but I won't stay and I won't return. I mean it, Jess."

"Can you forget me, Navarro?"

"I won't even try. Don't want to. My only good memories are of the times with you. But a memory is all you can be to me, and me to you. Accept that, Jess, or you'll be as miserable and bitter as I was for years. I kept fooling myself about what was important and real in life. Don't make that same mistake."

"What's real and important is us, Navarro."

"Don't, Jess, please." For the first time in his life, Navarro wanted to cry. He couldn't reveal any weakness before her. She had to be protected.

"I can help clear you, Navarro. I can get the money to bribe those other guards to silence. I can tell the law what a fine man you are, what you've done for us."

"What good would that do, Jess? I'm guilty! I'm a wanted, hunted man—a killer, an outlaw. You don't know what prison is like. I can't

risk having you sent there as my accomplice. I'd rather die than hurt
you. If the law finds me, it's either more killing as a means to escape
or surrender to the hangman. And I can't risk involving the people
I . . . like most in this world."

"You'll be safe here, Navarro. Arizona is long way off. The boys
like you. They're loyal to me. They'd help me protect you."

"You're forgetting about Fletcher's sketches and his detectives.
None of us would be safe with a condemned man around." He tried
another road to convince her. "I have sand in my boots and the law
on my back. It's riding time. Be strong and never look back, Jess.
Like the wind, I'll always feel you around me."

"You're too hard on yourself, Navarro. I don't care about your
birth or blood."

He had to make her care, or think she did. "You don't care I'm
part savage? You don't care my white blood butchered my Indian
blood and imprisoned the survivors on a filthy reservation? You
don't care I'm a bastard child? A killer?"

"I'm sorry about your mother's death and your father's cruelties."

"Don't be. They never loved me or wanted me."

"I love and want you, Navarro. You're good enough for me.
You're good enough for anyone. Don't be afraid to love, afraid to
take risks to claim happiness."

"I've taken plenty in my life, Jess, and they all hurt me."

She stepped closer to him. "I won't."

He backed away, determined to keep a clear head. "But I *could* hurt
you. I can't chance that, Jess. I left my evil father three times: at
twelve, twenty, and twenty-four. But I was never free of him; his
blood was always flowing in me, making me feel worthless. I saw
him gunned down, and I didn't even shed one tear."

"I don't blame you for feeling that way. But haven't you learned
that not everyone can feel or show love, Navarro? My own sister
is like that, and she didn't endure the harsh things you have. She
had a good life and a family who loved her, but they weren't
enough. Something happens to certain people to make them cold
and hard and selfish. Either your parents never learned about love
and all that goes with it, or things happened in their lives to kill
that emotion. Maybe it was the way they were raised, but you aren't
like them. Sure, you've made mistakes, but you've suffered enough
for them. I don't care if the law is after you."

"I have to care for both our sakes, Jess. I'm not what Miss Jessica

Lane needs. Think of your family and friends and hands. Think of the people you do business with. Think they want to deal with a half-breed bastard? Think we could keep me hidden on the ranch forever? The truth would come out one day, Jess. It's useless. What about children? You want to pass this evil Breed blood and peril on to them?"

"You aren't evil, Navarro. You gave up that kind of life, white and Indian."

"Blood don't leave your body unless you're dead, Jess. Your past can't be rubbed out like a message scratched in the dirt. What could you tell folks when they asked about me? Make up lies? Can you live like that for the rest of your life? Become hard and cold, like me? No, Jess. It isn't fair."

"I'll do whatever I must to have you."

"I'm no good for you or anyone," he stressed.

"You're perfect for me, Navarro Breed."

"You're wrong, blinded, Jess. I used to think it wasn't my fault, but partly it is. I could have run away as a boy. I could have left the Apaches anytime. I could have never returned to my father. Inside, I'm just as bad, selfish, and heartless as my mother and father were."

"Nothing in your past alters my opinion about the man you are today. You've changed, Navarro. Can't you see that? You didn't stay for the money. You aren't giving up what you want now for selfish reasons. Doesn't that tell you something about yourself? If you're selfish and heartless, how can you feel anything for me and the others? Why would our safety mean anything to an evil man? You have cause to be bitter and wary after what you've experienced. You have so much good and gentleness inside. No matter how hard you struggle to hide that, you can't. Don't try, my love. No matter how your parents raised you, you know the difference between right and wrong, between good and bad."

"My father and the Apaches taught me," he murmured, "when you see something you want, you take it and the risks be damned."

"Then why haven't you stolen me?"

"I have, Jess, in some ways."

"Are they enough for you?"

"They have to be. I've done lots of bad things in the past and made lots of enemies along my trail. If I stayed, it would only bring you even more heartache. How could I never step off this ranch or let anyone step onto it for fear of recognizing me? There could be—probably are—wanted posters out on me. You have seasonal hands in the spring and fall; you have cattle drives; you have contact with suppliers. I can't hide out, Jess. We can't seclude ourselves from the outside world. The more you expand, the more likely that someone who has seen my poster will arrive. You're listening, but you're not hearing me, Jess. It's too late for us. It's good-bye this time."

Jessie realized the truth in his tormenting words. She knew she couldn't stop him from leaving, but she would always go on hoping he would return. "No matter what you say, I'll wait for you. The law can't keep searching forever. Go somewhere safe and lay low. When enough time passes, come back to me. You can't change my mind about waiting. Can you love me one last time?"

"No, Jess; it would be too hard on us. Besides, the boys are stirring. There's no time left. You don't need a half-breed bastard outlaw fouling up your new life. You're chasing the wind. Let this wild and dangerous mustang go free to roam alone, or you'll get hurt trying to lasso and break him."

"You'll be back one day, Navarro. I believe that with all my heart. I want you to take something with you to remind you of me."

Navarro waited for her to fetch a locket with her picture inside. It was a tiny painting that she had commissioned for her grandmother's birthday. She opened it and showed it to him. "Would you like to have this?" she offered.

The fugitive took the necklace, stared at his love's image, snapped it shut, and pushed it into his pocket. He couldn't tell her he loved her; that wasn't fair with him deserting her. Anguish knifed his heart as he realized the wonderful life that was being stolen from him. He stroked her unbound hair and caressed her cheek, then dropped his hands to his sides. "I'm sorry, Jess. I'll miss you."

Tears glimmered in her eyes. "I'll miss you, too." She went into his arms and hugged him. "So much," she murmured. She lifted her head and rose on her tiptoes to kiss him. It was a bittersweet kiss that revealed love and torment, and he returned it urgently. She didn't try to cling to him when he pulled away, looked at her, then went and mounted his horse.

Jessie stood on the back porch, returned his last emotion-filled gaze, then watched his departure. She understood and shared his anguish and resentment. Something real and important had entered his life at last, but he couldn't grasp or keep it. This denial was the greatest cruelty of all, but she was helpless to save him. Not once had he said, *I love you,* though she knew it was so. If only she could be as convinced he would return one day. But somehow, a feeling of finality—like that of her father's death weeks ago—surrounded her. For the first time, hopelessness consumed Jessie. Tears escaped her eyes and flowed down her cheeks, and she hurried inside to let them flow freely, knowing her life was riding away from her this glorious day in June.

# CHAPTER
SIXTEEN

On Tuesday, Mary Louise came to the office where Jessie was awaiting her. The lawyer explained the papers and had both women sign them. There were three originals: one for each woman and one for the lawyer's files. Jessie gave her sister forty thousand dollars, and Mary Louise signed she had received it. Both agreed that the balance of payments were due in equal installments each June for eight years. He told them the deal was legal and final, then left them alone to talk.

Since they might never see each other again, Jessie said kindly, "It's done, Mary Louise. Why not part as friends? I love you, and I'm sorry life didn't work out for you here. I hope you'll be happy back East, and please be careful. You're a rich woman, and people might try to take advantage of you. Write us when you get settled."

"Don't be nice when it's too late, Jessica. If you're hoping I'll cancel your debt to me because I'm wealthy now, you're wrong. I'll never come home again. I hated it here. You and Father almost got us all killed."

Jessie was provoked by the girl's hostility. "Papa might still be alive if you hadn't framed Navarro and gotten him fired. If he hadn't been so troubled over his war with Fletcher and with you, he wouldn't have been there alone. You have your freedom and money, so I hope you enjoy them. They carried a big price."

"You fool. Father didn't fire him because of me. He knew I was lying. He did it to keep you and Navarro apart. You're all he's ever cared about and he couldn't risk losing you to another man. If you believed you could win a wild and dangerous man like that drifter, you're crazy. He's selfish and unfeeling. Tell me, what did you give him for this money?" she asked, tapping the bulging bag. "I know he stole it from Wilbur. I'm sure it had a big price, too."

"You're the one who's selfish and unfeeling, Mary Louise. I pity you. One day, money and looks won't be enough to protect you from life or make you happy."

"Says the miserable creature to the rich and respected widow. I'll bet you rolled in the grass with him many times. He's probably waiting for you in your room this very minute for a wild celebration."

"He's gone. His job is done. He left yesterday morning."

"Because you aren't woman enough to hold him. You're too much like Father."

"I'm sorry you resent me so much, little sister. I've suspected it for a long time, but I prayed it wasn't true. If Mama hadn't died when you were so young, maybe you would be different. Maybe you would possess a heart and a conscience. Maybe you would love home and family as the rest of us do."

"Mother's death isn't responsible for the way I am: Father is. He sent me away like unwanted baggage. I was alone and afraid. I made myself tough and smart. Then he forced me back to this savage land. He ignored me and was hateful to me. And to Tom. Only you pleased him and earned his love and respect."

"You're wrong, but I'm still not sure you know why. I'll tell you. Besides your sorry attitude and defiance, you're Mama's reflection. Haven't you noticed that in the mirror? You stare into it enough to have seen the truth. You were a constant reminder of what he lost. It was wrong, but he couldn't help himself. He loved her so much and he was so lonely without her. He loved you, too, but he didn't know how to show it, especially with you being so hateful and cold. The same is true of Tom. Papa blamed himself for Tom's problems. They made him feel helpless. It hurt him to watch Tom suffer. You've done your best to make everyone miserable. Go back East to the life you crave. I hope you find happiness there, and I hope you face the truth before it's too late."

"I will be more than happy; I'll be ecstatic. Wilbur's businesses and fortune are mine now. I'll live in grand style and leisure while you grub in the dirt and smelly manure to eke out a simple life. Be glad I accepted your meager offer until I could get my affairs settled. Be glad my marriage to him profited both of us."

"There's no need for us to continue this destructive talk. If you want to see Gran and Tom, do so; we'll be leaving in an hour. Goodbye, Mary Louise."

"Good-bye, Jessica. You've seen the last of me."

Jessie's intuition told her that last statement wasn't true, and she felt a surge of dread.

The following dawn, Jessie gathered the eggs and released the chickens from their coop so they could go scratching. She milked the cows and set them free in their confining pasture near the barn, then grabbed a pitchfork and tossed hay to the horses kept in the nearby corral. Several hands offered to assist her, but she declined their help. She needed hard work to occupy her mind. So many changes had occurred in her life lately, and she hadn't adjusted to them yet.

Matt witnessed the turmoil in Jessie and let her be without intruding. He went about his business, taking as much of the load as possible off her shoulders. Yet he found himself checking the horizon every so often to see if Navarro Jones was riding back to stake a claim on the woman they both loved.

When he sighted a lone rider that afternoon, he stiffened, but it was only Slim with the mail. He smiled as Slim handed him some letters without dismounting, tipped his hat, and left. He had forgotten this was one of the two days Slim was paid to deliver the mail each month.

Jessie ripped open the letter from the Cattlemen's Association and read it aloud to the foreman. "A little late, but good news," she remarked. "I wonder if I'm the first female rancher they've asked to join them."

"You going to?" he asked, noting the pleased and proud look in her gaze.

"Yep. I want as much power and influence as I can get before another Fletcher comes along. Besides, it's good business. I tried to get Papa to join, but he refused. After those Spanish Fever and Panic scares, I was surprised he didn't. I know it's only been in existence a few years, but banding together will make us all stronger. We'll attend their next meeting in Dodge after the cattle drive."

*   *   *

Thursday, Jessie, Matt, and some of her hands rode to the Bar F Ranch. The foreman selected which men he would keep on their payroll. Some were assigned to tend the pigs, chickens, stock, and garden. The chuckhouse cook was retained to feed them. Miguel and Carlos were asked to be assistant foremen over their new hands. Matt thought it wisest to mix the two sets of cowboys, and divided them between the two settlements as needed.

Jessie walked through the house with Matt. The first floor contained an enormous living area with a fireplace, couch, several chairs, tables with hand-painted oil lamps, costly paintings, fragile vases, a liquor bar with crystal glasses and a fine mirror, masculine desk, and billiard table. She envisioned a loving couple living there, then a happy family. Her mind easily pictured a husband stoking a cozy fire with children playing near its warmth on a wintry day. She imagined the couple snuggled together on the couch after their little ones were tucked in bed—kissing, talking, and sharing everything in their lives. Her mind's eye saw her filling the expensive vases with colorful flowers and filling the lovely lamps with oil.

The dreamy-eyed redhead cleared her tight throat and scolded her wandering thoughts as she realized the face of the man in her fantasy kept fading from Navarro's to Mathew Cordell's! She presumed it was because Matt was a homebody, a rancher, a familiar companion; while Navarro Breed was a camper and a drifter. It was difficult to imagine Navarro being comfortable in a house like this. Jessie cast aside such painful thoughts and comparisons.

She had never seen anything so grand. Matt followed her into a large dining room with Spanish furniture that matched the hacienda style of the house, then into a well-designed kitchen, and finally to a bathing closet on the back porch. They peeked inside and were amazed by the luxury they observed.

"He certainly enjoyed living high and fine, Matt. It's beautiful, all of it."

Matt liked the house and the emotions it stirred within him. He wondered why he wasn't uneasy in this opulent setting that should make a cowpoke feel as corraled as a Sunday suit and a choking necktie. He realized it was because Jessie was with him and because she liked the house, too, and fit perfectly into its surroundings.

Nothing of Fletcher's wicked aura lingered there. It was a tranquil and inviting home, one he would enjoy living in with her.

They went upstairs wide-eyed and in silence. They saw a spacious area with a fireplace to warm the second floor. It opened into two charming guestrooms, an extra room, and finally the master suite. At one end of the large yet intimate suite were a closet and a bathing room, and each had a window facing the front yard. At the other was an inviting, private sitting area. The furniture was massive and dark, but artistically carved. To her surprise, the decor was lovely.

Both gazed at the large bed that looked comfortable and enticing. Both imagined sharing it with a mate and making passionate love there.

Those sensual thoughts stimulated Matt. He walked into the bathing closet and glanced out the front window. He needed to master the runaway emotions that the seductive setting had aroused. He mustn't close in on Jessie until she pulled free of Navarro, and there hadn't been enough time for that. But Matt's romantic fantasy was powerful and tempting, and he yearned to make it a reality.

Jessie observed Matt's broad back and pondered his curious behavior. His body had stiffened, his gaze seemed guilty, and his face looked slightly flushed. Perhaps the intimate setting disquieted him or gave him romantic daydreams similar to those she was experiencing. She noticed how his brown hair teased at his collar and how well his garments fit his muscular frame. He was handsome and appealing, more so than she had ever realized. He would make some lucky woman a fine husband, and he would be a marvelous father. Jessie felt envious of the female who would share such love and happiness, when she herself was so denied. She hoped the woman would be worthy of Mathew Cordell.

Jessie's gaze returned to the bed. She couldn't help but wonder how different it would be to share it with Matt rather Navarro. Her foreman clearly had the traits of a loyal husband and good father. Would a wild and restless drifter like Navarro Breed feel tied down by such responsibilities? Could the fugitive change and settle down, if not for his peril? Her serene mood faded with such worries and doubts.

"Ready to go, Matt?" she asked, needing fresh air and a change of scene.

He turned and smiled. "Yep, but I sure do like it here. A fine home, Jessie."

"Yes, it is, Matt," she admitted. "For the right couple."

Outside, she glanced back at the facade of creamy red-trimmed stucco. Two arched windows were in the dining room and two in the living area. On the second floor, smaller versions were in the same places, in addition to one above the front door. A wall encircled the house, and colorful flowers and bushes were planted in spots along the matching stucco fence. She and Matt walked beneath the arched entrance, then smiled at each other, as if agreeing once more.

"I'll bet Mary Louise hated to leave this house," Jessie said. "Fletcher clearly put a lot of money and effort into it. Get Miguel and Carlos to lock it up for now. I'll decide what to do about it later. I'm sure some of the things inside are very valuable. Tell them to keep an eye on it." She took one last look at the place and left.

On Friday, Jessie wrote her letter of acceptance to the Cattlemen's Association and thanked them for inviting her to join. She related the news of Wilbur Fletcher's death and the circumstances behind it, proving her allegations.

Matt sent Big John Williams to oil the windmills around both properties, and Jefferson Clark went as his assistant. The foreman assigned several men to begin a new hayshed in the pasture and showed them where to construct it. Other hands were put to work on the garden, which was coming back nicely.

Tom was still either in bed or relaxing in a chair until his wound healed completely. Gran fussed over her two grandchildren every day.

As Jessie did the Saturday-afternoon milking, Matt returned from his tasks and joined her. She glanced up and said, "I still miss Sookie and Bess. I guess it's strange how milk cows become like pets. I miss Scout and Buck, too. I'd like to get another dog. You think any of the people in town have one?"

"Next time I go for supplies, I'll check around . . . You doing all right, Jessie?" he added hesitantly.

She caught his meaning. "Yes, but it's hard some days." Her hands halted their milking motions and she glanced at him over the cow's back. He was so kind and thoughtful, and she was grateful to have him. "It was terrible when Mama died, but it was worse with Papa. He and I were closer. His death was so violent, Matt. Do you think he suffered much?"

Matt rested his arms over the cow's back. "I pray not, Jessie. A wound like his usually kills fast. Try not to think about it."

She went back to work. "I can't help it, Matt. I keep wondering if his killer was punished. How do we know the murderer was one of the men with Fletcher that day? He could be free while my father's dead."

"You have to believe he was slain with the others, Jessie, or it'll drive you loco. If he wasn't, he'll get his due some day."

"I guess you're right." Jessie was pained by her recent losses, apprehensive about her enormous responsibilities, and soul-weary after the long struggle for survival and peace. There was so much to do. "Matt, you wouldn't ever . . ."

When she hesitated, the foreman coaxed, "Ever what, Jessie?"

"Leave again, would you? I don't know what I would do if you left me, too. I depend on you so much. You're my strength and courage, my right hand. I trust you for advice. You'd never let me fail or quit. Being with you and talking with you is so comfortable and easy. We've been good friends for a long time, Matt. I just want you to know how much I need you and appreciate you."

"Even if there's another war, I won't desert you, Jessie. I don't have any hankering to see other places. I'm happy here; this is my home and family."

"What about your brother? Do you hear from him much?"

"About once a year. I can't write him 'cause he's always on the move, like Navarro . . . You miss him, don't you?"

"Yes. He was a good friend. He risked a lot to help us. I wish he had stayed. He's a lonely and troubled man. We could have been good for him."

"He was trouble, Jessie. I can't explain how or what, but he had a devil on his back. A man trying to buck one of those off is dangerous to be around."

"You're right again, but I'm sorry you are. Let's drop all this depressing talk. We need to decide what to do about Fletcher's brand. There's no way we can change a bar *F* to a boxed *L*. I guess, just keep them with Fletcher's brand; we have proof of purchase. You still think it's all right for us to leave tomorrow?"

"Yep. The men have their orders. I put Rusty in charge over here,

Miguel and Carlos over there. They have plenty to keep them busy. If there's any minor trouble, we have enough hands to deal with it. We need to get to San Antonio and pick out those new bulls before breeding season. After we choose them, it'll take the boys weeks to drive them home across country."

"I'll be packed and ready to leave early tomorrow. The stage goes out of Fort Stockton at eight Monday morning. We'll be there in three days. That's a lot easier than horseback across country, and a much shorter trip. Maybe we'll have some fun there. Lord knows we need it and deserve it. You take your suit, and I'll take my prettiest dress. We just might kick up our heels, Mister Foreman."

As Jessie stretched out in her bed, assorted images and worries flooded her mind. It had been such a depressing day, and she didn't know why. The meeting with the new men at Fletcher's—no, *her*—ranch had passed without a hitch. Everything was going fine, except for Navarro's departure on Monday.

Yet, a terrible sensation of . . . She didn't know how to explain it, but an awful feeling of doom had attacked her two days ago and still lingered in her mind. She wished she could grasp its meaning, if it had one. Perhaps she was only exhausted and tense.

She must accept losing Navarro, as a life with him was impossible, would always be impossible. His parting words were wise and true. They had been rocks and havens for each other when each needed them desperately. Yet if they weren't meant to share a destiny, why was their love so strong and their separation so painful?

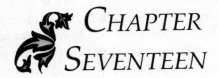

CHAPTER SEVENTEEN

Monday morning, June nineteenth, Jessica Lane and Mathew Cordell climbed into the stagecoach at Fort Stockton. Their horses would be boarded there and retrieved upon their return next week. They had eaten breakfast together, then headed out for San Antonio.

The stage traveled at a slow pace and halted every fifteen miles at swing stations to change teams. They headed eastward to the Pecos River, then southward to the crossing point, passing the ruins of Fort Lancaster on Live Oak Creek that had been evacuated in '61. Early afternoon, they stopped for a light meal, and finally around eight o'clock they pulled into a home station on the right bank of Devils River to spend the night. They could see the nearby ruins of Camp Hudson, deserted in '68. After a hearty meal cooked by the keeper's wife, the passengers went to their assigned places and turned in to sleep.

The bumpy journey continued southeastward after breakfast and followed the same schedule. They headed into the Hill Country where the stage often had to slow for rolling terrain. Hills and peaks were in all directions, and the coach seemed to roll as they did, but not as smoothly. The landscape was dotted with color from blue-bonnets, Indian paintbrush, purplish verbena, daisies, firewheels, cactus, and greenery. Mesquites, junipers, live oaks, and occasional red-buds and willows covered the hills. Sometimes early in the morning or late in the evening, they saw bobcats, javelinas, coyotes, deer, skunks, and badgers. When the stage was slowed by terrain, they even glimpsed rattlers, mice, and spiders. On nearly every bush and rock, a variety of lizards sunned themselves, undisturbed by their passing. It seemed as if this area was alive with vegetation and life, even if it was hot and dusty inside the jarring coach.

On the right side of the Las Moras Creek they passed Fort Clark, established in '52 and still occupied. Heading eastward, they crossed the Nueces River. Nearing eight again, they halted for the night at Uvalde Station near the ruins of Fort Inge on the bank of the Leon River. It was close to the junction of the road to Eagle Pass at the Rio Grande border. Uvalde had been notoriously dangerous in the fifties and sixties, and the driver said it wasn't much better these days. He didn't need to advise the weary, bone-sore passengers to stay at the station and get a good night's sleep. They did.

It was nearing dusk when Matt said, "We'll be there soon, Jessie. Looks like we'll make it without any trouble."

"Good. I'm ready for a nice meal, a hot bath, and a soft bed."

They hadn't traveled as far that day; their progress had been slower because of the hilly countryside. Matt pointed to San Antonio in the distance.

As Jessie watched the town come closer, she remarked, "It's so large. I love it every time I come here. I hope Mr. Turly has some good bulls for sale."

"He always does, so don't worry."

They hadn't talked much during the journey because of the other passengers. They had watched the scenery, and dozed. Reading, as Jessie quickly learned, was impossible because of the bouncing ride. She ached all over, even more than she did after eighteen hours or more in the saddle.

The stagecoach pulled into the station at the edge of town. Matt helped Jessie down. He hired a buggy driver to carry them and their luggage to a hotel. After they registered, they were guided to their rooms. They made plans to bathe, change, and meet for dinner downstairs.

When Jessie came down to join Matt, he was waiting at the base of the steps. His hair was combed and waved from his face and his chocolate eyes were bright with pleasure and admiration. He smiled, revealing white teeth that stood out against his deeply tanned face. His garments—white shirt, black vest, coat, and pants—fit him like a glove, displaying his broad shoulders and trim waist. Mathew Cordell "cut a fine figure," as her Papa used to say.

Enchanted, Matt gazed at the female approaching him. Even though she was beautiful dirty and in work clothes and with a braid, she sure looked different all dressed up. Her auburn tresses were pinned up in lovely curls that bounced when she walked. Her gown was slightly off her shoulders. He found that golden expanse of flesh enticing. The neckline, lower than what she normally wore, made her neck seem longer and silkier. The puffy short sleeves revealed arms that were also golden and firm from hard work. The waist was snug and exposed her slenderness. The flowing skirt moved with her, and he realized how graceful and feminine she was. Never had she appeared more like a ravishing woman than she did tonight. He couldn't take his eyes off her.

Jessie walked around the foreman, eyeing him up and down. She smiled and jested, "We clean up good for ranch hands, Matt."

"You're beautiful, Jessie. I've never seen that dress before, or your hair like that. I'll have to fight the men off you tonight."

Jessie mellowed under his gaze and compliment. She smoothed her skirt as she replied, "Gran made it for me from a Butterick catalogue pattern. This is the first time I've worn it. I love it, but it feels so . . . sinful," she teased as she fingered her bare neck, then laughed. "The woman had her hair this way in the same picture. Does it look all right? I feel strange all trussed up."

"Like I said, beautiful. I've never seen a prettier woman."

She knew he was being sincere. "Thanks, Matt. I had to do something to get me out of the dark hole I've been in lately. I must say, you look handsome yourself. Don't grow a mustache again. You look so good without it."

"Then it's gone forever, Boss Lady. You ready to eat?"

"Starving. It's been a long time since that skimpy meal at two. I want the whole barrel: steak, potatoes, bread, pie, and wine. We deserve to treat ourselves tonight. It's been a long battle, Matt."

He stroked her cheek and urged, "Don't go sad, Jessie."

"You know me so well, Mathew Cordell. I'm trying, really I am. I just need a little more time to get used to all the changes this war with Fletcher brought."

"You will, Jessie, and I'll be there every step to help you."

"That's the only reason I haven't lost courage, Matt. Help me keep from making mistakes. Speak up anytime. You know I trust you and depend on you more than anyone."

"I feel the same way, Jessie. I'll always be right beside you."

Matt guided her into the eating area. Heads turned and eyes widened as they touched on the auburn-haired beauty in her flowing blue gown. Whispers started as people asked who she was. As they skirted one table, Jessie heard a man repeat what the clerk had told him: "She's Miss Jessica Lane from the Box L Ranch. She's the owner. She's knows as much as men, more than some. She's in the Cattlemen's Association. Here to buy bulls. Smart woman. Real tough."

"All that and beautiful, too." Jessie grinned at his friend's response.

The redhead had never thought of herself as beautiful, but from the way the men in the room were staring at her, it seemed to be true. It both surprised and pleased her. As they were seated, men continued to stare at her or glance at her. When she caught their flirtatious gazes, they nodded and smiled. Jessie felt a surge of joy and pride, and a splash of power, wash over her at their reactions. She quickly warned herself not to become vain like her sister, who used her looks as a weapon. She laughed softly. When Matt questioned her, she smiled and whispered, "If they could see me like I usually look, they wouldn't take a second glance."

"You're wrong, Jessie. You look beautiful all the time."

"Sure I do, Matt, even when I'm covered in dirt and sweat in men's clothes."

"Have I ever lied to you?"

"No, but you're prejudiced."

"Am I?" he countered, then grinned.

Jessie looked at his handsome face and gleaming eyes. "Yes, you are, but thanks. If you'll notice, Mr. Cordell, I'm not the only one getting bold looks. I might have to fight off some eager women for your attention tonight."

"No, Jessie, you'd never lose me to another woman."

He seemed so serious. She tried to pass it off lightly. "Good. Let's see if we can get some service. I'm ravenous."

Matt smiled again, then looked over the menu he had been handed.

Jessie fretted over her foreman's reaction to her tonight. She recalled what Mary Louise and Navarro had said about Matt's feelings for her, and that reflection frightened and dismayed her. The man had never made a romantic overture toward her, and she didn't know what she would do if he did. She told herself she was mistaken, that Matt only loved her as a friend, as a girl he had been around since he was eighteen and she was seven. He had worked for her father for four years before going off to the War Between the States for two years, then he'd returned. He had been twenty-four, and she an impressionable thirteen. For the last ten years, he had been the foreman of their ranch. Jessie remembered all the years they had spent together, all the days and nights they had shared. They had been and were still close. She always felt safe around Matt. Although she had had a girlish passion for him years ago, she hadn't thought of him in a romantic way since then. Still, Matt was a handsome and virile man. There were eleven years between them, but it seemed less of a difference as the years passed. He had been a quiet, soft-spoken, serious, and reserved man—until Navarro's arrival on the scene. Now, it was as if he had been jarred awake, as if he had felt threatened by . . . Yes, a rival for her! No matter, her heart belonged to Navarro Breed, wherever he was.

As the pleasant and relaxing evening continued, Jessie found herself watching and listening to Mathew Cordell with great interest. It was strange how she had never seen or thought of him in this light before. Matt had always been there, always dependable, loyal, and hardworking, and always in the background. Lordy, she did not want to hurt him. She prayed that he didn't love her or want her, even though that would pinch her heart a mite. But it had only been ten days since Navarro had left, and she still couldn't believe she had lost him forever.

No, her heart cried, not forever. Yet Jessie realized the hopelessness of their situation. She remembered: "Don't wait, Jess. I won't be back, ever. I can't." She feared she had seen Navarro for the last time.

"Jessie? Is something wrong?" Matt asked for the second time.

The redhead looked at him and shook her head, causing her pinned curls to shimmer. "Just thinking about the past. I have to stop doing that. Sorry, Matt."

*   *   *

At Mr. Turly's breeding ranch, Jessie and Matt looked over the bulls he showed them. The bloodlines were excellent. They examined the animals' noses, ears, mouths, eyes, hooves, and bodies; they found all parts healthy. The man related his prices, then left the couple to speak privately and to take a final look at his superior stock.

When Turley rejoined them at the pens, Jessie said, "I'll take two of the Durhams and two of the Herefords." She pointed out which ones she wanted. "We've worked with Durhams, Booths, and Galloways before, but I hear others are having great luck with the Herefords. They're a fine-looking critter."

"Wise choices, Miss Lane. Some of the best breeding is being done between Herefords and longhorns. The meat is top grade and brings in a higher dollar."

Jessie eyed the white-faces, short horns, and red hide of the breed. "I believe you said the Durhams were two thousand each and the Herefords one each. That's six thousand dollars. Is it all right to send it with my men when they come for the bulls? I didn't want to travel on the stage with so much cash."

"The Herefords are younger; they'll need another year to fully mature for breeding. We have a deal. We'll sign the papers today. I trust you, Miss Lane. I've dealt with Jed many times. I'm sure sorry to hear he's gone. From the way he always bragged on his Jess, I'm sure you'll do fine."

"Thank you, Mr. Turly. Papa taught me a lot, and I have Matt to help me remember it all and do things right. I'll send the boys over as soon as I return home. They should arrive during the first week of the month."

Jessie and Matt spent two nights at the Uvalde and Devils River stations again. On the last day of their journey toward Fort Stockton, tired and sleepy, she dozed, her head falling against the foreman's shoulder.

Careful not to awaken her, Matt shifted toward the slumbering woman, slipped his right arm around her shoulder, and eased her head against his chest and neck. It felt good when Jessie snuggled closer to him and her temple nestled near his collarbone. Her left arm was between them and her hand lay on his right thigh. As she slept deeper, the redhead's right hand and arm moved across his lap and remained on his thigh. Her unbound tresses teased over Matt's hand and arm and against his chin. Jessie's familiar cologne wafted into his nose, and her body was warm next to his. As the stage jostled them, her left breast rubbed against his rib cage and he nearly jumped out of his skin.

Although the coach held six people and he was in the back left corner, Matt soon felt as if he and Jessie were alone somewhere, especially with his head leaning against the wood and with his eyes closed. His dreamy mind shut out all the surrounding sounds except her soft breathing. He felt the heat of her breath against his chest. He let his thirsting senses absorb the many sensations of Jessie. It was wonderful having her in his arms. He had longed for this moment for years, always loving her from a distance. But he had been afraid to approach her, unable to risk another tormenting rejection like the one that had driven him west at eighteen. He also hadn't wanted to back Jessie into a corner with an unwanted overture. Maybe it was time to take that risk. He yearned to kiss her. He could think of nothing more fulfilling than making love to her. He was in paradise, and he hoped the journey and her slumber would continue a long time.

The longer it lasted, the more Mathew Cordell was tantalized and enflamed. Sweat beaded on his face and dampened his entire body. He was as hot as a poker left in a roaring fire. His hands itched to stroke her silky hair and body, and it was a struggle to control those impulses. He wanted her so much, but feared how she would respond to his pursuit. Jessie was a unique woman: smart, honest, dependable, giving, and plenty of fun. When she smiled or laughed, tingles ran over him. It felt good just to be around her. He loved watching her do anything; she always enjoyed herself and did her best. He had seen her happy and sad, losing and winning, a playful tomboy and a ravishing woman, courageous and scared, gentle and tough.

As the yells from the jehu—driver—jingling harnesses, creaking coach, and pounding hooves stirred her foggy mind, Jessie found herself cuddled in Matt's arms. She was so drowsy and relaxed that she didn't care what the passengers thought of her behavior. It felt good to be held in strong, loving arms. That thought jarred her sluggish mind to reality. She straightened herself and squirmed to loosen her stiff body. She glanced at Matt, grinned, and said in close to a whisper, as others were sleeping, "You make a good pillow.

Sorry if I squashed you. I didn't realize I was so exhausted. I'll be glad to get home. How much farther?"

Matt removed his arm from her shoulder and flexed as much as the coach space allowed. "About two hours. Our last stop is coming up soon. When we get home, you should take it easy for a while. You're been working too hard."

"There's so much to do, Matt."

"You have plenty of hands for chores and plenty of time until roundup."

"I hope everything is all right at home."

He smiled and coaxed, "Don't worry; I'm sure it is."

Jessie was eager to get there. She hoped Navarro had changed his mind and returned. If not, perhaps there was a letter from him. Of course, she wouldn't get it until the end of the month when the man brought their mail during his semimonthly delivery. She doubted if one would come this soon from her sister. Yet, she wondered how both were and *where* they were.

Jessie and Matt reached the Box L spread before dark on Monday. The ride by horseback across terrain that was partly desert had been long and tiring. When they dismounted, jovial hands came to greet them and question their mission. Gran and Tom hurried to join the merry group.

Jessie told them about the deal with Turly. "I want Jimmy Joe, Jefferson, and Walt to go after them. You two are skilled with stubborn beasts, and Jimmy Joe will make a good guard for the bulls and money. I'll send it with you boys. It's six thousand dollars, so be careful with it."

"Guard it with our hides and souls, Jessie," the grinning towhead replied.

"That's why I chose you," she teased in return. "Everything all right?"

"Couldn't much be better, Jessie. No problems. Those boys on the Bar F are doin' fine. We'll haveta get used to peace ag'in."

"I just wish Papa were here to enjoy it with us."

"We does, too, Miss Jessie. We gots dem mills oiled an' spinnin' good."

"Thanks, Big John. If you boys will excuse me, I'm falling in my tracks. Thanks, all of you. As soon as the fall sale is over, you'll all get a five-dollar raise."

*   *   *

In the house, Jessie hugged her Grandmother and scolded her brother in a soft tone, "You shouldn't be up and about yet, Tom. I want that shoulder healed perfect before you go to pulling at it."

"I ain't no baby, Jessie. It's about well. I can help out now."

"Not yet, young man. It's only been three weeks, and it was a bad wound."

"Aw, Jessie, let me outta the house. I ain't no chicken to be cooped up."

"No, you're a brave young man. I won't scold you for being rash, because what you did that day took courage and wits. You and Gran probably scared those men off before they could ruin the entire garden. I'm proud of you, Tom."

"You are, Jessie?"

"You know I am. You're going to be a big help to me. We'll have to work hard to make this spread one of the best. You're old enough to start doing other things, but you have some learning to do first. Matt's going to help you. Is that all right, Thomas Lane?"

"More than all right, Jessie. I can be like a regular hand, can't I?"

"If you don't lag on your studies."

He caught her hint. "Yes, ma'am. I'll do both good. I promise."

Jessie touseled his auburn hair. "You best start with cleaning those glasses so you can see, young man. They're covered with dust and greasy fingerprints. I'm taking you with me on my next trip to a large town. We'll see if we can't get a better pair. Matt also suggested we talk to a bootmaker to see if he can make boots like those moccasins Navarro made."

"Real shoes?" he said in excitement.

Jessie wished she hadn't mentioned her love's name. "If it's possible."

"You think Navarro's coming back, Jessie?"

As the three of them sat down to eat, Jessie replied, "No, Tom, not ever. I'll tell you a secret you can't share with anyone. Anyone, Tom," she stressed, and saw she had his full attention and her grandmother's, too, whom she trusted with her life. "Navarro did some bad things when he was younger and got into trouble. The law is after him. That's why he couldn't stay long and can't come back. He doesn't want to get us into trouble for hiding him and helping him."

"Navarro wouldn't do nothing bad, Jessie. The law's wrong."

"Yes, it is, Tom, but he can't prove it."

"We finally proved Fletcher was bad. Navarro can find a way to clear himself."

Before taking a bite, Jessie refuted, "It isn't that simple for him, Tom. He got tangled up with the wrong men. When the law came to arrest the guilty ones, Navarro was with them at their hideout. The others were killed in a shootout, and the evidence of the robbery was there. No one is alive who can clear Navarro of those charges. He was tried and sent to jail. It was awful there, he said. He was beaten and starved. He busted out and was on the run when we met in San Angelo. He needed a place to hide and rest for a while; that's why he accepted my job offer."

"It ain't true, Jessie. He liked us. He helped us," the boy argued.

"Yes, he did. He does care about us. That's why he stayed so long. He hated to leave, but he had no choice."

"We coulda hid him and helped him."

Jessie put down her fork and explained about Fletcher's sketch and the detectives. "Don't you see, Tom? He was in even more danger than before, and so were we if he stayed and they came after him. He didn't want a shoot-out here."

"It ain't fair! He's my friend. I miss him."

"Me, too, Tom, but life isn't always fair."

"I know that. Look at me," he scoffed, slapping the leg with its bad foot.

"Don't get down on yourself again. Navarro liked you. Life hasn't been fair to him, either, but he's doing the best he can to survive. He wouldn't want you to hurt over him. I only wanted you to know why it seemed like he deserted us."

"It ain't his fault, Jessie."

"No, he isn't to blame, except for making mistakes that entrapped him. Just remember the fine things about him and all the good times you shared. There's nothing else we can do, Tom. I'm sorry it has to be this way."

"We can tell 'em how good he is. We haveta do something."

"If they didn't believe us, then they'd know where to start looking for him. It could help them track him down. They might think we know where he went. We can't risk more trouble, Tom. We can't make things worse for him."

"You know where he is?"

"No, honestly I don't." Jessie returned to her meal and drink.

"When did he tell you all about himself, Jessie?" Gran asked.

"He talked to me before he left, Gran. He wanted me to know why he couldn't stay. It was very hard for him to confess the truth. When I hired him, I suspected something was wrong, but I didn't care. We needed him, and I felt I could trust him, and I wasn't wrong. Navarro isn't guilty of that gold robbery. They shouldn't have tortured him. In his place, I would have done anything to escape and to stay free."

"I figured he was in some kind of trouble, too. A real shame. I liked that boy. I'm sure he's had a rough life." Gran passed the biscuits and gravy to Tom. "Eat, you two, before supper gets cold."

Jessie nibbled on the fried chicken. She cut a piece of biscuit smothered in gravy and put it in her mouth. It was so strange not having her father and sister around . . . and her lover. As she chewed, she realized that henceforth everything was her responsibility and duty. It was scary. What if another disaster struck? Could she handle it alone? Life was back to hard work with no special love to hold her in strong, passionate arms. Navarro had made her into a woman, and she wanted to remain one. She wanted children, love, a husband; and she wanted them all with the handsome fugitive. But—

For the second time, Gran asked, "Jessie, did you hear me?"

After swallowing the milk in her mouth, the distracted redhead asked, "What?"

She repeated her request. "Tell me about your trip with Matt."

Jessie smiled and said, "It was fun, Gran. I needed the diversion. I wore my new dress." And she happily told them all about her journey.

The next morning, Jessie sent the three men and six thousand dollars to San Antonio. She stood at the corral with the foreman and watched them depart.

No mail had arrived from Mary Louise or Navarro Breed.

July Fourth dawned clear and hot. Many of the hands were given the day off to go into town for the celebration. It was to be a big one, as America was one hundred years old. Matt was going in the buckboard and taking Gran and Tom. They all balked when Jessie said she wasn't accompanying them.

"Please go on," Jessie told them. "It's getting late. You want to make town before dusk. I don't feel well enough to make the trip. Something I ate Sunday didn't agree with me. Don't worry; I'm just tired and run down. I just plan to lie around resting and reading. I might even do some sewing; I have a few things that need repairs."

"Come with us, Jessie. You can lie in the back until we reach town. I'll bet you'd be better by then. Don't miss the fun," her brother urged.

"I felt awful yesterday and last night, Tom. If it didn't pass by the time we reached town, I'd have a terrible day. I don't want to take such a long and hot ride to sit in a hotel room being sick. I'd rather suffer here."

"I'll stay with you," her grandmother offered.

"No, Gran. You go and look at the material that came in last week. Tom needs new shirts. He's growing faster than the yearlings. And we want to make those curtains for the kitchen. We also can use fresh vegetables. Our garden has a ways to go after what Fletcher's boys did to it. And we'll need more canning jars soon. Go and shop. Then Matt and Tom can help you with the packages. You need a diversion, too. Please."

"You're right, child. We do need some things. Take care of yourself today."

Jessie kissed her cheek and promised she would.

As the others climbed into the buckboard, Matt approached her and asked, "You sure you'll be all right here alone? What if somebody comes?"

Jessie grasped his worry about Navarro. "I'll be fine, Matt. Some of the boys are around. I'd really like to be alone for a while. I need to get some things clear and settled in my head. There have been a lot of changes in my life, too much too fast. I need to think and plan."

"I see. I'll take care of Gran and Tom, then. Get rested. I'll bring you a surprise."

Jessie wandered around the house. it was so quiet with her grandmother and brother gone. Her father had been dead for six weeks, and his loss had not become any easier to accept. Navarro had been gone for three weeks, and it seemed forever. She missed them both terribly. She even missed her sister and wondered if the girl was all right. She couldn't imagine how it would be if anything happened to Gran or to Tom.

She felt lonely and denied. Life could be cruel at times. She wished this house was filled with her own family's laughter. She wished a baby were nestled in her arms and her husband at her side. With all hope gone for winning Navarro, what was she supposed to do? His words haunted her: "I won't be coming back. I'm not the settling-down kind. Be strong and never look back. Don't ruin the rest of your life because of me." If he wasn't to be the man in her life, who was? When? How? Surely God wouldn't leave her alone, as her father had been after losing her mother. Now she truly knew how lonely and heartsick Jed had been.

But Navarro wasn't dead. How could she forget him and fall in love with someone else? How could she marry another man and make passionate love to him as she had to the fugitive who had stolen her heart? Yet, since she couldn't spend her life with him— a reality she had to accept—she must look elsewhere for a loving mate, as Jessica Lane *was* the settling-down kind. She was in her mid-twenties, and life's clock wouldn't halt while she healed a broken heart.

Jessie's stomach churned. She told herself to worry over this matter later.

Matt, Gran, Tom, and the hands returned the following day. Her brother was elated over the new dog in his arms.

"His name's Clem, Jessie. Mrs. Mobley was going to live with her sister in North Carolina. She couldn't take him with her." Tom laughed and dodged the countless licks that the mongrel tried to put on his freckled face.

Jessie patted the creature's head and grinned. "He's sure lively. Hello, Clem."

The new pet was quick; he lavished moisture on her hand before she could move it. Jessie laughed at the ticklish antics and rubbed the pup's head. "You'll like it here, Clem. Lots of room to run around and play with Tom."

"Can he sleep with me tonight, Jessie? He stayed inside with Mrs. Mobley."

Jessie studied the energetic brown-and-white dog. She saw how Tom's eyes gleamed with happiness and new life. "If you give him a good bath first. You don't want a bed of fleas."

Tom hurried off with Biscuit Hank to tend to that chore.

Matt helped them carry the packages into the house. While Gran was putting away her things, Jessie looked at the foreman. "Thanks, Matt," she said.

"You're welcome, Jessie. I bumped into Mrs. Mobley and mentioned we were looking for a dog. She begged me to take Clem and give him a good home. I didn't think you'd mind getting a grown dog instead of a puppy."

"Not at all. Tom loves him already. It'll be good for him to have a pet to tend. It'll take his mind off everything that's happened."

"How are you?" he inquired, concern evident in his voice.

"Fine today. I needed that time alone. Thanks."

"You don't have to thank me for everything I do for you."

Jessie hugged him and kissed his cheek. "Yes, I do. How else can you know I'm grateful? If I started taking you for granted, you'd look elsewhere for a job."

"Never." He playfully yanked on her long braid. "I know how you feel. You have eyes and a smile that do a lot of talking—do it better than most words can."

"That's 'cause you've been around me so long and know me so well. I'll have to remember I can't keep secrets from you," she jested.

"No need to, Jessie; you can trust me with anything."

She gazed into his serious eyes and said, "I know, Matt, and thanks." The moment the word left her lips, they both laughed.

Gran returned and asked, "What's so funny?"

"Nothing, Gran," she said, then winked at the grinning foreman. "How about taking supper with us, Matt? You can all tell me about the doings in town."

Two days later, the hands were assigned to check the stock for screwworms. Every summer, their navels, noses, and wounds were examined for the pest that could sicken them. Any found with the larva were treated.

Jessie rode with Matt almost every day for exercise and distraction. She wondered when and if this feeling of emptiness would leave her. She warned herself she must come to terms with the changes she could not control. She knew Matt was doing his best to draw her out of her low mood, and sometimes he did make her laugh and forget for a while. But when she was alone or a certain task or object reminded her of Navarro or her father, it was difficult not to sink into her dark and lonely pit again.

On July fourteenth, the bulls and hands arrived from San Antonio. Everyone gathered around to look the beasts over and to congratulate Jessie for excellent choices. For a time, she was filled with pleasure, pride, and excitement, and she laughed and joked with the men like she used to.

Later, a letter was delivered from Mary Louise Fletcher in Boston. It briefly related her trip, her new address, and how glorious her life was in "civilization" and luxury. The blonde told them that everything she had dreamed of was coming true for her. An unbidden twinge of envy pinched at Jessie's nerves.

"Well, at least she's out of our hair and happy," Jessie remarked to Gran.

"Or she claims she is. Mary Louise would never tell us if things weren't working out for her, not after the way that girl fought to get there. It's been so quiet and peaceful lately. Even with chores, it's almost lazy living."

"I guess that's why I've been feeling so sluggish for the past week. We worked hard and long to get rid of Fletcher. We're back to routine now. Matt's giving most of the orders and taking the burdens and fears off my back. He almost makes it seem as if the ranch is running itself. The men aren't having any problems or complaints, not even those Bar F boys we took on."

Gran laughed and teased, "You almost make peace sound boring, Jessie. You need to get some excitement and happiness back inside you, child."

"That's easy to say, Gran, but so hard to do. Sometimes I feel so lonely, and edgy and listless. Everything is work, or planning future work. I want to have some fun, like Mary Louise. Not the kind she's having, but . . ."

"Why don't you have a party? That'll liven up this place."

Jessie sank into a chair and exhaled as if exhausted. "It's too soon after Papa's death, Gran. It wouldn't be respectful. Besides, I want people to take me seriously. I have to prove I can run this ranch."

Martha walked to her side and stroked Jessie's hair with a wrinkled hand. "You're not Jed's son, child. You're a woman. You have the right to behave and feel like one. Don't try so hard to prove you're strong and tough. You *are,* Jessie, and it will show to others. Just be yourself."

"I don't know who or what I am any more, Gran. I was like Papa's son for years. Just as I was becoming a woman, I had to go back to that role."

"No, Jessie, you don't have to."

"Yes, Gran, I do. If I dress like a fancy woman and behave like Mary Louise does, I'll have trouble with the seasonal wranglers and with every businessman I deal with. They wouldn't respect a frilly woman."

"Most of them know you, child. They like you. They know you helped my son run this ranch. A dress and loose hair won't change their minds."

"If you'd been in San Antonio with me and Matt when I wore that new gown and did up my hair, you wouldn't say that. Those men didn't see a cattle rancher; they saw a creature to chase and capture. How can I discuss business with a man when he's eyeing my figure or face? How can I get him in the corral when he's only wanting to get into my bed? Everything I do right, somebody else gets the credit. It was Papa when he was alive; it'll be Matt now. I have to show everyone that *I'm* the Box L Ranch."

Jessie was still in her strange mood when the next week began and she helped her grandmother with the washing and other household chores. As with each Monday, Jessie's troubled mind marked how long it had been since the week when Navarro had left: five today. Watching the weeks move by made the redhead realize her life was miserably slipping away with daily routine: dawn's chores, eat breakfast, chores, eat dinner, chores, eat supper, and sleep.

For months, Navarro had awakened and tantalized her desires, worked by her side, helped her defeat a terrible enemy, and given her hope for love and marriage. Now all of those things were gone forever. She ached for his companionship and touch; she yearned for his smile; she wanted to feel alive again, to taste his lips, to join her pleading body with his to find pleasure and contentment. She craved to share everything with him, but she was fast draining of hope.

For months, she had stayed on alert for danger. She had lived on the edge under Fletcher's threats of violence and death. Her wits and courage had been tested daily. Now life was back to the routine existence of running a successful ranch. She was glad the perilous trouble was over, but it had cost her the two men she loved most. And with Mathew Cordell in control and with the hands loyal and skilled, she had little out of the ordinary to do.

Something different came up at the end of the next week. Miguel sent word that most of Fletcher's garden was ready to be picked and canned. Early Thursday, Matt helped the two women load their things, and he drove them there.

As Jessie had ordered, the house was opened so fresh air could battle the late July heat. Wood was ready for use, and plenty of water was available. Jessie and Gran set up their supplies in the kitchen, and both admired the display.

Soon, men were bringing them baskets of corn, beans, tomatoes, okra, potatoes, and other vegetables to wash, pick, and prepare for canning. Others were outside helping with shelling and shucking, as they needed extra hands during the busy and fatiguing chore. All licked their lips in anticipation of the vegetables and soups they would enjoy this winter.

Matt entered the kitchen as Jessie finished stirring the huge pot of vegetable soup and began rubbing the muscles of her lower back. "You made Gran take a nap and the boys take a rest," he said. "Why don't you stop for a while, too? You look tired, Jessie."

"I have to get this work done, Matt. I don't want Gran overdoing."

"You can't overdo, either, Jessie. If you keep pushing yourself like this, you'll collapse. You have plenty of help, and it doesn't all have to be finished today, or even tomorrow. Turn around and let me work your back." Matt's hands urged her around and he massaged the muscles near her waist. His fingers curled against her sides while his thumbs pressed and stroked the taut flesh beneath them. "You're tighter than strung barbwire, Jessie. Relax. Let me ease the pain."

As the deft foreman labored on her aching back, Jessie closed her eyes and surrendered to his masterful touch. His pressure was firm and purposeful, yet gentle and persuasive. After a while, his hands moved to her neck.

"Lift your braid," he told her.

Jessie captured it, bent her head forward, and draped it over her face. His thumbs traveled up and down the stiff cords of her neck while his fingers rested on her collarbone. Jessie rolled her head to help loosen the sore area. Matt's hands drifted to her shoulders to give them attention and comfort. His knowing fingers eased the kinks in her upper torso. Soon, the redhead felt better.

"That's wonderful, Matt; thanks. Now I have to stir the soup before it sticks and burns." She went to tend that task, but hated to leave his soothing touch.

The foreman let her do her chore, then caught her right hand to pull her back to him. "I'm not done yet, Boss Lady." He guided her into a chair at the table, then sat down near her. "These hands need loosening, too."

Jessie watched Matt as he massaged the water-puckered skin and grumbling bones. His strong hands were rough from work. She didn't mind, as his touch was restorative and soothing. She gazed at his lowered head of dark-brown hair that fell in mussed waves toward a sun-bronzed face. Her gaze drifted down his neck to the hollow at its base. Dark hair was visible where the top buttons of his faded blue shirt had been undone in deference to the hot, dry day. The shirt fit snugly, emphasizing his broad shoulders. Where his sleeves were rolled to his elbows, she saw muscles honed from years of labor. She watched them move as his fingers worked on hers.

Jessie's eyes roamed upward to his face with its sunny smile and sparkling brown eyes. He was very gentle and soft-spoken for one so rugged in body and character. He was also quite handsome and virile. She wondered why Mathew Cordell had never wed. What had happened during his thirty-five years to keep him from choosing a wife and settling down on his own place? A woman couldn't find a better man than Matt to share her love and life, so why was he still unattached?

Matt glanced up to find the redhead's inquisitive gaze on him. "Is something wrong, Jessie?" he asked when she continued to stare at him.

Jessie liked the comforting sound of his voice. "No, just the oppo- site. I was thinking how lucky I am to have you around, Mathew Cordell." A broad grin came her way. His chocolate eyes softened and glowed. Yet, he looked suddenly shy and a little surprised by her words.

"Thanks, Jessie," he murmured, almost squirming in his seat.

Jessie warmed to his unfamiliar expression and mood. "No thanks are needed. It's the truth." He looked as if he wanted to say some- thing, but felt he shouldn't. Jessie decided not to intrude on his pri- vate feelings. "That's what I needed," she remarked, pulling her hands from his and flexing them. "I best get back to work. The next time you overdo, I'll return the favor."

Matt smiled and replied, "I'll hold you to that promise, Boss Lady. Fact is, I might cheat just to get it," he teased.

"Mathew Cordell be dishonest? The seasons would end first."

In a serious tone, he said, "It would shock you what some men would do for you, Jessica Lane." He stood and replaced his chair. "I'll get busy, too."

Jessie watched him leave, then returned to the simmering soup. She pondered his curious words. She asked herself if she could be the reason Matt had stayed on the ranch and never wed. That seemed unlikely in view of the fact he had never tried to court her. Yet, if he did have romantic feelings for her, she had to be careful not to hurt him.

The two women and men remained on the Bar F to continue their task. Hank stayed home to prepare supper for the cowhands. Tom was with him to tend the chores he had taken over from Mary Lou- ise. When the canning group halted that night, bodies were tired and hands were wrinkled from hours in water. The boys stayed in the bunkhouse. Gran spent the night in one of the guest rooms, Matt in another, and Jessie in the master suite.

She looked around before falling upon the inviting bed. She let her imagination wonder about the nights and days Wilbur Fletcher had spent in this room. Soon she should go through the clothes and possessions he had left behind. She would give Matt first choice, then pass the remainder to the other hands. She liked this lovely and comfortable Spanish-style house. It was a shame to leave it standing empty. Soon, she must also decide what to do about it.

As the redhead lay in the darkness, she wondered how Mary Louise had yielded to a man she hardly knew, a cruel and evil man. How many times had Fletcher and her defiant sister made love in this very room? What had it been like between them? Passionate and satisfying as with her and Navarro? Mary Louise was such a wild and reckless girl, such a greedy one. Would her sister miss her times with Wilbur as she missed hers with the desperado? Would Mary Louise seek to continue those carnal pleasures with another husband or a lover? Jessie couldn't imagine another man taking her lost love's place, but if she didn't allow one to do so, she would be alone for the rest of her life: lonely, empty, childless, and unfulfilled. Could she stand such a barren existence? She wished Navarro were there with her, holding her and kissing her and making love to her.

Jessie turned to her side. She couldn't get in a comfortable position. She was used to sleeping on her stomach, but her breasts were too sore to permit pressure on them. She realized she had missed her "woman's way" in early June and in July, too. She assumed all her troubles had affected her body. She felt puffy, and hoped her impending flow would ease the tension and discomfort she had been enduring recently. She wanted to be back to normal. She didn't like feeling queasy, exhausted and moody, like this. She had even halted her long rides with Matt because she was having to use the outhouse or chamber pot so frequently. It was bad enough to have her mind and heart not working right, but it was unbearably irritating to have her body fight her, too.

The canning was completed by Saturday afternoon. They left the filled jars in the kitchen, to be divided next week for use in both locations. They did have another round of canning to do soon when their own garden came in. They packed their things and were home before dark.

August arrived with a hot dryness that made the redhead even more miserable. She didn't want to worry Gran, but a strange illness was plaguing her. She prayed she hadn't caught a curious disease that would make her waste away. To hide it, Jessie rushed to the outhouse each time a wave of nausea came over her. She tried to conceal her fatigue and weakness. Sometimes she wanted to rest or sleep so much that she feared she would faint and expose her unnatural condition.

On Friday, a distraction came when Jimmy Joe asked if he could borrow a certain Mexican dress and mantilla to play a practical joke on Rusty Jones. When she saw Rusty arrive later, Jessie sneaked to the corner of the bunkhouse to catch the much-needed entertainment.

Jessie listened as the "woman" told the fiery-haired man with a beard that she was carrying his child as a result of the night he spent with her in the saloon two months ago. The confirmed bachelor didn't know what to say or do, except to ask her to repeat her astonishing story.

Jessie peeked inside for a quick look. The "girl's" back was to her uneasy victim. The thick, dark mantilla concealed the towhead's identity, who spoke low and soft to prevent too early discovery of the practical joke. Jimmy Joe spoke good Spanish, and Miguel translated at certain points. The story—based on a real incident—worried Rusty.

Jessie knew enough Spanish to comprehend most of the humorous conversation, and Miguel's assistance closed any gaps she or the other men had. At first she was amused, and she had to cover her mouth to silence any giggles.

"I don't follow your story, señorita," Rusty said in desperation.

The "girl" explained in Spanish, "I carry your child, Señor Rusty. I am not a soiled dove as the others who work for Señor Bill. You were my first and only man. After you left my bed, I ran away from the saloon. I could not do such things again with strangers for money. Do you not remember I was a virgin?"

Rusty glanced at his friends, looking embarrassed and nervous. He motioned for their help, but they all shrugged and grinned. He scowled at them.

"Do you not remember, Señor Rusty?" The question was asked again.

The bearded man cleared his clogged throat and replied honestly, "Yep, I was first to . . . sleep with you, señorita."

"First and last" was the soft correction.

"I didn't force myself onto you, señorita, and you weren't no prisoner there. You said I didn't hurt you. Why'd you come to me with your bad luck?"

"My father and brothers learned of my shameful secret. They say I must marry the child's father. You must help me."

"Help you?" Rusty asked, panicking more each minute.

"Yes. We must marry. I must stay here with you. If we do not, we will be in much danger." The "girl" pretended to weep in sadness and fear.

"In danger?" Rusty echoed, shifting about as if his whole body itched.

"Yes. They will come here and kill you for dishonoring our family."

Rusty's gaze grew wide and alarmed. He licked his dry mouth. His quivering fingers played with his red beard. His legs trembled. "K-k-kill me?"

"Sí" came the dreaded response.

Rusty's face became a bright red. His gaze pleaded for help from the observant men, to no avail.

"You must do right by her, Señor Rusty," Carlos said.

The others agreed, nudging the man nearby and nodding their heads.

"And for your baby, Señor Rusty," one added. "Don't forget about him."

"Who says that seed's mine? I ain't never heard of having to wed no soiled dove after one night's fun. How do I know I was last? How do I know she ain't laying a trap for me? If I knew for sure she's telling the truth, I'd marry her to give my child his rightful name. But this is suspicious." Rusty swallowed hard. He tapped the "girl's" shoulder and asked, "How can you be sure I'm to blame? How do you know you got a baby inside?"

When the "girl" related her symptoms, Jessie paled and shook as she recognized them as her own. She had been around animals mating and giving birth all her life, but she hadn't seen morning sickness or been around a woman in the early stages of pregnancy since she was ten and her mother had Tom. The truth of her condition struck her hard. She felt weak and shaky and and scared.

Before she escaped to her room, she heard Jimmy Joe burst into chuckles and tease Rusty. The others joined in and howled with laughter. Jessie fled the enlightening scene and hurried to her bedroom for privacy.

She closed her door and paced the floor. How stupid and naive she was, she scolded herself. She had missed her monthly flow before, during illness or from other unknown reasons, but this time her breasts were sore and her body was puffy. She had passed her queasiness off to bad food and her sluggishness to hard work and tension. She had even ignored her crazy moods because of all she had endured recently.

Jessie reflected on her "woman's way" and her nights with Navarro. She had missed the first one in June, right after her love's return during the storm. She had skipped her July one, and it hadn't appeared earlier this month. That meant she had to be over two months' pregnant. What, she wondered in alarm, could she do?

Navarro had been gone since June twelfth, almost nine weeks. She hadn't received any word from him and had no idea where he was. She doubted he would ever return. Even if he sent a letter, he wouldn't tell her where to locate him. She was carrying his child, and he would never know!

Jessie waxed between happiness and fear. She caressed her stomach and thought of their child growing there. Apprehension flooded her as she realized it would be born a bastard. Her child would be forced to fight the same stigma and heartache that its father had suffered. No, she couldn't allow her child to be tormented. She had to think of something, she fretted, but what?

Visions of disgrace entered her turbulent mind. She would soil the Lane name. She would become the topic of horrible gossip. Having a child out of wedlock would tarnish her, her family, her home, not to mention her child. Everyone would discover her "sin" with the fugitive drifter. Her beautiful love would become something ugly and shameful, something destructive, if she didn't prevent it.

Jessie knew she had to make a decision fast. She would be unable to hide her condition in a couple of months. She figured up the timing and decided the baby was due in early March. Tears rolled down her cheeks as she realized that was the month she had met Navarro Breed. If only he would return . . .

Jessie's tears and panic increased as she told herself that was a hopeless dream. This was a problem—a stark reality—she had to work out alone.

# CHAPTER EIGHTEEN

Saturday afternoon, Jessie let Tom go riding with Matt so she could speak with her grandmother alone. She could not put off telling her any longer. She had worried over it all night and had come up with an idea. Now she had to discuss it with Martha Lane. There was no use waiting and praying for Navarro to return in time to give their child a name before he had to leave her side again. She had stopped fantasizing he would ride up and pull her into his arms any day and make everything all right. But if he did, the redhead knew she would leave with him and take her family with them to begin a new life in a faraway place.

Jessie brushed her long hair to release part of her tension. She had been sick again upon arising, sicker than any morning thus far. But as the hours passed, so had her nausea. She put the brush aside, caressed her stomach, and whispered, "It's time, little one, to make plans to protect you from the hurt and shame your father endured."

Jessica walked into the kitchen. "Gran, I have something to discuss with you," she said. "I know you'll be hurt and disappointed in me, and I'm sorry. I'm in trouble, Gran, big trouble, and I don't know how to tell you about it."

Martha looked at the girl who stood there with lowered head and clenched hands. She went to her granddaughter and hugged her. "You're carrying Navarro's child," she said in a gentle tone to help Jessie begin.

Jessie's head jerked upward and she stared at the white-haired woman. Her blue eyes were wide and her mouth was open. "How . . . did you know? I only realized it yesterday."

Gran guided them to chairs in the eating area. She sat close and kept the redhead's cold, damp hands clasped in hers. Her voice and gaze were compassionate. "The Good Lord gave me three fine sons, but found it in His way to call them home to Him. A mother never thinks she'll outlive her children. I've borne and buried three children, Jessie, so I know the symptoms."

Jessie's eyes misted, her cheeks glowed, and her voice cracked with emotion. "Why didn't you say something? I must be stupid and naive, because I didn't make the connection until recently."

"How could you, child? You've been around men most of your life. I should have had a talk with you long ago, especially after I saw what was happening between you and Navarro." When Jessie looked surprised, the older woman continued. "I watched how you two reached out to each other. I've known you from birth, Jessie. I saw how he was changing you, and how you were changing him. But he's a drifter. I thought your feelings would pass after he left."

"If he hadn't had to leave, Gran, he would have married me. He loves me."

"I'm sure he does, Jessie, but that hopeless dream is over, gone with him. I knew you had troubles. I've seen you running for the outhouse many times, and I've seen how moody and weary you are. I was waiting for you to come to me."

"I would have come sooner, Gran, but I only learned what was wrong yesterday." Jessie explained how she had made her shocking discovery. "We love each other so much. We knew we didn't have much time together. At first I didn't know why. I didn't even believe Navarro when he kept swearing he couldn't stay long. When he came back that stormy night after Papa's death and the range fire, I needed him so much, and he needed me. I didn't understand how much until he told me he was leaving forever."

Jessie thought it was best for everyone if her grandmother were led to believe she had "sinned" only once, as Martha Lane was a firm believer in God and in right and wrong. It was hard enough for the older woman to learn about such a wanton weakness without having to be told it had happened several times. "I'm sorry, Gran."

"But you still love him and you're carrying his child," Martha reminded her.

"Yes, Gran, but I didn't want it to be like this. The best thing to do is move somewhere until the baby is born, or to live there permanently. I'll have to lie and say I'm a widow, so my child won't be treated as a bastard." Jessie related enough of Navarro Breed's history to let the woman know how he had suffered. "I'll wait another month to make certain Navarro won't change his mind and return. Then we'll leave before I start coming to season. We can decide afterward whether or not to return. I'm afraid people might guess the truth from the time of the baby's birth and its looks."

The older woman looked worried and distressed. "Sell the ranch, Jessie?"

"No, Gran. We worked too hard to keep it, and our family is buried out here. I plan to let Matt run it for us. In this fix, he'll do a better job than I could. Eventually I want to return and live here. This is our home. Maybe Navarro will find a way to end his trouble."

Martha squeezed her granddaughter's hands, then grimaced in pain from her arthritic condition. "Don't live in a dream world, Jessie. Face the truth, child; he can't ever return. He wouldn't, because he loves you and wants you safe. You'll be blooming soon, so you have to act quickly. A scandal can ruin the baby you're carrying and this ranch. You have a duty to them. Time is working against you, but there is another way. Do what you must, child."

"What is that, Gran?" she asked, near panic.

"Marry Mathew Cordell. He loves you, too. He'll understand and agree."

"Marry Matt?" she said, looking shocked. "Tell him about my trouble?"

"Soon words won't be necessary. Think about the baby, nameless and a bastard, even if you claim you're a widow. One day you'd have to lie to the child, too, or tell it the truth. Think of yourself, Jessie, shamed and ruined, alone and miserable, trying to raise a child without a father and away from your home. You don't know where Navarro is, and it's certain he won't return. Speak to Matt. He's a good man. He's loved you for years. He'll help; I'm sure of it."

"But it's wrong to use him, Gran. I'd be too ashamed to confess the truth. Matt thinks I'm a wonderful person. He'll be hurt and disappointed in me."

"Love is a strong and special gift, Jessie. It's forgiving and understanding. Let Matt give it to you and the baby," she urged.

"What if he doesn't want a soiled woman or to raise another man's bastard child? What if he was so angry he left us, Gran? Who would run the ranch for us then? I can't risk telling him and losing him."

"Don't down yourself, Jessie. You made a mistake during a hard time. Matt would never think badly of you, and he would never run out on you. Don't you realize he'll guess what's wrong when you desert the ranch? Isn't it better for the truth to come from you, child? He'll be hurt that you didn't trust him. You'd be surprised what some men will do to get the woman they love."

Matt had spoken similar words that day at the Bar F. Did he love and want her enough to take on such a burden? Should she give him a chance to help her out of a terrible predicament? Would he understand and marry her? Or would the truth destroy her in his eyes and heart? If he agreed, what would he expect in return? He would know she loved Navarro and had slept with him. How could he deal with such torments, if he truly loved her? Yet, her grandmother was right and wise. She had to act fast. Navarro was lost forever. She must think only of the baby, her family and home, and the Lane reputation. She had to take this risk, and pray she and Gran had not misjudged the foreman's feelings.

"All right, Gran; I'll talk to Matt tomorrow. If he refuses, but stays, we'll leave next week. If he leaves, I'll put Rusty in charge before we go."

Jessie and Matt rode to the scene of the range fire. Burned scrubs and trees had been cut and destroyed. Grass, wildflowers, and bushes were beginning to grow. Wind, rain, and cattle movements since that day in early June had scattered or trampled under the black surface. New greenery was taking hold. One had to look close to realize how much damage had been done.

Jessie glanced around and said, "The land is almost healed, Matt."

"Your heart will be healed soon, too, Jessie. Your father will always be with you, but the pain will soften more every week."

Jessie realized he misread her sadness. She dismounted and dropped Ben's reins to the ground. She walked to an unharmed tree and leaned her head against it. This task was harder than she had imagined, dreaded, it would be. She felt lonely and lost and and denied. She couldn't help feeling angry and bitter about all that had happened. A deep yearning for peace and safety chewed at her raw nerves and distraught mind. She needed someone to take away her pain. She wanted to be loved, held, kissed. She needed to feel special again. Could Matt fill those roles in her shattered life? Would he?

Matt joined her, sensing he had mistaken her problem. More than natural grief was tormenting his love. He longed to comfort her, to bring back his old Jessie. His hands grasped her trembling arms and turned her to face him. He saw tears rolling down her cheeks and moisture shining on her thick lashes. He pulled her into his arms and murmured, "Don't be sad, Jessie. You have me to take care of you and the ranch. What do you need so badly that hurts you this way?" Even as he asked his last question, he prayed her answer wouldn't be Navarro.

Jessie looked into his concerned gaze and more tears threatened to spill forth. She hated to hurt this unselfish man, but she was drawn to his tenderness and strength in her time of weakness. She was apprehensive about the challenges and responsibilities confronting her. She didn't want to face such burdens and fears alone. She had been a rock for others for years; now she wanted and needed a supportive pillar. She needed a powerful and dependable shoulder to lean on, someone to help her through the hard times ahead. She was in the arms of the best man for those tasks. She prayed that the awful truth would not turn him against her.

"I do need you so very much, Matt. You've always been nearby when I faltered. You've always been the one I could turn to for advice and loyalty and understanding. You know me better than anyone."

Aching to ease her anguish, Matt kissed her. His mouth was gentle, his kiss full of love and understanding, his arms protective and strong. The kiss was short, but filled with emotion.

Jessie pressed her face against his chest and cried softly. Her hands circled his waist and she clung to him for comfort and strength. When Matt embraced her and rested his cheek against her hair, his kindness flowed out to her.

He stroked her hair and coaxed, "Cry all you need, Jessie. Let all the suffering out. You've been strong for months for everyone else. I know how hard it's been for you. I'll do anything I can to lessen your pain and sadness."

Jessie looked up at him and said, "I wish you could, Matt. Nobody can help this time. I'm in bad trouble. I have to leave the ranch for a year or two. Will you take care of it while I'm gone? Gran and Tom are going with me." Jessie thought it was best if she exposed her problem, then let Matt decide how to deal with any part he wanted to take in solving it. She couldn't ask him to marry her; the suggestion had to be his. If he didn't make it, neither would she.

He was stunned by that news. "Leave? Why, Jessie?"

"I can't stay here, Matt. I'll be ruined."

He wiped at her tears. "No, you won't. I won't let you get hurt. The ranch is doing fine. *You're* doing fine. You're strong and brave and smart."

"Not as much as you think, Matt, and I have to get away soon."

"Give it time, Jessie. You can't run because you're scared. You aren't alone. I'm here. The boys are here. We won't let you fail."

"That isn't it, Matt."

He eyed her for a time, then asked, "Are you going to meet Navarro?"

Jessie lowered her head in guilt and apprehension. She was moving slowly, to prevent as much shock and anguish as possible. "No. He's gone; I don't know where, but he won't ever come back. But yes, it does have to do with him."

He was puzzled. "You can't stay because Navarro and your father are gone? Leaving is no answer. We'll handle whatever's wrong."

"That isn't it, either." Jessie turned away from his confused gaze. "It's me."

Matt was angry with himself for not realizing how much she had been suffering. He couldn't let her leave in this vulnerable state and have her meet someone else who might take Navarro's place. He had to be bold and persuasive to win her heart. First, he had to discover what was troubling his love. "What kind of bad trouble are you talking about, Jessie?"

Before she lost her courage, she confessed, "I'm . . . I'm pregnant, Matt."

"Pregnant?" he echoed in disbelief, that being the farthest idea from his mind.

Jessie faced him and rushed on. "Please don't think too badly of me. I had to tell you the truth because we're so close and I trust you like family. I have to go away to have the baby. We'll be ruined by disgrace if I stay and have it here. I don't know when I'll return.

Will you look after the ranch until I do? Please. I can trust you and depend on you. I don't want to sell it."

He was silent for a time as Jessie awaited his reaction and response. It seemed an eternity. If Matt loved her, this predicament had to be just as difficult for him. The hurt look in his somber brown eyes ripped into her soul. She wished she hadn't done this terrible thing to him. How could he understand and accept such wanton wickedness in her? In shame and anguish, she murmured, "I'm sorry, Matt. I shouldn't have told you. Please don't hate me. I couldn't bear to lose you, too. I'll be gone soon, and you won't have to look at me."

"Navarro's?" he asked in a strained voice.

"Yes." She told him the same amended story she had told her grandmother. It was also best for Matt to think it had happened only once. "I'm sorry, Matt. You must be terribly disappointed in me. I can't undo this mess, so I should leave before it's discovered and the news spreads. It was wrong to burden you with such a terrible matter. I just felt so alone and confused." She turned away again.

Matt didn't ask if she loved the drifter, as he knew she must to have made love with him. His anger at himself increased. If only he'd been there to fill her needs, she wouldn't have fallen prey to Navarro's wiles! But he *was* here now when her need was so great. "Leaving isn't best for you, Jessie. Or the baby. Or the ranch."

When he pulled her around to face him, she reasoned, "I created this problem, so I have to solve it, Matt. What else can I do?"

"Marry me," he responded. "I'm the man you need. You can trust me."

Jessie had hoped and prayed he would say that but she had feared he wouldn't, out of torment and bitterness. Her surprise showed more than her relief and joy. "But . . ."

His voice and expression were firm as he said, "But nothing, Jessie. You don't have much choice. This is where you need to be. I know you love him, and I know he loved you. Don't look shocked. I've been reading the signs since he arrived. I prayed I was wrong, but knew I wasn't. I was glad when he left and mad when he returned, because I was afraid he'd hurt you—and he has."

"It wasn't all his fault, Matt. He didn't trick me or assault me."

"But he pulled you to him, knowing he wasn't going to stay here."

"It was a bad time in both our lives. We were weak and suffering. We needed something from each other. Was that so terrible, so wrong?"

The pleading look in her blue eyes knotted his guts. Sunshine highlighted her auburn hair. Despite her flushed cheeks, her lovely face was pale. She needed so much from him, more than she realized at this dire time, and he was eager to help her. He dodged her last, loaded question. "If I had been more aware, this wouldn't have happened. Are you sure he's gone for good this time? He returned before, and things between you two were . . . even stronger than I realized."

Her honesty was apparent as she replied, "I'm sure. He's in trouble with the law—a fugitive fleeing a noose is what he told me that last day. To survive, he had to go, Matt, and he can't risk coming back. He'll never know about the baby."

Matt finally understood, and he almost felt sorry for the desperado who had lost so much. Yet he was furious with Navarro for taking advantage of Jessie when the man knew their future was impossible. "I suspected something was wrong. I knew he didn't want to leave, but I could tell he had to go. The sooner we get married, the better it'll be. How about Tuesday?" Matt wanted his claim settled on Jessie before his rival could sneak a visit and change her mind about this solution or take her with him far away.

Guilt chewed at Jessie. "I can't do this to you, Matt. It isn't fair to marry you under these conditions. I can't strap you with another man's burden."

"What wouldn't be fair is for me to let you uproot yourself and your family when I'm the answer to your problem. You wouldn't be strapping me down; I want to marry you. I love you, Jessica Lane; I have for years. I've waited too long to tell you. Become my wife, Jessie. I'll love you and take care of you forever."

The admission touched Jessie. Matt's clear gaze told her that every word was true. As he cupped her face with work-toughened hands and looked coaxingly into her misty eyes, his smile was reassuring and heartwarming. Yes, Mathew Cordell would make a lucky woman a perfect husband, and that woman could be her. She couldn't help but wonder what would have happened between them if Matt had revealed his love long ago. "Why haven't you said or done anything about your feelings for me?"

"Fear," he confessed, then sent her a wry grin.

She laughed and said, "I've never known you to be afraid of anything or anyone. Fear of what, Matt?"

"Rejection. Of causing a problem between us. When I came here at eighteen, I was running away from a busted love affair. I was going to marry a girl in Georgia, but she walked out the week of our wedding and married another man. I met Jed; we struck up a friendship, and I came to work for him. When I went back during the war, Sarah was there with her children. Her husband had been killed. She begged me to come back to her. I couldn't; it was over for me. My home was here. When I returned, you were thirteen and I was twenty-four. I watched you grow over the years. I've seen you in every mood and in every situation. I could tell you saw me only as an uncle or older brother. I was scared to approach you like this. If I had, maybe Navarro wouldn't have gotten to you. But things have a way of happening for the best. You've changed since knowing him, Jessie."

Matt's perceptions and gentleness evoked even deeper respect and affection from her. "I know," she concurred. "Before Navarro, I lived and worked as Jed's son. He made me realize I was a woman. Not many men have treated me that way, Matt, and it wasn't their fault. I was just one of the boys, not a female to be romanced."

Matt shook his head, causing shocks of brown hair to fall over one side of his forehead. His gaze seemed to sparkle with amusement at her mistake. For a time, the reason for their talk and his proposal vanished. Only the woman he loved and desired stood before him, toying with a loose button on his shirt. She was smiling at him with trust and affection in her eyes. "No female is more of a woman than you are, Jessie. You're beautiful. Don't ever doubt it again. Don't you remember that night in San Antonio? Men couldn't take their eyes off you, 'specially me. Every woman there was chewed up by envy."

"I must admit it turned my head a mite. I also recall how those women were eyeing my handsome escort. I was afraid one would steal you away."

"What would a fancy city lady want with an old cowpoke like me? I've lived in a saddle so long, I'm barely housebroken. Good thing you're a skilled rider. This wrangler needs training bad."

They laughed, and more tension left them.

Matt stroked her hair and waxed serious. "See, you can still smile and laugh. It sounds good to hear it again, Jessie."

His innocent remarks made her remember all that had saddened her, but she concealed her reaction. "You're so good for me, Matt, so good *to* me. I don't deserve such treatment, or a prize like you."

He grasped her hands and squeezed them. "That isn't true."

"Yes, it is. Look what a mess I've made of things."

"Trust me, Jessie; your pain will heal, just like this land healed. I should know. Lordy, Sarah hurt me bad, but I learned to live and love again. You can, too."

"I don't want to hurt you like she did, Matt. It's too soon to . . ."

"I know, but time passes every day. With Navarro gone and me here, I'll have the advantage. You won't be sorry, Jessie. I'll make you a good husband. I'll raise the baby as my own. I won't make any demands on you. If you come to love me and want me, I'll be here. But if we only stay close friends, I'll settle for that."

"You shouldn't have to settle for half a life, Matt. You're too special."

"But that life will be with the woman I love, Jessie. It's worth it to me. Besides, woman, you *do* love me. Not like I love you or hope you'll love me one day, but you love me nonetheless. Maybe that little seed will sprout and flourish."

Jessie gazed at his sparkling brown eyes. He was a dreamer, too. He wanted her as much as she wanted Navarro. If he had gotten over his anguish in the past, perhaps she would get over hers at some future time. What better man to share her life and love, to take Navarro's place? She could not help but return his appealing smile and catch his contagious mood. When his hand caressed her cheek and he entreated, "Marry me, Jessie," she relented. "All right, Mr. Foreman, I'll make you boss of the Box L Ranch and Lane family."

Matt whooped with joy. He lifted her around the waist and swung her around before kissing her. "I'll go hire the preacher tomorrow. We can marry Tuesday."

"What will the hands say?" she fretted, her fingers interlocked behind his neck. She enjoyed the way his adoring gaze engulfed her, the joy and relief he had given her, and the way he tempted her to stay in his embrace and to kiss him.

Matt savored the moment and the way Jessie was responding to him. Her behavior gave him hope about winning her love one day. "They'll think I'm the damned luckiest man alive. Have you forgot-

ten we were caught in the barn together with straw in our hair?"
he teased, that memory arousing him further.

"Everyone knows that was a trick," she refuted.

"What about all those nights we've been alone on the range? And
what about our trip to San Antonio together? They'll think we finally yielded to romance."

"What about my protruding belly in a few months?" she retorted
too quickly.

He saw her flush at the slip. He thought a minute, then said,
"You're two and a half months along. That'll put our baby arriving
first of March. We'll be on the cattle drive when you start showing,
Jessie. By the time we get back months later, nobody should suspect
anything. Babies do come early. But even if they guessed the truth,
the boys wouldn't say anything; they'd think it's mine. It *will* be
mine."

"You're such a rare and wonderful man. Are you sure this is what
you want, Matt? Don't get drowned trying to save a sinking person."

Matt clasped her face between his hands again. "I love you,
woman. This is all I want and need."

"What would I do without you?" she murmured.

"That's what I'm saying. I'll be good to you, Jessie."

"I know you will." She was about to hug and kiss him when he
spoke again.

"I do have to ask one question, Jessie. What happens to us if Navarro returns?"

"He won't. But if he did, it wouldn't change anything. I swear
it. The baby will be born and raised as yours with your name."

"What if you don't come to love me, and he wants you and the
child back?"

"We'll be a family until death, Matt; I promise. Navarro couldn't
stay here, and we couldn't go on the run with him. Our fates are
cast. Until death do us part; you have my word of honor. I also
promise to try to forget him and the past as quickly as possible, and
to try to love you like you love me."

"I know you're scared and hurting, Jessie. But you're a Lane. Be
strong and brave in the coming months. You can hide the pain until
it's gone."

"With you there beside me, Matt, I'm sure I can. Thanks."

Matt grinned. "This time I'm thanking you, Jessie."

*   *   *

Matt rode in with the preacher late Tuesday afternoon. Jessie and Gran had been working hard on preparations, and all was perfect when they arrived. The boys and Tom had collected wildflowers that were placed around the parlor. Food was ready for the party afterward.

Jessie was nervous. Her morning sickness had passed earlier, and she was relieved. She was wearing a lovely white dress with lace and ruffles. It fit her snugly at the waist and flowed into a full skirt. Her hair was pinned up, then cascaded down her back in ringlets that Gran had helped her make with the metal iron. Despite the hot and dry August heat, her hands were cold and shaking. She fastened her grandmother's pearls around her neck and settled them over her pounding heart. She knew she was supposed to remain in her room until summoned.

As she spent the last remaining minutes as a single woman, she tried to keep Navarro Breed off her mind. Once she committed herself to Mathew Cordell, it would be for life. For the first time, Jessie prayed that her lost love would never return. When he left, he had said it was too late for him. If he returned, it would be too late for *her,* for *them.*

Good-bye, my love. I'm doing this for our child. We can't ever think of ourselves again. For the rest of my life, I'll owe Matt loyalty for this sacrifice. I love you, Navarro Breed. Wherever you are, be safe and happy.

Jessie heard the fiddle and harmonica begin the music the boys insisted on playing for the occasion. Her pulse raced with her increased heartbeat. Her mouth went dry. She trembled. It was time to seal her future. At the tapping signal on her door, Jessie opened it and entered the room filled with her family, friends, and future husband. She approached the minister and Matt.

Matt took her hand in his and squeezed it. Jessie looked at him and saw love and joy written on his face. He had changed into a suit, and looked very handsome. She smiled.

Matt felt as if his heart would burst from the elation rushing through it. Jessie looked stunning, though her icy, quivering hands revealed her anxiety and her face was a little pale, her cheeks a little rosy. But everyone would think it was merely wedding shakes. He held her hand firmly to give her strength and courage and felt her tighten her fingers around his. He focused his attention on the preacher standing before them.

Reverend Adams motioned the music to halt. He cleared his throat, glanced at the couple, and looked down at his worn Bible. "Dear friends, we're gathered in this home to unite this man and woman in the bonds of holy marriage in the sight of God and these witnesses. I shall read from the book of Ruth, chapter one, verses sixteen and seventeen: 'And Ruth said, Intreat me not to leave thee or to return from following after thee; for whither thou goest, I will go; and where thou lodgest, I will lodge: thy people shall be my people, and thy God my God: Where thou diest, will I die, and there will I be buried: the Lord do so to me, and more also, if aught but death part thee and me.' From Ephesians five, verses twenty-two through thirty-three: 'Wives, submit yourselves unto your own husband, as unto the Lord. For the husband is the head of the wife . . .'"

Jessie's thoughts drifted as those serious words sank into her mind. She heard him quote, "For this cause shall a man leave his father and mother, and shall be joined unto his wife, and they two shall be one flesh." Again, she could not stop her mind from questioning the right or wrong of this marriage. Soon she would be vowing to Matt, before witnesses, and unto God . . .

"Mathew Cordell, do you take this woman to be your lawful wife?" Reverend Adams asked. "Will you love her, cherish her, protect her, support her, and guide her in all manners of sickness, health, in riches and in poverty, and amongst any perils unto death parts you as the Holy Scriptures command?"

Matt did not hesitate. "I do, until death," he said.

The minister asked the redhead, "Jessica Lane, do you take this man to be your lawful husband, to love, honor, obey, and cleave only unto him in all manners of good and bad, through health and sickness, for as long as you shall live as so commanded by the Bible?"

Jessie swallowed hard as those vows shot through her head. The baby. That was all that mattered, giving her child a name and fair chance. "I do, until death."

"Is there a ring?" the preacher inquired.

Gran removed her own wedding ring and handed it to the foreman. They'd decided to borrow hers until Matt could purchase one for Jessie. The redhead looked at the woman and smiled.

"A ring is a circle with no end, as love and marriage should be. It is the symbol of your vows before God. May your love remain as shiny and precious as this gold. Place the ring on her finger and say after me: With this ring, I thee wed."

Matt worked the gold band onto Jessie's finger and repeated the words.

"Hold his hand and say after me: I take this ring and thee I wed."

Jessie looked into Matt's eyes and repeated the words.

"By the authorities given to me by God above and by this state, I pronounce you husband and wife. As Matthew six commands: 'Wherefore they are no more twain, but one flesh. What therefore God hath joined together, let not man put asunder.' I congratulate you, Mr. and Mrs. Mathew Cordell. Let us pray."

All bowed their heads as the minister blessed the couple and their marriage. Afterward, the guests kissed the bride's cheek, shook the groom's hand, and gave them both merry advice. Tom hugged his sister and teased her, then talked with Matt. Gran and Jessie embraced for a lengthy time as the older woman whispered words of encouragement and comfort into the redhead's ear.

The festivities got underway with plenty of food and drink. Music and dancing started. Everyone was in a good mood.

Matt danced with his new bride. "That wasn't so bad, was it?" he murmured.

"It was a beautiful ceremony, Matt."

"You're what's beautiful today, Jessie. It'll work."

"We'll make it work." She snuggled close to him as she told herself this was the beginning of her new life. The preacher hadn't asked if anyone objected to the marriage, and no one had been there to do so. Navarro had left her over two months ago. If he had changed his mind, he would have returned by now. She had to face facts. That part of her life was over; Matt and the baby were her future. She was a wife and, in six and a half months, she would be a mother.

"You all right, Jessie?" Matt asked, looking down at her.

"Yes, my husband, I'm fine."

"You'll have to start taking it easier."

Jessie laughed. "It's not an illness, Matt, but I'll be careful."

Carlos, Miguel, Rusty, and Jimmy Joe claimed her hand for dances when the one with Matt ended. Guests ate and laughed and had a good time. When the hour grew late, the hands drifted out a few at a time. Finally, only the family and preacher were left inside, and he was to spend the night.

Gran and Jessie cleared away the food as the men and Tom chatted. Reverend Adams was shown to the room the two sisters had shared. Tom and Gran retired to theirs. Matt followed his lovely bride into Jed's old room.

"I was going to use Mary Louise's room, Jessie, but Preacher Adams has to stay over till morning. You sure you don't mind sharing with me tonight?"

"You have to stay with me every night, Matt, or people will wonder about us."

"I don't want you being uncomfortable. Who'll know if I use your old room?"

"Tom will be confused. I want him and everyone to believe our marriage is real and the baby is yours. We've known each other for years, and you are my husband. Hush now. We're both exhausted."

"I'll turn around while you change and get into bed."

"Always a gentleman," she teased, but was glad he was as she removed her dress and stood clad only in her chemise. "If I were always a lady, this wouldn't have happened."

Matt turned and scolded, "Don't ever say that again. Things like this happen, Jessie. Don't blame yourself."

The redhead didn't try to cover herself, but faced him boldly. "It required two of us, Matt, and we're both to blame. It was reckless and foolish."

Matt went to her, wrapped his arms around her, and urged, "Forget it, love."

"I'll try; honestly I will. I'm just so confused and shaky."

Matt's fingers stroked her bare shoulders. "You've been very busy. You need to rest. You aren't sorry you said yes to me, are you?"

"No, Matt, I'm not. Just give me time and your patience."

"You'll have them, Jessie,—as much as you need."

"I hate treating you this way. This isn't the wedding night you expected, I'm sure."

"What I never expected was to win you, Jessie," he refuted. "If it took Navarro to do that for me, I'm grateful to him. I only hope you'll want and need me one day as much as you did him. He came along when you were vulnerable. Now I'm doing the same thing.

The difference is, I won you, and I'll never do anything to make you regret marrying me."

"I do love you, Matt."

"I know, Jessie. Get to bed." Matt released her, and turned his back again.

Jessie looked at her husband. She was glad she had him, and somehow she had to prove it. One day, she would, she vowed. She undressed and slipped on her nightgown. She crawled into bed and pulled the light cover to her neck. "Ready, Matt."

The foreman doused the lamps, undressed in the dark, and climbed in beside her. Their arms and legs touched as they settled in place, and Matt hungered to pull her into his embrace. But he must wait until she came to him.

Jessie closed her eyes and took a deep breath. She couldn't offer herself to her new husband to appease her conscience or to show her gratitude. The minister's words from the Bible returned to haunt her. It was her wifely duty to submit to him. But not now, not yet, her heart and mind commanded stronger than those vows.

Soon, despite Matt's desires and Jessie's tensions, both were asleep.

It was hours later when Jessie began to toss and turn. Visions of Navarro in prison flickered through her restless mind. She saw him being beaten, starved, and thrown in that black hole he had told her about. She saw bugs and rats crawling over his flesh. She saw him raging with fever, and no one came to his aid. She saw him laboring under the hot sun and pleading for water. She saw him broken, tormented, alone. She saw him praying for her not to forget him.

Jessie bolted upright in bed, her body drenched in sweat and her heart pounding. Flashes from the nightmare shot through her head and chilled her.

"What is it, Jessie?" Matt asked from the shadows.

"Just a bad dream. It's so hot."

"The windows are open, but no air is stirring. We need a good rain to cool things off. It's as hot and dry as it was before that last thunderstorm."

"I hope we aren't in for another one. I'm sorry I awoke you."

"Lie down and go back to sleep."

Jessie was shaking. She didn't know why, but she had the awful feeling something was wrong, just as she had two days after Navarro left. She worried that he had been captured again. If that were true, he was . . . dead, hanged for murder. Could that be why he hadn't returned or sent word? How could she learn the truth? She dared not write the authorities about him. If the worst were true, she couldn't change it. Wasn't it better not knowing his fate? Wasn't it better to think he was safe and happy someplace far away?

"Matt, will you hold me? I'm so frightened."

Matt gladly gathered her into his embrace. "About what, Jessie?"

"I don't know. I just have the feeling something terrible is about to happen."

"You're safe with me, love. Relax and close your eyes."

Matt stroked her hair until Jessie settled down and was asleep again. It felt wonderful to have her in his reach, touching him. She smelled so fresh and was so soft. He recalled the day in the stage-coach when she had slept in his embrace. She was his wife now, and that thought thrilled him. Some day, she would turn to him, and he would be waiting there to claim her. But first, Navarro's ghost had to be taken from between them. He didn't know how to do that yet. All he could do was be close when she needed him.

When Jessie awoke, Matt was gone. She was relieved she was alone, for she was ill this morning. She jumped from bed, pulled the chamber pot from beneath it, and heaved over the container until her sides and throat hurt. She felt awful: nauseated, tired, achy, and tense. The door opened and her grandmother—neat and smiling—entered the room.

"I heard you stirring and thought herbal tea might settle your tummy. My ma and grandma used this recipe for years; they passed it along to me. When I was ailing with my boys those first months, it worked on my morning troubles."

"Thanks, Gran. I feel terrible. How long does this misery last?" Jessie took the cup, sipped the soothing liquid, praying it would stay inside.

"Another couple of weeks. Your body's changing. It's nature's way of telling you to go slow and easy for a while."

"What would I do without you, Gran? You're always here when

I need help the most. I've made so many mistakes, but you kept me from making another one."

"About leaving home?" the woman asked as she sat down beside the pale redhead and stroked her tangled hair.

Jessie was glad she hadn't said, "about running away." "I made the right choice, Gran, thanks to your wise advice. Matt's a wonderful man. I'll make this marriage work."

"What about Navarro, Jessie?"

"I have to forget him. I've settled my life. Navarro will have to do the same. We have to accept it's over for us."

"Is it over for you, child?"

"Don't look worried, Gran. It'll take time, but I have plenty of that. It hurts me and makes me angry that Navarro and I can't have each other, but I won't—I can't—dwell on the past. I can't become bitter. I have to give Matt the chance he deserves."

"That's a wise attitude, Jessie. You're a strong and courageous woman. You and Matt are good for each other. You're more alike than you and Navarro. Friendship and respect are important to a successful marriage. Matt and you have had those for a long time, so love will come if you let it."

"Gran, what if I never come to love Matt in that special way?"

Martha's gaze was gentle and encouraging. "Only take and give what your heart allows, Jessie. Don't be false with Matt. He wouldn't want you to pretend. Even if your love is never a blind, fiery one, you two will share a good life together. Sometimes a quiet and peaceful love is more rewarding than a dangerous and passionate one. Matt and Navarro are so different; that will help you not confuse them in your heart."

"I promise to give it my best, Gran; I owe Matt that much."

Jessie stayed in bed until her queasiness eased. She got up, bathed, and dressed. Gran prepared her a light meal so as not to upset her stomach again, which the redhead ate slowly. Afterward, she spent her time moving items to make room for her new husband's things.

When Matt returned after his chores, Jessie smiled and greeted him at the door. "If you'll get your possessions from the bunkhouse, I'll help you get moved in."

"You sure about this setup, Jessie?"

She laughed and said, "Of course, I am, Mr. Cordell. How can we get to know each other as we should if we live in different rooms?"

"I'm much obliged, Mrs. Cordell. I know this isn't easy on you."

Jessie looked into his eyes. "You make it easy for me, Matt. I promise to make you the best wife possible. There's only one difficult area, and we'll handle that after the baby's born. Is that all right?"

Matt looked at her rosy cheeks and bright blue eyes. He grasped her meaning. "I can wait for that day, Jessie. You just worry about staying safe and healthy."

Overcome with gratitude for his understanding, Jessie hugged him.

As Matt held her in his embrace, his spirits soared, knowing she was being honest and fair. "These next months will be busy ones, Jessie. I'm going to town next week to hire trained bronc peelers to get the cavvy broken in. If we're lucky, I'll find enough wranglers to hire on for the roundup and cattle drive."

"I'll let you tend to everything. I'm not in shape to help out these days."

"I'm not trying to take your or Jed's place, Jessie. I only want to do anything I can to take the work off you for as long as you need it."

"I know, Matt, and I'm grateful. I trust you completely; I always have. Besides, this ranch is ours now. You aren't the foreman any more; you're the boss."

"Rusty will be a good foreman. The boys like him and respect him. They won't have trouble taking orders from him."

"He was a good choice. Now let's get you settled before supper."

For the next few days, Jessica Lane Cordell continued to take things slowly. She remained at rest each morning until her misery passed, then helped her grandmother with housework or Tom with his book lessons. In a way, the redhead was enjoying her new womanly role. She could relax about her pregnancy with Matt to safeguard her and the child from scandal and heartache. Matt treated her with such tenderness and affection. She liked being made to feel special. She liked feeling feminine. The more she was with Matt, the more she adored him.

As he continued to court her with loving kisses and embraces, she had to admit she found his romantic attentions pleasurable. It was soothing to be held in his strong, cherishing arms. She had prayed that losing Navarro wouldn't embitter her to the point she couldn't feel passion and love for another man. She wanted her husband to stir the desires that Navarro had first awakened. She recalled how it felt to share herself with her lost love. She confessed that she wanted to experience those same passions and emotions again. Perhaps sex would be the final link in the chain to bind her and Matt together as they should be. Lovemaking had bonded her and Navarro, had proven and strengthened their trust. Yet, while she carried another man's child, she could not unite her body with Matt's. But she could work on giving herself to him emotionally until the time was right.

Late Friday, Jessie and Matt were standing on the porch watching a lovely sunset. He was behind her, his arms wrapped around her waist, hers clasped over them. She was leaning against his hard body with her head resting against the broad width of his chest.

"It's mighty hot and dry. Makes the men and stock restless," he said.

"But it's beautiful and peaceful," she remarked, gazing at the colorful horizon to the west. "Everything's settled down, Matt."

He bent his head downward to brush a kiss on her cheek. Jessie turned and nestled in his arms, her hands spread across his back. She listened to his heartbeat as her nearness increased its pace. His arms tightened, and he pressed his lips to her silky hair. She wondered which was better, to show her affection or to withhold it to keep from tantalizing him.

"Matt, does it make it harder on you when I get close? Should I stop?"

"I'm glad you can talk to me about anything, Jessie, and yep, it's hard being near you and not . . . You know what I mean. But it makes me happy to hold you, to have any part of you. Lean my way as much as you can," he coaxed.

Jessie pushed back enough to look into his brown eyes. "You're a very handsome man, Mathew Cordell. I'm lucky no girl lassoed you before I could. I do want you, but I have to wait until there isn't anyone between us."

"Navarro's ghost?" he asked.

"No, the baby. After it's born, I will become your wife in that way, too."

Matt's hands cupped her face, and he stared into her sincere gaze. He craved her so much, but her admission gave him the strength to wait for her. He understood and honored her feelings, her dilemma, her sense of duty to all of them. "I love you, Jessie. Much as I need you, our future is all that's important to me." His mouth covered hers with a soul-searing tenderness and power that stole her breath.

At the corral, Miguel nudged Carlos and remarked, "We were wrong, *amigo*. She could not love Navarro and surrender so sweetly to Matt. It is good. They have been close for many years. *Sí*, it is a good match."

"Where is the law that says a beautiful señorita cannot love more than one *hombre*? I think she turned to him from loneliness and fear. But, *chica* is an honorable woman; she would never hurt or betray our boss. I wonder if Navarro will ever return. What will he do when he sees he has lost her?"

"What can he do, Carlos? It is done."

Jessie awoke before midnight. She was restless and edgy. She didn't know what was wrong, but something more oppressive than the heat weighed upon her.

"What's wrong, love?" Matt asked from the darkness.

"I don't know. I can't sleep. I think I'll sit and read a while."

"It's just the weather and your condition. How about warm milk and a rub?"

"That isn't it, Matt. I have that dark mood again."

"Why don't I sit up with you? We can—"

A rumble in the distance caught their attention through the open windows. Both pairs of eyes darted in that direction. The noise came again, closer, louder.

"A storm's brewing. Maybe that's it," he suggested.

Jessie got out of bed, walked to the window, and looked outside. She saw lightning not far away and heard the rolling sound once more—deep, heavy, continuous until muffled by its retreat. Matt's arms encircled her body. She remained tense and stiff, staring at the ominous horizon.

Matt's gaze followed hers. From the look of it, they were in for a bad one. "I best go alert the boys. Don't want the stock spooked into a run."

The sky was dark and threatening. Thundercracks rent the hot air and roared off in all directions like angry beasts on the prowl. Lightning flashed, and branched into several limbs as it reached down from above to finger the land with its power. The house vibrated as the booming noises increased in volume and proximity. Shadows were dispelled for a time by flickers of brightness. Lightning attacked the terrain as rapidly as the peals of thunder shouted into the night. An eerie wind picked up and blew over the dry landscape, shaking anything in its aimless path.

"Don't go tonight, Matt. I want you with me. I'm . . . scared."

"You've never been afraid of storms, Jessie, but I'm here. Just let me get the boys to work, then I'll return." He hugged her, snatched on his clothes, and left.

Jessie kept her gaze on the sky. This was not a normal thunderstorm. Its strength was awesome; its warning was lethal. She trembled as lightning danced wildly in the sky, then sent forked tongues to lick at the earth. No Indian war drum could sound as intimidating as the claps of thunder over the house. She knew it was dangerous for any man or animal out tonight.

Jessie jumped and shrieked as she heard what sounded like an explosion nearby, bamming and echoing. The next siege began as soon as it was silent. The house seemed to sense danger and to shudder in panic. The windows rattled, their panes tinkling and their frames creaking in an odd way. Two loud bangs were discharged by a luminous thunderbolt that separated into several offshoots and struck the earth. Jessie jerked and screamed. She wished Matt would return. She was terrified, and she didn't know why.

The thunder and lightning were at full fury, foreshadowing a torrential rain. She wished moisture would pour down to cool the heat of the weather's rage. An ear-splitting blast charged through the house, causing it to tremble with alarm. Jessie knew it had been struck by lightning. She smelled smoke: fire!

Jessie rushed into the parlor, glanced about, and hurried toward the kitchen. Before she reached it, she saw the brilliance of flames from the back porch out the windows. Crackles said the hungry fire was spreading fast as it chewed at dry wood. In horror, she watched red devils jump from spot to spot to set them ablaze. The thirsting condition of the wood caused it to ignite and burn rapidly.

"Tom! Gran! Get out fast! The house is afire!"

Tom responded he was coming. Gran yelled she was yanking on clothes.

Jessie knew Matt was in the bunkhouse giving orders and didn't realize their peril, as the continuous claps and rolls were too noisy. She seized a bucket and pumped water as fast as she could, but it filled slowly from the lowered supply. She tossed the liquid at the blazing windows, then repeated her action. She realized it was futile, with the fire swift and the water sluggish. She saw ravenous flames licking or gnawing at the porch, bathing closet, and the roof. She knew it was already in the attic. "Tom! Can you hear me?" When he responded he was coming soon, she ordered, "Leave those things! Get down here! Now!"

Jessie reached the short hallway to her grandmother's bedroom. A surge of flames and blast of hot air swept from her old room and cut the redhead off from her target, forcing her backward a few steps. She held up her hands before her smarting face. Weakening beams overhead creaked and threatened to come crashing down before much longer. Tom moved slowly on his disabled leg. The kitchen was under attack, and his escape would be cut off soon. Frantic, she shouted above the noise of the fire and storm, "Gran! Keep your door closed! Fire in the hall! Get out the front window! Fast, Gran! I have to get to Tom before he's trapped!" Jessie did not get a response. She glanced toward the burning kitchen where Tom soon wouldn't be able to pass, then at the obstructed hall to her grandmother's silent room. In a split second, horrible thoughts raced through her mind. If she rushed outside to break the glass to rescue Gran, she could never reach her brother in time. If she went after Tom, they might be trapped upstairs and Gran in her room. Her baby. . . . All of the Lanes could perish tonight inside this raging oven. . . . Where was Matt? *God, help us!* She had to act, now.

# CHAPTER NINETEEN

Matt rushed into the house calling for Jessie. He hurried to her side and ordered, "Get to the barn where it's safe. I'll go for Tom. The boys are getting Gran out the front window. They're hauling water, but it looks bad. Too high to fight. Move, woman!" he shouted to spur her into motion.

Jessie didn't obey. She saw her husband run toward the kitchen, but returned to her room to save some of their possessions. She threw clothes on the spread, tied the corners, and tossed the bundle out the window. She threw more belongings and the ranch books onto the sheet and did the same with it. She jerked open drawers, scooped up items, and crammed them into emptied pillowcases. Out the window they went. She heard shouts as men passed orders and buckets. She smelled smoke and saw it wafting into her room like thick mist stirred by a brisk wind. Crackles and pops entered her ears. A crash told her the back porch was collapsing.

Matt hurried into their bedroom with an axe he had fetched. "Can't get through the kitchen! I'll have to chop through the wall to get to the attic steps. Get out, Jessie, before the ceilings fall." Matt slammed the tool with all his strength against the wall into the dining area. Wood splintered and flew in several directions. He worked quickly and desperately, knowing time was against him.

Jessie was panicked. The only way to her brother's room was by the steps in the far corner of the eating area. The sole window overlooked the back of the house where the blaze was raging at its worst, making a rescue ladder impossible. She couldn't leave until she saw Tom's face and knew he was safe. She prayed as Matt swung the axe and broke into the partition. When the hole was large enough for him to slip through, he vanished into the smoky room of flames, holding a soaked blanket over his head.

Jessie heard his boots clattering on the wooden steps. She heard the dog barking in fear. She heard her brother's voice. Her heart pounded and she clenched her hands. Soon two coughing males appeared, and she cried in relief.

"Let's go!" Matt carried Tom to the front window and outside.

Clem's frantic barks caught her attention. Jessie rushed to the hole calling to him, and the dog ran to her. She helped him through the opening which was too high for him to leap over to safety, then carried him to the window and leaned over to place him on the porch. Clem took off toward the yard. As Jessie bent to crawl out, the window gave way and struck her head. Everything went black.

Gusts of wind whipped the flames into a wild frenzy. It swirled dry dirt and smoke into everyone's eyes. "No use, boys!" Matt shouted. "Pull back!" The men stopped fighting the determined fire and rushed to collect the family's possessions that had been tossed out the windows. Bundles were carried to safety in the barn.

"Where is Jessie?" Gran shouted.

Flames leapt into the dark sky over their home and brightened the wanton area. Smoke billowed. Walls and sections of roof gave way. Over the thunderclaps, voices, wind, barks, and pops of burning wood, Matt heard Gran and looked around for his wife. He saw Jessie's head in the bedroom window. He ran to the porch, jumped onto it, and shoved the sash upward. He held it in place with his knee while he pulled Jessie into his arms, then carried her down the steps. A loud crash followed them and sent fiery coals and ashes into the air. One burned through Matt's shirt and seared his flesh. He halted for Miguel to toss water on the area.

Matt entered the barn and placed Jessie on a blanket on the hay. By lanternlight, he checked her head. The wound wasn't bad, but it had rendered her unconscious. "She'll be fine in a while, Gran," he told the worried woman. "Watch her for me."

Matt left the barn. He watched helplessly as flames engulfed and destroyed it. He wished the rain would hurry. It was too late to save their home, but a downpour would protect other structures on the ranch from flying sparks. "Watch the other buildings. That wind is gusting embers all over."

"Sorry, Boss, but she's riding high and bucking stubborn," Rusty said.

The men stared at the consuming blaze. Lightning flashed in all directions. Peals of thunder followed each display of powerful light. More walls and sections of roof rumbled to the floor. Heat reached them even at their distance. Rain started, slow at first; soon, it was drenching them fast.

Jessie roused and sat up to find everyone observing the fire that was fighting for its life against ever-increasing rain. She saw bundles nearby. She stood, battled her dizziness, and walked to the doorway.

Matt steadied her with an arm around her waist. Jessie leaned her head against his shoulder. She watched the storm rage into full force. Her home was gone, like her father and Navarro. "Damn," she swore in distress. "I hate fires! This isn't fair. It's the third one we've had. That's more than our share. Why didn't He send the rain sooner to help us?"

"Don't get bitter, love. We still have more than most people do. We'll bed down here in the barn tonight, then figure what to do come morning."

The hands rushed to the bunkhouse to get out of the storm and to change into dry garments. Matt coaxed his wife and Tom and Gran from the grim scene and closed the barn doors. "Let's get dry and get some rest," he suggested.

Jessie looked at the four of them: filthy with soot, smelling of smoke, exhausted, and depressed. The soaked animal in Tom's arms gave off its own doggy smell. "Why, Matt? Haven't we been tested enough?"

"Don't, Jessie. Accidents happen. There was nothing we could do."

"He could have," she remarked with anger, glancing upward.

"We don't question the good Lord's ways, child," Martha told her. "Not everything, good or bad, is His doing and bad things aren't always His tests or punishments. Be thankful we're all alive and safe."

Jessie lowered her aching head and replied, "You're right, Gran. You, too, Matt. You saved my life and Tom's. It's just been such a long and hard fight to end this way."

"It isn't over, love. You have Fletcher's home. We can move there. Either we can stay there or we can rebuild here."

"That's a crazy twist of fate: Fletcher came after our home and land, but we wound up with his. We'll use his place until we decide what to do."

"*Our* place," Gran corrected, then sent her an encouraging smile.

Matt turned his back while the two women changed nightgowns. Then they did the same while he and Tom changed. He pulled bedrolls from the tackroom and spread them on piles of hay. "Let's turn in," he said.

Jessie took the roll beside her husband and pulled protective cover over her shaking body. She saw Clem snuggle next to Tom's warm body. Fatigued, she realized her grandmother and brother were soon asleep. Jessie curled closer to her husband's side, needing his strength and comfort. He turned toward her and wrapped his arms around her. His hair and skin still smelled of smoke and his face was smudged. She wriggled closer to whisper, "I'm glad you're here, Matt."

He looked over at her misty gaze and weary expression. "Me, too, Jessie." His mouth closed over hers and kissed her deeply, soothingly.

Jessie's hand caressed his dirty cheek, and she returned the more-than-pleasant kiss. As one drifted into another, she rolled to her back and her husband lay half atop her. His mouth worked a stimulating path across her face before returning to her lips. Jessie warmed to his touch. She did not once think of Navarro Breed. She closed her eyes and dreamily realized how skilled Matt was with kisses and caresses, and she enjoyed them for a time.

"I love you, Jessie," Matt murmured in her ear. "I'll always protect you."

She hugged him tightly and replied, "I love you, too, Matt."

As if knowing it was perilous to continue his amorous behavior, Matt halted it and cuddled her in his embrace. "Sleep, love."

Jessie was grateful for his caution. She knew now that she could respond to him when the right time came, but that was months away. Relaxed, despite the raging storm and devastating fire, she closed her eyes.

*   *   *

Jessica Cordell stared at the wet, blackened ruins of her home. The storm had ceased at dawn, but the ground was muddy from it. She walked around the fallen house twice, and saw nothing more could be saved than the few bundles they had tossed outside last night. The rock foundation and chimneys stood firm in place amidst dark debris. Broken glass lay here and there from heat-shattered windows. The stench of destruction hung heavy in the cooled air. She took a deep breath to settle her edgy nerves. Maybe a move would be a new and challenging beginning for her marriage to Matt, away from the room where her father had been washed and wrapped for burial and where she had slept with Navarro during the last violent storm. All that was gone; it was time to look to the future.

They had eaten earlier in the chuckhouse, and Gran was helping Biscuit Hank with the chores there. The other hands were out checking herds and fences to see how they had weathered the storm. Matt was hitching up a wagon to drive them to their new home a few hours away. When it was loaded, he joined her.

"Come away now, Jessie. Don't look any more."

Jessie turned to her husband and smiled to let him know she was all right. She was fortunate that morning sickness had not attacked her on this challenging day. She reached for his hand and curled her fingers around his. After what had happened between them last night, she felt a little shy with him. To cover it, she behaved more boldly than usual. "It's over here, Matt. Let's go home."

A broad smile made creases near his brown eyes and enticing mouth. He guided her to the wagon and helped her aboard. He fetched Gran and Tom. When all were ready, he flicked the reins and off they went.

Jessie put away their clothes in Wilbur Fletcher's old bedroom. Gran and Tom did the same in the two guestrooms across the hall. After warning his wife to take it slow and easy, Matt returned to the other ranch to give orders.

Hours passed as the two women took inventory of their new possessions. The windows were open wide to air the stuffy place. Jessie had men move the billiard table to the old foreman's dwelling, a large one-room structure on the other side of the bunkhouse, to the left of the hacienda-style home. Other furniture was moved by the men as the women rearranged the large parlor.

Jessie checked every area for fire safety. There were plenty of windows for quick escape. Yet she knew the stucco facade and the flat roof with *canales* for drainage wouldn't catch fire, so that eased her fears of another dangerous blaze. Jessie recalled the terror and helplessness that had overwhelmed her during the fire, and she never wanted to feel that way again. She would make certain everyone was careful with the lamps and candles—anything that could ignite.

After a bath and shampoo to remove the smell of last night's disaster and the sweat from her labors today, Jessie donned a simple cotton dress. As she brushed her hair, her gaze slid to her flat stomach. She tried to imagine it protruding with a child. "Ouch," she muttered as the brush was ensnared in her tresses.

As she worked with the auburn tangles, she walked to a small extra room beside hers that would be nice for the baby. She looked into the area and tried to envision a cradle and rocker there, and her child playing. She wondered what sex it would be and how it would look. Jessie admitted to herself that she was anxious about giving birth and about raising a child. She was glad she had Matt's help and love, as he would make a wonderful parent.

More so than the troubled Navarro, she admitted, as he had had poor experiences with his home life. She was glad she wasn't on the run in her condition, that she was safe and comfortable here. She knew that Navarro still had bitterness to resolve, something only he could do for himself, so it was probably best they had parted. The trouble that had drawn them together could have made them too dependent upon each other. Months ago, they had needed each other desperately. Now Matt could fill her needs. She and Matt were so similar, whereas she and Navarro had been so different. Yet Navarro had opened her heart and life so Matt could enter them. Yes, Matt would be a better father than—

"Anything the matter, Jessie?" Matt asked from the stairs.

She leaned against his strong body after he joined her in the doorway and kissed her cheek. "I was just thinking about what a good father you'll be."

The answer delighted Matt. He couldn't forget how she had felt in his arms last night, how she had responded to him. "You'll be a good mother, Jessie."

"I hope so. This new job is a scary one," she admitted.

"I agree. We'll work hard to do it right. Have you given any thought to whether you'd prefer to live here or try to rebuild on the other property before spring?"

Her husband followed her into their new bedroom. "Yes, I've been thinking about that all afternoon. We've got broncbusting, fall roundup, and the cattle drive soon. When you and the boys get back from Dodge, it'll be only a few months before the baby's due. That isn't the best time for construction or moving, or for spending a lot of money on materials and extra men. I don't think we should make any decisions until next spring, after roundup and branding. Let's see how we like it here this winter. It's a lovely, safe house, and large enough for our family. We have so much to do between now and March."

"Sounds good to me. I don't want you working so hard. You have to be careful of lifting heavy things."

"You worry about me too much," she teased with a grin, glad he did.

"That's a new job I'm loving, Jessie."

"Me, too," she concurred, knowing deep inside it was true.

On Monday, Jessie had some of the men begin work on a new smithy. She didn't like the location of the old site next to one of the two barns. It was a fire hazard that Fletcher had overlooked, one she didn't want. Her husband had agreed that the structure should be in a clearing by itself, as on the Lane property.

Matt left early that morning for town to buy supplies, things the women needed in their new home, and to hire seasonal workers for the impending tasks.

In bed alone that night, Jessie realized it felt strange not to have him at her side. She was already accustomed to his presence after only a week of marriage. The bed seemed larger with only her to occupy it. She missed his company and the sense of security it gave her. She was glad she had never shared this bed with Navarro. Nothing in this house could remind her of the missing desperado, except the child she carried. She told herself this was the last night, last time, she would think of him. She owed Matt her life, Tom's twice, her family name, her love, her earnest attempts to make him happy, and her fidelity of heart and mind and body.

You have to leave me in all ways, Navarro. I can't keep thinking about you. I must be true to Matt; he deserves that and more from me. Good-bye, my love.

When Matt returned late Tuesday, he found Jessie and Martha in the kitchen preparing supper. "I'm home, love," he called from the doorway.

Jessie dried her hands and hurried to greet him with a hug and kiss.

"I have several surprises for you," he hinted.

"What?" she asked. Excitement and anticipation brightened her pale face. She had been ill again both mornings during his absence, but was better by now.

"This is first." He pulled a gold band from his pocket and slipped it on her finger. "There, Mrs. Cordell. It's my brand," he teased.

Jessie eyed the wedding ring with delight. "It's beautiful, Matt. Thank you." She hugged him again. "What else?" she inquired, recalling he had mentioned several surprises.

"I hired wranglers for the roundup and drive. Had to offer 'em top dollar, forty a month. They'll be here a week from Sunday." Matt knew the long drive to market meant they would be separated for months, and he dreaded that time alone on the trail. Even more, he hated leaving Jessie in her condition to run the ranch and in new surroundings that might tempt her to do more work than she should. But mostly he was anxious over the possibility of Navarro's return during his absence. Yet Jessie had vowed she was his wife forever . . . To conceal his lingering worry, Matt continued with his news. "I got two broncbusters coming Sunday to break in the cavvy. I promised 'em five dollars a head. Between them, Jimmy Joe, Miguel, and Carlos, we'll have the horses ready in a week or less."

"That's wonderful, Matt. Papa would be proud of us. Things are finally getting back to normal. I'm glad."

"Me, too. Word spread about Fletcher's death, so drovers headed this way again. We have a big job before us, and I didn't want to lose 'em to other ranchers. I wired our old trail boss, and he accepted my offer. I promised him a bonus if he gets us there on time and without much trouble. You don't mind, do you?"

"Certainly not. He's worth every dollar. We need him." Jessie stroked Matt's stubbled chin and said, "This is *our* ranch now, Matt, so you don't have to check everything with me. Besides, you were the best foreman any ranch could have. Marriage hasn't made you lose that magic touch. We have plenty of stock ready for market, so we can afford the best hands. I want you, the boys, and our herd safe on the trail. And back home as soon as possible," she added.

Matt grinned in pleasure. "My last surprise is for you and Gran. With me taking both cooks, that'll leave you two tending the boys left behind for chores and protection. I don't want either of you working that hard so I hired extra help for the house and hands. She's waiting outside."

"She?" Jessie echoed.

"Margaret Anne James. She's all alone, Jessie, an orphan. Just eighteen. You know what jobs are around for women on their own. Annie is nice and kind. They were letting her go at the hotel. Most men will be gone for months this time of year, so they don't need two girls. I heard Annie pleading to stay on just for meals and board until business picked up again; she said there weren't any other jobs around and she didn't have money to travel to another town where there might not be any, either. I felt sorry for her, Jessie, and we can use her. I figured we could move the billiard table into one of the barns and let her have the old foreman's house. We need a strong back and extra hands to take the load off you and Gran. Annie can help with the housework and cooking, and whatever else has to be done. This way, you and your grandmother can get more rest—and especially you, love. You'll need it in the coming months. You've also got a lot of sewing and planning to do for the baby. Annie can help you tend him after he's born."

Jessie was moved by her husband's thoughtfulness. But a twinge of jealousy pricked her. She had never heard Matt talk so much about another woman . . . and so caringly. She admonished herself for her foolishness. Matt had a tender heart, and great concern for his wife. She didn't care to have another woman, a stranger, in the house, but the girl was needed. She hoped this Annie would work out for everyone, as she didn't want Matt disappointed. "Bring her in so we can meet her."

"Did I make a bad decision?" he asked, as she had hesitated a while. For a moment, he suspected he read jealousy in her gaze. Was that—

Jessie broke into his thoughts, "No, Matt, a good one. You're right, and you're the kindest man I've ever known. I'm a lucky woman to have you."

While Matt was fetching the girl, Jessie told her grandmother, "If we don't like her and she doesn't work out, Gran, wait until Matt's gone before we handle the matter. I don't want him hurt or embarassed."

"You're a good-hearted woman, Jessie."

Matt returned with Annie, who looked a little shy and worried. She had thick brown hair, grass-green eyes and dimples set in a lovely face. At five seven, she was taller than Jessie and had a fuller figure. The girl appeared to be older than eighteen, but Jessie assumed a hard life had aged and matured her beyond her years. Those unbidden twinges pricked her again as she eyed the young beauty at her smiling husband's side.

After Matt introduced them, the girl dipped at the knee, nodded her head, and said in a southern accent, "Pleased to make your acquaintance, ma'am. I want to thank you for this job, Mrs. Cordell. I need it badly. I promise I'll work hard. I don't drink strong spirits, use bad talk, steal, or sneak off to play."

Jessie warmed to the blushing female with trembly voice and earnest gaze. She smiled to relax her. Annie's green eyes were clear and honest. She spoke well and had good manners. She deserved a chance to prove herself. "Welcome to our home, Annie. I'm sure you'll do fine here. Matt will have the boys prepare your place for you. I'm sure you're tired after your long journey, so go along with him to get settled in. We'll go over your chores in the morning. Did you and Matt discuss wages?"

"Yes, ma'am. He offered the same as the hotel, twelve dollars a month. If that's too much, you can pay me less. I had to use my earnings for boarding and meals, so it's more than I was making in town."

"No, that's fine. I think you'll like it here, Annie. Just remember we have lots of men around who can be tempted by a pretty face. I wouldn't want to lose you and one of them about the time I get used to having good help."

The girl smiled at Jessie's teasing tone. "Yes, ma'am. You have a beautiful home. I've only seen a few as grand."

"Thank you. We've only been here a few days. Ours burned last Friday. We owned this one, too, so we moved here. Gran and I have some changes we want to make. You can help us with them later.

Matt, see that Annie's settled in, then return for supper. I'll bring you a plate after we eat. If you need anything, you can tell me when I come over."

"You're all very kind. I'll do my best here."

"I'm sure you will, Annie."

The girl left with Matt. Jessie and her grandmother exchanged smiles of acceptance. They returned to their chore, chatting about Matt's actions. Tom joined them soon, and Jessie sent him to wash up for the evening meal. By the time the food was on the table, Matt walked in and took his place at one end.

"What do you think of her?" he asked the two women.

Tom replied first. "She's mighty pretty. I like her."

"We do, too, Matt," Jessie said reassuringly. "We're glad you brought her home with you. She'll be a big help, and you spared her from a terrible fate in the saloon."

"That should make her even more loyal and hardworking," Gran added.

"I'm sure it will, Gran." Jessie turned to Matt and asked, "What else did she tell you about herself? I didn't want to ply her with questions she'd already answered for you. She was a mite skittish, but I don't blame her. If I had refused her the job, she would have been in for a bad time."

Matt buttered his bread as he responded. "Her parents moved from South Carolina to El Paso when she was twelve. They died two years back when she was sixteen. Annie doesn't have any other family, and didn't know many people in town. Seems her father wasn't liked much and died in heavy debt. Men he owed took most of what she had to settle his accounts."

"That's awful, Matt. How did she live, alone and so young?"

"She helped a seamstress for over a year until the lady closed shop and left town; Annie had been living in her back room. The woman gave her enough money to survive on until she got another job. She worked in the El Paso Hotel until five months ago. The owner was mean and . . . demanding," he said, choosing the word carefully for Tom's adolescent ears. He knew the two women would understand his meaning. "She'd saved enough to take the stage as far as Davis. She was about out of money when she was hired at the hotel. Didn't last long with business going down."

"Why haven't I see her in town? How long was she there?"

"She worked at Morley's place at the far end of town. We never stayed there. Annie came about four months ago. She tried to get another job in El Paso first, but that spiteful man made certain nobody hired her."

"I'm sure he was trying to force her back into his employ." With her young brother sitting there with keen ears, Jessie didn't say what she felt about the wicked man and his doings. Yet it angered her to think of a young girl in such a helpless situation. She was glad Annie was a good girl and hadn't given in to the lustful beast. "Most women are vulnerable if they don't have a family."

"Unless they're strong and smart like my wife, who has her own ranch."

Jessie laughed and retorted, "Unless they have wonderful husbands who keep them from losing their . . . skins to men like that hotel owner and Fletcher."

"You could run this ranch without me, woman, and we both know it."

"Perhaps, but I wouldn't want to find out. I like being married to you, Mathew Cordell, and we shouldn't have waited so long to have so much fun."

Matt's eyes glinted with pleasure and desire. "We haven't had much of that since our marriage last Tuesday, but we will."

"Last Tuesday?" she repeated in amazement. "It seems so much longer."

Matt laughed heartily at her expression. "Because so much has happened. I guess I'm already like a comfortable old shoe. I've been around a long time."

Jessie was seated to her husband's right, with Tom across from her and with Gran at the other end. As Jessie turned toward Matt it was easy to forget the others were there as she lost herself in their teasing conversation. "Better that, Mr. Cordell, than a tight and painful new boot that doesn't fit and is paid for."

Matt grinned and grasped her left hand. He gazed at the gold band on her finger, his heart swelling with pride and love. Jessie had never seemed more relaxed and happy than she did tonight. It was apparent she had accepted him in her new life, and that she was trying her hardest to be a good wife. In time, their marriage could only get better. If Navarro didn't return and spoil it.

Jessie observed the tormented look that flashed in Matt's brown eyes like lightning before a storm. His grip on her hand tightened for a moment as something distracted and alarmed him. Her astute mind went over the clues—marriage, ring, claim on her—and realized what her husband feared could happen to his new life. Jessie squeezed his hand, capturing his attention, and gazed into his troubled eyes. "I love you, Matt," she said, "and I'm glad I said yes to your proposal."

"Oh, no, Gran, they're gonna get squishy on us. Wait till after supper."

Everyone looked at Tom's wrinkled nose and comical expression, and laughed.

"Sorry, little brother, but I am a new bride. We act crazy like this."

"He'll understand when the love chigger digs into his hide like it did mine."

"Oh no, they never will," the boy vowed with wide eyes enlarged by thick glasses.

"I'll remind you of that claim one day, young man, when you're chasing some lucky girl's skirt," Jessie warned in a playful tone.

Tom shook his auburn head. "I ain't gonna act loco over no girl."

"Love ain't loco, Tom; it's wonderful and magical. It's very special."

"Matt's right," Gran concurred, smiling at the man. "You'll see one day."

The boy didn't look convinced, but stayed quiet and returned to his meal. The others did, too. When the table was cleared and the dishes were done, Jessie headed for the one-room house where Annie was lodged.

The door was open, so Jessie called out and walked inside. "Here's your food, Annie. How is everything?"

"It's more than nice, ma'am. Thank you."

Jessie saw how misty her green eyes were. She realized what a difficult and frightening life Annie had had. But the girl was strong, brave, and smart enough to take care of herself for years and to seek a new start each time she had to. Jessie's tender heart went out to Margaret Anne James, as Matt's had in town. "I'm glad you like it. I hope you'll be with us a long time."

"Is there anything . . . you want to know about me?"

"Matt's told us what you related to him," Jessie admitted. "I'm sorry you've had such a bad time of it. That's over now, Annie. The boys here are good men; they won't give you any trouble. If anyone does, come to me. Most of them have worked for my family for years, but we do have a few new hands from the past owner of this ranch, so I don't know them well."

Annie caught her meaning. "I won't give them any reason to approach me, Mrs. Cordell. Sometimes manners and kindness are mistaken for overtures, so I'll be careful. I'll try not to make any mistakes here."

"Come to the house about seven in the morning. We'll start then."

As the redhead turned to leave, Annie said, "Thank you again, ma'am."

"You're welcome, Annie," Jessie replied. "See you tomorrow."

Wednesday morning, Jessie and Gran talked with Annie and showed her around the house. They discussed the daily schedule, went over the list of chores, and told the girl how they wanted them done.

The three women took to each other quickly. Over the midday meal, Jessie gave Annie a brief sketch of their family history. She told the girl she had only been married a short time, but didn't give a date. Of course, she might guess her secret one day, or someone could reveal the conflict in timing by accident. Jessie couldn't worry about what Annie or the hands would think about a seven-month baby. Surely everyone saw how happy and compatible she and Matt were, and they were aware how long the couple had known each other. She knew, with the men about to go away, the truth would be safe until spring. And as babies sometimes came early, perhaps others would be fooled when it arrived in early March instead of mid-May. But even if the hands suspected her secret, none of them would speak ill of her and Matt, and hopefully wouldn't suspect who the child's father was.

Annie and Gran finished talking about Wilbur Fletcher. "You're a strong and courageous woman, Mrs. Cordell," Annie said. "You're lucky your father was a good man. Mine wasn't. We had to leave Carolina because he was always into trouble over gambling debts. It wasn't any better in El Paso. If he and Mother hadn't eaten tainted food and died, I don't know what would have happened to us. Creditors came and took everything as soon as he was buried. It was awful. I know a lot about sewing, so I can help make clothes. A seamstress taught me."

Jessie didn't mention she would especially need that skill and assistance in two months when her figure started expanding. She also didn't comment on how Annie had changed the subject in a rush. "Please call me Jessie," She coaxed. "I'm only six years older than you. Mrs. Cordell sounds so matronly."

"And I'm Gran to everyone, child," Martha added.

"You're all so good and kind. I'm so happy Mr. Cordell was in town to rescue me. Some men can be so wicked, but I knew I could trust him. You're lucky, Mrs.—I mean, Jessie."

The redhead sensed the sad-eyed girl had secrets of her own, but she didn't pry into them. "Yes, I am. You will be too one day, Annie. You're sweet and lovely. You'll see that all men aren't like your father and that hotel owner."

The rest of the week went by fast as the women changed Wilbur Fletcher's house into the Cordell home. Jessie also spent time on Tom's neglected lessons, as Matt had purchased new books in town. Annie helped out on occasion, something young Thomas Lane seemed to like. He did his best to impress the girl.

Each evening, Margaret Anne James served their dinner in the dining room, ate in the kitchen, and did the dishes before retiring. Jessie told her she wasn't a servant and it wasn't necessary to wait on them, but Annie seemed to enjoy the task and insisted upon doing it.

The professional broncbusters—peelers—arrived on Sunday. Matt introduced them to his wife, then showed the two men where to bunk during their brief stay.

The remuda—cavvy—of half-broken and wild horses was corraled near the barn and ready for busting and training to begin tomorrow. Hands had gathered them over the last few days for the seasonal task of preparing them for roundup and the long drive on the Western Trail to Dodge City, Kansas.

Each man needed three horses for gathering steers and for cowpunching on the trail, a total of one hundred ninety horses. Excluding their regular mounts—which made four apiece—that left the Cordells one hundred and fifty horses to break. Each man was responsible for all the care his four animals would require along the way: thinning and shortening tails, trimming and shodding hooves, treating injuries and sickness, currying sweaty hides, and feeding them.

Geldings were used, as stallions and mares were moody and undependable. The remuda was allowed to roam the range until it was needed in the fall. Most were seven to ten years old; the older were more experienced and easiest to retrain for the next time. Each had its own personality. Some made good cutting horses that were superior at culling market-ready steers from the herds. Night horses were steady of foot in the dark. Rope horses seemed to know when and how to keep lassos tight around stock's necks. Herd mounts were adept at working with steers during drives and skilled at remaining calm and masterful and sure-footed during terrifying stampedes.

The dusty, exhausting, and perilous task of training the horses would begin after breakfast tomorrow. An aura of suspense and excitement already hung over the area as everyone awaited the event.

Jessie joined Matt and others at the corral. They talked a while, then parted as he went to handle the chore. She waved to Miguel, Carlos, and Jimmy Joe as they prepared themselves to risk life and limb while challenging half-wild creatures to prove who was master. Hands perched on the fence, ready to lend help if an unseated rider was in danger of being trampled and eager to shout jests and encouragement during the episodes.

Five areas were sectioned off so all the busters could work mounts at the same time. The professional peelers took on six to eight of the wildest beasts a day, while the Cordell hands rode three to four half-broken creatures into renewed submission. Each man had a helper to rope the right animal and to assist the rider with saddling and mounting a frantic critter.

Jessie stepped onto the bottom rail and looped her arms over the top one to observe the action. This time, she didn't sit atop the fence and risk a fall.

"Tame them good, Miguel," she said to the Mexican who was dressed in his finery to put on a good show.

"Do not fret, amiga; I will be resting by high noon," he vowed with a grin.

"On a busted arse!" one of the men joked, then chuckled.

"You wish to make a bet on who gets tamed?" Miguel retorted.

"Yep! Fifty cents for every hoss that throws ye."

"Done" was the confident reply. His dark eyes twinkled with anticipation of earning the wager.

Miguel's assistant pulled a wide-eyed horse to the snubbing post. The animal snorted, backed until a taut noose halted him, then jerked his captive head several times to free it. His mane shook, but the lariat held firm. The critter's ears twitched and he moved his hooves in restless panic.

Miguel tried to calm him with a soft and soothing voice. As he did so, he eased forward and slipped a hackamore onto its head. With caution, he put on the blanket and saddle. While the helper talked to the animal, then twisted an ear to hold its attention, Miguel mounted. The instant the horse felt weight upon its back, he began bucking. His front hooves slammed into the hard ground and his back legs kicked up and out, fast and hard. The beast hunched and reared and bawled in outrage and fear.

Dirt and pebbles were flung in all directions. Dust clouds went into the air. Hands yelled and chuckled. Some waved hats above their heads and rocked their bodies on the fence as if helping the rider who pitched and swayed in a frenzied dance. The area was charged with emotion, and with prayers for safety.

Jessie knew what a jarring strain such a wild ride was on a man. It was as hazardous to his teeth, spine, neck, and innards as a crushing fall could be.

Up and down and around went the pair as the roan and vaquero challenged each other's will and stamina. The Mexican used a quirk and spurs to master the animal, but was careful not to injure the creature. Miguel's hair, bandanna, and batwings flapped about—as did the gelding's tail and mane—as the two whirled and bounced to the music of broncbusting which played inside their heads.

In the end, the beast tired and calmed. Miguel rode him around the area for a time. The procedure would be repeated every day until the buster was certain the animal was tamed. Then its special skills would be cultivated.

Later, Gran and Annie joined the redhead to watch the action and join the fun. Jessie saw how the girl gazed at Miguel. She had seen the two talking several times during the past week, and she suspected a romance was in the making. Jessie witnessed how the Mexican glanced their way and how his admiring gaze lingered on Annie.

Concern nipped at Jessie as she noticed an unnatural cockiness enter the Mexican at the girl's presence. The vaquero grinned and mounted his last horse. It only took the panicked chestnut a few leaps and bucks to send the inattentive rider to the ground. Its back legs kicked ominously near the fallen man's head as it tried to buck off the saddle, too, then, failing, raced around the enclosure while venting its fury. Jessie heard Annie's squeal of fear and the thud as Miguel hit the ground.

"That's three fur you and one fur me!" the wagering hand shouted.

Miguel jumped from the dirt, dusted off himself, and glanced at the group in embarrassment. "Double or nothing I do not eat dirt again, *amigo!*" he shouted.

The gambling hand looked at the frantic horse, then back at Miguel. He saw, as did everyone, that the vaquero limped toward his helper, who had captured the gelding's reins and was having trouble controlling the beast. "That high roller'll toss ye agin. Ye got a bet, *amigo,*" he chuckled, then spit tobacco.

Jessie saw the determination and pride in Miguel's expression. "You're wasting good money, Slim; he won't be thrown a second time. I know that look." She was right. When the vaquero had the animal calmed and trotting around the enclosure, she said to the women, "Let's get back to our chores." The others weren't finished yet, and she decided against watching more of the action. She didn't want a distracted rider injured while trying to impress the green-eyed beauty. "See you later, boys," she called out and left with Gran and Annie trailing her.

Over dinner preparations, Annie asked questions about the men and broncbusting. Jessie knew why. She talked about her times with the hands and explained the seasonal chores and schedule of ranch life. She guided the conversation to Annie's obvious object of interest.

"You've met Miguel, the rider we were watching earlier. He's one of our best hands, one of my best friends. He's an expert with guns and horses. He's one of the most skilled ropers and cutters I've known."

"What's a cutter?"

"That's when horse and rider work as one to separate certain steers from the herd. Both must have a natural instinct for that task. I'm sure you realize he's Mexican. He's been with us since he was twenty."

"How old is he now?"

"Twenty-seven."

"Does he . . ."

"What?" Jessie coaxed.

"Does he have a sweetheart?"

"Not that I know about. He is a man to catch women's eyes. You caught his today; that's why he took that spill, showing off for you."

The girl blushed and said, "I'm sorry. I didn't mean to . . . cause an accident. I won't go near the corral again."

Jessie laughed and replied, "No need to stay away, Annie, not if you let him know you're just as charmed by him as he is by you. If he doesn't have to worry about other hands catching your interest and he doesn't have to impress you, he won't get cocky again. I don't want him hurt or killed."

"Killed? It's that dangerous?"

"If a rider's careless or distracted, he can break his neck in a fall. Miguel's good. He doesn't usually act that way. But I can't blame him. You're a beauty."

"Thank you, Jessie. But I know little about romance and men like him."

"Then Gran and I will have to teach you. Of course we won't if you aren't interested in him or ready to learn."

Annie thought a minute, smiled, and admitted, "I'm both." She frowned and asked, "What if *he* isn't interested or ready?"

Jessie and Gran laughed. "I've known him for years," the redhead told her. "He's both, too. Trust me; I'm sure."

By dusk Saturday, the broken cavvy was ready to tackle the tasks ahead of it. The peelers were paid and thanked for a job well done. The three Cordell hands were given bonuses for their additional labors, skills, and dangers. The extra drovers and trail boss were due to arrive tomorrow to begin Monday's roundup.

*   *   *

Jessie and Matt took a stroll after dinner. Holding hands and chatting, they paused near the corral to observe the sun's last appearance of the day.

Matt watched the fading rays on his wife's hair. Its golden soul shone through the dark-auburn strands. Her skin glowed in the enhancing light. She seemed tranquil to him tonight. He knew her serene mood came from a successful week, having Annie's help in the house, and the disappearance of her morning sickness a few days ago. "You're beautiful, Jessie," he murmured. "I'm gonna miss you."

Her calm blue gaze met his adoring brown one. She smiled and said, "I'll miss you, too, my comfy old shoe."

They shared laughter at her rhyming reply.

He stroked her hair and cheek. "It's working for us, isn't it, Jessie?"

She nestled against him. "Yes, Matt; it is."

His arms crossed her back and he rested his chin against her sweet-smelling hair. "I'm happier than I ever dreamed I could be, thanks to you, woman."

"Me, too. Everything is going so well for us. We make good partners, Matt."

"Then you aren't sorry I talked you into staying and marrying me?"

"No, I made a good bargain." When his head lifted and he stiffened, she knew she had used the wrong word. She was denied a chance to correct herself.

His voice was strained as he said, "We both got a good deal."

Jessie tried to rectify the mistake, but her meaning went astray. "After the baby's born, it'll be a better one for you."

He sounded sad and serious as he argued, "You don't owe me more than you've given so far, Jessie."

"But you want and need more, don't you, Matt?" she challenged.

He remained quiet for a while, and both knew he was deciding how to respond.

His mood worried her. She tried again to better it. "I know how hard this has been on you, Matt. You're the most unselfish and caring person I've ever met."

"That's more true of you than me, Jessie."

"No, it isn't." She leaned away to look into his eyes. "I've been selfish and unfair just to protect myself, the baby, and the ranch.

I've taken advantage of your love and kindness. You've done so much for me, Matt, and I'm truly grateful. How could I help but love you and respect you? And want you? Don't look surprised and doubtful. It's true, Matt. I've always had deep feelings for you, and they've grown since . . . in the last few months. They're getting stronger and clearer. I just need more time to get over the past. After the baby's born, I'll be a real wife to you. I promise."

Matt released her and stepped to the corral. He leaned against it, his back to her. "Don't rush yourself, Jessie. The hurt goes away; I know from experience, but not this fast or this easy. Let it work itself out. I'll be here when the right time comes. When it does, you'll know." He turned to face her. "I don't want Navarro's place, Jessie; I want my own spread in your heart and life. Until you can surrender that terrain for the right reason, let's leave our life as is."

# CHAPTER TWENTY

The drovers and trail boss—Jake Bass—gathered on the ranch Sunday evening. Jake was tough and wise, with quick reflexes and keen instincts. The hands respected and obeyed him without question or hesitation. He kept the men relaxed, but still working hard. He was an expert horseman and gunman. He knew the territory they traveled with the herd: where to find the best grass, ample water, how to avoid the worst perils. He knew cattle, their quirks and needs. Experienced and in great demand, they were lucky to hire him again this year. At one hundred twenty-five dollars a month, he was well worth his high pay.

Matt met with the men and gave the orders. Returning men and Cordell hands separated into groups to talk over old times, tell tall tales, play jokes, and relate their experiences since they'd last worked together. New men joined in to laugh and learn. They would be on the trail for six to eight weeks, so it was important to build good rapport and trust. Matt spent most of the evening with them, enjoying old acquaintances and making new friends.

Jessie watched them for a time from the front porch. She saw Annie and Miguel taking a stroll, and smiled in pleasure. It was obvious to everyone that the couple was smitten with each other. She liked the girl and trusted her. She was in favor of a match between the two, but it was happening awfully fast.

Fast? her mind taunted as she went to her room for privacy. Instant love and attraction were things she knew too well. The moment she had gazed into Navarro's eyes, she had been lost to him. Each hour in his company had entrapped her more, until she hadn't wanted to escape. In all honesty, she had tried to forget Navarro. She had tried to make the hurt and anger go away. Each time he returned to her mind, she had closed the door. Yet cracks around the jamb had allowed parts of him to slip past her barrier. Her mind told her it was wrong and unfair to pine over him and the life they could have shared, but her heart couldn't help but do so at weak moments.

She wanted and needed to get over her lost dream, to embrace her reality, but it was so hard, more than she had realized. Sometimes his memory was so vivid that it seemed as if he would return from a day on the range at any moment, just as on some days she briefly forgot her father was gone forever. Yet Jed's loss was more real than Navarro's was, and she didn't know why. Perhaps because she knew Navarro was still alive somewhere and could reappear before her. She was forced to admit she still loved and desired Navarro Breed, and she still yearned and watched for his return.

Jessie knew that was foolish, and cruel to her husband. It would soon be three months since Navarro had gone. She resented him for not sending word, not letting her know he was safe, that he was suffering as she was—that he still loved her and hadn't changed his mind about returning. She needed a last message from him before she could truly break with the past. The silence was eating at her nerves.

Matt sensed that turmoil, she decided, even though she herself hadn't been aware of it. She had been so caught up in other matters and emotions that she hadn't realized how hard she was struggling to keep Navarro out of her mind; when, all the while, he was lurking in her heart and waiting to spring on her.

That wasn't her fault, she vowed. She wasn't to blame for loving the desperado. Love wasn't something that came and went on schedule like the seasons. It wasn't an emotion that could be controlled. She wasn't guilty of not trying to make a new life and not trying to turn to a new love. But, did innocence and determination matter? She didn't know, but she wanted it to.

Matt was a good man. He deserved more than half of her, more than a marriage in name only. But Matt was right: she couldn't rush the healing process or make him a substitute for Navarro. Her husband had to win her heart before she could yield her body to him. But was he right about keeping her at a distance?

At times she was tempted to surrender to her husband. She truly desired Matt, and she yearned to free the passions that Navarro had once unleashed. Mathew Cordell stirred them to life some nights with his touch, kisses, and tenderness. He often made her head spin, and her body tremble, but he never tried to make love to her. He seemed content as things were. Perhaps, she worried, he didn't desire her as Navarro had.

She had accused herself of being wanton for thinking of Matt that way so soon after Navarro's departure. But was she so wrong? Wicked? Unnatural? How so, when Matt was her husband? When she had known him forever? When, perhaps, she had always loved and desired him and failed to recognize her feelings? Perhaps it was because the two men and situations were so different.

Navarro had been a wild and urgent temptation. She had been helpless to resist his allure. He had ridden into her heart and life when she was vulnerable and felt so trapped by her role as Jed's "son." He had made her feel strong, alive, and free. He had given her adventure, romance, and her womanhood. He had come along at the right time to become her confidant, partner and solace. Maybe, she mused, those were meant to be his only roles in her life.

Perhaps Mathew Cordell was her real destiny. Matt's love was different. It was calm, tender, safe, and nourishing. It was honest and pure. She knew everything about Matt; no shadows surrounded him. She and Matt were compatible in personality and background, but she hoped not too much alike to prevent sparks of excitement and mystery. Yet, after only a short marriage, they were like a long-time couple. Their marriage was comfortable and tranquil. But what about passion, romance, temptation? Amidst the steady coals, there had to be occasional sparks of fiery sensuality to ignite her soul, to make her burn with desire. Yet she had to think of the fugitive as a turbulent and brief adventure, and Matt as a serene and permanent haven.

She felt her flat stomach. It was hard to believe she was pregnant with another man's child. Often, Navarro seemed only a dream to her. Matt was reality. She had a good life and family. It would be stupid to ruin them. If only she knew how she would feel if she ever saw Navarro again. What if he rode up, took her in his arms, and said, "I love you. I'm free. I can stay forever if you still want me,"?

Jessie knew she could never go on the run with the fugitive. But what if Navarro could return to her side? Could she break her vows to Matt and to God and to herself? And break Matt's heart a second time?

Jessie searched her soul and realized the answer was no. Yet, she comprehended that it would take all her strength to turn Navarro down should he return for her. But Mathew Cordell and their life together was worth that painful sacrifice.

Her conversation with Matt last night returned to haunt her troubled mind. She had accepted his words and had agreed with them, at least verbally. In silence, they had returned to the house. They hadn't touched in bed or kissed good night as usual. All day he had been quiet, serious, and reserved, like the old Matt. She knew he was hurting, and her heart ached for things beyond her control.

Jessie closed her teary eyes and prayed for the next six months to pass swiftly and mercifully. Until Navarro's child was born, her body and life were tied to the past. All she could do was wait, hope, and pray she didn't lose her second love while imprisoned by her first bittersweet experience.

The men left for roundup the next morning. While Annie was hanging up wash, Jessie and Gran did the dishes and talked. The distressed redhead told her grandmother of her thoughts.

"What am I going to do, Gran? I feel so helpless. I'm trapped between them. I love them both, but in different ways. I can't have Navarro, but I have Matt. Navarro is a landslide, but Matt is stable ground. I want him and need him, Gran, but he won't reach out to me as long as he thinks I'm bound to Navarro."

Martha sympathized and comforted her troubled granddaughter. "Matt's right, Jessie," she said, "Time is all you need."

"It can work against us as much as for us, Gran. So much happened with Navarro; so many unfamiliar emotions were involved. I was lost in a sandstorm before I knew what was happening to me. I was too susceptible to Navarro's spell, too inexperienced and naive. I was just one of the boys, Jed's 'son' and heir. I'd never had such feelings before. Now, every time I dam them up, something happens to let them break free again. I've honestly tried to forget him, and I usually do a good job at it. But Matt can't forget our past together. It's so hard for him to accept the fact Navarro had me as he hasn't yet."

"He loves you, Jessie. He wants to be the only man in your heart and life."

"It's too late for that, Gran. I wish I could change what happened, but I can't."

"Then you and Matt must learn to accept it."

"I hope we can. I do love him and want him, Gran, but I'm not sure he believes me. I'm so afraid I'll lose him before he realizes the truth. You know how stubborn and destructive pride can be."

"He needs time, love, and patience, too, child."

"Time!" Jessie exploded. "That damned word sounds as dangerous and frightening as our old enemy Fletcher was!"

"Don't work yourself up, Jessie. It isn't good for the baby."

"Good for the baby? Everything I've done lately has been for the baby. Navarro's child is ruining my life with Matt. I wish it were his, Gran; I really do."

"Don't blame an innocent child, Jessie," she scolded in a soft tone.

"I'm sorry, Gran. You're right, as always. I do love it and want it. It's mine. But sometimes it seems so unreal," she said, glancing at her slim waist.

"That's because the daily sickness is gone and you aren't showing yet. Living with Matt while it grows inside you will make it feel like his."

"To me, yes; but to him, no. I'm afraid he'll always see it as Navarro's. Maybe it was a mistake to let us believe it will be ours."

"No, Jessie, it wasn't a mistake. You'll see."

"Will I, Gran? How can Matt bear to watch me bloom from another man's seed? He'll come to hate me. I would rather Navarro feel that way than my Matt. What am I going to do, Gran? How can I hold Matt's love and respect until I become his wife? Losing him would be far worse than losing Navarro." She began to cry.

In a few minutes, Matt called out from the parlor, "Jessie! I'm back! I forgot something! Where are you?"

Jessie panicked. She couldn't let him see her like this. She wiped her eyes on her apron and yelled, "In here, Matt!"

He came to the kitchen, glanced at her, Gran, then back to Jessie again. He came forward and asked, "What's wrong?"

"Something in her eye," Gran said, which wasn't totally untrue: there had been tears.

Matt tilted her head upward and gazed into her eyes. He read anguish and panic in them. "It's gone now. You must have washed it out. I came back for my duster. It gets cool some nights on the range. We'll be back in a few days. If you need anything, send one of the hands. We'll be in the south pasture."

"I'll be fine, Matt. Don't worry about me."

"That's a husband's job. Walk me upstairs?" he asked.

"Of course." With his arm around her waist, Jessie accompanied him.

Jessie leaned against the wall near the bedroom door as Matt fetched his duster from the closet. As he walked toward her, their gazes locked. Matt dropped the boot-length garment of water-resistant canvas to the floor. He stepped in front of her and propped one hand against the wall over her head. The other hand lifted a henna curl and toyed with it. Jessie was baffled and mesmerized.

"I also forgot to tell you I love you," he murmured just before his mouth covered hers. His hand released the curl and shifted behind her head to hold her close.

Matt's kiss was deep and passionate. His other hand left the wall and both cupped her face as his mouth continued to pleasure and stimulate hers.

Jessie was astonished, taken off guard. Going almost limp, she leaned against the wall for support. Matt pressed closer, his full length snug against hers, and his mouth worked hungrier at its tasty feast. Jessie felt dizzy, weak, and breathless. A hot flush spread over her quivering body. She was lost in a golden swirl of emotions. Her hands slipped up his back. She clung to him and returned her husband's tantalizing kiss with an ardor that surprised both of them. A soft moan escaped her throat as Matt spread a fiery trail over it. She trembled with longing for more, much more. She wanted him to carry her to the bed and finish what he had started—a sensual journey to discovery.

Instead, Matt's hands drew her head to his chest and held it there. He kissed her hair, then took several deep breaths. Jessie felt the tension and craving in him. She heard his heavy breathing and thudding heart. She felt the strength of his hard body.

"I love you, Jessie, now and always. Nothing will ever change

that. Take care of yourself and our baby. I'll see you in a few days."
He scooped up his duster and left in a hurry.

Jessie sank against the wall—enflamed, confused, and shaky.
Matt had never kissed her or behaved like this before; and she wondered what it would be like to make unrestrained love to him. Wild,
fiery sensations begged her to explore that astonishing mystery. So
much, she concluded, for thinking Matt's passions were calm and
cozy!

Jessie raced after him. He had secured his duster to his saddle and
mounted. She rushed to his horse and looked up at him, flustered
and dazed. She just kept staring at him, as if seeing him fully for
the first time.

Matt looked down at his wife's rosy cheeks. Her gaze held a mixture of bafflement and desire. "Did I forget something else?" he
asked.

His voice returned hers. "You're quite a surprise, Mathew Cordell."

A broad grin revealed his white teeth and played mischievously
in his dark eyes. "I figured it was past time I stopped being just a
dependable, nice friend and started showing you how I really feel
about you, woman. You asked me if I wanted and needed more from
you, and I didn't answer. Well, I do, Jessie. I'm not a martyr. My
head was clear when I staked my claim on you. I was the one who
took advantage during a hard time, not you. But I realized you were
believing you owed me something. I must be loco, because I haven't
been doing anything to help you get over Navarro and turn to me.
If I stand back, it'll take longer to heal and will hurt more. *I'm* the
medicine you need, Jessie, not time. From now on, woman, I'm
gonna work on proving I can be anything and everything you need
in a man, in a husband. Between today and next spring, I'm gonna
chase you, romance you, and tempt you until you can't resist me.
That's a warning and a promise, Mrs. Cordell."

After the initial shock of his stirring words, Jessie was smiling
so much her eyes sparkled. "I'll hold you to both, Mr. Cordell. I love
you."

Matt leaned over and Jessie lifted herself on her tiptoes so they
could kiss. When they parted, Matt said, "I love you, Jessie."

"Good-bye, Matt. Be careful. You owe me a lot."

"Don't worry; I always pay my debts, and collect what's due me."
Matt rode off with love, pride, and hope in his heart. He was glad
he had overheard Jessie's enlightening talk with Gran. It warned

him that he certainly couldn't win his wife by leaving her alone. He had to show Jessie he was more of a man than she realized. He couldn't do that by behaving like her brother. After that accidental eavesdropping and the passionate scene upstairs, he knew she loved him and wanted him. Whatever it took, he would defeat Navarro's ghost!

Matt returned Thursday afternoon. Jessie heard his voice and hurried to greet him. She eyed three days' stubble on his face, grinned, and fingered it. "I let you out of my sight and care for a while and look what happens," she teased.

"You know how we boys are on the trail. I only stopped by to tell you we're on the way to the north pasture. We'll cull the steers there, move the others to the west section, and get ready to pull out next Wednesday."

She toyed with the buttons on his shirt. "I miss you already."

"Good."

"Can't you stay home tonight?"

"Nope, not a good idea. You're too tempting, and my clever plan's working."

"Good . . . I think." They both laughed, and Jessie remarked, "We need to increase our vocabulary, Mr. Cordell; we're overworking *good.*"

"But it's such a . . . good word." Matt chuckled and changed the subject. "Best I can tell, we have between eight and eleven thousand head ready for market. If the price is good"—they both grinned—"we'll have a nice deal."

"I hope so. A weak market could hurt us this year. Our cash will be low soon. If we do, Matt, I want to pay off Mary Louise for the ranch. I don't want to risk problems with her later. You know how she can be. Is that all right with you?"

"It's your cattle and money, Jessie. The decision is yours."

"It's all *ours,* Matt. Tell me what you think. I trust your opinion."

"It's a smart idea. Sorry, Jessie, but I don't trust your sister, either. The sooner our deed is clear, the better. I best ride before the boys get too far ahead."

"You'll be leaving for over two months soon. Will I see you again before you go?"

"Yep. I'll visit before we head out."

"Visit?"

"The less time I spend with you right now, the more you'll miss me, woman."

"Part of that clever plan of yours to drive me loco?"

"Not loco, just into my arms."

"You already have that much."

"Yep, but like I said, I want you craving me something fierce."

"More than I already do?" she challenged.

"Yep, a whole lot more."

"That's cruel, Mathew Cordell."

"Nope, just smart."

"I like you this way," she murmured. "Possessive, masterful, and cocky."

"I've only gained a little confidence about you, Jessie."

"Good. It's about time." They laughed again.

"Yep, it is. See you soon." He brushed her lips with his and mounted.

"See you soon, my love," she murmured, watching his departure.

Matt rode in Monday afternoon with Miguel. Jessie excused Annie from her chores so she could visit with the vaquero before he left for the months-long mission. She also wanted privacy with her husband, which Gran and Tom respected.

"By the time you get back, you'll have a beard and long hair, Matt. All you men'll look like drifters before you get home and cleaned up. I wish I could go with you."

"Me, too, but it's too hard and dangerous this time. You need anything?"

She stroked his coarse jawline. "Besides you, my stingy husband?"

He backed away with hands raised and jested, "Behave yourself, Jessica Cordell. We have to get back. We're heading off at dawn Wednesday."

"Why can't you stay home tonight?" she urged.

He waxed serious. "You know why."

"That's no longer a reason, Matt. You can't make it back to camp by dark."

Matt was afraid of hurting Jessie and not giving her pleasure in her condition. He didn't know much about such things. When they came together the first time, he wanted it to be special, passionate, and fulfilling. He wanted only the two of them in bed, not anything of Navarro's sharing it. He dared not tempt them tonight, because he wanted her too badly and she was willing to surrender. "Not yet, Jessie. We need to get closer first. We'll work on it when I return."

By the time he returned, Jessie knew she would be showing. It would then become impossible to forget she was pregnant with Navarro's child. She feared how Matt would react. She wanted him to have her now. She wanted him to know she belonged to *him*. She also felt it would make the baby seem more like his. How could it if they'd never made love? How could he want her so much and hold off taking her?

Matt interrupted her obvious worrying. "We'll ride most of the night. We can catch a nap in camp tomorrow while the boys finish up. Don't work too hard or take any risks while I'm gone," he said as he took her hand and walked to the door. He had to leave before she became even more tempting.

Jessie knew she couldn't stall him. "Be careful, Matt. You know there are all kinds of dangers on the trail: Indians, rustlers, stampedes . . ."

"I'll be home by Thanksgiving." He looked Jessie over and smiled. "The chuckwagons pulled out this morning. They'll load up and join us at Fort Stockton."

"Don't you go visiting those naughty saloons in Dodge, Mr. Cordell. You're a married man now. You need a ring to show my claim on you, like yours on me."

"This lasso around my heart is strong and tight enough to hold me true."

Jessie shook her finger at him and jested, "You try loosening it any to play around and I'll treat you like male calf at spring branding."

"Ouch!" he yelped and grimaced playfully. "I best shout for Miguel and hightail it before you try something foolish, woman."

"That was sweet of you to bring him along. I think he and Annie have picked up that love chigger you mentioned to Tom."

"I think you're right. I'm glad."

"Me, too. Everybody should be in love."

"Yep." Matt kissed her, took a last look, and left. He and Miguel rode off with Jessie and Annie watching their retreat until they were out of sight.

"Well, Annie," Jessie said with a sigh, "it'll be a long and lonely wait for them."

A week later, Jessie was answering Annie's questions about the long drive to Dodge City. "There's about ten thousand steers, two hundred horses, two chuckwagons and cooks, and over sixty men. They spread out for miles across the terrain, Annie; you can't let them bump horns and hooves. It's an awesome sight. But it's loud, dusty, and tiring. At times, the journey seems endless. It's eighteen-hour days and short, chilly nights. By the time you make camp, you swallow your grub and hot coffee, then fall onto your bedroll, to start it all again in a few hours. They won't be back for two and a half to three months."

"It takes that long?" Annie murmured.

"I'm afraid so. They have to cross dangerous rivers and harsh country. In the Oklahoma Territory, you have to pay Indians to keep them from scaring off stock just so they can charge you to round them up again. White men try to pull that same trick some-times. Storms or thirst can spark a herd into stampedes along the way. If you don't stop them fast, the steers can be injured, lose valu-able weight, or get killed. A few times, we had trouble with irate farmers and other ranchers not wanting us to cross their land. If you're used to stopping for water and grazing there and have to cir-cle a wide path, it can be bad. Of course, I can't blame them; several large herds during a season can do a lot of eating and trampling. And you always have rustlers trying to pick off a thousand or two. It's exciting, Annie, but exhausting and hazardous." Jessie took a deep breath. "Mercy, it's a slow pace. You almost get rocked to sleep in the saddle, unless you're one of the drag riders responsible for strays and sluggards. Then you eat dust and stay busy."

"You've been with them?"

Jessie grinned. "Many times. Papa was teaching me what I needed to know to take over for him one day."

"But you're such a . . . I was going to say 'delicate woman,' but you aren't."

"I was raised as Jed's son, as one of the boys. Papa and the hands always forgot I was a girl. Sometimes they said and did things they shouldn't because they were so used to having me around." Jessie laughed.

"How could they forget? You're so beautiful and feminine."

"In boy's clothes, a pigtail, and dirty face, I looked the role I had to play."

"Had to play?"

Jessie exhaled loudly in the ensuing silence. "I was Papa's heir. I grew up on our ranch doing anything and everything the hands do. Until this year, I almost forgot I was a woman. I opened everyone's eyes when I started wearing girl's clothes, leaving my hair down, and acting like a lady."

"Because of Matt—and love?" Annie hinted with a smile.

"Yes, because of love. It's surprising how first love affects a female."

"I'm learning that more and more every day. When you've been independent like me and you, it's scary seeing how much you can lean on another person, how much you want them to share everything with you."

Jessie nodded and agreed. She left the painful area of first love by saying, "We'll be safe while the men are gone. Matt left plenty of hands for chores and protection. And we won't have wasted milk; they took two cows with them. But we'd better get busy with the hands' supper before they're moody with hunger."

The following Tuesday, Jessie dropped a bottle of cologne. It struck the shelf in her private water closet and shattered. Fragrant liquid and glass shot in all directions. "Tarnation," she muttered.

With caution, she gathered the broken pieces. She poured water from a pitcher into a basin and set it on the floor. She wiped up the cologne, then removed the items in the cabinet and placed them atop it. With a bathing cloth, she worked to clean up the mess. As she leaned inside to reach the back and corners, she noticed a packet tucked beneath a support board.

Jessie tossed the cloth into the basin. She worked the packet free from its snug and secret hiding place and leaned against the wall and opened it. She withdrew a map, several papers, and a few letters. Unfolding the map first, she gazed at it.

Jessie's eyes widened in confusion, then narrowed in understanding and anger. The map revealed a proposed rail line right through the Lane ranch, past Fort Leaton, and into Mexico. There was a spur to Fort Davis that traveled onward to Fort Quitman and El Paso, and a spur into the Chinati Mountains that were southwest of them. She saw an X marked in the last area. She read the papers. One related the profitability of shipping cattle and supplies to the posts and across the border, and of transporting Mexican precious metals and goods into America. The other exposed that rich silver mines in the Chinati region were owned by the Fletchers! Now she knew why Wilbur Fletcher had craved the Box L Ranch. His motive had been greed, as his railroad and mine could earn him enormous wealth and power. The Lane property was the best route because of easy terrain and ample water and wood for the engines, and proposed stops were marked on the map.

Jessie studied the map and papers. No company names were listed so she assumed it was a private venture by the Fletchers. That was a relief, else any partners might try to finish what Wilbur had failed to accomplish. Worry nipped at her as she realized Fletcher could have accomplices somewhere, waiting until the Lanes were lulled into complacency before starting new attacks. With Matt and most of the hands away for months, she prayed that wasn't true.

Jessie opened the letters to read them, seeking clues as to any future threat. They were from his brothers back East. Dread filled the redhead as she realized they had been in on the plot.

Mary Louise was there now. Jessie had written her late last month to tell her about her marriage to Mathew Cordell, the fire, and their move here. She had mentioned they were in the midst of broncbusting, and that the men were leaving soon for roundup and market. The blonde must have received it about the time Matt left for Dodge. Had her sister shared that news with Fletcher's wicked brothers? If Mary Louise had responded immediately, a letter could arrive with the twice-monthly mail this Saturday.

Jessie wondered how the Fletcher men had taken the news of their brother's marriage, his death, then his widow's arrival to claim her husband's possessions from them. Jessie owned this entire area now, so what destructive action could they take against her? With this evidence in her grasp, they had better not try anything! Yet she had little help and protection available with the others gone, and Mary Louise might have told them she'd be vulnerable now. It would be wise to warn the remaining hands to stay alert, and she would do so today. If nothing more, the villains might want to make certain any evidence against them was destroyed.

Jessie asked herself if she should write Mary Louise again and warn her sister about the Fletchers. No, she decided, as the men might get their hands on the revealing letter and harm Mary Louise. It was best to keep this evidence a secret in case she needed it to stop the Fletchers. She needed to find a good hiding place for it. She also needed to alert Sheriff Toby Cooper of possible danger and a need of assistance. She would send one of the men in the morning. She must do all in her power to prevent another siege.

"I wish you were here, Navarro. I'm scared, and I might need your help again," she murmured to herself.

The moment she spoke these words, Jessie grimaced. She prayed he wouldn't return. She couldn't work with him again; it was too dangerous for him and for them, particularly with her husband away for so long.

Jessie met with their new foreman Rusty Jones when he returned from the range. She showed him the papers, map, and letters. "This could be big trouble, Rusty. I want you to take this evidence to the line shack and conceal it under the floor. Then I want you to ride into Davis and explain matters to Sheriff Cooper. Bring him to the old house. I'll meet him there and go over the situation. I don't want Gran, Tom, and Annie to know about this. I don't want them to worry. I trust you, Rusty, so I need you to handle it personally. Put the men on alert, but tell them to keep quiet. At least Matt took all of Fletcher's old hands with him, so we don't have to worry about traitors if his brothers should arrive. I want this information safe. After that trick Fletcher pulled with the bankers, I don't dare risk letting them lock them up for me. Hopefully I'll get a letter from Mary Louise this week."

Jessie told Rusty about the letter she'd sent to her sister. "By now they all know what's happened here. Hopefully they won't take over where Fletcher failed."

"If they do, Jessie, we'll be waiting for 'em. I got a notion they won't try anything soon. They won't know how many men Matt left behind to guard the place. Let's take every precaution we can. We don't want 'em trying to force this proof out of your hands. You women best stay close to the house. Be ready to lock 'er up and have guns nearby. I'll keep one of the men around all day and I'll leave at first light. After I hide this packet on the way, I'll ride into town. Me and Toby should be back Thursday afternoon afore three."

"I'll be waiting over there for you. Be careful, Rusty."

Jessie was apprehensive for two nights and the next day. She managed to conceal the reason for her strange mood by pretending it was loneliness and worry over Matt. While Gran was napping Thursday after their midday meal, Jessie saddled Ben and rode several hours to the burned-out site of her old home. She had told Annie she was going for a leisurely ride and would return later. She had also sent Tom out with one of the men to keep him in the dark about her actions.

Jessie dismounted, dropped Ben's reins to the ground, and strolled around the blackened ruins. She hadn't been there since the devastating fire almost six weeks ago. Her heart ached at seeing the tormenting reminder of her home.

Her parents had died here, as had two brothers and her grandfather. She had loved and lost Navarro here. She had battled Fletcher here. She had discovered her pregnancy here. She had watched her sister walk out the door.

But there had been happy and special times, too. She had to forget the painful memories and only remember the good ones. She was making a new life in a new place. As with the house and loved ones, the past was dead.

Ben's whinny and movement alerted Jessie to riders approaching. She shielded her eyes from the sun to check their identity. She was holding a rifle, her piebald was alert and protective, and she was a skilled horseman, so she hadn't been afraid to come here alone.

She waved to Rusty and Toby as they joined her. "Good to see you back safe."

Toby Cooper removed his hat and said, "Rusty explained everything, Mrs. Cordell. We'll stay on watch until Matt and the boys return. Then, you should turn that evidence over to the law and let them handle the matter. I always say, head off trouble before it strikes if you can. Once they're unmasked, they won't be a threat to you again. Unless you want to go ahead with it now."

Jessie wanted to wait for her husband's return. She wanted to let Matt take care of the problem. That would increase his pride and confidence. She wanted to use the situation to show she needed him. She was strong, smart, and brave. She could handle the matter, but she wanted Matt to believe she leaned on him for protection and strength and courage. With the sheriff involved, there shouldn't be any danger for a while.

"I'll let my husband settle it, Sheriff, unless there's trouble before his return. I simply wanted you informed in case Fletcher's brothers arrive to cause problems. The Fletchers are rich and powerful. It would be dangerous to challenge them while Matt and the boys are away. We can't even prove they were involved with the fight here; we can only prove they knew what Fletcher was doing to us and why. I'm not sure that makes for a strong case against them. They have plenty of money for smart lawyers and for bribes. I wouldn't want to challenge them alone. It's best to keep quiet for now."

"I agree," Toby said. "If you see anything suspicious, send word. I'll keep my eyes open for strangers in town. I can bring soldiers if you need help."

"Thank you, Sheriff Cooper."

Rusty and Jessie watched the lawman mount and head back toward town.

"I hope we can trust him, Rusty. You know what a rail line could do for Davis and the fort. I only hope none of the men there were involved with Fletcher's plot to bring it in. Big contracts offer big money to businessmen and posts. I didn't want to tell him that I didn't know whom we can trust. I just keep remembering how sluggish he and the Army were about exposing Fletcher."

"Toby's a good man, Jessie. So is Captain Graham. I wouldn't worry about them betraying you and siding with that snake's brothers."

"I'm sure you're right, but I don't want to take any chances. When Matt and the hands get back, we'll have plenty of guns and men. He'll know what to do."

Jessie received another shock on Saturday in the mail. There were two letters. One was from Wilbur's brothers. She went to her room, closed the door, and ripped open the envelope. Her eyes widened as she read it. She tore open Mary Louise's, and had the same stunned reaction.

Jessie realized she had to share this news with her grandmother.

She called down the steps for the woman to join her for privacy. She and Martha sat on the small couch in the bedroom sitting area. Jessie related how she had found the packet of evidence, what she had done about it, and the gist of today's letters.

"Can they take the house and ranch back?" Before Jessie could respond, Martha asked, "Where will we go till Matt returns? We'll have to separate everything that's been mixed, and put up that boundary fence again."

"Don't be worried, Gran. It's just a bluff. Mary Louise claims her husband's will left everything to his brothers and she had no legal right to sell it to us. She warns us to leave pronto. The Fletchers have threatened to recover this ranch in court if we refuse to get out and turn it over to them. They say they don't want to sell, and we know why, thanks to Wilbur's carelessness. They don't care about this spread; they just want to recover their foothold here. Naturally they offered to buy the Box L again. They're awaiting my answer before starting legal action against us. They're in for a fat surprise."

"What are we going to do, Jessie?" Martha asked in alarm.

Irate, the flushed redhead declared, "Give them an answer, but not one they expect! Will or no will, this land is ours. I don't care if a wife can't inherit without one. That's a stupid law! It isn't right that a man's family can walk in and take over after the husband dies! We aren't in the dark ages any more. Women work as hard on spreads as men do, sometimes harder. If anything happens, she should get the land and home, not his kin. Matt insisted our deed remain in my name, and I see why. He wanted me protected from such injustice. I'll bet my best boots Mary Louise is in the saddle with them!"

"How could she do this to us, Jessie?"

"Because she's just as wicked and greedy as they are! She claims she invested the money I paid her and lost it, so she can't return it. That's a lie! She says she's living off their charity and support, so she has to take their side. More lies, Gran. The deceitful witch even apologized for her *mistake!* She said she didn't get any of Wilbur's holdings and money back there. That could be true or his brothers' trick, but it's the only part of her letter I'm inclined to believe."

"Didn't she tell them about the sale when she got there? Why did they wait so long to threaten us?"

"I'm sure she did. They waited until Matt and the boys were gone. They think I'll panic and run. When they learned we'd moved here, they must have panicked. This means her last letter was nothing but more lies. I should have suspected something was up when she didn't send a boastful one every week!"

"What if we can't fight that will, Jessie? What if the law sides with them?"

"They can't battle us from prison, Gran. I have that evidence, so I'm going to call their bluff. I'll send word we have proof against them and they had better not threaten me or challenge me again! I'll even blackmail them if I have to. We don't know if they're telling the truth about wills and inheritances. I'll let them know I've already seen the Sheriff, and I'll fight them in court. I'll claim I have all of their old letters to Wilbur and have his incriminating journal. That should scare them. I'll threaten them with a scandal and imprisonment."

Martha's blue eyes widened. Her face paled. "That's too dangerous, child. They might come after you. Wait until Matt returns."

Jessie frowned in dismay. "I was going to, Gran, but that's months away. I have to act fast. I don't want them coming here and starting another battle while we're low on men. I have to protect you and Tom and the ranch, not to mention the baby. If I notify the governor, Army, the Rangers, the U.S. marshal, and a lawyer and tell them I've done so, that should at least frighten them into holding off for a while. Hopefully for good."

"Send a letter or telegram to Matt. He'll get it when he reaches Dodge."

"No, Gran; that'll only worry him. Being so far away and hearing we've been in danger for months will frighten him. And there's nothing he can do from there. He'll blame himself for us being in danger. It'll be two months before he's home, and the Fletchers are almost knocking at our door."

"You think we should move into town until he's back?"

"No, Gran; nobody is going to force me off my land or out of my home. If we run scared, they'll smell it and pursue us. We take a stand and don't budge."

Martha clasped the redhead's hands in hers and confessed, "I'm afraid for you and the baby, child, and for Tom. I'm an old woman. I've lived a long and good life. My safety doesn't matter. What if they hurt you? These are violent and desperate men, Jessie."

"I know, Gran. But we took a stand against Wilbur and won, and we'll do the same with his brothers. Lane blood and spirit run in my body; I'm no quitter or coward. After they're exposed, we'll be safe. Don't worry."

Jessie met with the foreman and hands. She explained the new predicament. She handed Rusty the letters to the authorities she had mentioned to her grandmother, a terse letter to her treacherous sister, and a bold one to the Fletchers. "These will put our daring plan into motion, Rusty. I pray they work. You men stay on full alert, but don't take any chances."

Jessie returned to the house and related the trouble to Tom and Annie. "I think we'll be safe, but keep your eyes and ears open. Annie, if you want to go into town for a while, I'll pay your expenses there until it's safe to return. You weren't part of this trouble and I can't ask you to risk your life for us."

"I'm staying here, Jessie. All of you are more of a family to me than my parents ever were. If those buzzards come, we'll show them how women clip wings."

"I think you should stay in the house with us. We'll put up a cot in the extra room upstairs. I don't want you out there alone."

Over two weeks passed without trouble. Jessie, Gran, and Annie occupied themselves making clothes for the baby and working on Jessie's garments, as she had told the girl about her pregnancy and let Annie think the child was Matt's. She did not give any details about her due date, but she knew Annie would realize how far along she was in a few weeks.

Jessie knew her letters had reached the Fletchers and the authorities by now, and she wondered what was happening.

It was five weeks since Matt left home, and she was anxious for his return. She prayed for his safety on the trail, and she missed him. Some nights she found her hand stroking his side of their bed, and she wished he were lying there in his arms. It was strange, but she thought and dreamed about him more now than Navarro.

Yet a few times she had allowed herself to think and worry about the desperado. She hated to think of him alone, bitter, and in danger. There had been moments when she was tempted to write the

Arizona governor to see if she could help exonerate him. Each time she warned herself it was too risky. It could stir up new interest and a search for him. She could be the reason he was captured and hanged. It might bring the authorities to her ranch.

Navarro had told her that day at the windmill she needed a man raised as she was, a rancher. He had pointed out Matt's love for her several times. Had he knowingly pushed for this union? Navarro had said, "Be strong and never look back," so how could he blame her for believing and obeying him? His failure to return or write had proven she had made the right—the only—choice.

Tuesday, October seventeenth, a rider approached the house with Rusty. Jessie walked outside to see who it was and what he wanted. Her heart pounded in dread.

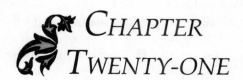# CHAPTER
TWENTY-ONE

Jessica Cordell studied the stranger. It was obvious to her that he was not a horseman from the awkward way he sat the saddle and dismounted. His neat brown suit and white shirt suggested he was a businessman. His looked aggravated and uncomfortable. As he straightened his clothes, dusted himself off, and walked toward her, she read arrogance and purpose in his gaze and stride. The Fletcherss' lawyer? she posited.

Rusty accompanied him to Jessie and said, "I found him heading this way, so I rode in with him. Says he's here to fetch Annie."

"That's right. Where is she? I've come a long way and I'm in a hurry."

Jessie took an instant dislike to the impatient and unfriendly man. There was something about him that made her uneasy. "Who are you, sir?"

"I'm Jubal Starns from El Paso. I've come to fetch her home. Call her out."

It was the hotel owner who had given Annie a hard time. "Home, Mr. Starns? Annie *is* home; she lives here with us."

"I assume you're Mrs. Cordell?"

"That's right. How can I help you?"

"You can't. I'm here to speak with Annie and take her back to El Paso."

"Annie didn't like El Paso, Mr. Starns; that's why she moved here. I'm sure she has no intention of leaving her new home with us."

"That's not for you to say, Mrs. Cordell. Call her out," he demanded.

"Everyone on this ranch is my responsibility, sir. She doesn't want to see you."

"That's none of your business, woman. I insist you not interfere."

"I'm afraid it *is* my business. I know why Annie left El Paso and your employ. I'm positive she doesn't want to see you or speak with you again, and I agree with her. You should leave. I don't like your manner."

Starns glared at Jessie. "I'll discuss this with your husband."

"He's away on business. However, I am the owner of this ranch, not him, so you'll have to deal with me. Annie isn't leaving here with the likes of you."

He puffed with anger and his eyes narrowed. "You can't keep her prisoner here. I'll fetch the law if necessary. You can't keep me from my fiancée."

"I'm not your fiancée!" Annie shrieked from the doorway and joined them.

The man turned to face her. "You promised to marry me, girl, after my wife died. I buried her two weeks past. You have to keep your word to me. Get your things and let's go. I'll buy a horse for you to use. The folks in town told me I couldn't make this ride in a carriage."

"While your wife was dying, you asked me to marry you, but I didn't accept. I never will. I hate you, Mr. Starns. And you know why."

"Don't be airing our private affairs before strangers, girl," he warned.

"I know all about you, Mr. Starns. Annie told me," Jessie informed him. More anger and now embarrassment colored his expression. "Rusty, show Mr. Starns the way back to town."

"I'm not leaving without her," Jubal announced coldly.

"Yes, you are," Jessie stated.

"If you don't come, Annie, you'll leave me no choice but to put the law on you. I don't want to do that, girl, but I will."

That threat infuriated Jessie. "For what reason?" she asked.

"Annie knows" was his reply as he stared at the wide-eyed girl.

"What is he talking about, Annie? Maybe I can help."

"I borrowed—"

"She ran out on a legal debt," the man interrupted. "It's against the law to flee a creditor. I had a man track her to Davis, then here. As soon as time allowed, I came after her. Since she couldn't repay me, I told her I would forget the loan if she married me. I understood her answer to be yes."

"That's absurd, Mr. Starns!" Jessie declared. "A woman like Annie James doesn't sell herself into marriage. She could have repaid you, if she hadn't quit your employ because you were forcing your unwanted attentions upon her. You also made it impossible for her to get another job in El Paso. She had no choice but to move to another town. You have no legal claim on her."

"I have a contract that says she owes me money. I thought Annie was honest and reliable, so I trusted her. Her father cheated lots of men out of money. Some folks in El Paso still hold a grudge against him. The law wouldn't be lenient with his kin doing the same."

"That wasn't my fault," Annie cried. "When Father died, his creditors took all I had but for my clothes. After what you did to me, I had to move to support myself."

"And flee without telling me? And no word since. Can you pay me off, girl?"

"No, sir, but I'll send you money every month until it's settled."

"The contract says it must be repaid within a year. Your time has lapsed. Cost me more money to track you here. If you don't settle up today, I can have you jailed for escaping your debt. You sneaked off without telling me and making arrangements to honor your liability. That's the same as cheating or stealing. The law is on my side. Think hard, girl. Me or debtor's prison?"

Annie looked terrified of the man and of going to jail. "Please, Mr. Starns, give me more time. I promise to repay you, but I can't marry you."

"A deal is a deal, girl. If I leave without you, I'm going straight to the law."

"How much did you borrow, Annie, and why?" Jessie inquired.

"One hundred dollars. It was to pay off a debt of my father's or go to jail."

"I don't understand. A sixteen-year-old isn't responsible for her parents' debts. Who told you such a lie?"

"Mr. Hobbs. He said he talked to the sheriff and a lawyer. They told him I had to pay the bill or go to jail. I was already working for Mr. Starns, so he agreed to loan me the money. I was to repay him out of my salary. By the time I paid for boarding, meals, and clothes, there was little left. The same was true in Davis. I was going to start sending him money this month to avoid trouble."

"But you went to work for a seamstress after your parents died," Jessie reasoned. "Why did Mr. Hobbs wait so long to approach you?"

"I don't know. He said he was giving me time to heal and work."

"Did you speak to the sheriff and lawyer?"

"No, Jessie; I was afraid to cause trouble."

"I see," the redhead murmured. "Are Mr. Hobbs and Mr. Starns good friends?"

"Yes, they—"

"Hold on a minute! What are you implying, Mrs. Cordell?"

"You know what I'm charging, sir. You had this man frighten and trick Annie into a corner so you could take advantage of her. She can't be held accountable for her father's old debts. She was almost a child."

"I don't know about the law or if Hobbs tricked her, but I made a legal loan."

"Did you, sir? I wonder what the El Paso sheriff, that alleged lawyer, and Mr. Hobbs will say when I contact them. Better still, when the U.S. marshal does."

"How dare you threaten me or insinuate I'm a liar!"

"I think you're despicable, sir. If you press this matter, so will I. However, I am willing to see if Mr. Hobbs lied and Annie's debt to you is real. If it is, I'll gladly send you the money to settle her account. Please give me their names and addresses. I'll have my lawyer check it out and handle it for us."

"You're making a big mistake intruding in my affairs!"

Jessie saw how flustered and outraged he was. "No, sir, you made all the mistakes in this offensive matter. You dared to push yourself onto a helpless girl. Worse, while your wife lay dying! You had a man trick her into an illegal debt. You tried to ruin her life by driving her into poverty and desperation. You dared to come here and threaten her. Get off my land. If we ever hear from you again, sir, you'll be the one in court, then in jail."

"Try to do something nice for someone, and this is what happens!"

"You don't have a nice bone in your body, sir."

"If your answer to my proposal is no, Annie, I'll be leaving."

"It is," the girl replied, having gained courage from her boss and friend.

The defeated man slyly eyed Jessie and Rusty, then said to the girl, "I guess I should apologize for being so mean. I love you and want you so much, Annie, that I lost my wits. You're what's important, not the money. If you change your mind, you know where to find me. If you're scared to travel alone, just send for me. You were a good worker, so I'll cancel your debt to me."

"That would be wise," Jessie said, although she didn't trust him.

"Good-bye, Mrs. Cordell. Annie." Jubal Starns went to his mount and struggled onto its back with difficulty. Then he rode away from the watchful group.

"Thank you, Jessie," the tearful girl said, then embraced the redhead.

"You'll never see that vile beast again, so forget him," Jessie advised.

After Annie returned to her chores, Jessie remarked to the foreman, "I thought Sheriff Cooper was going to alert us to strangers in town, especially one who asks for directions to our ranch. I'm surprised that greenhorn made it alone. Of course the sheriff might not have been around to take notice."

"I'm willing to bet Toby never saw Starns in town. He would have come along."

"You're probably right. At least we solved one nasty problem. I'm sure Annie's been afraid something like this might happen. She can relax now."

"That was a low-down man, Jessie. He needs a good lashing with a whip."

"I know. It's a shame there are so many like him around who take advantage of vulnerable females. I'm glad Matt found her and brought her here."

Rusty grinned. "So is Miguel."

"I've noticed. I think they'll be good for each other . . . Any problems on the range?" she asked, leaving the subject of romance behind them.

"None, but the boys are still on alert."

"We should have news by the end of the month. Hopefully we can settle it as quickly and easily as we handled Mr. Jubal Starns."

*   *   *

On Monday, October thirtieth, Jessie hurried to meet the mail deliverer, as she had been watching for him all morning. She took the twine-bound letters, thanked him, and returned to the house. She hadn't bothered to put on a wrap, as the days in southwest Texas were still pleasantly warm. She closed the front door and sat in the parlor to learn the news.

Jessie dreaded opening the letters. There were so many of them today. She began with the ones from the authorities she had written for help. She sighed in relief as the Texas Rangers and U.S. marshal offered any assistance needed to avert more trouble with the easterners and revealed that the Fletchers had been notified of such intentions. She smiled as the governor said he would never sign permission for a rail line across her ranch, and particularly if something happened to drive the Cordells off their land. He also related that he had informed the authorities back East of the charges against the Fletchers and that he would press for an investigation of them if Mrs. Mathew Cordell was harmed in any way.

Jessie's smile and satisfaction increased as she read a letter from the lawyer who had handled the sale from Mary Louise Fletcher. He was certain it was legal and would stand up in court. He offered his services to fight the case for her.

Feeling confident, Jessie ripped open the missive from the Fletchers. Her gaze traveled it rapidly, then slowly, to absorb each word. It was apparent the Texans had reached the eastern men with their warnings before this letter was written. It was also obvious that the brothers feared challenging the "alleged evidence" she possessed. They retreated by giving the ranch to Wilbur's widow, to dispose of as she desired. They even apologized for the "shameful trouble" with their "headstrong and misguided" brother! And they swore they were not involved in that attempted landgrab and could prove it. They had assumed Wilbur was obtaining the land needed for the proposed railroad by legal means. To prevent a "scandalous, time-consuming, and costly battle in court," they suggested the matter be dropped.

Jessie whooped with elation and victory. Gran came to see what was wrong. "Nothing, Gran. I'm just excited. We won! They backed down." She read the letters to the older woman, who laughed and cried in joy.

"We beat them this time without a bloody fight. Matt will be so relieved. I can't wait until he gets home, so I can share all this wonderful news with him."

"You've got a long wait, child, at least another month," Gran reminded.

"A busy one, too. My waist and tummy are changing. I'd better work faster on my clothes. I'll be five months on Wednesday and I'll start getting fat."

"It doesn't happen overnight, child. Your waist will thicken slowly and your tummy will begin to round. You won't be very big when Matt returns."

"I hope not. I want him around as it happens; then, it won't be such a shocking change. I should write Mary Louise about the baby, but I hate— I forgot; we haven't read her letter yet. Let's see what little sister has to say about all this trouble. I dread to," she murmured, ripping open the last envelope.

Dear Jessica, You have no idea how much trouble, misery, embarrassment, hard feelings, and money your actions have caused me. The Fletchers have now refused to grant me any support and friendship. They are making my social life and acceptance here impossible. It's all your fault. How could you accuse such fine men of such wickedness? Just because Wilbur made a mistake, that gave you no right or reason to attack them. They will have nothing to do with me now, and are encouraging everyone to ostracize me. I shall have to move to another city to begin a new life for a second time. I will send you my address when I'm settled. I shall expect my yearly payments on schedule or I shall be forced to confiscate the ranch for your debt. If you've read the Fletchers' letter, you know they gave Wilbur's ranch to me. That means, dear sister, you still owe me forty thousand dollars as the balance of our deal. Family or not, it is a legal contract that states I regain possession if you happen to default. Tell Gran and Tom hello.

The letter was signed, Mrs. Mary Louise Fletcher.

"What a little bitch she is," Jessica said in exasperation to her grandmother. "If she ever steps foot here again, I'll take a whip to her buttocks!"

"And I'll hold her for you," Gran replied. "Such an ungrateful and selfish girl. How could she have turned out so badly?"

"That fancy school and those so-called friends filled her head with crazy ideas. I'm glad she's gone. Sometimes I can't believe she's my sister. There isn't any Lane in her. How can she say the Fletchers gave her no widow's support, when they deeded her the ranch. And I paid her forty thousand dollars cash four months ago, and she'll get five more every year for eight years. How much money does that girl need?

"My sister better lasso herself another rich husband before she spends all her money. I won't give her a dollar more than I owe her or another pinch of sympathy. She's trampled our love and loyalty into the ground. She'll never be welcome here again. I'm finished with her. I'll settle my debt with her as soon as Matt returns with the money, all of it. I want the ranch title clear of any threat from her and those devious Fletchers."

"Don't get yourself so worked up over her, Jessie. It isn't good for the baby. Mary Louise made her choice; she deserted and betrayed us. One day she'll be sorry. The Good Lord always punishes such wickedness."

Jessie tried to calm herself. "I used to feel sorry for her, Gran. I tried to believe her problems weren't her fault. But they are. She made herself and us miserable. She wanted to capture a dream that she'll discover in the future is a nightmare. Love and family are the most important things in life. She's turned her back on them for pleasures of the flesh. Heaven only knows what's in store for my little sister."

Thursday, against her grandmother's pleas, Jessie rode into Davis with Rusty to get rid of Mary Louise for good . . .

In mid-November, the three women and Tom were sitting in the parlor after dinner before a cozy fire. Jessie giggled and caressed her stomach.

"What is it?" Gran asked, looking at her glowing granddaughter.

"The baby—it moved. I thought it was my imagination the last few times. It's like . . . a feather tickling my insides."

"Baby?" Tom echoed, dropping his book and coming to sit beside her.

Jessie smiled at her brother and said, "Yes, Tom; Matt and I are expecting a baby next spring. You'll be an uncle."

"You'll be a mother," he said, amazement shining in his wide gaze.

"That's right." She ruffled his hair and grinned.

"This is exciting!" he shouted. "Annie, my sister's gonna have a baby!"

"I know, Tom. Isn't that wonderful?"

"Am I the last one to learn anything around here?" he asked, feigning anger.

Gran cuffed his chin and said, "It's women's business until it shows, Tom."

"Does it hurt?" he asked, gazing at her stomach.

"Not yet, but I hear birth can give a few pains," she jested.

"Don't be funny. You'll be all right, won't you?"

"Of course. Having babies is woman's work, a natural thing. When he's born, you can play with him. Would you like that, Uncle Tom?"

"Is it a boy?" he questioned, seriousness filling his gaze and voice.

"I don't know. Unborns are usually called *he,* but it might be a girl."

"I bet she'll be as pretty as you and Annie," he remarked.

"It could be a boy. Then he'd be like a little brother to you."

"I'll be fourteen. Big boys don't play with babies."

"Said who, Mr. Thomas Lane?" she teased.

As if enlightened to something wonderful, he replied, "You're right, Jessie. Can I feel him move?"

"Not yet, just me. When he starts kicking hard, I'll let you feel him."

His eyes were full of wonder, then panic. "Will he be all right, Jessie?"

"What do you mean?" she inquired.

"Will he be good?"

"Good?"

"Not broken like I am. Or die like my brothers."

Martha grasped Tom's hand and squeezed it. "He'll be a fine baby, Tom."

The boy looked at his silent sister. "I'm sorry, Jess. I didn't mean to scare you. He'll be perfect. Won't he, Annie?"

"I'm sure he will, Tom. Why don't I help you with that arithmetic?" the girl offered.

After the two went to Tom's room, Jessie glanced at her grandmother and asked, "He will be all right, won't he, Gran? God wouldn't punish an innocent child for my wickedness?"

"I'm sure he'll be fine, Jessie. But if he isn't, you won't be to blame."

"Are you certain, Gran? You said God punishes wickedness."

"What you did with Navarro was love, Jessie, not evil. It should come after marriage, but that doesn't make it any less special."

"I did love him, Gran."

"Did?" the older woman repeated.

"Do," Jessie admitted. "But it's different now. I still think about him, but most of the pain and bitterness are gone. I just want him to be safe and happy like I am. I accept we can't share a life together. I have Matt now, and I'm happy."

"I'm glad, Jessie. But if you want to keep the baby safe, you should stay home. Riding is hard and dangerous for both of you."

"I had to go into town, Gran. I wanted Mary Louise paid off, so I wouldn't have to worry about her treachery any more. That puts us low on money, but Matt will be home in a few weeks to replace it."

"It was risky, child. What if the market was bad or they get robbed? You should have waited and talked it over with your husband."

"Perhaps, but I'd rather owe the bank than any Fletcher, Gran. If the worst happens, we can get a loan until next season, or sell stock to the Army and miners. I wanted that debt and title cleared."

"You sure you trust that Brazel detective you hired to carry it to her?"

"Yes, Gran, I do. While he's there, he's to check out the Fletcher brothers. I have to make certain they've really backed down. I don't trust men like them. Or that Jubal Starns. I'm having him checked on, too. Before we start a new year, I needed all those problems laid to rest. They will be soon."

Jessie heard the commotion of men and horses outside and realized—after over ten weeks—her husband and the hands had returned. Joy was her first reaction and she started to race outdoors to welcome the boys and Matt. Panic halted her. She fretted over how Matt would take her news. Men were considered the heads of homes, the protectors, and the decision-makers. They wanted wives to be dependent upon them, and submissive.

Jessie had known Mathew Cordell for ages, but she wasn't sure of his innermost views on marriage, and a wife's role. What, she asked herself, if he was annoyed and disappointed with her? The forty thousand dollars she had withdrawn and spent was theirs. What if he considered her action impulsive and hasty? What if he had decided not to pay off Mary Louise in a lump sum?

Time passed, and Matt didn't join her. Jessie began to pace the bedroom and wonder what was delaying him. Why hadn't he rushed to her side? She wanted to have their reunion in private. If he didn't come soon, she would go downstairs to greet him.

Jessie went into the water closet and glanced out the window that overlooked the front yard. She saw her husband talking with Rusty Jones. She had asked the new foreman and longtime hand to let her be the one to relate the news to Matt. She wondered if Rusty was obeying. Judging from Matt's face and his rigid stance, he was pretty upset. She saw Matt yank off his hat and run his fingers through tousled, shoulder-length brown hair. He hadn't shaved since the first week of September when roundup began, three months ago. His clothes were dusty and wrinkled. He tooked tired and distressed.

When Matt glanced toward the front door, then up at the window, Jessie jerked aside and her heartbeat increased. She admonished herself for her silly reaction. She wasn't actually spying on him. So why did she feel guilty and devious? Why did she wish so hard that she could overhear them? Why did she have this oppressive feeling that something terrible was wrong?

Jessie turned from the window to check her appearance in the mirror. Her freshly washed hair was brushed and hanging free. Her complexion was clear, but her cheeks were a little too rosy. At least the let-out waist and full skirt of her dark-blue dress didn't blatantly show her condition. Yet her bosom was noticeably fuller. She knew the bodice was snug and revealing, as there had been no excess seam to enlarge. This dress would have to be put away soon, if her sensitive breasts grew any more. But it was too late to change clothes.

What are you doing out there, Matt? Hurry, so I can get my confession over with, so we can enjoy your homecoming. The timing is perfect: tomorrow's Thanksgiving. I don't want to spoil your return. What is Rusty telling you?

*   *   *

Matt felt an urgent need to speak with his wife about his visit to the jeweler, and, even more, his strange talk with Rusty Jones echoed through his mind:

"Been any trouble, Rusty?"

"Let Jessie tell you everything. She's anxious to see you, Boss."

"Anything wrong?"

"She'll explain."

"Why don't you tell me, so I won't have to tire Jessie?"

"I promised Jessie she could give the news."

"Any visitors while I've been gone?"

"Not many."

"Who were they? What did they want?"

"Why don't you go on inside, Boss, and let Jessie talk to you? I ain't the one to speak in her place."

Rusty hadn't exposed anything, but Matt had perceived that plenty was afoot. His anxiety mounted when Gran refused to give any clues, and Tom didn't come greet him. Even Annie wasn't in the kitchen, and he suspected she had sneaked out the back door to avoid him. Something was wrong.

Matt trudged upstairs and entered their bedroom. He closed the door and glanced at his wife as she left the water closet. She didn't run into his arms as he'd hoped and dreamed since leaving her side. She, too, looked worried and wary.

"Has Navarro returned, Jessie? Is he here now?"

Stunned at those queries, Jessie stared at him in confusion. "No, why?"

"Are you sure?" he pressed.

"Yes, Matt, I'm positive. Why would you think about him? Or doubt me? I swear I haven't seen him or heard from him since he left over five months ago."

"Did you give him this?" he asked, withdrawing her locket from his vest and dangling it before her pale face.

Jessie's quivering hands took it. She opened the catch, stared inside, then asked, "How did you get it back? Did you see him? Where is my picture?"

"It was sold to a jeweler in Dodge, where your father bought his last watch. I went in to buy you a Christmas gift while the papers were being drawn up for the cattle sale. I saw it and realized I hadn't seen you wearing yours since the fire. I figured you'd lost it that night, and it would be nice to have a new one for the baby's picture.

The jeweler said he hadn't been able to sell it because it was marked with the last owner's initials: JML. Said he'd make me a good deal on it if we didn't mind. JML, Jessica Marie Lane," Matt ventured. "Right?"

Jessie swallowed hard. She was confused, and frightened for Navarro. She was also hurting for Matt. "Yes, it's mine. And yes, I gave it to Navarro. It was a farewell gift, Matt. I don't understand. Why would he remove the picture and sell it? He must have needed money badly."

"The man who sold it didn't fit Navarro's description. He told the jeweler he won it in a card game in New Mexico in late June. That means Navarro headed that way after leaving here."

"I don't know where he headed or where he is now. I swear it. Maybe the man stole it from him, or maybe it didn't mean anything special to Navarro, or maybe that man took it after he . . ."

"Killed Navarro?" Matt finished for her. "A man like that lives by his guns, Jessie, and usually dies by them."

"Don't say that!" she shrieked.

Matt looked and sounded crushed by her reaction. "I'm sorry this hurts you so deeply, Jessie. I know you still love him and hope he isn't dead. Maybe he isn't. Maybe he's on the way here now, after you."

"Don't say that, either, Matt. It isn't true. Even if it were, it wouldn't change anything between us. I'm your wife; I'll always be your wife. I love you."

"But you loved him first; you love him more," he remarked sadly.

"First, yes; but more, no. You must believe that, Matt. I don't want him killed or hanged, but I wouldn't leave you for him. There had to be a good reason why he gave up the locket. I'm afraid for him, but I'm happy you bought it. Maybe this is fate's way of proving to us that it's over between me and Navarro. Maybe he didn't love me as much as he thought he did. Maybe he's found someone new to love. If he truly cared about me, don't you think he would have at least sent me word that he's safe? I think it's time I told you the whole truth about Navarro Breed, so we can forget about him."

"Breed? I thought his name was Jones."

"No, Matt, it isn't. Navarro Breed is a fugitive from an Arizona prison. He was convicted of a gold robbery. He killed a guard to escape a few months before we met." Jessie related Navarro's life history to her shocked husband. "If he's recaptured, he'll hang. But he swore he would never let them take him alive. That's why he left and why he can't ever come back. Never, Matt."

Matt paced the room, deep in thought. Everything made sense now. He knew Navarro loved Jessie and had given her up to protect her. The desperado hadn't betrayed and deserted Jessie. Losing and leaving her must have been the hardest thing he'd endured in his grim existence. Matt felt a wave of sympathy for the fugitive. "I'm sorry. I didn't know or understand how hard it had been on both of you."

"Matt, I don't want him to return to me, but I do want him to be safe and happy somewhere far away. He's no threat to you; I promise."

He walked to her and caressed her cheek. "I'm glad you told me the truth, Jessie. I can relax now. I was plenty worried. When Rusty acted so crazy and wouldn't answer my questions, I thought Navarro was back."

"That isn't what I asked Rusty to let me tell you. I'm glad you're home, Matt. So much happened while you were gone. I wanted to wait until you got back so we could handle the situation together, but I couldn't. Please don't be angry with me. I did it all for us. I had to."

"Did what, Jessie?"

She explained about finding Wilbur Fletcher's packet of information in the water closet two weeks after his departure. Matt looked shocked to hear about the railroad line. She told him about her meeting with Sheriff Toby Cooper and about hiding the evidence in the line shack. She explained that she had planned to wait for him before taking action against the villains, but the letters from the Fletcher brothers and Mary Louise had forced her hand. She told him what she'd written to the authorities, Fletcher's brothers, and her sister, and about the answers she'd received. She hurriedly went on to tell how she had withdrawn the forty thousand dollars, sent it to her sister, hired detectives to check on the brothers and on Jubal Starns, and what had happened with the hotel owner.

"I should have Mary Louise's receipt soon; then the ranch title will be clear. Gran was upset with me for paying her off without asking you, but I just wanted it over with, Matt. And I had to be sure the Fletchers and Starns wouldn't try anything else against us, especially before your return."

"Mercy, a lot happened while I was gone. I should have stayed home, Jessie. I should have let Jake Bass handle the drive. He's the best trail boss in the west. You could have been hurt. You shouldn't have had to deal with this by yourself."

"Are you angry because I did all that without you?"

Matt gathered her into his arms. "No, my love. You're strong and smart. I knew you could take care of yourself and the ranch. That's why I didn't worry much leaving you here. But I thought the trouble was over or I wouldn't have gone. You've always run or helped run everything for Jed. Your strength and courage are parts of you that I love and respect. I don't want to change you, Jessie. I don't feel less of a man because you can manage alone. I'm relieved, in case anything ever happened to me."

"Most men don't feel that way about their wives, Matt. Most men would be furious about a woman taking control."

"I'm not most men, Mrs. Cordell," he said, then chuckled as he hugged her.

"I thought I knew you, Matt. But you surprise me more and more."

"I hope in a good way."

"Yes, a very good way." She nestled closer to his broad chest.

"You see, Jessie, I always had to hide my feelings and real self around you. Jed was always ordering me to watch out for men trying to get their hands on what you'd inherit one day. I knew he liked me and trusted me, but I was afraid of how he would react to me pursuing you. He didn't want anybody taking you away from him. After your mother died, he was even more possessive and scared about losing you to a man. He didn't mean to be like that. He loved you and needed you. He felt steady and strong with you at his side. He fired Navarro because he sensed a threat from him, not because he believed your sister."

"I know, but it doesn't matter now. Except . . ."

"Except what, love?" he coaxed her to finish.

"Papa might still be alive if Navarro hadn't been sent away. I think he was at Mama's grave alone because he felt guilty over what he'd done. But we can't change the past. Let's not think or talk about it again. You don't have to worry about Navarro's return or my feelings for him. I'm yours forever, Matt."

His body ached with desire for her, but he was a mess. He didn't want to hold her or kiss her until he'd had a chance to clean himself up. "I'll never doubt that again, Jessie." He released her and said,

"It's civilizing time. This beard and hair have to go. I need scrubbing head to foot. I'm about as filthy as a pig wallowing in mud, and stink about as bad. I'll go over the trip with you after I'm clean and fed."

Friday, Jessie and her husband sat down to insert the drive expenses and profit into the ranch book. Matt figured and called out amounts for his wife to enter.

"Salaries for the sixty drovers at forty a month, forty-eight hundred. Trail boss at one-twenty a month and bonus, four hundred. Supplies, five thousand. Indian pay, three hundred. No tricks or troubles this time, Jessie. Paying them to cross their lands is a lot better than having them spook the cattle. We lose less time and no beeves this way. Meal and lodging for our boys in Dodge, two hundred," he said. The seasonal hands had left them after receiving their pay to look for their next jobs. "Feed and holding pens, $8,823. He charged twenty-five cents a day each for four days. That's the highest so far. Supplies for the return trip, three hundred. Bonuses, four twenty-seven. Total expenses, $20,250.00."

"That's wonderful, Matt, less than last time."

"Thanks, Jessie. We got thirty dollars a head, and we had 8,823 by the time we reached market. Didn't lose many this trip. Our profit is $244,440. That'll give us plenty to use until next year."

"Sounds as if four is our lucky number this year," Jessie remarked.

"Yep. I'll assign shifts to give the boys a few days off apiece. They deserve it. They worked hard."

"Oh, Matt, I'm so excited and pleased. I have so many dreams about our spread." Her eyes glowed as she spoke. "We'll give the boys those raises we promised. And I want to add a large room onto the bunkhouse with a fireplace, billiard table, comfortable chairs, and a couple of poker tables. A sitting room will be nice for them, especially in the winter. They've been loyal to us for years. I'd like to show our appreciation. I also want to buy more bulls, and some Hereford cows. It's time we start improving our bloodlines like Papa planned. And we can purchase blooded studs. A hearty breed will sell good to the Army. And I want to raise or buy more hay this year; Fletcher's grasslands aren't as good as ours for so much extra stock. We'll need more windmills here and on the southern range in case of drought. We can keep them shut down until needed. I want to replace the things we lost in the fire. We'll be so successful. Things are finally brighter than a sunny day for us. And I want to build a new entrance to the ranch, a large arch of stone with a new sign: L/C Ranch; it'll be our new brand," she finished, almost breathless from her rush of words.

Matt chuckled at her exuberance. "Whoa, Jessie," he teased. "Money only goes so far. We can't do everything in one good year. The next one or two could be bad. We'd better hold plenty back for emergencies and hard times."

Jessie gazed at her handsome husband who was smiling ear to ear. His brown eyes shone with love, joy, and pride. He looked rested and at ease today. "That's why I married my expert foreman, to keep me from leaping onto a runaway stallion," she jested.

"We'll do it all, Jessie, just not at once. We have plenty to be thankful for."

"Yes, we do," she agreed, then reflected for a few minutes on their happy Thanksgiving yesterday. Her parents had always made it a special event. She would continue that family tradition.

"What are you thinking about now? More dreams?" he asked.

"Yesterday, and all our years to come. They'll be good ones, Matt."

"I know. I love you, Jessie."

"I love you, too, Matt."

Feeling aroused by her adoring gaze and nearness, Matt suggested, "Let's get finished here, so we can make those dreams come true one day."

Christmas was a wonderful time for the Cordells and Lanes. Annie and the hands joined them inside the night before to sing and eat and drink. At seven months, Jessie's pregnancy was showing. The men shared their joy with their bosses at the blessed event. Small gifts were given to the regulars and Annie. In turn, Matt and Jessie were presented with a cradle that Big John had made. The hands had contributed money for the materials and for the covers inside it, which Margaret Anne James Ortega had selected in town.

Miguel and Annie had wed on Saturday, so that added to the party spirit. He had moved into the small foreman's house with her. Everyone was pleased.

There was more for the family to celebrate. Reports had come in from the Brazel detectives that week. They learned that Jubal Starns had died during a stage holdup on his return to El Paso, so he couldn't cause future trouble. They discovered that the Fletcher brothers had sold their holdings and moved to England, so vengeance from that distance should be impossible. Mary Louise had moved to Philadelphia, and had sent a receipt for the balance that Jessie had owed her for the ranch. Now the title was free of any threat from her sister and Wilbur's kin.

Jessie had given Matt a light wool shirt that she had made, and he wore it Christmas day. He presented her with a lovely wool shawl he had purchased in Dodge, feeling the locket was only a return of her property.

When the special day was over, Jessie and Matt stood gazing down at the cradle in the extra room beside theirs. It and her protruding stomach made the baby's impending arrival more of a reality. The redhead leaned her back against Matt's body and nestled her head to his neck. Matt's arms overlapped hers.

When the baby began to kick, Jessie shifted their arms to let him share the sensation. "Feel it?" she murmured in wonder, her hands covering his.

"Yep. He's getting stronger and busier. Anxious to bust outta his cell, too. I hope it's a girl who looks just like you."

"What if it's a boy who looks just like his father?"

She and Matt both reacted to her slip. She feared from his last two sentences that he was thinking about Navarro again. She hoped and prayed not. "I'm sorry, Matt, but I think of you as his father."

He smiled, knowing she was being honest. "That's how it should be, Jessie. I love you and I'll love the baby. Let's get you to bed. It's been a busy season."

Matt's soft snoring told Jessie he was asleep. She hoped she hadn't hurt him tonight with her accidental remark. He was her husband and was with her all the time, and she had come to think of the baby as theirs. Matt was a good man, a special man. Every day she realized how lucky she was to have him. She only wished her parents were there to share the joy of her success, her child, and her marriage. A new year was approaching, and she must put the past behind her, behind *them.*

But tonight had brought back thoughts of Navarro Breed. She

wondered where and how he was. He could be cold, miserable, and alone. She couldn't forget about Fletcher's sketch. She wondered why nothing had come of it. Perhaps it hadn't fallen into the right hands, or more accurately, the *wrong* ones. Perhaps Fletcher had lied about it to scare the skilled gunslinger away. If not for the sketch, perhaps Navarro wouldn't have left her, or he might have returned by now, at least for a brief visit.

What would Navarro have done if he'd learned about their baby? What could he have done with the law on his back and the threat of a noose hanging over his head? It would have hurt him deeply to learn he had put her into such a bind. Had he forgotten her? Had he met someone else to love, someone with no responsibilities who could run off with him? Had he realized he didn't truly love her as much as he had thought?

If only he'd sent a letter by now that he was alive and well. Surely six and a half months were long enough to go without a single word. But maybe he felt writing to her was unfair and cruel. He had told her to forget him, to seek a new start with another man, that he could never return. Had he meant those tormenting words? Or had something terrible happened to him on the trail?

Jessie asked herself for the hundredth time if she should contact the Arizona authorities about him. Her letters to the Texas authorities had helped her out of a dangerous situation with the Fletchers. Perhaps she could help Navarro by sending the truth to the Arizona governor, U.S. marshal, and prison officials. If they learned he had been sentenced and imprisoned unjustly and had been forced to escape, it could save his life and clear his name.

But she was afraid to act on her hopes. If they didn't believe her or if it didn't change things for him, it could stir up a new search for the fugitive. If the prison was as bad as Navarro said, the men there would want to silence him. It could also spur those lawmen to come here to probe about the desperado, to stir up the painful past. To protect all of them, Jessica Cordell asked herself, shouldn't she let the matter go?

CHAPTER
TWENTY-TWO

Jessie's back had ached for hours, since early morning. Contractions hardened her stomach every ten to fifteen minutes, like her insides were twisting into painful knots. She was tense and scared. She'd told Gran and Annie that she suspected her labor had begun, and everything was prepared on this still chilly day in March. All she could do was wait, and try to ease her fears.

Jessie wished Matt would hurry home. He was due back anytime from the range. It was almost four o'clock. Gran had explained the birthing process. She was ready to get started, to see her first child, to get the pain behind her. Her stomach was so large. She had been miserable and uncomfortable for weeks. Getting up and down was difficult now. Sleeping was almost impossible, so she was tired and edgy.

It had been a long wait. Once the baby was born, she and Matt could settle down to their life together. So many times she had desired him, and she was looking forward to their first night of lovemaking. That would make her truly and finally his, something she needed and wanted.

More time passed, and the pains increased in frequency. Each one hurt more than the last. Jessie paced her bedroom floor to distract herself. But each knifing slice through her body reminded her of what was in store. She dreaded the suffering she must endure to bring a new life into the world. She hoped and prayed she would be brave, that the child would be safe and healthy. She groaned, held her distended belly, and gasped for breath. Tears blurred her vision. Standing was hard on weak legs, but sitting was worse. Besides, Gran told her that moving around would help lessen the agony.

Every few minutes, Gran or Annie checked on her. They kept Tom away so his nervous jabbering wouldn't bother her. Water was kept hot on the stove. Cloths, sheets, cord, scissors, and basin were ready for use nearby.

Jessie glanced out the window and wondered what was keeping Matt. She wanted him there to keep up her strength and courage, to help her keep silent. She wanted to scream with each pain, yet she didn't want Tom and the men outside to hear her yells. Each time, she clamped her hand over her mouth to keep her torment from escaping. Gran said it could take all day, and Nature was trying her best to prove the woman right.

Jessie was in a loose nightgown and was barefoot. Her hair was braided to keep it out of the way. She grabbed a bathing cloth to wipe the beads of moisture from her flushed face. When Gran entered the room, Jessie murmured through clenched teeth, "It hurts so bad, Gran. They just keep coming and coming."

Gran patted her hands and comforted, "It'll be over soon, child."

Jessie moaned and gripped her stomach, bending forward as if that helped, which it didn't. Gran spread old covers on the bed and told her to lie down. Jessie crawled onto the bed and curled to her side.

Martha handed her a knotted rag and said, "Bite on this when it strikes."

Jessie seized it and obeyed; she felt as if she were being ripped apart.

Gran timed the contractions. Five minutes apart. "Let's get you ready. Won't be long." She helped Jessie work up her nightgown to the waist. She covered her bare bottom with a sheet. "I'll tell Annie to be ready when I shout."

"Gran, I'm scared," the suffering redhead confessed.

"I know. Try to think of something pleasant."

"How can I?" she gritted out as she bit into the cloth and groaned.

Matt hurried into the room. He sat down on the bed, gazed at his wife, and captured her hand in his. Although she gripped his tightly, he felt her tremble. He was worried and frightened by her pale, wet face and flushed cheeks. "We had to pull some calves out of the mud. You doing all right?"

Jessie was about to answer when she stuck the rag into her mouth, closed her eyes, stiffened, and groaned. The labor pain was long, deep, and hard.

"Jessie?" he hinted in panic.

"She's fine, Matt. You're just used to seeing and helping deliver animals. We women make a little more noise than they do. Watch her until I get back."

Matt wiped her brow with his hand. "I love you, Jessie. Don't worry."

When Martha came back, he asked, "Have you sent for the doctor yet?"

"No need. The baby'll be here before he could make it from town. I know what to do, son. Relax. It'll be a while. Why don't you get some coffee and food?"

"I can't leave her like this, Gran."

"Go ahead, Matt. I'll be fine," Jessie encouraged.

Matt obeyed, but reluctantly. When he heard Jessie scream, he dropped his fork and took the steps two by two to get to her side. "What is it?"

"Sorry," she murmured, breathing hard and fast. "It caught me by surprise."

"They're close, Matt. You'll have your first child soon."

But hours passed, Jessie's torment mounted, and no baby entered the world. She had been in labor since eight that morning; it was now eleven. Jessie was writhing in agony. Matt was frantic. Gran was worried.

The older woman bathed her granddaughter's brow with a cool cloth. Jessie's hair was soaked, as were her gown and the bedding. She looked pale, weak, and frightened. She had suffered too long without release.

"Matt, I think you should send for the doctor," Gran whispered.

Jessie halted her rolling motions and stared at her grandmother. "Why, Gran?"

"It's taking longer than I expected. We might need help," she admitted.

"Is something wrong with my baby?" Her eyes were large and dark.

"I don't think so, but he's being stubborn," she tried to jest to calm her granddaughter.

Matt kissed her cheek and left to send one of the boys into town.

"Tell me, Gran, what's wrong," Jessie persisted during his absence.

"I think he might be turned wrong. He might need help getting out."

Jessie's water broke and saturated the area beneath her. Blood flowed onto the wet padding. "What was that?"

Gran reminded her of the birth process. "That's a good sign."

The contractions were coming fast and lasting long. Matt lifted Jessie while Gran and Annie pulled the soaked padding from beneath her and placed a new one there. Gently he lowered his wife to the bed. Gran kept the cover aside to watch for the baby's head.

Jessie was too dazed and was hurting too much to think of modesty or to realize this was the first time her husband had seen her nakedness.

More time passed, and still the baby refused to be born. Labor was almost one continuous agony now. Jessie was exhausted and terrified. Her braid had loosened itself during her thrashings, and her hair was damp and tangled. Her body was covered in perspiration. Her breathing was harsh and loud. She no longer tried to silence her screams, and her throat and lips were dry from them. She yanked on the loops Matt had tied to the bed at Gran's instruction.

By noon the next day, the fatigued and alarmed rider returned to the ranch. Matt hurried to meet him. "Where's the doctor?"

"Not there, Matt. He's in El Paso getting some supplies."

While her husband was outside and Annie was downstairs, Jessie asked, "Is my baby going to die for my sins, Gran? Am I going to die, too?"

"No, child. You'll both be fine."

Matt returned and gazed at his weakened wife. He feared he was going to lose her. He came to the bed and told the older woman, "If the baby's breech, what can we do to get it out? We can't let her go on like this. It's dangerous for both of them. I've turned and pulled out plenty of calves and colts."

"It isn't that easy with a woman, Matt."

"I've got to try it, Gran." Matt moved between Jessie's legs. He examined her stomach, then tried to push the baby into another position. Matt slipped his fingers inside his dilated wife. He felt a foot.

Trying not to increase Jessie's pain, his fingers gently searched for the other one. Locating it, he shoved it near the first. With care, he tugged on them inside the expanded area. The baby moved downward. Matt prayed he wasn't injuring the child or his wife. "Hold on, Jessie; it's coming now."

Jessie ordered herself to be brave. Those ripping pains grew worse. She felt as if her womanly opening was splitting asunder when the baby's legs and hips were expelled. She took deep breaths and shoved with all her might to assist the action. She felt Matt's fingers helping those tiny shoulders outside, but they felt as wide as her own at that trying moment. Jessie pushed and grunted several more times between prayers . . . and the baby was delivered. With the pain and pressure gone for a time, she gasped for breath and collapsed into the bed. She let go of the grabbing loops and tossed the biting knot aside.

Matt hurried to clear the child's nose and mouth. He popped its bottom to make it inhale its first breath of air. When it did so and began to cry, he laughed and whooped with joy and relief. "A boy, Jessie, a fine son."

She tried to lift herself to see him. "Is he all right?"

"Beautiful and healthy," Matt promised. "Lie still. We aren't done yet."

"I'll finish up," Gran told the smiling man. She tied off the cord in two places an inch apart and close to the baby, then cut the umbilical link to its mother. "You and Annie tend him while I do a woman's work here."

A nervous Matt accepted the tiny boy. It took twenty minutes for the placenta to pass, but luckily with little bleeding. While Matt and Annie cleaned and dried the infant, Gran bathed Jessie and cleared away the cloths and afterbirth. She called Matt to help her get Jessie into a fresh gown and to help put clean covers on the bed.

Jessie ignored her pain and exhaustion. "Let me see him." She struggled to raise herself.

Matt brought the blanket-wrapped infant to his wife and placed him in her arms.

Jessie cuddled the child close and gazed at him in amazement and love. He had lots of hair, black fuzz. What little she could see of his eyes were dark, too. She moved aside the covering to look him over from head to foot. She saw nothing to worry her. He was wrinkled and pale, and crying in a high baby pitch. She smiled and nestled him against her. "He's perfect, Matt. Let's call him Lane, Lane Cordell."

That brought a broad grin to Matt's face. "It's a good, strong name."

"You saved our lives, Matt," she remarked, love and gratitude shining in her eyes. "Our son. Our first child," she added, and smiled at him.

He beamed with pleasure. "Get some rest. You've worked hard, Jessie."

Gran took the baby from her. "We'll tend him while you sleep a while."

"You're all as exhausted as I am." Her weary lids looked heavy.

"We can take turns napping and watching Lane. Get some rest before he's hungry and shouting for his milk."

Matt bent over, kissed her forehead, then her lips. "I love you, Jessie."

"I love you, too," she replied, drifting off to sleep.

Jessie finished bathing and dressing Lane, then nursed him and put him down to nap. She gazed at the sleeping infant of two and a half months. He was a healthy baby, and a good baby, a joy to tend. His hair was still dark, and she believed his eyes would be hazel, like his father's.

Jessie and Matt loved him so much that neither minded that resemblance. If anyone else had noticed, nothing had been said to them or within their hearing. Of course, it helped that Matt had dark hair and eyes. The baby had been so small that everyone believed he had arrived early.

Jessie realized that Lane Cordell had been born on the very day she had met his father a year ago. She felt as if it were God's way of replacing Navarro in her heart and life. It had been a difficult birth, but she and the baby were fine now. She had Matt's quick thinking to thank for their survival.

Today was June first of 1877, a year after she became pregnant by Navarro Breed. It was the right day for beginning her life as Matt's wife. She had thought of her husband all morning and afternoon. He had taken such excellent and gentle care of her since Lane's arrival. He had waited upon her, bathed her, washed her hair, and helped tend their son. Nature had healed her body, and time had healed her heart.

It was time to settle her life and love, time to belong fully to Mathew Cordell. She would always love and remember Navarro Breed, but it was totally and finally over between them. She hadn't heard from the desperado in almost a year. If he ever returned, she would remain Matt's wife. Matt was her life and love now.

Or would be tonight, she decided. Jessie bathed and donned a lovely dress. She splashed on fragrant cologne. She brushed her hair and let it tumble down her back. She planned a special meal for dinner, including wine from Wilbur Fletcher's old stock. Everything was prepared for a romantic evening.

When Matt entered the house, his gaze widened. Candles were lit on the dining-room table, which was set for two. He walked into the kitchen to find Jessie humming as she worked on their meal. "What's going on?" he asked.

"I thought we would enjoy a quiet meal alone tonight. Lane doesn't need attention for another few hours. Tom is camping on the range with the boys. Gran wanted to turn in early. I gave Annie the night off with Miguel. It's just you and me, if that's all right," she said with a sly grin and twinkling eyes.

"It's more than all right," he replied in a hoarse voice. He noticed how beautiful she was tonight and sensed her strange and tantalizing mood.

"I heard you arrive, so I got everything ready for your bath in the closet outside," she remarked, motioning to the room for bathing on the back porch near the kitchen door. "I couldn't carry water upstairs, so I prepared your bath down here. Get busy, sir; dinner's almost ready."

"Is there something I should know?" he inquired, his gaze and tone hopeful.

"You said I would know when the time was right for us," she said. "That's tonight, Mathew Cordell, if you're ready and willing to make a fresh start with me."

Matt's mouth fell open and his brown gaze enlarged. "Are you saying . . ."

"Yep, and about time, don't you think?" she teased.

Matt felt a tingle and flush race over his body. His heart pounded in joy and suspense. "Are you sure, Jessie?"

"More than sure, Matt," she replied with confidence. "Get along," she coaxed.

Jessie grinned to herself as the happily confused male left the room. All day she had fantasized about tonight. She had day-dreamed of what it would be like to be in Matt's arms, unrestrained and passionate. She was eager to make love with her handsome and virile husband. She had envisioned them in bed with his fingers and lips working magic upon her body. She had made a lovely gown for this special event, and couldn't wait for Matt to see it on her. She wanted to hurry the meal; yet, she wanted to prolong the entic-ing prelude to the wonderful evening ahead.

Matt returned and glanced at Jessie. She sent him an encouraging smile. He followed her into the dining room, and they took their places with her next to him. Jessie passed him the food, and his hands trembled slightly as he handled the dishes. He watched her pour two glasses of wine.

"To us, Matt, and our bright future," she toasted and tapped their glasses, but only took a small sip or two since she was nursing the baby.

"Delicious," he murmured, but his appetite was whet for a differ-ent kind of meal. He tried not to eat too fast, but it was hard. He had been waiting for this night for almost a year. No, he had wanted Jessica Lane for much longer. Joy and anticipation coursed through his body.

Jessie noticed how excited and pleased Matt was. The meal was wonderful, but not nearly as wonderful as what was in store for them later. She watched candlelight dance on his bronzed face and in his deep brown eyes. She realized he was nervous, and that touched her heart. As they finished the dinner, she suggested, "Why don't we have our pie and coffee later—much later—Mr. Cordell?"

He agreed, then said, "I'll help you with the dishes."

"I'll put them in hot soapy water and do them later. Why don't you go up and get ready for bed? I'm sure you're tired," she jested.

The eager Matt followed her request.

When Jessie entered their bedroom, only candles were burning, casting a soft glow that enhanced the romantic mood. She closed and bolted the door. She didn't want anything or anyone to disturb them for hours. The redhead gazed at the man awaiting her. He was propped against the headboard, resting on a pillow. His bare torso was exposed, but a light sheet concealed his lower half.

Jessie started to enter the bathing closet to change into her new gown, but changed her mind. She sat on the small couch instead and removed her shoes. She unbuttoned her dress and peeled it off her shoulders, then worked it over her hips. She placed the garment over the couch back. Jessie was aware that Matt was watching her with speechless surprise. She found that undressing before him aroused her as much as it did him. She unlaced her chemise and slipped it off her arms. Her breasts were full and taut. She eased off her knee-length bloomers and stood naked before him. She had gained little weight during her pregnancy, and her figure was almost back to normal.

"You're beautiful, Jessie," he murmured in pride and desire.

Mathew Cordell stared in wonder as she walked to the bed. Her auburn hair cascaded over her shoulders like a dark-red river over creamy sand. Her enticing eyes looked bluer than usual. Her body was no longer that of a tomboy. She was bewitching and seductive, knowing and innocent. She appeared soft and fragile, but Matt knew she was firm and strong. He ached to get his hands and lips upon that silken skin.

Jessie sat down near him. She trailed her fingers over his hairy chest, making tiny dark curls along her way. She felt his heart beating at a swift pace. As her fingers journeyed upward, they paused a moment on the pulse point at the base of his throat to feel it racing beneath them. She traced over his jawline, avoiding the small nick from his hasty shave. They traveled down his straight nose and teased over his wide mouth. "I was around you for so many years, but failed to realize how handsome you are." When he smiled, she said, "You have the most beautiful smile in the world. It makes your eyes light up."

"Only when I'm looking at you, Jessie." His hand lifted to caress her cheek.

"I wish I had known about your feelings for me sooner. We wasted so many years. Let's not waste any more," she said, then sealed her mouth to his.

Matt grasped her body and rolled her over his to place her at his side. The cover twisted around his hips as he lay half atop her. His mouth and tongue worked with hers to send their senses spinning. His fingers drifted over her silky flesh, trailing down her arm and over her back. They entangled themselves in her lush mane and didn't seek freedom for a time.

Their bare torsos met and Jessie gasped at the sensation. They explored each other's bodies with equal and rising passion.

Matt's mouth left hers to roam the smooth flesh of her neck, then traveled downward to move slowly and purposefully toward one beckoning breast. He brushed his lips over its peak, his hot breathing enflaming the taut bud and causing it to stiffen. His tongue lavished sweet nectar upon it, and he felt Jessie quiver in pleasure. His hand drifted over her hip and lower, to the very center of her passion. With skill and tenderness, he teased and caressed her moist, satiny flesh.

Jessie closed her eyes and savored the blissful sensations her husband was creating. His hands and lips were skilled and knowing. If ever she had doubted she loved and desired Matt Cordell, those qualms were gone. If ever she had doubted she could respond to him in this way, she had been mistaken. Her body was sensitive and receptive to every move he made. She wanted to touch him, to pleasure him, to tantalize him, too. The cover prevented her bold explorations. She yanked at it and Matt caught her intention.

Without taking his lips from her body, he grasped the edge and tossed it aside, leaving nothing between them. He felt Jessie's hands stroke his back, tease over his buttocks, and seek his throbbing hardness. He sucked in air and stiffened a moment when she touched him.

Jessie smiled at his reaction and her hand curled around him. As her desire increased, her fingers roamed up and down his hot, hard length. Her mind was dazed by the wall of fire around her. Her body was engulfed in passion's flames. She wanted to be consumed by them. "I want you so much, Matt."

Jessie didn't have to tell him she was ready to receive him; her actions spoke for her. Matt moved atop her and when she eagerly parted her thighs, he thrust into her with a cry of ecstasy.

Jessie groaned with pleasure as their bodies united and worked as one. Their hands and lips continued to heighten their hunger. Their lovemaking was blissful and stirring. But they had waited a long time and were unable to restrain themselves. They moved with urgency, their hearts and bodies demanding to be sated.

"I love you, Jessie. It's more wonderful than I dreamed."

"Oh, yes, Matt, it feels wonderful." she murmured as the bittersweet sensations charged through her writhing body. "You're driving me crazy."

Unable to hold back any longer, he carried them to the edge of restraint and into paradise itself. Together, they shared a rapturous delight, then lay contented in each other's arms, savoring the glowing aftermath of their first union.

Jessie teased her fingers over her husband's damp chest. "Mathew Cordell, you're one surprise after another. Why did you keep me starving so long?"

He laughed. "Don't you know food tastes better when you're hungriest?"

"Ah, yes, that devious scheme of yours to conquer me," she jested.

"Seems it worked," he retorted, hugging her possessively.

"I must admit it did, and most delightfully."

Matt rolled to his side and propped on his elbow. He gazed down into Jessie's radiant and serene face. "And I'll confess that was worth waiting for."

"You're right. We did need time to get this close. I'm yours now."

As he studied her gaze and mood, he knew that was true in all ways.

Jessie heard the baby cry. She laughed and said, "Now, our son wants his dinner. For a while, we'll have to work our schedule around his. I won't be long. Keep the bed warm, my love." Jessie rose and donned her gown. "On second thought, Mr. Cordell, keep yourself warm until I get back. Seems I haven't had my dessert yet."

Jessie nursed Lane and tended his needs. As she rocked him to sleep, she smiled and hummed. She realized it was possible to love two men. There was still a special place in her heart for Lane's father, but her life was with Matt. Surely Matt was her destiny.

She wouldn't allow the bittersweet past and her lost first love to torment her again. She wouldn't dream of how it could have been with Navarro. She wouldn't fantasize about his eventual return. She would live in the present and for the future. She was lucky to have captured a beautiful second chance.

Jessie tucked in her son and gazed at him for a short time. Lane Cordell had been meant to be born, and she would no longer scold herself for making a sinful mistake. He would be loved and nurtured by two happy parents. That was more than Navarro had had and more than Lane would have had if she'd escaped with the fugitive that day long ago.

Despite sharing love and passion, she and Navarro had been too different to have made a life together. She would have been lost in Navarro—overwhelmed by him. But she and Matt were equal halves that made a healthy whole.

No doubt Navarro had realized such truths, too, and that was why he hadn't visited or written: to let them both heal and forget. With all her heart, she wished Navarro well, but she loved Matt and their happy life. There would always be a small corner in her heart that only Navarro had touched and where he would reside. She would always be grateful to him for what he had done for her and for her family. There was no shame or sin in such pure love and harmless loyalty. Yes, things were as they should be.

Matt was awaiting her return to share more pleasure. Peace ruled their ranch and lives, Miguel and Annie Ortega were expecting their first child next year. Everyone was safe and happy.

Jessie took one more glance at her son, smiled, and left to rejoin Matt. Her life was perfect, and nothing or no one could spoil it . . .

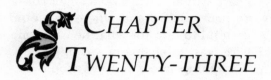

CHAPTER TWENTY-THREE

Matt entered the parlor where Jessie and Gran were sewing and chatting. Tom was in his room doing lessons. The November day was cool, and a cozy fire glowed on the large hearth. Lane sat on a rug near his mother's feet playing with wooden toys that Big John Williams and other hands had carved for him. Annie was in her small home tending to her new infant. The two women halted their hands and looked at Jessie's husband as he approached them.

He scooped up the twenty-month-old boy and said, "How's my fine son tonight? Getting bigger and smarter every day."

Lane laughed and squealed with delight as Matt played with him for a time.

After Matt set him down and kissed Jessie's cheek, he withdrew an envelope from his pocket. He held it out to his wife and said, "A letter from Mary Louise."

The redhead stared at the mail as if it were a viper about to strike her, and that was just how she felt. With reluctance, she took the envelope. She glanced at her grandmother, then at Matt, and murmured, "I wonder what she wants. It's been two and a half years of peace. I hope she isn't going to try to end it for us."

Jessie exhaled in dread. "Might as well get it over with." She ripped open the missive and read it to the others. The redhead blinked and shook her head, doubting what her eyes and wits were gathering. No one had spoken. She realized Matt and Gran were as shocked by the news, too. "I don't believe it."

"She sounds sincere, Jessie," Gran remarked.

"I have to admit, I think she does too," Matt added. "Never thought to see the day when she would change."

"It must be a trick," Jessie said, but somehow didn't believe it was.

"What would she have to gain with this offer?" Matt reasoned.

"Matt, watch Lane for me. He's curious about fire, so don't take your eyes off of him," she advised. "I want to study this closely." Jessie went into the kitchen, sat down at the table, and read her sister's letter once more:

Dear Jessica, Gran, and Tom,

You must be surprised to hear from me again after all these years of silence. I beg your forgiveness for the wicked things I did. I realize I was a terrible person, and I'm sorry. I was selfish, defiant, impulsive, and cruel. If you can't find it in your hearts to forgive me, I shall understand. You're wondering what caused this drastic change in me. Love, Jessica, something you can understand. But not only love.

I was so confused when I returned home from school and left home years ago. I had convinced myself Father hated me and that I had to escape. I was so mean to myself and all of you. Being on my own and alone was frightening, but I could not admit it, not after the awful way I behaved there. When I reached Boston and related my news, the Fletchers took the money you gave me. Wilbur's will left them everything. He lied to me and used me, as you warned. He sent his money here and made an iron-clad will the day we wed to keep the Lanes from getting his estate! I was forced to survive off their charity and had to aid their cause to get it. I couldn't confess my stupidity and dire straits to you. They composed that wicked letter I wrote to you. When you called their bluff, I told them you couldn't be tricked or scared off your land. When they were forced to yield, they blamed me, and my life worsened.

I used the final payment you sent for survival and a second escape. I fled to Philadelphia and was fine for almost a year. But I had more to learn, all the hard way. I sought another rich man and profitable marriage. Again, I was used and discarded by several targets. Looks and wiles aren't enough without a good heart behind them. I was living high to gain attention and success, so my money was running out fast. Then a terrible thing happened to me. I was robbed and beaten, and worse. I nearly died. I wanted and needed my family, but I had betrayed them. I feared you would think it was only a trick to get more money or sympathy. I was so ashamed and scared. A wonderful and gentle—and handsome, too, Jessica—doctor saved my life and tended me like a child. Under his care, I realized love and family are what's important in life. He's so like Matt, a good and kind man. His name is John Blye. He's thirty-three.

After I'd healed, John dismissed me. He had heard what an awful person I was, and he wanted to escape my greedy clutches. But I had fallen in love with him. I chased him until I convinced him I had changed. We had a glorious courtship, and we married. He has an office in our home. Many times I help him with patients. We love each other so much and we're so happy. Each day I changed even more. I'm so like Jessica now that no one at home would recognize me.

But I'm writing for another reason, too. I told John about Tom's problems. John is certain he can help improve them or find a specialized doctor who can. If you'll send Tom to us, we'll help him. He can live with us during treatments, for as long as it requires. Please allow him to come. His life can be so much better.

Jessie put the letter down and rubbed her eyes, tired from sewing all day. She heard Lane and Matt playing in the parlor and smiled. She wanted to join them, but she had a serious decision to make. She lifted the astonishing letter again and read on about Mary Louise's life and work with Dr. John Blye, about her experiences before and after her marriage, about her many changes, and about her dreams for helping their brother.

Jessie got up to pour herself a cup of coffee, then sat down to think. She yearned to believe she could trust her sister. She prayed it was possible to treat Tom's clubfoot and bad eyes. She hated to think of him going so far away to endure pain and loneliness in his effort to seek a better chance in life. Yet Tom deserved any help he could receive. Jessie knew he would want to take this risk when he learned of this opportunity. He was going on sixteen, but times weren't much different for him today than years ago. He didn't want to be a rancher, and could never manage a spread on his own. Yet, if surgery and treatments couldn't improve his conditions, she didn't want to give him false hopes. But it was Tom's choice to make, not hers.

Jessie took the letter and headed for the parlor stairs. She told Gran and Matt she was going to talk with Tom. Neither tried to discourage her. Jessie knocked on his door, then entered after he responded. She looked at her brother. He was tall and lanky, and sat erect. His dark-auburn hair was mussed from running his fingers through it countless times while studying. Many of his childhood freckles had vanished, but there was still a charming smattering of them across his nose and cheeks. He had become quieter and more serious over the last year. He spent a great deal of time reading and studying.

"Yes, Jessie?" he asked in a voice that seemed to deepen more each day.

Jessie sat on his bed. He was such a nice and smart young man, with excellent manners. When she remained silent, he squinted to see her better through his thick glasses.

"Is something wrong?" he pressed.

"I have some news to share with you, Tom."

When she hesitated once more, he grinned and asked, "Another baby?"

Jessie laughed and sent him a sly grin. "Yes, but don't tell Matt before I do. Due next fall, you perceptive young man."

"He'll be excited. Why tell me first?"

Jessie noticed how his grammar had improved due to all his hard work and her assistance. "That isn't what I came to say, but you're so clever to have guessed my secret. I was waiting to make certain before I told Matt. But what I wanted you to know is that we received a letter from our sister today."

Tom frowned. "What does she want now?"

"That was my first reaction, but we're wrong this time. I want to read it to you, then discuss her suggestion." Jessie read the letter to a shocked Tom. As she lowered it to her lap, she asked, "Do you want to think about it for a while, or talk about it now?"

Tom glanced at his disabled foot, then removed his glasses to rub his strained eyes. He replaced them and looked at his older sister. "Do you think it's possible?"

"I don't know, Tom. But I doubt a doctor would say he could help if he knows for certain he can't. He will have to examine you first to make sure. I hope he can, but I don't want to raise your hopes."

Tom drifted into deep thought. His eyes darted about as he deliberated this unexpected opportunity. "He can't make things worse, but he might make them better. It's a risk, Jessie, but I want to take it. When did she say to come?"

Jessie was not surprised by his choice. "There's a train from Dallas on December second. Mary Louise will meet it in Philadelphia on the chance you're on it. That'll give us time to get your things ready. I'll send Rusty with you."

"I'm not a baby, Jessie. I can travel by train alone."

"But it's such a long trip, Tom. You've never been away before. You aren't grown yet, little brother."

"I'll behave and study all the way. Will you and Gran and Lane be all right without me? She said it'll probably take a year of surgery and exercises."

"We'll miss you terribly. It's going to be scary, hard, and probably painful, Tom. You'll have to be brave and work hard to get well. You'll also have to be patient and not push too fast to recover. I would go with you to get things started, but you know why I can't. There's Lane and . . ." She patted her stomach.

"Don't worry, big sister. I can take care of myself. I can take the pain and work to be normal. Even if Dr. Blye can't cure me, Jessie, can I stay there to go to college? Could I get in and do the work?"

Jessie's eyes widened. "You want to attend college back East?"

"More than anything," he confessed. "I've dreamed about it. This is my chance to make it come true. Please, Jessie, say yes. I'm not dumb."

"Of course you aren't. I'm sure you can do it, but it would keep you away so much longer. It takes years, Tom."

"Only a few. I don't want to ranch or farm, Jessie. I want to study business and lots of other things. I want to be around other students. I want to learn and do fun stuff. I want to see what it's like over there. Please."

"So many surprises in one day," she murmured. Jessie studied Tom's pleading look and realized how sincere and serious he was. "I'm sure John could help. And I'll give you the funds, if this is really what you want."

"Whoopee! It is, Jessie. I'll make you proud of me; I promise."

Jessie returned his impulsive embrace. "I *am* proud of you, Tom."

"But it'll be better for me after I'm fixed and educated. Even if the doctor can't repair me, who laughs at somebody who's been to college? This will give me the chance to be somebody, to get respect, to stop the jokes. I'll become too smart for them to hurt me or ignore me anymore. I can live at school, Jessie, so I won't be any trouble for Mary Louise and her husband."

"You've learned enough at home to do any of their lessons."

"Then, it's all right?"

"Why not gamble for the whole pot while you're at the table?" she quipped. "I'll bet John tries to talk you into medicine or law. Just don't let that eastern school ruin you like it did Mary Louise."

"Don't worry; I'll only change for the better. I swear."

"If you're sure about this, we'll start preparing for your departure tomorrow."

"I'm sure, Jessie. You and Mary Louise have good lives now. I have to seek mine."

"I'll write Mary Louise tomorrow, so she can get things prepared for Tom's arrival. I just hate to see him hurt and disappointed if John can't help him. Science and medicine are so tricky, but they change all the time."

"We'll hope and pray for the best," Matt replied.

"Do you think I'm doing the right thing, Matt? It's so serious. Tom's never been away from home before. Is he too young to face so much alone?"

"I don't think so, Jessie. He's mature for his age, and he's smart. He'll have Mary Louise and John with him. He needs this chance to prove himself. We can afford to send him for treatment and school. That rail strike last year didn't hurt us. And our sale this time was good," he added, referring to the long drive from August to November that he had completed two weeks past.

"I'm glad you started the roundup and drive early this year, so you're home now to advise me on this. We were lucky that cattlemen's war in New Mexico didn't affect us at market. This is the third season I've missed."

"Lane keeps you busy at home, love. Surely you don't miss the hard riding and trail dust," he teased.

"Sometimes I do. I was used to being a ranch hand. It takes a while to adjust to being a mother and wife who stays home. I miss the excitement and good times with the boys. I don't feel much a part of my old life anymore."

"What about missing me?" he jested.

She smiled. "I miss you most of all during market season."

"Two weeks hasn't caught me up for what I missed for three months."

"Me, either," she responded. Jessie slipped off her garments and got into bed fast to avoid a chill. "Let's make up for lost time," she hinted.

Matt grinned. "I'll check the fire in the hall and make sure Lane's asleep."

Jessie snuggled under the covers. She was glad Big John Williams had made a sturdy crib for their son, who loved to climb on things and investigate every curiosity. Jessie had worried over Lane falling down the steps or exploring the fire in the second-floor hearth. John had constructed the bed so the small boy would stay put and not get into dangerous mischief.

Matt closed the door behind him and joined his wife in bed. He nestled her close to his naked body. "Cold?" he whispered.

"Not anymore."

Matt's mouth met hers. He kissed her many times before sending his hands on a skilled search for pleasure. His fingers and lips teased and tantalized his responsive wife until she was riding with him toward bliss.

Jessie's hands roamed Matt's well-muscled body as she trailed kisses over his neck and face. Sometimes their lovemaking was calm and leisurely. Sometimes it was urgent and swift. Sometimes it was a mixture of both. But every time it was fulfilling and pleasurable. She had come to love him more each day since their marriage. Both had mellowed, and she knew it was because they were a good match. They were friends and partners and mates. Lane was like their son. She was eager to share her other news with him later, as he would be ecstatic to learn she was carrying his child this time.

Matt's touch brought her attention back to the spell he was weaving. She soared with him, knowing he gained as much satisfaction as he gave. She stroked his hard back where muscles rippled with his movements. She arched to meet each thrust he made into her welcoming womanhood. She loved being with him in this special way that bound their bodies and hearts as one. He was such a gentle and skilled lover. He knew what to do to drive her mindless with desire. She enjoyed the taste of his mouth on hers and savored each caress.

And Matt could never seem to get enough of Jessie. He wanted to be near her every day, if only to see her smile. He savored the way she clung to him and responded with such eagerness and passion. He had no doubts that she loved him, desired him, and found ecstasy in his arms. To realize he could reach her so deeply thrilled him. At first he had worried he couldn t or might not satisfy her like Navarro had. But those doubts and fears had vanished. He was confident that Jessica Cordell was his forever.

Matt and Jessie rode the waves that crashed over, around, and through them. Their lovemaking became more frenzied as the power of it urged them higher, then carried them to ecstasy. They kissed and embraced until they lay exhausted and breathless but happy.

Matt turned and kissed her ear. "You're the most precious treasure a man could have, Jessie," he whispered.

She stroked his cheek. "Isn't it strange how lovemaking gets better each time. You'd think it would become commonplace after so many times. But the feelings just get stronger. It's almost as if it's new and different each time, but . . . It's strange and wonderful," she finished, unable to describe how marvelous each union was.

"I feel the same way. We're perfect for each other."

"Yes, we are. By the way, you left a gift behind before the drive. Thank you."

"A gift? I don't recall one," he said in confusion.

Jessie grinned, candlelight revealing her expression. "I'm three months' pregnant, Matt. You'll be a father again in early May."

"A baby?" he murmured, gazing into her merry eyes.

"Yep, cowboy, you've saddled me with another child," she teased. "It happens when two people make love as often as we do. In fact, it took longer than I imagined it would. It's been quite a while since you and I started these delightful bouts in bed, and Lane is nearly two. Aren't you pleased?"

A mixture of elation and dread filled Matt. "You had such a hard time with Lane's birth. Will you be all right, Jessie? I'm worried."

She caressed his face and kissed him. "I'm fine now, Matt. First babies can be difficult. Don't be afraid. Your child would never give its mother trouble."

"My child," he murmured. "That's wonderful, Jessie."

"It'll be a busy time with spring roundup and branding."

"Don't worry. I'll stay home. Rusty and the boys can handle the roundup of calves and colts next year. I want to make certain I see our child born."

"Want to play doctor again, huh?" she jested.

He chuckled, then responded, "I'll be satisfied just to be in the house this time. I don't want you to suffer like you did with Lane."

"Gran said it's only hard the first time. The others come fast and easy."

"I hope so. You scared me last time. I can't lose you, Jessie."

"You won't, Matt, not ever."

"I wonder if it'll be a boy or a girl."

"Does it matter?"

"Nope." He ran his fingers through his hair. "This is good news, woman."

Jessie spread kisses over his chest. "We have months to get used to it and make our plans. With Tom leaving for school, we can put Lane in his room. Then the nursery will be ready for use again."

"I want to fill up this house with our children."

"Whoa, boy, one at a time, please. If I get too busy with lots of children, that'll leave less time for you, for us. For this," she added, then moved atop him.

March thirteenth of 1881 was a lovely spring day. The last two years and four months had been successful and happy ones for the Lanes and Cordells. Matt was outside with four-year-old Lane, keeping the boy busy while his birthday meal and cake were being cooked. Alice Cordell—named after Jessie's mother—was napping in the nursery. At twenty-two months, she was a beautiful child, with Matt's brown eyes and Jessie's red hair. Gran was tickled to have a little girl to help raise, and Alice's father adored both child and mother.

Gran was stiffer these days from her arthritis, but she still insisted on doing chores. Jessie did as much as possible, but the two children took much of her time and energy. Matt had suggested hiring another girl, as Annie Ortega had two children of her own to tend. With Gran now seventy-five and with Jessie three months pregnant with a third child, the redhead knew she should seek hired help soon.

"Did you write to Tom and Mary Louise about the new baby?" Martha inquired.

"Not yet. Mary Louise is depressed about not getting pregnant so far. She's afraid she can't have children. She thinks she's being punished by God or tested to see if she'll make a good mother. I told her not to worry. It'll happen."

"How much longer does Tom have at school? And is he walking again?" she asked. She was forgetful some days.

Patient and loving, Jessie gave the same answers again. "He'll be home next summer. He's already talking about starting a business in town. Matt and I told him we'll back him. I'm so glad the surgery worked, Gran. Tom says he only has a slight limp now. His foot is almost straight. One of his greatest pleasures in life is wearing shoes, even if they are specially made. I can't wait to see his new glasses; he says he can see so much better. Things are going wonderfully for him. He's happy. Mary Louise and John are happy. All of us are happy and safe."

"We wouldn't be safe if those soldiers and Rangers hadn't whipped those renegades. They sure we won't have no more trouble?"

"We're fine, Gran. It's been two years since Victorio went on the warpath. We were lucky the Apaches liked to cross into Mexico between Fort Davis and El Paso, instead of over here like the Comanches did. I was nervous when Fort Davis was made the headquarters for West Texas. But Captain Baylor and his Rangers did more than the Army to stop the outbreak."

"I remember. They licked the Apaches good at Quitman Canyon in July of last year. Then they got 'em good again at Rattlesnake Spring in August."

Jessie smiled at the woman who sometimes thought clearly and other times was muddled. "That's right, Gran. Then Victorio was beaten in October by the Mexicans. The survivors took a last stand in January at Quitman Canyon, but Baylor and his men defeated them. The papers say Indian wars are over for Texas."

"What about those two chiefs who escaped?"

"Nana and Geronimo are living and raiding farther west, Gran. They won't be any trouble to us. Besides, we still have those Apache symbols painted on our fence posts. If any renegades came our way, they honored them."

"I still think we should keep on extra men to be sure."

"We did, Gran. Matt doesn't want to take any risks until the other chiefs and renegades are stopped or back on the reservations. You can't blame the Indians for wanting to roam free like their ancestors did. I read that some of those reservations are terrible. I think the Apaches prefer the Warm Springs location to San Carlos. It's a shame we can't all live in peace. A lot of people have died from these wars."

"I bet Navarro could lick a whole band by himself."

Jessie stiffened, and her hands stopped spreading icing on her son's cake. It had been five years ago today that she had met the desperado, and four since she'd borne their child. Gran had mentioned his name several times to her lately. She hoped the aging woman didn't do the same with Matt or Lane. She didn't know why Navarro Breed was on her grandmother's mind so much these days, unless it was because Lane was favoring his real father more and more. Jessie always ignored the mentions with hopes they would pass out of the woman's head as fast as so many other things did.

Not today. "He sure beat that Fletcher good," Gran added.

"Yes, he did. Are the biscuits finished?" Jessie asked to distract her.

"Does Matt know he's Lane's father?"

Jessie halted her task and took her grandmother's gnarled hands in hers. "Yes, Gran, but we don't talk about that secret. Someone might overhear." The redhead worried over slips the aging woman might make in front of others. Jessie fretted over the clouding of the woman's memory, and her occasional bouts of stubbornness, which the doctor had said couldn't be helped. This was one of those irrational moments. Gran looked at her and scowled.

"A boy should know who his father is, Jessie."

"Matt is Lane's father, Gran. Matt is rearing him. You must keep this secret." Jessie explained the past and their need to protect Lane Cordell.

The cloud lifted for now. "You're right, Jessie. I'm sorry."

"Let's get finished before Lane's cake is a mess."

By Monday, Navarro and Gran were still on Jessie's troubled mind. In her condition, Jessie knew she didn't need this tension plaguing her. It was making her miserable and edgy. Perhaps the only way to get it behind her was to do what she had thought about years ago: send letters to the authorities to help clear Navarro. She had succeeded with those against the Fletcher brothers, whom they hadn't heard from since she had taken that action. Perhaps, if Navarro was still alive and free, she could end his torment.

If she wrote the President, the Arizona governor, the U.S. marshal, and the Arizona law, perhaps things could be changed for the fugitive. It could initiate an investigation into the false charges against him and the brutalities at the prison. If she could get Navarro pardoned, then if she ever heard from him again, she could tell him he was free. That would pay any debt she owed the man for his being denied a life with her and their son and for all his years of suffering.

Too, if Lane ever discovered the truth about his birth, it would be better if his real father wasn't a wanted criminal. If Lane learned his heritage was Breed, it would be better if that name was cleared of its blackness and shame.

Navarro had given her a new life, and she owed him one. He had refused to carry her away and to sweep her into his perilous existence. He had refused to intrude by letter or visit. It was time to pay him back for his generosity.

Matt was confident enough now in their love to endure any questions the authorities might ask. She was carrying his second child, and he trusted her. She had to take this risk for Navarro and their son.

But, she fretted, what if Navarro was pardoned and returned? How would she feel when she saw him again? She honestly didn't know. How would seeing her married with children affect him? She didn't know that, either. But if he was the man she believed him to be, he would thank them and leave to make a fresh start elsewhere. She had been compelled to start over, and it had worked for her. She had found a rich, fulfilling love and a happy life; that would show him that he could, too. A pardon would give Navarro a new beginning.

Yet all he would need was one look at Lane for him to guess the truth. Was it fair for her to protect herself and family at Navarro's expense? Was it just for him to keep suffering while she was free and happy? Especially when she might could change all that for him with a few letters? She could tell the authorities his side and what kind of man he truly was. At least she might get his sentence reduced so he'd only have to serve a few more years.

The more Lane favored his father, the more her secret was in jeopardy. If her son learned the truth, how would he feel about her not helping his father? Faith, hope, love, and charity: she believed in those things, and tried to practice them. Yes, she decided, it was worth the risk to help Navarro, even if the fugitive never discovered she had done so. And, what better day than the momentous March thirteenth to begin her task?

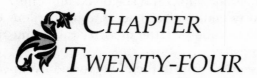

CHAPTER TWENTY-FOUR

On an early June day in 1881 Mathew Cordell rode to the old Lane settlement and dismounted. He and Jessie had discussed building a few small houses on this location for the hands who married so they wouldn't have to leave their employ, as several had reached that age and inclination. Last night they had sketched out their plans and figured the construction cost. Reasonable rent would give them enough to pay the bank note each month, and the chosen amount wouldn't be a hardship on the families. Both had decided it would be nice to have neighbors and other families nearby. Workers' children would give the Cordell family playmates. Matt had ridden over to check the location.

As Matt worked and made notes, he knew it was an excellent spot. The site had plenty of water and fertile gardening space. They would start with three houses, and perhaps later increase it to five. If spaced and arranged creatively around the existing structures as Jessie had suggested, each family would have its own yard and privacy. The couple knew the men's wives and children would be safe in this area, as some of the wranglers and a cook still occupied the Lane bunkhouse. Since there was so much work in this area and beyond, it made their schedules easier. Presently those hands were off riding herd and fence. Their cook was at the river fishing, to give the men a change in their diet while he enjoyed himself.

It was a quiet and peaceful setting with no one around an hour past the noon meal. The sky was clear and blue in all directions.

A gentle breeze wafted over him and the sun-drenched landscape, stirring grass and bushes as it passed. With sufficient rain so far this year, everything was green and growing. The ranch structures still in use were kept in excellent condition. Flowers that Jessie and Gran had planted long ago and a variety of wild ones bloomed here and there to add color and beauty. Chickens scratched and a milk cow grazed contentedly at a distance, occasionally sending forth a few clucks and moos. Only the stone foundation and chimneys of the original Lane home were standing; the charred debris had been cleared long ago to prevent an eyesore. They could use the stones for future construction, but not build over them, as the old Lane home was larger than the cozy houses they were planning.

Jessie had wanted to come with him; but in the sixth month of her pregnancy, both knew horseback riding was unwise and a leisurely carriage trip would have taken six hours over and back. Matt hurried his task, eager to get back to her.

As he completed it, galloping hooves caught his attention. Matt looked in that direction and saw a man heading toward him. As the rider neared the location, dread filled the rancher. Matt realized his only nightmare was coming true: Navarro Breed was back. He had feared his past rival's return ever since he gave Jessie permission to write the authorities three months ago on Navarro's behalf.

As Matt awaited his approach, he wondered if the fugitive knew about their efforts to help him. He wondered if those letters had worked in Navarro's favor, or if the loner was unaware of them and was stealing a visit. Matt had suspected this event would take place one day, but his tender-hearted wife had convinced him with little effort that it was the right thing to do.

At least, Matt admitted, he was being given the chance to speak with Navarro first. Hopefully he could persuade the man to do the right thing, too: keep riding without seeing and upsetting Jessie in her condition. Not that Matt distrusted his wife's loyalty or doubted her feelings for him, but there was time later for her to learn the truth, after the baby's birth when she was well. *Lord help us both do the right thing for everyone,* he prayed.

Navarro dismounted and joined the unsmiling rancher. Neither spoke for a short time. Sweat beaded on both men's faces and dampened their shirts. Both had dark tans, white teeth, strong features, and matching garments; but they didn't favor each other in the least. Both were strong, proud, and skilled, but the confidence of both men was shaky at that moment. At six foot two, Navarro stood taller than Matt, but they had about the same build.

"Hello, Matt," Navarro finally greeted him, perceiving that the man was anything but happy to see him return. "Where's Jessie? And what happened here?" he asked with a worried look, nodding toward the ruins of the Lane home where he had bid his beloved Jessie good-bye.

"A fire, two months after you left," Matt replied. He prayed again for the power and words to handle this trying situation.

Panic filled Navarro and showed in his expression. "Was Jessie hurt?"

"No, she's fine. Everyone got out safely."

"Where is she? I have to see her."

"She moved to Fletcher's place. She bought it, remember?"

"I'll ride over," he said as he turned to mount.

Matt's hand on Navarro's arm halted his intention. "Don't," he said simply.

Navarro man stared at Matt. "Why not?"

"Jessie is married now. The past is over. Leave her be."

Navarro couldn't conceal his shock and dismay. "Married? To whom?"

"To me. For years," Matt added, trying to feed him the truth in small bites.

Navarro couldn't swallow that bitter piece. "I don't believe you."

"It's true. If you love her, stay out of her life."

The loner knew that Matt had loved and wanted Jessica Lane years ago. Could she . . . "How did you manage that? Take advantage of her after this fire and my leaving?"

"We got married before the fire," Matt hinted.

"Before? But you said it was two months after I left. She wouldn't have."

"She did. She needed me."

Navarro was confused and angry. He couldn't accept that Jessie had wed so soon after his departure. "You made her think she did! I'm going to see her, your wife or not!"

"Don't do this, Navarro. We have children. Don't spoil our lives."

"She married you and had your children! How could she? She said she loved me. She said she'd wait for me."

"For how long? It's been five years without word or a visit."

"But she didn't even wait a few months! I thought she was honest and special. How could she have loved me, then turned to you so soon?"

Matt read the man's bitterness and resentment, and knew he would feel the same in Navarro's place. He tried to be kind and gentle, to avoid involving Jessie. "She *is* honest and special. She *did* love you. When you deserted her and never contacted her again, she didn't think you'd ever return."

"She could have waited for a while! Longer than two months! She'll have to tell me herself why she betrayed me. I risked everything for her."

Knowing Navarro's past from Jessie, Matt used the only weapon he could use on the man to defeat him. "If she had waited for you to return, seeing as how it took five years, your son would have been born a bastard like his father."

Navarro's heart pounded. "Son? What are you talking about?"

Matt prayed that Navarro's love was strong and pure, that his rival would make the right sacrifice for his wife and child. It was a risk worth taking, since Navarro would recognize the truth if he saw Lane. Matt tried to work on the loner's conscience. "You deserted Jessie while she was carrying your child. You left her alone and in a mess. You never came back to help her. What did you expect her to do? Live in shame? Run off somewhere to have the child, where nobody knew she wasn't married and where she had no friends around to protect her? If you're the man I think and hope you are, you wouldn't have wanted her life to be that way."

The stunned man asked in a strained voice, "Why didn't she tell me? Was she afraid I'd think she was trying to trick me into staying?" Yet Navarro suspected it was all because of what he'd told her during their last meeting. His confession had silenced hers, as she realized they couldn't wed. She had let him leave without knowing of their child, then married Matt to protect them both. Cruel life had given her no choice, but how he wished he had known about his child.

Matt had waited a few minutes for the news to settle in. "She didn't know she was pregnant until August. You were long gone by then, and she didn't know where to locate you. I know why you left, Navarro; Jessie told me all about your past and troubles. I'm glad you didn't draw her into them. I know how hard it was to give her up, but you did the right thing. She couldn't wait any longer to see if you'd ever be back. Time was against her. Even if she had waited and you'd returned for a visit, what did a fugitive have to offer her and the child? Nothing but trouble and danger. She was frantic and sick. She had everything put on her shoulders: the ranch, her family, the baby, and losing you and Jed. She was going to move somewhere, claim she was a widow, and have the baby. She asked me to take care of the ranch until she could return. I persuaded her not to give up her home, to stay here where me and the boys could protect her and help her, to marry me to give your child a name. Jessie didn't want to take advantage of me, so I had to talk long and hard to convince her it was the best path to take. I loved her and wanted her; I was even glad you'd shoved her into my arms. She agreed to marry me and stay home. As time passed, she came to love me. She was right not to wait; it's been five years!"

Navarro exploded from guilt and bitterness. "I didn't desert her! I couldn't put her in danger by staying or by taking her with me. I told her everything, and she understood. But she vowed to wait anyway, and I believed her. We both hoped something would happen to clear me so I could come back to her. I was captured by the law two days after leaving here. I was on my way back to tell Jessie I loved her when they trapped me and carried me back to that Arizona prison. I realized it wasn't fair to leave her without telling her something that important. I'm sure she knew the truth, but I never said those words aloud. I wanted her to hear from me how I felt. I never wanted her to think I had selfishly taken so much from her without loving her. I said I'd never return, but we both knew I would. It had to hurt her bad to think she was wrong about me."

Navarro grimaced and clenched his teeth. "Fletcher's sketches helped them catch me. Did she tell you about them?" When Matt nodded, he continued. "I couldn't send word about my capture because I didn't want the law to think she'd been hiding me and get her into trouble. I've been in that stinking hole for five years. They made sure I had no chance to escape again. I was released two weeks ago. The governor started an investigation into that place; he cleaned out the vermin and set me free. I came straight here. I have to see her and explain everything, Matt."

Matt was glad to hear the news about the prison reform, and he felt compassion for all Navarro had endured for years—no, since the man's ill-fated birth. Yet protecting Jessie was the most important thing on his mind. "Don't, Navarro. She's accepted your loss. Don't stir up new pain for her. Seeing you can't change anything now. We have a good and happy life. Besides your son, we have a daughter two years old and another child on the way."

"You said you married her to give my child a name. Now you're telling me you're a real husband to her. How could she love me and be a wife to you?"

"*Loved* you, Navarro, long ago. She loves me now. Time heals wounds and changes lives. If you love her, let her be. Think what you'll do to her and Lane if you suddenly appear or try to lay claim to them. That's cruel and selfish."

"Lane?"

"Your son, Lane Cordell. *My* son. I've raised him as my own for four years, Navarro. He's smart and good. He favors you, but that doesn't trouble me. I love him. I'm a good father to him, a good husband to Jessie."

"But he's my son. She's my woman. You stole them while I wasn't around to guard them."

Matt reasoned with the distressed man. "Would you rather I had stood back and let your baby be born a bastard? Let Jessie be shamed? Let her run off and be alone? I've always loved her. If you hadn't come along and stolen her from me, she'd have been mine first. Be satisfied with the time and love you shared with her. You have us to thank for getting you out of prison." Matt related what they had done to help Navarro and why. "Repay us by leaving us in peace."

Learning that his beloved was behind his release made Navarro wonder. "What if Jessie still loves me and wants me? Is it fair not to give her a choice? Is it fair to keep the truth about me from her?"

"She would never leave her family for you, even if she did love and want you more than me. But she doesn't, Navarro; believe me. She's expecting another baby in a few months. Confronting you after all this time could be dangerous for them both. She almost died giving birth to Lane. She suffered bad after you left. Don't make her hurt like that again!"

"I'm a free man now," Navarro broke in. "Let her choose between us. I can settle down with my son and the woman I love. I'd raise your children like you've raised my son."

"If Jessie and I didn't share a real marriage and our children, I would agree. I know how you must be suffering. But others have suffered, too, Navarro. They'll suffer more if you don't back down. Lane thinks I'm his father. If you ride up and spill the truth, he'll be hurt and confused. You'll ruin Jessie's name if people learn our secret. You have a responsibility to protect both of them. Think about them, not yourself," Matt urged.

Navarro had to work through his anguish, guilt, and disappointment. "Like you did years ago when you laid claim to what's mine? You're thinking of yourself now, Matt. You don't want to lose Jessie and all you have with her. You can't know what I've endured. You've never been thrown into prison for something you didn't do. You haven't been beaten and starved. You were never treated like a half-breed bastard. You've never had to give up everything you ever wanted and needed when it was in your grasp because you thought it was too late to keep it. You had a home, a family, a good life. You've had Jessie for years, and my son. I can be blamed for many things in my past, but not for deserting my love and child. How can you ask me to walk away, to never see them, to not explain? How can you expect me to give up this second chance?"

"You're right about some things. You had a bad life, and I'm sorry about that. But I thought Jessie had changed you. I guess prison undid all the good she did you. Call it back to mind, Navarro. Think and feel with your heart. Be unselfish—for her and Lane. Doesn't it matter how much she loved you and suffered?"

"If Jessie had loved me as I love her, she couldn't have turned to you so quickly. I understand why she married you. But how could her love for me die? How could she love you and truly become your wife so soon?"

Matt grasped the crux of his confusion and torment. "It wasn't soon or easy, Navarro. Our love came from sharing years of days and nights together, tending each other when sick, giving help and comfort in times of trouble and hardship, raising our children, planning for our future, and in providing each other with hope and courage and strength. It came from all of those things that draw two people together over a period of time. We didn't sleep together as man and wife until a year after you'd been gone. Before she could turn to me, Jessie had to lay your ghost to rest. That was a hard and painful battle, Navarro, for both of us."

The rancher knew that hearing such facts and details was rough on the troubled man before him, but Navarro didn't interrupt. Matt continued in a soft-spoken and understanding tone. "You know what kind of woman Jessie is; you can grasp why she finally accepted your loss and why she wanted and made a new life with me.

She had so much to give, and it was crying for release. I was the one there to receive it."

"Because I wasn't around to defend my claim on her and Lane."

"Partly, but face the whole truth, Navarro. Even if you hadn't been recaptured, you couldn't have built a good life with Jessie, not the kind she deserves. You wouldn't have risked staying and you wouldn't have taken her on the run. You wouldn't have sentenced your love and child to a miserable existence of stolen visits. I think you're more of a man than that and your love is stronger than that, too. Don't punish her for seeking the safe and happy life you wanted for her, the kind you wanted with her but couldn't have. I know it's hard to see another man in her life. I felt that way about you from the moment you arrived here long ago and I saw that gleam in her eyes for you. I held her in my arms and comforted her while she cried over you. I watched her bloom with your seed. I was with her when she almost died bearing your child. I delivered your baby and tended both of them. Yes, I know what it's like for the woman you love to belong to another man. But all those days we spent together and all those things we shared made us cling to each other."

Matt saw his rival was listening closely to him. "We always liked each other and respected each other. I watched Jessie grow from a tomboy into a woman. I saw her open up and come alive because of you. She was hurting, and needed me for comfort and strength. You two met at a time when each needed the other. That time has passed, Navarro. You and Jessie have different destinies. You have to seek yours elsewhere, but hers is with me, here with our children. Your relationship was meant to help you both change and grow, to prepare you both for your real destinies."

"She was my destiny, Matt," Navarro argued. "She *is* my destiny."

The rancher shook his head. "No, each of you was a marker on the other's trail to point the way, but not a final destination. She loved you, but she had to get over you. I helped her do that. I admit I did everything I could to slay your ghost. You'd have done the same in my place. Surely you didn't want her to pine and suffer for years. I swear to you we love each other and have a good life together. I don't think it could be the same for you and her because you can't have a real life based on fiery passion alone. You have to have all of that time and those things that Jessie and I have shared."

"I was denied them because of prison, Matt."

"For whatever reason, Jessie was taken from your arms and put into mine. Be honest with yourself, Navarro—what kind of life could you have given her for the past five years, even if you hadn't been recaptured? What would it have been like if she'd run off with you? Or been like for her as Jessie Breed, wife of a prisoner or widow of a hanged man? You didn't want such an existence for her; that's why you left, left alone. You told her you wouldn't return, to start a new life. Now you act as if her doing so was a sin and betrayal."

Those words stung, because Matt was right. Navarro had told Jessie he was never coming back, not to wait for him. He had pushed her toward another man, toward Matt. Jessie and Gran had said Matt was a lot like him, and Matt had been like part of their family for a long time. He had witnessed their closeness. How could he blame Jessie for turning to Matt for love and comfort?

"I need her, Matt. She is my heart. Dreams of her kept me going in prison."

"That's over and you have to wake up. What you need is what she's already done for you. Don't ask for more; I'm begging you."

Navarro knew he had lost this vital battle, but he made one last thrust at his rival. "If you aren't afraid she'll pick me over you, why can't I see her and let her choose? At least explain the truth and say a final good-bye? If you're so confident and what you've said it true, what difference can our meeting make?"

Matt perceived his victory, but he didn't gloat. "Jessie doesn't deserve to be pulled between us, and I don't want to put her under such tension. I told you she's expecting another child. It could be hard on her to see you and talk to you, knowing she had to hurt you again. There's also the men, our hands; if they see you with Lane, much as you two favor each other, they'll guess the truth. You don't want them to know about the truth of his birth. They'll wonder why you left Jessie in that condition and why you never returned. If you didn't relate the whole truth about your past and prison, they'd think badly of you. They liked you and respected you, Navarro; leave it that way."

"But I want Jessie to know the truth, Matt. I don't want her to hate me for what she thinks I did."

"She doesn't, Navarro. Can't you see that in how she helped with your pardon? You were Jessie's first love; she'll always have special feelings for you. After she has the baby, I'll tell her everything, I swear it. I'll even walk farther with you: when you get settled somewhere, send me your address and I'll keep you informed about Lane and Jessie. If either of them ever needs you, I'll let you know. But you'll need to pick a name to use until I can tell her everything. And if anything happened to me, I'd make certain Jessie knows how to reach you."

"I was offered a job by the Arizona governor. Seems the remaining Apaches, under Nana and Geronimo, are raiding again. They know I'm part Apache so they think I can help them prevent more bloodshed. I've scouted before."

"Do it, Navarro; make your new chance work. Use all the things Jessie taught you." He told him about the loss of his own first love and his acceptance of it. "I found a second love; Jessie did, too. So can you, Navarro. A life with Jessie isn't possible for you now, so why torment all of us? It's in your power to be kind or cruel. I won't try to stop you from seeing Jessie and Lane, but I'm pleading with you to leave us in peace."

Navarro paced as he considered Matt's words. He comprehended what it took for a strong, proud man like Mathew Cordell to beg, and he grasped the man's true motives. His heart ached over this unexpected dilemma. He had been so happy when he was exonerated and set free. Now he felt as if he were staked to a frozen earth and talons of fire were ripping his body apart. "Before I decide, tell me what's happened during the last five years. How's Tom, Gran, and the boys?"

Matt told him all he could. He finished by telling Navarro about the locket incident.

Navarro explained. "When I was trapped, I knew I'd be searched once they'd captured me . . . or killed me. I removed Jessie's picture and hid it in a small crevice in the rocks. I didn't want the law to learn about her. While I was distracted, one of the lawmen sneaked up and clobbered me senseless. When I reached prison, one of the prison guards took the locket. I guess he was the man who gambled it away. I surely could have used its comfort while I was there." He didn't tell Matt he had recovered the picture, worn and faded.

"Why didn't they hang you? Jessie said you killed a guard to escape."

"I was lucky, for once. Another prisoner escaped that same day and he got blamed for that bastard's death. He was shot, so the law never knew I did it. That's why I was returned to prison, not swung from a rope. If I'd known I wasn't charged with murder, I would have turned myself in and finished my sentence so I could earn freedom to return to Jessie. She'd have waited for me."

"Don't you see that it wasn't meant to be for you two? You were cleared of all charges, Navarro. You have an important job offer, a new chance for a fresh beginning. Go after them without hurting everyone here. We're part of your past, too. Let it die, all of it. Please."

Navarro paced again in deep thought. If he were the same man he had been years ago, he wouldn't hesitate a moment before slaying this obstacle to his dream. But he wasn't the Navarro Breed of five years ago; he had changed because of Jessica Lane. As he lived and breathed, he wanted her with every part of his being!

But, Navarro confessed to himself, Jessie must have changed, too, because their long separation had changed everything. Their destiny was no longer as one. Their trails had parted. It was cruel and wrong to force himself into her new life. He couldn't think about what might have been; he had to accept reality. He must make this choice—sacrifice—for his love and his child. Jessica Lane . . . Cordell had earned a new life, and he could not destroy it and her.

Navarro halted and faced his love's husband. "You win, Matt. You're right. I love Jessie too much to hurt her again. I love my son, too, even if I've never seen him and didn't know about him until today. Promise me you'll take care of Jessie and Lane. Promise you'll send word if they ever need me. You can reach me through the Arizona governor; I'll accept his job offer. That'll give me a starting point."

The rancher shook Navarro's hand, knowing how hard his decision had been. "You have my word of honor, Navarro. I love them and want what's best for them. If I believed that was you, I'd step aside. When the time's right after the baby's born in September, I'll tell Jessie everything about today. Thanks, Navarro," Matt said with a smile of gratitude and tear-filled eyes.

"No, Matt, you can't tell her about today. That would cause trouble between you two."

Shocked, Matt argued, "But that isn't fair to either of you. I can't lie to my wife."

"Staying quiet to prevent trouble and heartache isn't lying."

"It's cows in the same pasture," Matt refuted. "I'd feel dishonest."

"Listen to me," Navarro persisted. "Jessie is a proud and tender-hearted person. She'll be upset we didn't let her make the choice about seeing me or not. She won't believe she needed this kind of protection from either of us. She'll think we treated her like a child. If she learns I was recaptured while trying to return to her, she'll blame herself for what happened to me after I left here. She'll feel guilty and tormented for all the years I had to suffer in prison; I told her what that place was like. If she learns her letters got me freed, she'll feel worse for not trying to help me sooner. I'm sure that's how she'll react. She can't find out you were involved today. She'll be angry at you for withholding the truth for months and for excluding her from our decision today. I don't want Jessie to suffer again, or to cause trouble between you two."

"But—"

"There's a better way for her to hear only what she needs to learn," Navarro interrupted. "Around Christmas, I'll write her a letter. I'll tell her I've been cleared and have a new life. She doesn't have to learn about my troubles of the past five years. I'll tell her I'm fine and safe. I'll say a friend checked on her for me. I'll tell her I'm glad she's married to you, has children, and is doing so well. I'll thank her for all she did for me, but say it's best if we don't meet again. That'll let her know I'm all right and won't be back, let her know I'm aware things are good for her. Hearing about today and the last five years would do more harm than good for Jessie and for your marriage. For her to learn you convinced me to leave without seeing her will make her think you doubted her loyalty, love, and strength; she may think I love her more than you do." Navarro saw the older man grimace at those words. "You told me not to be cruel and selfish, so you do the same. Every time you're tempted to confess, think of the damage the truth can do to your marriage. We both want her happy and protected; this is the best way, the only way, Matt. A short letter will tell her all she ever needs to know about what happened after we parted."

When Matt looked worried and reluctant, Navarro added, "If I can accept and conceal the truth because it's best for Jessie, Lane, and your marriage, so can you. Be strong and generous, Matt; that's what you're asking of me. It's only fair that we partner up this last time to share the responsibility of Jessie and Lane. How could you feel bad about doing what's right for everyone?" Navarro reasoned.

"But you're asking me to deceive my wife. Jessie and I have always been honest with each other."

"Don't be foolish, Matt; it could cost you the same things my mistakes have cost me. You can't just tell Jessie part of what happened here today; if you tell her all of it, you'll hurt her beyond reason. What happens when she comes to find me to make sure I'm all right? What will happen when we talk and try to comfort each other? I'm afraid I wouldn't be able to resist her. You'd have her all confused about love and loyalty, gratitude and guilt. Let it go, Matt, for all our sakes. All I ask is that you contact me if Jessie or Lane ever need me. Otherwise, forget the past, forget today, and forget about me."

Matt contemplated the man's words. He admitted they made sense, but for another woman, not his Jessie. Navarro didn't grasp how it was with married couples who loved and trusted each other. Matt was certain his wife would understand and concur with his decision to protect her in her condition. Matt realized that Navarro hadn't known Jessica Lane well enough long ago, and she had changed—matured—over the years since then. She would not react as the man believed. But Matt was happy and relieved that Navarro was being so unselfish. To prevent fears and worries or Navarro changing his mind, the rancher pretended to agree. "We'll do it your way, Navarro. Thanks." Yet Mathew Cordell knew he would reveal the truth about the other man and today as soon as possible.

It was dark outside the Cordell home, but the children were still up, as Matt's tardy return had made the evening meal late. While Jessie and Gran sewed, the rancher read a bedtime story to Lane and Alice, named after Jessie's beloved mother. Sometimes he did the storytelling; other times it was Jessie or her grandmother. A story always settled down the children after an active day.

Lane sat on one leg and Alice on the other, with Matt's arms around them and his hands holding the book they were using tonight: *Adventures of the Smallest Pony.* It had been read many times before, but they never tired of hearing it again. Matt's delivery was entertaining as he used several voices for the different characters and created sound effects for the creatures and events. The children smiled and laughed, and sometimes halted their father to ask the same questions or to make the same comments as in past readings.

With love and patience, the rancher replied with the same answers. Often he glanced at his wife and grinned or winked. Jessie would return his smile with adoring eyes. Neither scolded the children for interrupting or quelled their enthusiasm.

"Got out," Alice squealed with joy when the pony escaped a brush enclosure. "See, run," she said, giggling and clapping her pudgy hands.

At two, the girl's vocabulary increased every week. Jessie and Matt were proud of both their children.

"I wanna pony, Papa," Lane informed his parents as he had done countless times.

"Get a little bigger first," the soft-spoken Matt told him.

"When I'm five?" the four-year-old asked, eyes wide with hope.

"Six is better, son. These legs have to get longer," Matt explained, releasing one hand from the book to playfully shake the boy's knees, then tickle his tummy.

"Why, Papa?" Lane inquired.

"To reach the stirrups. You have to use them for balance when learning to ride. If you don't, you fall off and get hurt."

"I'm going with you tomorrow," Lane reminded Matt.

"Yep, I haven't forgotten, son. We'll ride over to check on the horses after breakfast."

"Me go," their daughter stated, looking at her father with bright eyes.

Matt kissed her forehead and smiled. "Not tomorrow, Alice. You'll get to go on the picnic Saturday to the new pond the boys dug."

"Let your father finish the story, children," Jessie said. "It's very late."

After Matt did so, Lane coaxed, "Read it again, Papa."

He put the book aside. "Another night, son. It's off to bed with you two."

As the couple and their children talked a few minutes, no one noticed the man hiding outside the nearby window who was observing the poignant scene. Navarro Breed had left his mount at a safe distance, then sneaked to the house to see his son and his lost love before riding out of their lives. His secrecy was aided by the wall around the home and bushes near the structure. The hands were all inside the bunkhouse.

Navarro witnessed the love and closeness of the family he was observing. Bittersweet emotions tugged at him. He wished it were he enjoying this family and this special life. He knew for certain now that Mathew Cordell had not lied to him; that made him feel both good and bad.

He gazed at his son as Matt gathered the boy into his arms to put him to bed. Lane did resemble his real father, and that pleased Navarro. He devoured every word, movement, and expression his son used. It hurt to hear the boy call another man "Papa," but the love and rapport those two shared was undeniable. The little girl favored Jessie; Alice was pretty, bubbly, and delightful. Navarro saw Lane hug and kiss his little sister, and the action made the man smile.

Gran, looking older and weaker, took charge of Alice to put her to bed for Jessie. The white-haired woman and Matt left the room to do their tasks. Gran had bid them good night, as she was turning in, too.

Navarro's hungry eyes consumed every inch of Jessica Lane Cordell as she put toys and sewing away. She was more beautiful than five years ago. She wore a loose dress that did not conceal her pregnancy, and Navarro imagined that was how she had looked carrying his son. Her auburn hair was unbound; it flowed silky and wavy down her back. She still kept it cut shorter on the sides and top as she had done for her disguise so long ago in San Angelo. Her skin was smooth and flawless, and glowed with her happiness. Her expressive eyes seemed bluer and clearer; no doubt from peace and joy, he decided. How lovely she was, and he yearned to kiss her and hold her one last time . . . No, he wanted her forever. But that could not be. Once more, it was too late for them. Years ago, he had lost his love because of his dark past. Now, he would lose her again because of her bright future, into which he could not intrude.

Navarro remembered all Jessie had taught him and all she meant to him. When he had met her, he hadn't loved or needed anybody. That was no longer true. She had inspired love, compassion, unselfishness, and courage. He had learned about what makes a home and a family from this unique woman. She had made him laugh and smile, even learn to dance. She had gotten him a pardon and job, even though the law hadn't revealed her part in it when they set him free. Even after thinking he had deserted her, she didn't hate him.

On her ranch, he had made real friends. He had shared a special bond with her brother, one that had helped both of them. But he was not a part of their lives anymore, and that saddened him.

If he hadn't met Jessica Lane and fallen under her influence, his existence would be bleak today. He wouldn't have cared about life or even a new chance. He would still be on the run or dead. He would have been in and out of trouble for the rest of his miserable life. She had saved him and changed him.

He had a fine son. He had beautiful memories. He had a fresh start. Hard as it was to ride away, this time forever, he must and he would. One day his son would own this splendid ranch. Lane would have a better life with Matt than he himself could have offered; and it wasn't right to confuse and hurt the boy now. Lane had a loving and wonderful mother, a good father, and kin. Lane would be happy, respected, be somebody important: things his natural father had been denied. Matt had promised to contact him if trouble arose in the future, and he trusted the rancher. It was time—

Navarro watched as Matt returned to his wife and embraced her. "All done, love."

They sat on the couch and talked, cuddled together. Matt's arm was around Jessie, and her head rested on his strong shoulder. The couple discussed their construction plans for the hands' homes; they spoke of their future, of the child Jessie was carrying. They talked of how much they looked forward to seeing Tom after college ended. They spoke of Mary Louise Lane Blye, who wanted children and who would be visiting them with her physician husband next summer. Matt joked about Miguel and Annie Ortega trying to catch up with them, as they were expecting their third child, too. Jessie reminded Matt of their intention to replace Annie before their next child was born, as Annie had her hands full with her own family. The couple smiled when Matt related that Biscuit Hank, their chuckhouse cook, had finally proposed to a lovely widow in town.

"It's perfect timing, Matt. Hank and his bride can move into one of the new houses, so he can remain with us. Annie and Miguel have asked for one; they need more room. If we get busy, they can be settled before Christmas."

"It shouldn't take long, Jessie. It was a good idea. You're always thinking about everybody else. That's why I love you so much, woman."

"I just want everyone to be as happy and comfortable as we are. If the . . ." She halted and laughed. "The baby's moving. It tickles. Maybe it's a son. Feel."

"Doesn't matter, love; I have a fine son, the best a man could want."

Jessie nestled closer to him. "You're a good father to Lane, Matt."

"It's easy; I love him. Jessie . . ." he began rather hesitantly. "If the day ever comes when Lane needs to know about his real father, we'll tell him the truth. Navarro would be proud of Lane. He left to protect you, so that proves he's a good man. After the baby's born, do you want me to get you the truth about him?"

Jessie turned her head and gazed into her husband's warm brown eyes. "That isn't necessary, Matt. We've done all we can for him. After he left years ago, I had terrible feelings and nightmares that he was in danger. Maybe there was some kind of mental connection to him because I was carrying his child. But lately, especially today, I have this strong feeling that he's all right. I can't explain it, but I sense he truly is safe and free. It's almost as if he knows the truth about us and accepts it. I hope so. It would be so hard to face him and hurt him again. Navarro doesn't deserve more pain and sacrifice. He was a special part of my life, but that was long ago. I'm glad you don't feel threatened by our past. I love you for being so kind and understanding."

Matt kissed her brow. "Perhaps Navarro knows the truth and that's why he's left us alone. He wouldn't do anything to hurt you and Lane. You gave him the strength and courage to fight for a fresh start. Navarro's a special man; he'll win this time. Wherever he is, he knows he's done what's best for all of us."

"I honestly hope so, Matt; that's what I want to believe. Let's get to sleep. The children will be up at dawn and pulling us from our bed."

Matt stood and helped Jessie to her feet. The rancher doused the lamps. With their arms around each other, they headed for the steps and a cozy bed.

Neither saw the man who eased away from the open window, sneaked over the stucco and stone wall, and slipped from their happy life without turning it inside out. Navarro Breed mounted his horse and rode toward Arizona to capture a new dream.

Upstairs, Mathew and Jessica Cordell peeked in on their children. All was quiet. The couple entered their room. Matt undressed and eased into bed. Jessie donned a pretty cotton gown and joined him. They snuggled and kissed.

"Sweet dreams, Jessie," Matt murmured into her ear.

"You, too, my love," she replied, at last feeling as if that was the only kind she would have forever. *You, too, Navarro,* her peaceful heart added.

EPILOGUE

Mathew and Jessica Cordell stood before the new entrance to their ranch. A large sign hung from the stone arch over the dirt road to their home, one that said L/C Ranch: their stock brand, ranch name, and the initials of their two sons. Matt was behind Jessie, his arms wrapped around her slender waist. Both gazed at the sign and thought of the bond it represented.

Jessie reflected on all that had brought them to this September day in 1882. She knew her father and mother would be happy, and proud of her. She had never learned who had slain Jedidiah Lane six years ago, but she had to believe his killer had met justice. At least, the man who ordered his murder had been punished.

Jessie didn't want to dwell on sad matters today. She had two fine sons: Lane and Lance Cordell, brothers who would share this magnificent and profitable spread one day. She had a beautiful vivacious daughter who would be given the chance to choose her own path; Alice would never be treated or viewed as a son, as she herself had been for twenty-four years. Yet the redhead was not bitter about the way she'd been raised. Jed had never meant to harm any of his three children. They all loved him. She knew her father must be resting easier now that Mary Louise and Tom were so much happier.

So much had happened this summer. A healthy and happy Thomas Lane had returned from college in June, with only a slight and almost unnoticeable limp. His new glasses provided perfect vision and looked appealing on the handsome auburn-haired nineteen-year-old. Tom had brought home a lovely girl named Sarah Jane Tims, and the engaged couple had wed in late July. With the Cordells' backing, Tom and his bride had opened a mercantile store in Davis that was doing well.

Mary Louise and Dr. John Blye had accompanied Tom home. They had visited with her family until after the wedding. Everyone, but particularly Jessie and Gran, had been astonished and pleased by the good changes in the beautiful blonde who radiated with happiness. Powerful love, Jessie decided, was a great medicine for the sick in heart, spirit, or body. Since returning home to Philadelphia, news had arrived by letter this month revealing Mary Louise's first pregnancy. Both the Blyes and Cordells were thrilled.

Gran, at seventy-six, still insisted on doing chores in the house. She loved her grandchildren and great-grandchildren, and was happy all the family were friends at last. The few bouts of forgetfulness or confusion she had these days were harmless.

Most of the original Lane hands still worked for them. Five couples—including Annie and Miguel Ortega, Hank Epps and his wife, and Jefferson Clark and his new bride—occupied the cozy houses on the site of the old homestead. It was nice having good neighbors for the adults and playmates for the children. Since both towns—Davis and Stockton—were so far for daily travel and both schools were crowded, Jessie and Matt had decided to construct a small schoolhouse on their property for all the children.

As Jessie had thought over the last six years, she realized how one dream had been exchanged for another, one man for another. She could not help but wonder how Navarro Breed was doing.

Following Lance's birth a year ago, Matt had told her about Navarro's visit and the men's talk last June. Jessie had been relieved and saddened to learn why Navarro had been unable to contact her or return to her. At last she was able to understand and forgive. She was proud of her role, and Matt's, in his new life. She believed the two men had made the right and kindest decision for everyone last year. She understood why Navarro hadn't wanted Matt to tell her about their meeting, but dear Matt knew her so well, as it should be between a husband and wife.

Hopefully Navarro had found real peace and happiness, as his brief letter last December had indicated. Jessie wanted those things for him; she prayed his claims were true, not just meant to protect her from some awful truth. More and more Lane favored his real father; but the dark-haired, hazel-eyed boy had Mathew Cordell's personality. In all but blood, Lane was Matt's son.

In his letter, Navarro had told how he'd been exonerated of all charges, found a good job and a contented life. He had said he stayed away all those years to protect both of them and to give each a chance for a fresh start alone. He had revealed that he'd checked on her to make certain she was all right. Since she was also doing so well, he had felt it was best not to meet again and stir up the past. He had thanked her for her role in changing him. He had intended to let the past stay buried, but her letters to several Arizona authorities—passed on to him because of his job—encouraged him to write so she wouldn't worry about him any longer. He had mentioned prison reforms, and she was delighted about them. He had said he was happy for her, and knew she'd feel the same for him.

Jessie was relieved Navarro had written instead of visiting. Yet she hated that he would never know his son, even though it was important for everyone's happiness. He was living and working in Arizona as a scout, translator, and peacemaker between the whites and Apaches. She was relieved the skilled half-white warrior was there to keep the raiding Apaches from heading this way. But she hadn't tried to contact him, as gently ordered. Jessie was glad Navarro Breed had made a fresh start, and she treasured not only his sacrifices of six years ago but the final one of last year. Knowing he was alive and well gave her peace and joy.

For most of her life, she had lived as Jed's "son," as Jess Lane. Navarro had ended her passionless existence. She had loved him wildly and freely, rashly and blindly. If he had returned in time, she would have lost herself again as Navarro's woman.

With Matt, she had found her real self, the woman she was meant to be. She had grown and matured; she had stayed strong, and had gotten stronger. She loved her husband and needed him, just as he loved and needed her. They were so alike, so special as one. Mathew Cordell was her destiny. A turbulent life was behind her. A good life was with and before her.

Jessie turned to face her husband. She hugged him tightly. When he laughed and questioned the meaning of her emphatic squeeze, she gazed into his eyes and said, "For so long I was searching for a beautiful dream, and it was right before me when I awoke from my girlish sleep. I love you, Matt; I think I always did. I just had to become a woman before I could understand that. I'm glad you gave me time to grow up and you let me capture you."

The grinning man returned her smile. "I love you, too, Mrs. Cordell." Matt could not help but think about the man—the half-breed drifter—who had helped make this blissful life possible. He knew Navarro would keep his word about staying away. Yet, if trouble came down the road one day, Jessie knew where and how to locate Navarro Breed for help, protection, and comfort.

Jessie cuddled closer to her husband. With Matt at her side and in her arms, the L/C Ranch would become famous far and wide. Jessie lifted her head and kissed him deeply. She had sought to follow the wind with a daring desperado, but now she possessed a beautiful and priceless love.